ALSO BY THOMAS PYNCHON

INHERENT VICE

THOMAS PYNCHON

JONATHAN CAPE
LONDON

Published by Jonathan Cape 2009

2 4 6 8 10 9 7 5 3

Copyright © Thomas Pynchon 2009

Thomas Pynchon has asserted his right under the Copyright, Designs
and Patents Act 1988 to be identified as the author of this work

First published in Great Britain in 2009 by
Jonathan Cape
Random House, 20 Vauxhall Bridge Road,
London SW1V 2SA

www.rbooks.co.uk

Addresses for companies within The Random House Group Limited can be found at:
www.randomhouse.co.uk/offices.htm

The Random House Group Limited Reg. No. 954009

A CIP catalogue record for this book
is available from the British Library

(Hardback edition) 9780224089487
(Trade paperback edition) 9780224089753

The Random House Group Limited supports The Forest Stewardship
Council (FSC), the leading international forest certification organisation. All our
titles that are printed on Greenpeace approved FSC certified paper carry the FSC logo.
Our paper procurement policy can be found at:
www.rbooks.co.uk/environment

Mixed Sources
Product group from well-managed
forests and other controlled sources
www.fsc.org Cert no. TT-COC-2139
© 1996 Forest Stewardship Council
FSC

Printed and bound in Great Britain by
Clays Ltd, St Ives PLC

Under the paving-stones, the beach!

INHERENT VICE

ONE

SHE CAME ALONG THE ALLEY AND UP THE BACK STEPS THE WAY
she always used to. Doc hadn't seen her for over a year. Nobody had.
Back then it was always sandals, bottom half of a flower-print bikini,
faded Country Joe & the Fish T-shirt. Tonight she was all in flatland
gear, hair a lot shorter than he remembered, looking just like she swore
she'd never look.

"That you, Shasta?"

"Thinks he's hallucinating."

"Just the new package I guess."

They stood in the street light through the kitchen window there'd
never been much point putting curtains over and listened to the thumping of the surf from down the hill. Some nights, when the wind was
right, you could hear the surf all over town.

"Need your help, Doc."

"You know I have an office now? just like a day job and everything?"

"I looked in the phone book, almost went over there. But then I
thought, better for everybody if this looks like a secret rendezvous."

Okay, nothing romantic tonight. Bummer. But it still might be a paying gig. "Somebody's keepin a close eye?"

"Just spent an hour on surface streets trying to make it look good."

"How about a beer?" He went to the fridge, pulled two cans out of the case he kept inside, handed one to Shasta.

"There's this guy," she was saying.

There would be, but why get emotional? If he had a nickel for every time he'd heard a client start off this way, he could be over in Hawaii now, loaded day and night, digging the waves at Waimea, or better yet hiring somebody to dig them for him . . . "Gentleman of the straightworld persuasion," he beamed.

"Okay, Doc. He's married."

"Some . . . money situation."

She shook back hair that wasn't there and raised her eyebrows *so what*.

Groovy with Doc. "And the wife—she knows about you?"

Shasta nodded. "But she's seeing somebody too. Only it isn't just the usual—they're working together on some creepy little scheme."

"To make off with hubby's fortune, yeah, I think I heard of that happenin once or twice around L.A. And . . . you want me to do what, exactly?" He found the paper bag he'd brought his supper home in and got busy pretending to scribble notes on it, because straight-chick uniform, makeup supposed to look like no makeup or whatever, here came that old well-known hardon Shasta was always good for sooner or later. Does it ever end, he wondered. Of course it does. It did.

They went in the front room and Doc laid down on the couch and Shasta stayed on her feet and sort of drifted around the place.

"Is, they want me in on it," she said. "They think I'm the one who can reach him when he's vulnerable, or as much as he ever gets."

"Bareass and asleep."

"I knew you'd understand."

"You're still trying to figure out if it's right or wrong, Shasta?"

"Worse than that." She drilled him with that gaze he remembered so well. When he remembered. "How much loyalty I owe him."

"I hope you're not asking me. Beyond the usual boilerplate people owe anybody they're fucking steady—"

"Thanks, Dear Abby said about the same thing."

"Groovy. Emotions aside, then, let's look at the money. How much of the rent's he been picking up?"

"All of it." Just for a second, he caught the old narrow-eyed defiant grin.

"Pretty hefty?"

"For Hancock Park."

Doc whistled the title notes from "Can't Buy Me Love," ignoring the look on her face. "You're givin him IOUs for everything, o' course."

"You fucker, if I'd known you were still this bitter—"

"Me? Trying to be professional here, is all. How much were wifey and the b.f. offering to cut you in for?"

Shasta named a sum. Doc had outrun souped-up Rollses full of indignant smack dealers on the Pasadena Freeway, doing a hundred in the fog and trying to steer through all those crudely engineered curves, he'd walked up back alleys east of the L.A. River with nothing but a borrowed 'fro pick in his baggies for protection, been in and out of the Hall of Justice while holding a small fortune in Vietnamese weed, and these days had nearly convinced himself all that reckless era was over with, but now he was beginning to feel deeply nervous again. "This . . ." carefully now, "this isn't just a couple of X-rated Polaroids, then. Dope planted in the glove compartment, nothin like 'at . . ."

Back when, she could go weeks without anything more complicated than a pout. Now she was laying some heavy combination of face ingredients on him that he couldn't read at all. Maybe something she'd picked up at acting school. "It isn't what you're thinking, Doc."

"Don't worry, thinking comes later. What else?"

"I'm not sure but it sounds like they want to commit him to some loony bin."

"You mean legally? or a snatch of some kind?"

"Nobody's telling me, Doc, I'm just the bait." Come to think of it, there'd never been this much sorrow in her voice either. "I heard you're seeing somebody downtown?"

Seeing. Well, "Oh, you mean Penny? nice flatland chick, out in search of secret hippie love thrills basically—"

"Also some kind of junior DA in Evelle Younger's shop?"

Doc gave it some thought. "You think somebody there can stop this before it happens?"

"Not too many places I can go with this, Doc."

"Okay, I'll talk to Penny, see what we can see. Your happy couple— they have names, addresses?"

When he heard her older gent's name he said, "This is the same Mickey Wolfmann who's always in the paper? The real-estate big shot?"

"You can't tell anybody about this, Doc."

"Deaf and dumb, part of the job. Any phone numbers you'd like to share?"

She shrugged, scowled, gave him one number. "Try to never use it."

"Groovy, and how do I reach you?"

"You don't. I moved out of the old place, staying where I can anymore, don't ask."

He almost said, "There's room here," which in fact there wasn't, but he'd seen her looking around at everything that hadn't changed, the authentic English Pub Dartboard up on the wagon wheel and the whorehouse swag lamp with the purple psychedelic bulb with the vibrating filament, the collection of model hot rods made entirely of Coors cans, the beach volleyball autographed by Wilt Chamberlain in Day-Glo felt marker, the velvet painting and so forth, with an expression of, you would have to say, distaste.

He walked her down the hill to where she was parked. Weeknights out here weren't too different from weekends, so this part of town was already all ahoot with funseekers, drinkers and surfers screaming in the alleys, dopers out on food errands, flatland guys in for a night of hustling stewardesses, flatland ladies with all-too-grounded day jobs hoping to be mistaken for stewardesses. Uphill and invisible, traffic out on the boulevard to and from the freeway uttered tuneful exhaust phrases which went echoing out to sea, where the crews of oil tankers sliding along, hearing them, could have figured it for wildlife taking care of nighttime business on an exotic coast.

In the last pocket of darkness before the glare of Beachfront Drive, they came to a pause, a timeless pedestrian gesture in these parts that usually announced a kiss or at least a grabbed ass. But she said, "Don't come any further, somebody might be watching by now."

"Call me or something."

"You never did let me down, Doc."

"Don't worry. I'll—"

"No, I mean really ever."

"Oh . . . sure I did."

"You were always true."

It had been dark at the beach for hours, he hadn't been smoking much and it wasn't headlights—but before she turned away, he could swear he saw light falling on her face, the orange light just after sunset that catches a face turned to the west, watching the ocean for someone to come in on the last wave of the day, in to shore and safety.

At least her car was the same, the Cadillac ragtop she'd had forever, a '59 Eldorado Biarritz bought used at one of the lots over on Western where they stand out close to the traffic so it'll sweep away the smell of whatever they're smoking. After she drove away, Doc sat on a bench down on the Esplanade, a long slopeful of lighted windows ascending behind him, and watched the luminous blooms of surf and the lights of late commuter traffic zigzagging up the distant hillside of Palos Verdes. He ran through things he hadn't asked, like how much she'd come to depend on Wolfmann's guaranteed level of ease and power, and how ready was she to go back to the bikini and T-shirt lifestyle, and how free of regrets? And least askable of all, how passionately did she really feel about old Mickey? Doc knew the likely reply—"I love him," what else? With the unspoken footnote that the word these days was being way too overused. Anybody with any claim to hipness "loved" everybody, not to mention other useful applications, like hustling people into sex activities they might not, given the choice, much care to engage in.

Back at his place, Doc stood for a while gazing at a velvet painting from one of the Mexican families who set up their weekend pitches along the boulevards through the green flatland where people still rode horses, between Gordita and the freeway. Out of the vans and into the calm early mornings would come sofa-width Crucifixions and Last Suppers, outlaw bikers on elaborately detailed Harleys, superhero badasses in Special Forces gear packing M16s and so forth. This picture of Doc's showed a Southern California beach that never was—palms, bikini babes, surfboards, the works. He thought of it as a window to look out of when he couldn't deal with looking out of the traditional glass-type one in the other room. Sometimes in the shadows the view would light up, usually when he was smoking weed, as if the contrast knob of Creation had been messed with just enough to give everything an underglow, a luminous edge, and promise that the night was about to turn epic somehow.

Except for tonight, which only looked more like work. He got on the telephone and tried to call Penny, but she was out, probably Watusi-ing the night away opposite some shorthaired attorney with a promising career. Cool with Doc. Next he rang up his Aunt Reet, who lived down the boulevard on the other side of the dunes in a more suburban part of town with houses, yards, and trees, because of which it had become known as the Tree Section. A few years ago, after divorcing a lapsed Missouri Synod Lutheran with a T-Bird agency and a fatality for the restless homemakers one meets at bars in bowling alleys, Reet had moved down here from the San Joaquin with the kids and started selling real estate, and before long she had her own agency, which she now ran out of a bungalow on the same oversize lot as her house. Whenever Doc needed to know anything touching on the world of property, Aunt Reet, with her phenomenal lot-by-lot grasp of land use from the desert to the sea, as they liked to say on the evening news, was the one he went to. "Someday," she prophesied, "there will be computers for this, all you'll have to do's type in what you're looking for, or even better just talk it in—like that HAL in *2001: A Space Odyssey?*—and it'll be right back at you with more information than you'd ever want to know, any lot in the L.A. Basin, all the way back to the Spanish land grants—water rights, encumbrances, mortgage histories, whatever you want, trust me, it's coming." Till then, in the real non-sci-fi world, there was Aunt Reet's bordering-on-the-supernatural sense of the land, the stories that seldom appeared in deeds or contracts, especially matrimonial, the generations of family hatreds big and small, the way the water flowed, or used to.

She picked up on the sixth ring. The TV set was loud in the background.

"Make it quick, Doc, I've got a live one tonight and a quarter ton of makeup to put on yet."

"What can you tell me about Mickey Wolfmann?"

If she took even a second to breathe, Doc didn't notice. "Westside Hochdeutsch mafia, biggest of the big, construction, savings and loans, untaxed billions stashed under an Alp someplace, technically Jewish but wants to be a Nazi, becomes exercised often to the point of violence at those who forget to spell his name with two *n*'s. What's he to you?"

Doc gave her a rundown on Shasta's visit and her account of the plot against the Wolfmann fortune.

"In the real-estate business," Reet remarked, "God knows, few of us are strangers to moral ambiguity. But some of these developers, they make Godzilla look like a conservationist, and you might not care to get into this, Larry. Who's paying you?"

"Well . . ."

"All on spec, eh? big surprise. Listen, if Shasta can't pay you, maybe that means Mickey's dumped her, and she's blaming the wife and wants revenge."

"Possible. But say I just wanted to hang out and rap with this Wolfmann dude?"

Was that an exasperated sigh? "I wouldn't recommend your usual approach. He goes around with a dozen bikers, mostly Aryan Brotherhood alumni, to watch his back, all court-certified badasses. Try making an appointment for once."

"Wait a minute, I ditched social-studies class a lot, but . . . Jews and the AB . . . Isn't there . . . something about, I forget . . . hatred?"

"The book on Mickey is, is he's unpredictable. More and more lately. Some would say eccentric. I would say stoned out of his fuckin mind, nothing personal."

"And this goon squad, they're loyal to him, even if when they were in the place they took some oath with maybe a anti-Semitic clause in it here and there?"

"Drive within ten blocks of the man, they'll lie down in front of your car. Keep coming, they'll roll a grenade. You want to talk to Mickey, don't be spontaneous, don't even be cute. Go through channels."

"Yeah, but I also don't want to get Shasta in trouble. Where do you think I could run into him, like, accidentally?"

"I promised my kid sister I'd never put her baby in the way of danger."

"I'm cool with the Brotherhood, Aunt Reet, know the handshake and everything."

"All right, it's your ass, kid, I have major liquid-liner issues to deal with here, but I'm told Mickey's been spending time out at his latest assault on the environment—some chipboard horror known as Channel View Estates?"

"Oh yeah, that. Bigfoot Bjornsen does commercials for them. Interrupting strange movies you've never heard of."

"Well, maybe your old cop buddy's the one who should be taking care of this. Have you been in touch with the LAPD?"

"I did think of going to Bigfoot," Doc said, "but just as I was reaching for the phone I remembered how, being Bigfoot and all, he'd probably try to pop *me* for the whole thing."

"Maybe you're better off with the Nazis, I don't envy you the choice. Be careful, Larry. Check in now and then just so I can reassure Elmina that you're still alive."

Fucking Bigfoot. Well, wouldn't you know. On some extrasensory impulse, Doc reached for the tube, switched it on and flipped to one of the off-network channels dedicated to long-ago TV movies and unsold pilots, and sure enough, there was the old hippie-hating mad dog himself, moonlighting after a busy day of civil-rights violation, as pitchman for Channel View Estates. "A Michael Wolfmann Concept," it read underneath the logo.

Like many L.A. cops, Bigfoot, named for his entry method of choice, harbored show-business yearnings and in fact had already appeared in enough character parts, from comical Mexicans on *The Flying Nun* to assistant psychopaths on *Voyage to the Bottom of the Sea*, to be paying SAG dues and receiving residual checks. Maybe the producers of these Channel View spots were desperate enough to be counting on some audience recognition—maybe, as Doc suspected, Bigfoot was somehow duked into whatever the underlying real-estate deal was. Whatever, personal dignity didn't come into it much. Bigfoot showed up on camera wearing getups that would have embarrassed the most unironical hippie in California, tonight's being an ankle-length velvet cape in a paisley print of so many jangling "psychedelic" hues that Doc's tube, a low-end affair purchased in Zody's parking lot at a Moonlight Madness sale a couple years ago, couldn't really keep up. Bigfoot had accessorized his outfit with love beads, shades with peace symbols on the lenses, and a gigantic Afro wig striped in Chinese red, chartreuse, and indigo. Bigfoot often reminded viewers of legendary used-car figure Cal Worthington—except where Cal was famous for including live animals in his pitch, Bigfoot's scripts featured a relentless terror squad of small children, who climbed all over the model-home furniture, performed insubordinate cannonballs into the backyard pools, whooped and hollered and pretended to shoot Bigfoot down, screaming "Freak Power!" and "Death to the Pig!" Viewers were ecstatic. "Those li'l kids," they would cry, "wow, they're really something, huh!" No overfed leopard ever got up Cal Worthington's nose the way these kids did Bigfoot's, but he was a pro, wasn't he, and by God he would soldier through, closely studying old W. C. Fields and

Bette Davis movies whenever they came on to see what tips he could pick up for sharing the frame with kids whose cuteness, for him, was never better than problematical. "We'll be chums," he would croak as if to himself, pretending to puff compulsively on a cigarette, "we'll be *chums*."

There was now sudden hammering on the front door, and briefly Doc flashed that it had to be Bigfoot in person, about to kick his way in once again as in days of old. But instead it was Denis from down the hill, whose name everybody pronounced to rhyme with "penis," appearing even more disoriented than usual.

"So Doc, I'm up on Dunecrest, you know the drugstore there, and like I noticed their sign, 'Drug'? 'Store'? Okay? Walked past it a thousand times, never *really saw* it—Drug, Store! man, far out, so I went in and Smilin Steve was at the counter and I said, like, 'Yes, hi, I'd like some drugs, please?'—oh, here, finish this up if you want."

"Thanks, all's 'at'll do 's just burn my lip."

Denis by now had drifted into the kitchen and started looking through the fridge.

"You're hungry, Denis?"

"Really. Hey, like Godzilla always sez to Mothra—why don't we go eat some place?"

They walked up to Dunecrest and turned left into the honky-tonk part of town. Pipeline Pizza was jumping, the smoke so thick inside you couldn't see from one end of the bar to the other. The jukebox, audible all the way to El Porto and beyond, was playing "Sugar, Sugar" by the Archies. Denis threaded his way back to the kitchen to see about a pizza, and Doc watched Ensenada Slim working one of the Gottlieb machines in the corner. Slim owned and operated a head shop just up the street called the Screaming Ultraviolet Brain and was a sort of village elder around here. After he'd won a dozen free games, he took a break, saw Doc and nodded.

"Buy you a beer, Slim?"

"Was that Shasta's car I saw down on the Drive? That big old ragtop?"

"She stuck her head in for a couple minutes," Doc said. "Kind of weird seeing her again. Always figured when I did, it'd be on the tube, not in person."

"Really. Sometimes I think I see her at the edge of the screen? but it's always some look-alike. And never as easy on the eyes, of course."

Sad but true, as Dion always sez. At Playa Vista High, Shasta made Class Beauty in the yearbook four years running, always got to be the ingenue in school plays, fantasized like everybody else about getting into the movies, and soon as she could manage it was off up the freeway looking for some low-rent living space in Hollywood. Doc, aside from being just about the only doper she knew who didn't use heroin, which freed up a lot of time for both of them, had never figured out what else she might've seen in him. Not that they were even together that long. Soon enough she was answering casting calls and getting some theater work, onstage and off, and Doc was into his own apprenticeship as a skip tracer, and each, gradually locating a different karmic thermal above the megalopolis, had watched the other glide away into a different fate.

Denis came back with his pizza. "I forget what I asked for on it." This happened at the Pipeline every Tuesday or Cheap Pizza Nite, when any size pizza, with anything on it, cost a flat $1.35. Denis now sat watching this one intently, like it was about to do something.

"That's a papaya chunk," Slim guessed, "and these . . . are these pork rinds?"

"And boysenberry yogurt on pizza, Denis? Frankly, eeeww." It was Sortilège, who used to work in Doc's office before her boyfriend Spike came back from Vietnam and she decided love was more important than a day job, or that's how Doc thought he remembered her explaining it. Her gifts were elsewhere, in any case. She was in touch with invisible forces and could diagnose and solve all manner of problems, emotional and physical, which she did mostly for free but in some cases accepted weed or acid in lieu of cash. She had never been wrong that Doc knew about. At the moment she was examining his hair, and as usual he had a spasm of defensive panic. Finally, with an energetic nod, "Better do something about that."

"Again?"

"Can't say it often enough—change your hair, change your life."

"What do you recommend?"

"Up to you. Follow your intuition. Would you mind, Denis, actually, if I just took this piece of tofu?"

"That's a marshmallow," Denis said.

BACK AT HIS PLACE AGAIN, Doc rolled a number, put on a late movie, found an old T-shirt, and sat tearing it up into short strips about a half inch wide till he had a pile of maybe a hundred of these, then went in the shower for a while and with his hair still wet took narrow lengths of it and rolled each one around a strip of T-shirt, tying it in place with an overhand knot, repeating this southern-plantation style all over his head, and then after maybe half an hour with the hair dryer, during which he may or may not have fallen asleep, untying the knots again and brushing it all out upside down into what seemed to him a fairly presentable foot-and-a-half-diameter white-guy Afro. Inserting his head carefully into a liquor-store carton to preserve the shape, Doc lay down on the couch and this time really did fall asleep, and toward dawn he dreamed about Shasta. It wasn't that they were fucking, exactly, but it was something like that. They had both flown from their other lives, the way you tend to fly in early-morning dreams, to rendezvous at a strange motel which seemed to be also a hair salon. She kept insisting she "loved" some guy whose name she never mentioned, though when Doc finally woke up, he figured she must've been talking about Mickey Wolfmann.

No point sleeping anymore. He stumbled up the hill to Wavos and had breakfast with the hard-core surfers who were always there. Flaco the Bad came over. "Hey man, that cop was around looking for you again. What's that on your head?"

"Cop? When was this?"

"Last night. He was at your place, but you were out. Detective from downtown Homicide in a really dinged-up El Camino, the one with the 396?"

"That was Bigfoot Bjornsen. Why didn't he just kick my door down like he usually does?"

"He might've been thinking about it but said something like 'Tomorrow is another day' . . . which would be today, right?"

"Not if I can help it."

DOC'S OFFICE WAS located near the airport, off East Imperial. He shared the place with a Dr. Buddy Tubeside, whose practice consisted largely of injecting people with "vitamin B_{12}," a euphemism for the physician's own blend of amphetamines. Today, early as it was, Doc still had to edge his way past a line of "B_{12}"-deficient customers which already stretched back to the parking lot, beachtown housewives of a certain melancholy index, actors with casting calls to show up at, deeply tanned geezers looking ahead to an active day of schmoozing in the sun, stewardii just in off some high-stress red-eye, even a few legit cases of pernicious anemia or vegetarian pregnancy, all shuffling along half asleep, chain-smoking, talking to themselves, sliding one by one into the lobby of the little cinder-block building through a turnstile, next to which, holding a clipboard and checking them in, stood Petunia Leeway, a stunner in a starched cap and micro-length medical outfit, not so much an actual nurse uniform as a lascivious commentary on one, which Dr. Tubeside claimed to've bought a truckload of from Frederick's of Hollywood, in a variety of fashion pastels, today's being aqua, at close to wholesale.

"Morning, Doc." Petunia managed to put a lounge-singer lilt onto it, the vocal equivalent of batting mink eyelashes at him. "Love your 'fro."

"Howdy, Petunia. Still married to what's-his-name?"

"Oh, Doc . . ."

On first signing the lease, the two tenants, like bunkmates at summer camp, had tossed a coin for who'd get the upstairs suite, and Doc had lost or, as he liked to think of it, won. The sign on his door read LSD INVESTIGATIONS, LSD, as he explained when people asked, which was not often, standing for "Location, Surveillance, Detection." Beneath this was a rendering of a giant bloodshot eyeball in the psychedelic favorites green and magenta, the detailing of whose literally thousands of frenzied capillaries had been subcontracted out to a commune of speed freaks who had long since migrated up to Sonoma. Potential clients had been known to spend hours gazing at the ocular mazework, often forgetting what they'd come here for.

A visitor was here already, in fact, waiting for Doc. What made him unusual was, was he was a black guy. To be sure, black folks were occasionally spotted west of the Harbor Freeway, but to see one this far out of the usual range, practically by the ocean, was pretty rare. Last time anybody could remember a black motorist in Gordita Beach, for example, anxious calls for backup went out on all the police bands, a small task force of cop vehicles assembled, and roadblocks were set up all along Pacific Coast Highway. An old Gordita reflex, dating back to shortly after the Second World War, when a black family had actually tried to move into town and the citizens, with helpful advice from the Ku Klux Klan, had burned the place to the ground and then, as if some ancient curse had come into effect, refused to allow another house ever to be built on the site. The lot stood empty until the town finally confiscated it and turned it into a park, where the youth of Gordita Beach, by the laws of karmic adjustment, were soon gathering at night to drink, dope, and fuck, depressing their parents, though not property values particularly.

"Say," Doc greeted his visitor, "what it is, my brother."

"Never mind that shit," replied the black guy, introducing himself as Tariq Khalil and staring for a while, under different circumstances offensively, at Doc's Afro.

"Well. Come on in."

In Doc's office were a pair of high-backed banquettes covered in padded fuchsia plastic, facing each other across a Formica table in a pleasant tropical green. This was in fact a modular coffee-shop booth, which Doc had scavenged from a renovation in Hawthorne. He waved Tariq into one of the seats and sat down across from him. It was cozy. The tabletop between them was littered with phone books, pencils, three-by-five index cards boxed and loose, road maps, cigarette ashes, a transistor radio, roach clips, coffee cups, and an Olivetti Lettera 22, into which Doc, mumbling, "Just start a ticket on this," inserted a sheet of paper which appeared to have been used repeatedly for some strange compulsive origami.

Tariq watched skeptically. "Secretary's off today?"

"Something like that. But I'll take some notes here, and it'll all get typed up later."

"Okay, so there's this guy I was in the joint with. White guy. Aryan Bro, as a matter of fact. We did some business, now we're both out, he still owes me. I mean, it's a lot of money. I can't give you details, I swore a oath I wouldn't tell."

"How about just his name?"

"Glen Charlock."

Sometimes the way somebody says a name, you get a vibration. Tariq was talking like a man whose heart had been broken. "You know where he's staying now?"

"Only who he works for. He's a bodyguard for a builder named Wolfmann."

Doc had a moment of faintheadedness, drug-induced no doubt. He came out of it on paranoia alert, not enough, he hoped, for Tariq to notice. He pretended to study the ticket he was making out. "If you don't mind my asking, Mr. Khalil, how did you hear about this agency?"

"Sledge Poteet."

"Wow. Blast from the past."

"Said you helped him out of a situation back in '67."

"First time I ever got shot at. You guys know each other from the place?"

"They were teachin us both how to cook. Sledge still has about maybe a year more in there."

"I remember him when he couldn't boil water."

"Should see him now, he can boil tap water, Arrowhead Springs water, club soda, Perrier, you name it. He the Boilerman."

"So if you don't mind an obvious question—you know where Glen Charlock works now, why not just go over there and look him up directly, why hire some go-between?"

"Because this Wolfmann is surrounded day and night with some Aryan Brotherhood army, and outside of Glen I have never enjoyed cordial relations with those Nazi-ass motherfuckers."

"Oh—so send some white guy in to get *his* head hammered."

"More or less. I would of p'ferred somebody a little more convincing."

"What I lack in *al*-titude," Doc explained for the million or so -th time in his career, "I make up for in *at*-titude."

"Okay . . . that's possible . . . I seen that on the yard now and then."

"When you were inside—were you in a gang?"

"Black Guerrilla Family."

"George Jackson's outfit. And you say you did business with who now, the Aryan Brotherhood?"

"We found we shared many of the same opinions about the U.S. government."

"Mmm, that racial harmony, I can dig it."

Tariq was looking at Doc with a peculiar intensity, and his eyes had grown yellow and pointed.

"There's something else," Doc guessed.

"My old street gang. Artesia Crips. When I got out of Chino I went looking for some of them and found it ain't just them gone, but the turf itself."

"Far out. What do you mean, gone?"

"Not there. Grindit up into li'l pieces. Seagulls all pickin at it. Figure I must be trippin, drive around for a while, come back, everything's still gone."

"Uh-huh." Doc typed, *Not hallucinating.*

"Nobody and nothing. Ghost town. Except for this big sign, 'Coming Soon on This Site,' houses for peckerwood prices, shopping mall, some shit. Guess who the builder on it."

"Wolfmann again."

"That's it."

On the wall Doc had a map of the region. "Show me." The area Tariq pointed to looked to be a fairly straight shot from here eastward down Artesia Boulevard, and Doc realized after a minute and a half of mapreading that it had to be the site of Channel View Estates. He pretended to run an ethnicity scan on Tariq. "You're, like, what again, Japanese?"

"Uh, how long you been doing this?"

"Looks closer to Gardena than Compton, 's all I'm saying."

"WW Two," said Tariq. "Before the war, a lot of South Central was still a Japanese neighborhood. Those people got sent to camps, we come on in to be the next Japs."

"And now it's your turn to get moved along."

"More white man's revenge. Freeway up by the airport wasn't enough."

"Revenge for . . . ?"

"Watts."

"The riots."

"Some of us say 'insurrection.' The Man, he just waits for his moment."

Long, sad history of L.A. land use, as Aunt Reet never tired of pointing out. Mexican families bounced out of Chavez Ravine to build Dodger Stadium, American Indians swept out of Bunker Hill for the Music Center, Tariq's neighborhood bulldozed aside for Channel View Estates.

"If I can get ahold of your prison buddy, will he honor his debt to you?"

"I can't tell you what it is."

"No need."

"Oh and the other thing is I can't give you nothin in front."

"Groovy with that."

"Sledge was right, you are one crazy white motherfucker."

"How can you tell?"

"I counted."

TWO

DOC TOOK THE FREEWAY OUT. THE EASTBOUND LANES TEEMED with VW buses in jittering paisleys, primer-coated street hemis, woodies of authentic Dearborn pine, TV-star-piloted Porsches, Cadillacs carrying dentists to extramarital trysts, windowless vans with lurid teen dramas in progress inside, pickups with mattresses full of country cousins from the San Joaquin, all wheeling along together down into these great horizonless fields of housing, under the power transmission lines, everybody's radios lasing on the same couple of AM stations, under a sky like watered milk, and the white bombardment of a sun smogged into only a smear of probability, out in whose light you began to wonder if anything you'd call psychedelic could ever happen, or if—bummer!—all this time it had really been going on up north.

Beginning on Artesia, signs directed Doc to Channel View Estates, A Michael Wolfmann Concept. There were the expected local couples who couldn't wait to have a look at the next OPPOS, as Aunt Reet tended to call most tract houses of her acquaintance. Now and then at the edges of the windshield, Doc spotted black pedestrians, bewildered as Tariq must have been, maybe also looking for the old neighborhood, for rooms lived in day after day, solid as the axes of space, now taken away into commotion and ruin.

The development stretched into the haze and the soft smell of the fog component of smog, and of desert beneath the pavement—model units nearer the road, finished homes farther in, and just visible beyond them the skeletons of new construction, expanding into the unincorporated wastes. Doc drove past the gate till he got to a patch of empty contractor hardpan with street signs already in but the streets not yet paved. He parked at what would be the corner of Kaufman and Broad and walked back.

Commanding filtered views of an all-but-neglected branch of the Dominguez Flood Control Channel forgotten and cut off by miles of fill, regrading, trash of industrial ventures that had either won or failed, these homes were more or less Spanish Colonial with not-necessarily-load-bearing little balconies and red-tile roofs, meant to suggest higher-priced towns like San Clemente or Santa Barbara, though so far there wasn't a shade tree in sight.

Close to what would be the front gate of Channel View Estates, Doc found a makeshift miniplaza put there basically for the construction folks, with a liquor store, a take-out sandwich place with a lunch counter, a beer bar where you could shoot some pool, and a massage parlor called Chick Planet, in front of which he saw a row of carefully looked-after motorcycles, parked with military precision. This seemed the most likely place for him to find a cadre of badasses. Plus, if they were all here at the moment, then chances were Mickey was, too. On the further assumption that the owners of these bikes were here for recreation and not waiting inside drawn up in formation prepared to kick Doc's ass, he breathed deeply, surrounded himself with a white light, and stepped in the front door.

"Hi, I'm Jade?" A bubbly young Asian lady in a turquoise cheong-sam handed him a laminated menu of services. "And please take note of today's Pussy-Eater's Special, which is good all day till closing time?"

"Mmm, not that $14.95 ain't a totally groovy price, but I'm really trying to locate this guy who works for Mr. Wolfmann?"

"Far out. Does he eat pussy?"

"Well, Jade, you'd know better'n me, fella named Glen?"

"Oh sure, Glen comes in here, they all do. You got a cigarette for me?" He tapped her out an unfiltered Kool. "Ooh, lockup style. Not much eating pussy in there, huh?"

"Glen and I were both in Chino around the same time. Have you seen him today?"

"Till about one minute ago, when everybody suddenly split. Is there something weird going on? Are you a cop?"

"Let's see." Doc inspected his feet. "Nah . . . wrong shoes."

"Reason I ask is, is if you were a cop, you'd be entitled to a free preview of our Pussy-Eater's Special?"

"How about a licensed PI? Would that—"

"Hey, Bambi!" Out through the bead curtains, as if on a time-out from a beach volleyball game, strode this blonde in a turquoise and orange Day-Glo bikini.

"Oboy," Doc said. "Where do we—"

"Not you, Bong Brain," Bambi muttered. Jade was already reaching for that bikini.

"Oh," he said. "Huh . . . see, is what I thought is, here? where it says 'Pussy-Eater's Special'? is what that means is, is that—"

Well . . . neither girl seemed to be paying him much attention anymore, though out of politeness Doc thought he should keep watching for a while, till finally they disappeared down behind the reception desk, and he wandered away figuring to have a look around. Out into the hallway, from someplace ahead, seeped indigo light and frequencies even darker, along with string-heavy music from half a generation ago from LPs compiled to accompany bachelor-pad fucking.

Nobody was around. It felt like maybe there had been, till Doc showed up. The place was also turning out to be bigger inside than out. There were black-light suites with fluorescent rock 'n' roll posters and mirrored ceilings and vibrating water beds. Strobe lights blinked, incense cones sent ribbons of musk-scented smoke ceilingward, and carpeting of artificial angora shag in a variety of tones including oxblood and teal, not always limited to floor surfaces, beckoned alluringly.

As he neared the back of the establishment, Doc began to hear a lot of screaming from outside, along with a massed thundering of Harleys. "Uh-oh. What's this?"

He didn't find out. Maybe it was all the exotic sensory input that caused Doc about then to swoon abruptly and lose an unknown amount of his day. Perhaps striking some ordinary object on the way down accounted for the painful lump he found on his head when at length he awoke. Faster, anyhow, than the staff on *Medical Center* can say "subdural hematoma," Doc dug how the unhip Muzak was silent, plus no Jade, no Bambi, and he was lying on the cement floor of a space he didn't recognize, though the same could not be said for what he now ID'd, far overhead, like a bad-luck planet in today's horoscope, as the evilly twinkling face of Detective Lieutenant Bigfoot Bjornsen, LAPD.

"CONGRATULATIONS, HIPPIE SCUM," Bigfoot greeted Doc in his all-too-familiar 30-weight voice, "and welcome to a world of inconvenience. Yes, this time it appears you have finally managed to stumble into something too real and deep to hallucinate your worthless hippie ass out of." He was holding, and now and then taking bites from, his trademark chocolate-covered frozen banana.

"Howdy, Bigfoot. Can I have a bite?"

"Sure can, but you'll have to wait, we left the rottweiler back at the station."

"No rush. And . . . and where are we at the moment, again?"

"At Channel View Estates, on a future homesite where elements of some wholesome family will quite soon be gathering night after night, to gaze tubeward, gobble their nutritious snacks, perhaps after the kids are in bed even attempt some procreational foreplay, little appreciating that once, on this very spot, an infamous perpetrator lay in a drugged stupor, babbling incoherently at the homicide detective, since risen to eminence, who apprehended him."

They were still within sight of the front gate. Through a maze of stapled-together framing, Doc made out in the afternoon light a blurry vista of streets full of newly poured foundations awaiting houses to go on top of them, trenches for sewer and utility lines, sawhorse barricades with lights blinking even in the daytime, precast storm drains, piles of fill, bulldozers and backhoes.

"Without wishing to seem impatient," the Lieutenant continued, "any time you feel you'd like to join us, we would so like to chat." Uniformed toadies crept about, chuckling in appreciation.

"Bigfoot, I don't know what happened. Last I recall I was in that massage parlor over there? Asian chick named Jade? and her Anglo friend Bambi?"

"Wishful figments of a brain pickled in cannabis fumes, no doubt," theorized Detective Bjornsen.

"But, like, I didn't do it? Whatever it is?"

"Sure." Bigfoot stared, snacking amusedly on his frozen banana, as Doc went through the wearisome chore of getting vertical again, followed by details to be worked out such as remaining that way, trying to walk, so forth. Which was about when he caught sight of a medical examiner's crew with a bloodstreaked human body supine on a gurney, settled into itself like an uncooked holiday turkey, face covered with a cheap cop-issue blanket. Things kept falling out of its pants pockets. Cops had to go scramble in the dirt to retrieve them. Doc found himself freaking out, in terms of his stomach and whatever.

Bigfoot Bjornsen smirked. "Yes, I can almost pity your civilian distress—though if you had been more of a man and less of a ball-less hippie draft dodger, who knows, you might have seen enough over in the 'Nam to share even my own sense of professional ennui at the sight of one more, what we call, stiff, to be dealt with."

"Who is it?" Doc nodding at the corpse.

"Was, Sportello. Here on Earth we say 'was.' Meet Glen Charlock, whom you were asking for by name only hours ago, witnesses will swear to that. Forgetful dope fiends should be more cautious about whom they choose to act out their wacko fantasies upon. Furthermore, on the face of it, you have chosen to ice a personal bodyguard of the rather well-connected Mickey Wolfmann. Name ring a bell? or in your case shake a tambourine? Ah, but here's our ride."

"Hey—my car . . ."

"Like its owner, well on the way to impoundment."

"Pretty cold, Bigfoot, even for you."

"Come come, Sportello, you know we'll be more than happy to give you a lift. Watch your head."

"Watch my . . . How 'm I spoze to do that, man?"

THEY DIDN'T GO downtown but, for reasons of cop protocol forever obscure to Doc, only as far as the Compton station, where they pulled in to the lot and paused next to a battered '68 El Camino. Bigfoot got out of the black-and-white and went back and opened the trunk. "Here, Sportello—come and give me a hand with this."

"What, excuse me, the fuck," Doc inquired, "is it?"

"Bobwire," replied Bigfoot. "An eighty-rod spool of authenticated Glidden four-point galvanized. You want to take that side?"

Thing weighed about a hundred pounds. The cop who'd been driving sat and watched them lift it out of the trunk and stash it in the bed of the El Camino, which Doc recalled was Bigfoot's ride.

"Livestock problems out where you live, Bigfoot?"

"Oh, you'd never use this wire for actual fence, are you crazy, this is seventy years old, mint condition—"

"Wait. You . . . collect . . . barbed wire."

Well yes, as it turned out, along with spurs, harness, cowboy sombreros, saloon paintings, sheriffs' stars, bullet molds, all kinds of Wild West paraphernalia. "That is, if *you* don't object, Sportello."

"Whoa easy there Jolly Rancher, ain't looking for no drawdown 'th no bobwire collector, man's own business what he puts in his pickup ain't it."

"I should hope so," Bigfoot sniffed. "Come on, let's go inside and see if there's a cubicle open."

Doc's history with Bigfoot, beginning with minor drug episodes, stop-and-frisks up and down Sepulveda, and repeated front-door repairs, had escalated a couple of years ago with the Lunchwater case, one more of the squalid matrimonials that were occupying Doc's time back then. The husband, a tax accountant who thought he'd score some quality surveillance on the cheap, had hired Doc to keep an eye on his wife. After a couple days of stakeouts at the boyfriend's house Doc decided to go up on the roof and have a closer look through a skylight at the bedroom below, where the activities proved to be so routine—hanky maybe, not much panky—that he decided to light a joint to pass the time, taking one from his pocket, in the dark, more soporific than he had intended. Before long he had fallen asleep and half rolled, half slid down the shallow pitch of the red-tile roof, coming to rest with his head in the gutter, where he then managed to sleep through the events which followed, including hubby's arrival, considerable screaming, and gunfire loud enough to get the neighbors to call the police. Bigfoot, who happened to be out in a prowl car nearby, showed up to find the husband and the b.f. slain and the wife attractively tousled and sobbing, and gazing at the .22 in her hand as if it was the first time she'd seen one. Doc, up on the roof, was still snoring away.

Fast-forward to Compton, the present day. "What concerns us," Bigfoot was trying to explain, "is this, what we in Homicide like to call, 'pattern'? Here's the second time we know of that you've been discovered sleeping at the scene of a major crime and unable—dare I suggest 'unwilling'?—to furnish us any details."

"Lot of leaves and twigs and shit in my hair," Doc seemed to recall. Bigfoot nodded encouragingly. "And . . . there was a fire truck with a ladder? which is how I must've got down off the roof?" They looked at each other for a while.

"I was thinking more like earlier today," Bigfoot with a touch of impatience. "Channel View Estates, Chick Planet Massage, sort of thing."

"Oh. Well, I was unconscious, man."

"Yes. Yes but before that, when you and Glen Charlock had your fatal encounter . . . when would you say that was, exactly, in the sequence of events?"

"I told you, the first time I ever saw him, is he was dead."

"His associates, then. How many of them were you already acquainted with?"

"Not normally guys I'd hang with, totally wrong drug profile, too many reds, too much speed."

"Potheads, you're so exclusive. Would you say you *took offense* at Glen's preference for barbiturates and amphetamines?"

"Yeah, I was planning to report him to the Dope Fiend Standards and Ethics Committee."

"Yes, now your ex-girlfriend Shasta Fay Hepworth is a known intimate of Glen's employer, Mickey Wolfmann. Do you think Glen and Shasta were . . . you know . . ." He made a loose fist and slid the middle finger of his other hand back and forth in it for what seemed to Doc way too long. "How did that make you feel, here you are still carrying the torch, and there she is in the company of all those Nazi lowlifes?"

"Do that some more Bigfoot, I think I'm gettin a hardon."

"Tough little wop monkey, as my man Fatso Judson always sez."

"Case you forgot, Lieutenant, you and me are almost in the same business, except I don't get that free pass to shoot people all the time and so forth. But if it was me over there in your seat, I guess I'd be acting the same way, maybe start in next with remarks about my mother. Or I guess *your* mother, because you'd be me. . . . Have I got that right?"

It wasn't till the middle of rush hour that they let Doc call his lawyer, Sauncho Smilax. Actually Sauncho worked for a maritime law firm over at the Marina called Hardy, Gridley, and Chatfield, and his résumé fell a little short in the criminal area. He and Doc had met by accident one night at the Food Giant up on Sepulveda. Sauncho, then a novice doper who'd just learned about removing seeds and stems, was about to buy a flour sifter when he flashed that the people at the checkout *would all know what he wanted the sifter for* and call the police. He went into a kind of paranoid freeze, which was when Doc, having an attack of midnight chocolate deficiency, came zooming out of a snack-food aisle and crashed his cart into Sauncho's.

With the collision, legal reflexes reawakened. "Hey, would it be okay if I put this sifter in with your stuff there, like, for a cover?"

"Sure," Doc said, "but if you're gonna be paranoid, how about all this chocolate, man . . . ?"

"Oh. Then . . . maybe we'd better put in a few more, you know, like, innocent-looking items. . . ."

By the time they got to the checkout, they had somehow acquired an extra hundred dollars' worth of goods, including half a dozen obligatory boxes of cake mix, a gallon of guacamole and several giant sacks of tortilla chips, a case of store-brand boysenberry soda, most of what was in the Sara Lee frozen-dessert case, lightbulbs and laundry detergent for straight-world cred, and, after what seemed like hours in the International Section, a variety of shrink-wrapped Japanese pickles that looked cool. At some point in this, Sauncho mentioned that he was a lawyer.

"Far out. People are always telling me I need a 'criminal lawyer,' which, nothing personal, understand, but—"

"Actually I'm a marine lawyer."

Doc thought about this. "You're . . . a Marine who practices law? No, wait—you're a lawyer who only represents Marines. . . ."

In the course of getting this all straight, Doc also learned that Sauncho was just out of law school at SC and, like many ex-collegians unable to let go of the old fraternity life, living at the beach—not far from Doc, as a matter of fact.

"Maybe you better give me your card," Doc said. "Can't ever tell. Boat hassles, oil spills, something."

Sauncho never officially went on retainer, but after a few late-night panic calls from Doc he did begin to reveal an unexpected talent for dealing with bail bondsmen and deskfolk at cop stations around the Southland, and one day they both realized that he'd become, what they call de facto, Doc's lawyer.

Sauncho now answered the phone in some agitation.

"Doc! Have you got the tube on?"

"All's I get here's a three-minute call, Saunch, they've got me in Compton, and it's Bigfoot again."

"Yeah well, I'm watching cartoons here, okay? and this Donald Duck one is really been freaking me out?" Sauncho didn't have that many people in his life to talk to and had always had Doc figured for an easy mark.

"You have a pen, Saunch? Here's the processing number, prepare to copy—" Doc started reading him the number, real slowly.

"It's like Donald and Goofy, right, and they're out in a life raft, adrift at sea? for what looks like weeks? and what you start noticing after a while, in Donald's close-ups, is that he has this *whisker stubble*? like, growing out of his beak? You get the significance of that?"

"If I find a minute to think about it, Saunch, but meantime here comes Bigfoot and he's got that look, so if you could repeat the number back, OK, and—"

"We've always had this image of Donald Duck, we assume it's how he looks all the time in his normal life, but in fact he's always had to go in *every day* and *shave his beak*. The way I figure, it has to be Daisy. You know, which means, what other grooming demands is that chick laying on him, right?"

Bigfoot stood there whistling some country-western tune through his teeth till Doc, not feeling real hopeful, got off the phone.

"Now then, where were we," Bigfoot pretending to look through some notes. "While suspect—that's you—is having his alleged midday nap, so necessary to the hippie lifestyle, some sort of incident occurs in the vicinity of Channel View Estates. Firearms are discharged. When the dust settles, we find one Glen Charlock deceased. More compellingly for LAPD, the man Charlock was supposed to be guarding, Michael Z. Wolfmann, has vanished, giving local law enforcement less than twenty-four hours before the feds call it a kidnapping and come in to fuck everything up. Perhaps, Sportello, you could help to forestall this by providing the names of the other members of your cult? That would be ever so helpful to us here in Homicide, as well as the chance of a break for you when that ol' trial date rolls around?"

"Cult."

"The *L.A. Times* has referred to me more than once as a Renaissance detective," said Bigfoot modestly, "which means that I am many things—but one thing I am not is stupid, and purely out of noblesse oblige I now extend this assumption to cover you as well. No one, in fact, would *ever* have been stupid enough to try this alone. Which therefore suggests some kind of a Mansonoid conspiracy, wouldn't you agree?"

After no more than an hour of this sort of thing, to Doc's surprise, Sauncho actually showed up at the door and started right in with Bigfoot.

"Lieutenant, you know you don't have any case here, so if you're going to charge him, you better. Otherwise—"

"Sauncho," Doc hollered, "will you dummy up, remember who this is, how sensitive he gets— Bigfoot, don't mind him, he watches too many courtroom dramas—"

"As a matter of fact," Detective Bjornsen with the fixed and sinister stare he used to express geniality, "we probably *could* take this all the way to trial, but with our luck the jury pool'd be ninety-nine percent hippie freaks, plus some longhair sympathizer of a DDA who'd go and fuck the case all up anyway."

"Sure, unless you could get the venue changed," mused Sauncho, "like, Orange County might be—"

"Saunch, which one of us are you working for, again?"

"I wouldn't call it work, Doc, clients pay me for work."

"We're only detaining him for his own good," Bigfoot explained. "He's closely connected with a high-profile homicide and possible kidnapping, and who's to say he himself won't be next? Maybe this'll turn out to be one of those perpetrators who *specially like* to murder hippies, though if Sportello's on their list, I might have a conflict of interest."

"Aww, Bigfoot, you don't mean that. . . . If I got knocked off? think of all your time and trouble finding somebody else to hassle."

"What trouble? I go out the door, get in the unit, head up any block, before I know it, I'm driving through some giant damn *herd* of you hippie freaks, each more roustable than the last."

"This is embarrassing," said Sauncho. "Maybe you two should find somewhere besides an interrogation cubicle."

The local news came on and everybody went out to the squad room to watch. There on the screen was Channel View Estates—a forlorn-looking view of the miniplaza, occupied by an armored division's worth of cop vehicles parked every which way with their lights all going, and cops sitting on fenders drinking coffee, and, in close-up, Bigfoot Bjornsen, hair Aqua-Netted against the Santa Anas, explaining, ". . . apparently a party of civilians, on some training exercise in anti-guerrilla warfare. They may have assumed that this construction site, not yet being open for occupancy, was deserted enough to provide a realistic setting for what we must assume was only a harmless patriotic scenario." The Japanese-American cutie with the microphone turned fullface to the camera and continued, "Tragically, however, live ammunition somehow found its way into these war games, and tonight one ex–prison inmate lies slain while prominent construction mogul Michael Wolfmann has mysteriously vanished. Police have detained a number of suspects for questioning."

Break for commercial. "Wait a minute," said Detective Bjornsen, as if to himself. "This has just given me an idea. Sportello, I believe I shall kick you after all." Doc flinched, but then remembered this was also cop slang for "release." Bigfoot's thinking on this being that, if he cut Doc loose, it might attract the attention of the real perpetrators. Plus giving him an excuse to keep tailing Doc in case there was something Doc wasn't telling him.

"Come along, Sportello, let's take a ride."

"I'm gonna watch the tube here for a while," Sauncho said. "Remember, Doc, this was like fifteen billable minutes."

"Thanks, Saunch. Put it on my tab?"

Bigfoot checked out a semi-obvious Plymouth with little E-for-Exempt symbols on the plates, and they went blasting through the remnants of rush hour up to the Hollywood Freeway and presently over the Cahuenga Pass and down into the Valley.

"What's this?" Doc said after a while.

"As a courtesy I'm taking you out to the impound garage to get your vehicle. We've been over it with the best tools available to forensic science, and except for enough cannabis debris to keep an average family of four stoned for a year, you're clean. No blood or impact evidence we can use. Congratulations."

Doc's general policy was to try to be groovy about most everything, but when it was his ride in question, California reflexes kicked in. "Congratulate this, Bigfoot."

"I've upset you."

"Nobody calls my car a *murderer,* man?"

"I'm sorry, your car is some kind of . . . what, pacifist vegetarian? When bugs come crashing fatally into its windshield, it . . . it feels remorse? Look, we found it almost on top of Charlock's body, idling, and tried not to jump to any obvious conclusions. Maybe it intended to give the victim mouth-to-mouth."

"I thought he was shot."

"Whatever, be happy your car's in the clear, Benzidine doesn't lie."

"Well yeah . . . does make me kind of jumpy though, how about you?"

"Not the one with the *r* in it"—Bigfoot fell for this every time—"oh,

31

but here's Canoga Park coming up in a few exits, let me just show you something for a minute."

Off the exit ramp, Bigfoot hooked a U-turn without signaling, went back under the freeway and began to climb up into the hills, presently pulling in at a secluded spot that had Shot While Trying to Escape written all over it. Doc began to get nervous, but what Bigfoot had on his mind, it seemed, was job recruitment.

"Nobody can predict a year or two hence, but right now Nixon has the combination to the safe and he's throwing fistfuls of greenbacks at anything that even looks like local law enforcement. Federal funding beyond the highest number you can think of, which for most hippies is not much further than the number of ounces in a kilo."

"Thirty-five . . . point . . . something, everybody knows that— Wait. You, you mean like, *Mod Squad,* Bigfoot? rat on everybody I ever met, how far back do we go and you still don't know me any better'n 'at?"

"You'd be surprised how many in your own hippie freak community have found our Special Employee disbursements useful. Toward the end of the month in particular."

Doc took a close look at Bigfoot. Jive-ass sideburns, stupid mustache, haircut from a barber college out somewhere on a desolate boulevard far from any current definition of hipness. Right out of the background of some *Adam-12* episode, a show which Bigfoot had in fact moonlighted on once or twice. In theory Doc knew that if, for some reason he couldn't imagine right away, he wanted to see any other Bigfoot, off camera, off duty—even married with kids for all Doc knew, he'd have to look in through and past all that depressing detail. "You married, Bigfoot?"

"Sorry, you're not my type." He held up his left hand to display a wedding ring. "Know what this is, or don't they exist on Planet Hippie."

"A-and, you have like, kids?"

"I hope this isn't some kind of veiled hippie threat."

"Only that . . . wow, Bigfoot! isn't it *strange,* here we both are with this *mysterious power* to ruin each other's day, and we don't even know anything *about* each other?"

"Really profound, Sportello. Aimless doper's driveling to be sure, and yet, why, you have just defined the very essence of law enforcement! Well done! I always knew you had potential. So! how about it?"

"Nothing personal, but yours is the last wallet I'd ever want money out of."

"Hey! wake up, it only looks like Happy and Dopey and them skipping around the Magic Kingdom here, what it really is is what we call . . . 'Reality'?"

Well, Doc didn't have the beard, but he was wearing some tire-tread huaraches from south of the border that could pass for biblical, and he began to wonder now how many other innocent brothers and sisters the satanic Detective Bjornsen might've led to this high place, his own scenic overlook here, and swept his arm out across the light-stunned city, and offered them everything in it that money could buy. "Don't tell me you can't use it. I am aware of the Freak Brothers' dictum that dope will get you through times of no money better than vice versa, and we could certainly offer compensation in a more, how to put it, inhalable form."

"You mean . . ."

"Sportello. Try to drag your consciousness out of that old-time hard-boiled dick era, this is the Glass House wave of the future we're in now. All those downtown evidence rooms got filled up ages ago, now about once every month Property Section has to rent more warehouse space out in deep unincorporated county, bricks and bricks of shit stacked to the roof and spilling out in the parking lot, Acapulco Gold! Panama Red! Michoacán Icepack! numberless kilos of righteous weed, name your figure, just for trivial information we already have anyway. And what you don't smoke—improbable as that seems—you could always sell."

"Good thing you're not recruiting for the NCAA, Bigfoot, you'd be in some deep shit."

AT THE OFFICE NEXT DAY, Doc was listening to the stereo with his head between the speakers and almost missed the diffident ring of the Princess phone he'd found at a swap meet in Culver City. It was Tariq Khalil.

"I didn't do it!"

"It's okay."

"But I didn't—"

"Nobody said you did, fact they thought for a while it was me. Man, I'm really sorry about Glen."

Tariq was quiet for so long that Doc thought he'd hung up. "I will be, too," he said finally, "when I get a minute to think about it. Right now I'm conveying my ass out of the area. If Glen was a target, then so am I, I would say in spades, but you folks do get offended so easy."

"Is there someplace I can—"

"Better not be in no contact. This is not some bunch of fools like the LAPD, this is some heavy-ass motherfuckers. And if you don't mind a piece of free advice—"

"Yeah, care in motion, as Sidney Omarr always sez in the paper. Well, you too."

"*Hasta luego,* white man."

Doc rolled a number and was just about to light up when the phone rang again. This time it was Bigfoot. "So we send some Police Academy hotshot over to the last known address of Shasta Fay Hepworth, just a routine visit, and guess what."

Ah, fuck no. Not this.

"Oh, *I'm* sorry, am I upsetting you? Relax, all we know at this point is that she's disappeared too, yes just like her boyfriend Mickey. Isn't that odd? Do you think there could be a connection? Like maybe they ran off together?"

"Bigfoot, can we at least try to be professional here? So I don't have to start callin you names, like, I don't know, mean-spirited little shit, somethin like that?"

"You're right—it's the federals I'm really annoyed with, and I'm taking it out on you."

"You're apologizing, Bigfoot?"

"Ever known me to?"

"Uhhm . . ."

"If anything does occur to you about where they—so sorry, *she*—might've gone, you will share that, won't you?"

There was an ancient superstition at the beach, something like the surfer belief that burning your board will bring awesome waves, and it went like this—take a Zig-Zag paper and write on it your dearest wish, and then use it to roll a joint of the best dope you can find, and smoke it all up, and your wish would be granted. Attention and concentration were also said to be important, but most of the dopers Doc knew tended to ignore that part.

The wish was simple, just that Shasta Fay be safe. The dope was some Hawaiian product Doc had been saving, although at the moment he couldn't remember for what. He lit up. About the time he was ready to transfer the roach to a roach clip, the phone rang again, and he had one of those brief lapses where you forget how to pick up the receiver.

"Hello?" said a young woman's voice after a while.

"Oh. Did I forget to say that first? Sorry. This isn't . . . no, of course it wouldn't be."

"I got your number from Ensenada Slim, at that head shop in Gordita Beach? It's about my husband. He used to be close to a friend of yours, Shasta Fay Hepworth?"

All right. "And you're . . ."

"Hope Harlingen. I was wondering how your caseload's looking at the moment."

"My . . . oh." Professional term. "Sure, where are you?"

It turned out to be an address in outer Torrance, between Walteria and the airfield, a split-level with a pepper tree by the driveway and a eucalyptus out back and a distant view of thousands of small Japanese sedans, overflowed from the main lot on Terminal Island, obsessively arranged on vast expanses of blacktop and destined for auto agencies across the desert Southwest. TVs and stereos spoke from up and down the streets. The trees of the neighborhood sifted the air green. Small airplanes went purring overhead. In the kitchen hung a creeping fig in a plastic pot, vegetable stock simmered on the stove, hummingbirds out on the patio poised vibrating in the air with their beaks up inside the bougainvillea and honeysuckle blossoms.

Doc, who had a chronic problem telling one California blonde from another, found an almost 100-percent classic specimen—hair, tan, athletic grace, everything but the world-famous insincere smile, owing to a set of store-bought choppers which, though technically "false," invited those she now and then did smile at to consider what real and unamusing history might've put them there.

Noticing Doc's stare, "Heroin," she pretended to explain. "Sucks the calcium out of your system like a vampire, use it any length of time and your teeth go all to hell. Flower child to wasted derelict, zap, like magic. And that's the good part. Keep it up long enough . . . Well."

She got up and started pacing. She was not a weeper, but she was a pacer, which Doc appreciated, it kept the information coming, there was a beat to it. A few months back, according to Hope, her husband, Coy Harlingen, had OD'd on heroin. As well as he could with a doper's memory, Doc recalled the name, and even some story in the papers. Coy had played with the Boards, a surf band who'd been together since the early sixties, now considered pioneers of electric surf music and more recently working in a subgenre they liked to call "surfadelic," which featured dissonant guitar tunings, peculiar modalities such as post–Dick Dale *hijaz kar,* incomprehensibly screamed references to the sport, and the radical sound effects surf music has always been known for, vocal noises as well as feedback from guitars and wind instruments. *Rolling*

Stone commented, "The Boards' new album will make Jimi Hendrix *want* to listen to surf music again."

Coy's own contribution to what the Boards' producers had modestly termed their "Makaha of Sound" had been to hum through the reed of a tenor or sometimes alto sax a harmony part alongside whatever melody he was playing, as if the instrument was some giant kazoo, this then being enhanced by Barcus-Berry pickups and amplifiers. His influences, according to rock critics who'd noticed, included Earl Bostic, Stan Getz, and legendary New Orleans studio tenor Lee Allen. "Inside the surf-sax category," Hope shrugged, "Coy passed for a towering figure, because he actually improvised once in a while, instead of the way second and even third choruses usually get repeated note for note?"

Doc nodded uncomfortably. "Don't get me wrong, I love surf music, I'm from its native land, I still have all these old beat-up singles, the Chantays, the Trashmen, the Halibuts, but you're right, some of the worst blues work ever recorded will be showing up on the karmic rap sheets of surf-sax players."

"It was never his work that I was in love with." She said it so matter-of-factly that Doc risked a quick scan for eyeball shine, but this one was not about to start in with the faucets of widowhood, or not yet. Meantime she was running through some history. "Coy and I should've met cute, with cuteness everywhere back then and all of it up for sale, but actually we met squalid, down at Oscar's in San Ysidro—"

"*Oh* boy." Doc once or twice had been in—and through the mercy of God, out of—the notorious Oscar's, right across the border from Tijuana, where the toilets were seething round the clock with junkies new and old who'd just scored in Mexico, put the product inside rubber balloons and swallowed them, then crossed back into the U.S. to vomit them back up again.

"I had just gone running into this one toilet stall without checking first, had my finger already down my throat, and there Coy sat, gringo digestion, about to take a gigantic shit. We both let go at about the same time, barf and shit all over the place, me with my face in his lap and to complicate things of course he had this hardon.

"Well.

"Even before we got to San Diego, we were shooting up together in the back of somebody's van, and less than two weeks later, on the interesting theory that two can score as cheaply as one, we got married, next thing we knew here came Amethyst, and pretty soon this is what we had her looking like."

She handed Doc a couple of Polaroid baby pictures. He was startled at the baby's appearance, swollen, red-faced, vacant. Having no idea of what kind of shape she was in at present, he felt his skin begin to ache with anxiety.

"Everybody we knew helpfully pointed out how the heroin was coming through in my breast milk, but who could afford to buy formula? My parents saw us locked into a dismal slavery, but Coy and I, all we saw was the freedom—from that endless middle-class cycle of choices that are no choices at all—a world of hassle reduced to the one simple issue of scoring. And how was shooting up any different from the old folks and their dinner-hour cocktails anyway? we figured.

"But actually when did it ever get that dramatic? Heroin in California? my gracious. Stepped on so often it should have 'Welcome' written across every bag. There we were happy and stupid as any drunk, giggling in and out bedroom windows, cruising straightworld neighborhoods picking out strange houses at random, asking to use the bathroom, going in and shooting up. 'Course, now that's impossible to do, Charlie Manson and the gang have fucked that up for everybody. End of a certain kind of innocence, that thing about straightworld people that kept you from hating them totally, that real desire sometimes to help. No more of that, I guess. One more West Coast tradition down the toilet along with three percent product anymore."

"And so . . . this thing that happened to your husband . . ."

"It wasn't California smack, for sure. Coy wouldn't've made that mistake, using the same amount without checking. Somebody had to've switched bags on him deliberately, knowing it would kill him."

"Who was the dealer?"

"El Drano, up in Venice. Actually Leonard, but everybody uses the anagram because he does have that sort of caustic personality, plus his effect on the finances and emotions of those close to him. Coy had known him for years. He swore up and down it was local heroin, nothing out of the ordinary, but what does a dealer care? Overdoses are good for business, suddenly herds of junkies are showing up at the door, convinced if it killed somebody then it must be *really good shit*, and all they have to do themselves is be careful and not shoot quite so much."

Doc became aware of a baby, or technically toddler, risen quietly from her nap, holding on to a doorjamb and watching them with a big expectant grin in which you could see some teeth already in.

"Hey," Doc said, "you're that Amethyst, ain't you?"

"Yep," replied Amethyst, as if about to add, "what's it to you?"

Bright-eyed and ready to rock 'n' roll, she bore little resemblance to the junkie baby in the Polaroids. Whatever dismal fate had been waiting to jump her must've had a short attention span and turned aside and gone after somebody else. "Nice to see you," Doc said. "Really nice."

"Really nice," she said. "Mom? Want juice."

"You know where it is, Juicegirl." Amethyst nodded vigorously and headed out to the fridge. "Ask you something, Doc?"

"Long as it ain't the capital of South Dakota, sure."

"This mutual friend you and Coy have. Had. Is she, like, some kind of ex, or were you just dating, or . . . ?"

Who did Doc have to talk to about any of this that wasn't stoned, jealous, or a cop? Amethyst had found a cup of juice waiting in the fridge and climbed up onto the couch next to him, looking all set for a grown-up to tell her a story. Hope poured more coffee. There was too much kindness in the room all of a sudden. Doc had learned only a thing or two in the business, but one of them was, kindness without a price tag came along only rarely, and when it did usually it was too precious to accept, being too easy, for Doc anyway, to abuse, which he was bound to. So he settled for, "Well, sort of an ex, but now she's a client, too. I promised her I'd do something, and I waited too long, so the party she ended up with, scumbag developer and all, could be in some bad trouble now, and if I'd just taken care of business—"

"As one who's been down that particular exit ramp," Hope advised, "you can only cruise the boulevards of regret so far, and then you've got to get back up onto the freeway again."

"Thing is, though, now Shasta's disappeared too. And if she's in trouble—"

Amethyst, realizing this wasn't going to be her idea of entertainment, climbed down off the couch, threw Doc a reproachful look over her juice, and went off into the next room to watch the tube. Soon they could hear Mighty Mouse's dramatic treble.

"If you're on this other case," Hope said, "busy with it or something, I understand. But the reason I wanted to talk to you," and Doc saw it a half second before she said it, "is I don't think Coy is really dead."

Doc nodded, more to himself than to Hope. According to Sortilège, these were perilous times, astrologically speaking, for dopers—especially those of high-school age, who'd been born, most of them, under a ninety-degree aspect, the unluckiest angle possible, between Neptune, the dopers' planet, and Uranus, the planet of rude surprises. Doc had known it to happen that those left behind would refuse to believe that people they loved or even only took the same classes with were really dead. They came up with all kinds of alternate stories so it wouldn't have to be true. Some ex–old lady had hit town, and they'd run away together. The emergency room had mixed them up with somebody else, the way maternity wards switched babies around, and they were still on some intensive-care ward under another name. It was a particular kind of disconnected denial, and Doc figured he'd seen enough by now to recognize it. Whatever Hope was showing him here wasn't it.

"Did you ID the body?" He figured he could ask.

"No. That was one peculiar thing. Whoever called said somebody from the band already did it."

"I think it's supposed to be next of kin. Who called you?"

She had her diary from that period, and she'd remembered to write it down. "Lieutenant Dubonnet."

"Oh yeah, Pat Dubonnet, we've transacted one or two pieces of business."

"Sounds like he ran you in."

"Not to mention over." She was giving him one of those looks. "Sure, I had this hippie phase. Everything I really did, I got away with, and nothin they picked me up on was ever my doing, because the only description they had was Caucasian male, long hair, beard, multicolored clothing, bare feet, so forth."

"Just like the one of Coy they read me over the phone. It could've been a thousand people."

"I'll go talk to Pat. He might know something."

"There's this other thing that happened. Look." She brought out an old bank statement from shortly after Coy's alleged overdose, for her account at the local Bank of America, and pointed to a credit.

"Interesting sum."

"I called, I went in and talked to vice presidents, and everybody insisted it was correct. 'Maybe you lost the deposit slip, did the math wrong.' Ordinarily don't look a gift horse, you know, but this was creepy. They kept using exactly the same phrases, over and over, I mean, talk about denial?"

"You think it was something to do with Coy?"

"It showed up so close to his . . . his disappearance. I thought, maybe somebody's idea of a payoff? Local 47, some insurance policy I didn't know about. I mean, you wouldn't expect it to be anonymous, would you. But here's this mute set of figures in a monthly statement and some obviously jive-ass story the bank came up with to explain it."

Doc wrote the date of the deposit on a match cover and said, "Is there a picture of Coy you could spare?"

Was there. She pulled out a liquor-store box full of Polaroids—Coy sleeping, Coy with the baby, Coy cooking heroin, Coy tying off, Coy shooting up, Coy out under a shade tree pretending to cower away from a 454 Big Block Chev engine, Coy and Hope out on the beach, sitting in a pizza joint playing tug-of-war with the last slice, walking down Hollywood Boulevard just as the streetlight was coming on.

"Help yourself. I should've probably thrown 'em all away a long time ago. Detach, right? move on, hell, I'm always lecturing everybody else to. But Ammie likes them, likes it when we look through them, I'll tell her a little about each one, and she should have something anyhow, when she gets older, to remind her. Don't you think?"

"Me?" Doc remembered how Polaroids have no negatives and the life of the prints is limited. These, he noticed, were already beginning to shift color and fade. "Sure, sometimes I'd like to have one for every minute. Rent, like, a warehouse?"

She gave him one of those social-worker looks. "Well, that . . . might be a little . . . Are you seeing, like, a therapist?"

"She's more of a deputy DA, I guess."

"No, I meant . . ." She'd picked up a handful of photos and was pretending to arrange them in some meaningful way, the gin hand of her brief time with Coy. "Even if you don't know what you've got," she said slowly after a while, "act sometimes like you do. She'll appreciate that, and even you'll be better for it."

Doc nodded and picked up the first picture to hand, a shot of Coy holding his tenor, maybe taken during a gig, the lighting inexpensive, out-of-focus elbows and shirtsleeves and guitar necks poking in at the edges. "Okay if I take this one?"

Without looking at it, Hope said, "Sure."

Amethyst came running in, revved up. "Here I am," she sang, "to save the day!"

LATER IN THE AFTERNOON Doc drifted up to the Tree Section to his Aunt Reet's place, where he found his cousin Scott Oof out in the garage with his band. Scott had been playing with a local group known as the Corvairs, till half of them decided to join the northward migration of those years up to Humboldt, Vineland, and Del Norte. Scott, to whom redwoods were an alien species, and Elfmont, the drummer, decided to stay on at the beach and went around sticking up ads on different school bulletin boards till they'd assembled this new band, which they called Beer. Playing mostly covers in bar gigs around the area, Beer were now actually almost paying their rent month to month.

At the moment they were rehearsing, or today actually trying to learn the correct notes to, the theme from the TV western *The Big Valley,* which had recently gone into reruns. The shelves of the garage were lined with jars of purple pork rind, sure-fire bait for the depraved reservoir bass Aunt Reet went off periodically to Mexico after and came back with the trunk full of. Doc wasn't sure, but in the dimness the stuff always appeared to be glowing.

Beer's front man Huey was singing, while the rhythm guitar and bass filled in behind him,

"The . . . Big . . .
     Valley!
[*Guitar fill*]
   The
BIG Valley! [*Same guitar fill*]
         just
How big, is it, well go, visit sometime . . .
Ride all night, till,
Dawn-and-what will
     you find?

The Big Valley! Yes! Even more-of— the
Big Valley! *no* place to score in— the
Big Valley! big? that's for sure, it's— the
Big Val-ley!

"It's like my roots," Scott explained, "my mom hates the San Joaquin,
but I don't know, man, every time I go up there, gigs at the Chowchilla
Kiwanis or whatever, there's this strange feeling, like I used to live
there. . . ."

"You did live there," Doc pointed out.

"No, like in another life, man?"

Doc had considerately brought along a shirtpocket full of prerolled
Panamanian, and soon everybody was wandering around drinking cans
of supermarket soda and eating homemade peanut butter cookies.

"Anything on the rock 'n' roll grapevine," Doc inquired, "about a
surf saxophone player named Coy Harlingen who used to play for the
Boards?"

"OD'd, right?" said Lefty the bass player.

"Allegedly OD'd," Scott said, "but there's also been a strange rumor
going around, is that he really survived? they brought him back in some
Beverly Hills emergency room, but everybody kept it quiet, some say
they paid him to go on pretending he's dead, and he's out there someplace right now walkin among us in disguise, like with different hair and
so forth—"

"Why would anybody go to that much trouble?" Doc said.

"Yeah," said Lefty, "not like he's some hot-lookin singer every chick
wants to ball, some kick-ass guitarist who'll change the business forever,
just another surf-band sax player, easy to replace." So much for Coy.
As for the Boards, they'd been making piles of money lately, living all
together in a house up in Topanga Canyon, with the usual entourage—
groupies, producers, in-laws, pilgrims who'd journeyed long and hard
enough to be taken in as part of the household. The resurrected Coy
Harlingen was darkly rumored to be one of these, though nobody

recognized anyone there who might be him. Maybe some thought they did, but all was fuzzed, as if by the fog of dope.

Later, as Doc was getting in his car, Aunt Reet stuck her head out the bungalow office window and hollered at him.

"So you had to go talk to Mickey Wolfmann. Nice timing. What did I tell you, wise-ass? Was I right?"

"I forget," Doc said.

THREE

THE COP WHO'D CALLED HOPE HARLINGEN WITH THE NEWS ABOUT Coy's overdose, Pat Dubonnet, was now top kahuna at the Gordita Beach station. Doc located behind his ear a bent Kool, lit up, and considered aspects of the situation. Pat and Bigfoot had come up at around the same time, both having begun their careers in the South Bay, practically on Doc's own stretch of beach, back in the era of the Surfer-Lowrider Wars. Pat had stayed, but Bigfoot, quickly picking up a rep for stick-assisted pacification solid enough to look to the folks downtown like an obvious draft choice, had moved on. Doc had been around long enough now to watch a few of these hotshots come and go, and to note that they always left behind them some residue of history. He also knew that Pat had more or less fucking hated Bigfoot for years.

"Time for a visit," he decided, "to Hippiephobia Central."

He drove past the Gordita Beach station house twice before he recognized it. The place had been radically transformed, courtesy of federal anti-drug money, from a pierside booking desk with a two-coil hot plate and a jar of instant coffee into a palatial cop's paradise featuring locomotive-size espresso machines, its own mini-jail, a motor pool full of rolling weaponry that would otherwise be in Vietnam, and a kitchen with a crew of pastry chefs working around the clock.

After threading his way among a crew of trainees chirping around the place squirting mist at the dwarf palms, Wandering Jews, and dieffenbachias, Doc located Pat Dubonnet in his office, and reaching into his fringe shoulder bag, withdrew a foil-wrapped object about a foot long. "Here you go Pat, expressly for you." Before he could blink, the detective had grabbed, unwrapped, and somehow ingested at least half of the lengthy wiener and bun within, which had also come with Everything On It.

"Hits the spot. Amazed I have any appetite. Who let you in, by the way?"

"Posed as a drug snitch, fools 'em every time, all 'em bright new faces, still naïve I guess."

"Not enough to stay here any longer than they have to." Even though Doc was watching carefully, somehow the rest of the hot dog had disappeared. "Look at this miserable place. It's The Endless Bummer. Everybody else will move on, but guess who, for his sins, will remain stuck out here forever in Gordita, nothin but penny-ante collars, kids under the pier dealing their moms' downers, when I should be in West L.A. or Hollywood Division, at least."

"Center of the cop universe for sure," Doc nodding sympathetically, "but we can't all be Bigfoot Bjornsen can we—ups I mean who'd want to be him anyway?" hoping this wasn't pushing things, given Pat's mental health, frail on the best of days.

"At this point," Pat replied grimly, a quiver in his lower lip, "I'd settle for a life swap even with him, yes trade what I've got for what's behind the door where Carol is standing you might say, even if it turns out to be a zonk—in Bigfoot's bracket how bad of a deal could that be?"

"Weird, Pat, 'cause what I hear is, is he's scuffling these days. You'd know better than me, o' course."

Pat squinted. "You're awfully inquisitive today, Sportello. I would have noticed sooner if I wasn't so upset with career issues which are no doubt beyond you. Is Bigfoot giving you problems again? Call the Internal Affairs Hot Line, it's toll-free—800-BENTCOP."

"Not that I'd ever file a complaint or nothin, Lieutenant, understand, but how *desperate*, man, blood out of a turnip, even the most wasted spare-change artist up on Hollywood Boulevard knows enough to pass *me* by anymore, but not that Bigfoot, oh no."

You could see a struggle going on here in Pat's mind, between two major cop reflexes—envy of another cop's career versus hatred of hippies. Envy won out. "He didn't actually quote you a *sum*?"

"He listed some expenses," Doc started improvising, and saw Pat's ears definitely change angle. "Personal, departmental. I told him I always thought he was better connected than that. He got philosophical. 'People forget,' is how he put it. 'No matter what you may have done for them in the past, you can never count on them when you need them.'"

Pat shook his head. "And with the risks he's taken . . . A lesson to us all. Some real ungrateful fuckers in *that* business, huh?" He had this Art Fleming look on his face, like Doc was now supposed to guess which business, exactly.

Doc in turn made with the blank hippie stare that could mean anything, and which if held long enough was sure to unnerve any quadrilateral in uniform, till Pat shifted his eyes away, mumbling, "Ah. Yeah I get you. Groovy. 'Course," he added after some reflection, "he's got all them residuals."

Doc by now had very little idea what they might be talking about. "I try to stay awake for those reruns," he hazarded, "but somehow I always crash before Bigfoot's are on."

"Well, Mr. News At Ten's got himself another case of the century now, since Mickey Wolfmann's gorilla got wasted. . . . Let the others have Benedict Canyon and Sharon Tate and them, for the right chief investigator this one could be a bottomless source of cash."

"You mean . . ."

"It's bound to be a Movie for TV, ain't it, whatever happens. Bigfoot can end up with script and production credits, even play himself, the asshole, but ups, eleventh-commandment issues, ignore that I said that."

"Not to mention if he gets Mickey back, he's a big public hero."

"Yeah, if. But what if he's too close to this? Some point it begins to fuck with your judgment, like doctors ain't supposed to operate on family members?"

"Mickey and him are that tight, huh?"

"Ace buddies, according to legend. Hey. You think Bigfoot's Jewish, too?"

"Swedish, I thought."

"Could be both," Pat dimly defensive. "There can be Swedish Jews."

"I know there's Swedish Fish." Basically only trying to be helpful.

FOUR

ON CERTAIN DAYS, DRIVING INTO SANTA MONICA WAS LIKE having hallucinations without going to all the trouble of acquiring and then taking a particular drug, although some days, for sure, *any* drug was preferable to driving into Santa Monica.

Today, after a deceptively sunny and uneventful spin up through the Hughes Company property—a kind of smorgasbord of potential U.S. combat zones, terrain specimens ranging from mountains and deserts to swamp and jungle and so forth, all there, according to local paranoia, for fine-tuning battle radar systems on—past Westchester and the Marina and into Venice, Doc reached the Santa Monica city line, where the latest mental exercise began. Suddenly he was on some planet where the wind can blow two directions at once, bringing in fog from the ocean and sand from the desert at the same time, obliging the unwary driver to shift down the minute he entered this alien atmosphere, with daylight dimmed, visibility reduced to half a block, and all colors, including those of traffic signals, shifted radically elsewhere in the spectrum.

Doc went automotively groping in this weirdness east on Olympic, trying not to flinch at what came popping up out of the gloom in the way of city buses and pedestrians in altered states of consciousness. Faces came sharpening into an intensity usually seen only at area racetracks, their trailing edges prolonged, some of them, in quite drastic hues, and often taking some time to clear the frame of the windshield. The car radio didn't help much, being able to pick up only KQAS, playing an old Droolin' Floyd Womack single Doc had always had conflicted feelings about, on the one hand trying not to take it personally just because he'd chased down a debtor or two, but then again finding himself going back over wrongs and regrets—

> Th' repossess man comes
> Bouncin through that
> Win-dow! just
> Layin' his hooks on ev'rything he can—
> There goes my 19-inch!
> My ride's up on some winch!
> Good-bye and cheeri-o
> To my ol' stere-o!
>   Wohh,
> The repossess man, he
> Never will be
> Hap-py,
> Till he's got ev'rything I need that
> Gets me through. . . .
> 'Cause it's all just out on loan,
> Never really your own,
> Look out!
> That repossess man, he's comin' after you!

Just out of Ondas Nudosas Community College, Doc, known back then as Larry, Sportello had found himself falling behind in his car payments. The agency that came after him, Gotcha! Searches and Settlements, decided to hire him on as a skip-tracer trainee and let him work the debt off that way. By the time he felt comfortable enough to ask why, he was in too deep.

"This is fun," he remarked once after about a week on the job, as he and Fritz Drybeam were parked up in Reseda someplace on what was proving to be an all-night stakeout.

Fritz, in the business twenty years and seen it all, nodded. "Yep and wait till you start with the Inconvenience Premiums."

This being Milton the bookkeeper's term. Fritz, as graphically as possible, went on to describe some of the forms of motivation that clients, typically those who loaned at high interest, often asked the agency to provide.

"*I'm* supposed to kick somebody's ass? How believable is that?"

"You'll be authorized to carry a weapon."

"I never fired a gun in my life."

"Well . . ." Reaching under the seat.

"What—kind of a 'weapon' is that?"

"It's a hypodermic outfit."

"I knew that, but what am I supposed to load it with?"

"Truth serum. Same kind the CIA uses. Just stab 'em anyplace that's easy to reach, and before you know it they're jabbering like speed freaks, won't stop, telling you all about assets they never even knew they had."

Larry decided to stash the outfit in a sinister-looking red faux-crocodile shaving kit he'd found at a yard sale up in Studio City. It wasn't long before he noticed how many of the delinquents he and Fritz visited seemed unable to keep their eyes off of it. He understood that if he was lucky, he might not have to so much as unzip it. It never quite became a tool of his trade, but did develop into a useful prop, in time earning him the nickname "Doc."

Today Doc found Fritz banging around under the hood of a Dodge Super Bee preparing to go out on a collection run. "Hey there Doc, you look like shit."

"Wish I could say the same for you, bright eyes. Keepin all 'em carburetors straight?"

"Wholesome thoughts and don't smoke nothing 's been grown in a combat zone, that's my secret and it could even work for you, that's if you had any self-control."

"Uh-huh, well my good luck today that your brain's all dialed in, because I need to find somebody in a hurry—my ex–ol' lady Shasta Fay."

"I think you mean Mickey Wolfmann's girlfriend. This is Dr. Reality's office calling, you're way overdue for your checkup?"

"Fritz, Fritz, how have I offended you?"

"Every cop in the LAPD and the Sheriff's is out looking for both of them. Who do you think will find them first?"

"Judging by the Manson case, I say any random idiot off the street."

"Well come on in and check this out," motioning Doc into the office. Milton the bookkeeper, wearing a flowered Nehru jacket, several strings of cowrie shells around his neck, and vivid yellow shooting glasses, glanced up with a wide smile out of a haze of patchouli scent and waved slowly as they headed for the back room.

"He looks happy."

"Business has been picking up, and it's all because of—" He flung open a door. "Tell me how many random idiots you know got anythin like this."

"Wow, Fritz." It was like being inside a science-fictional Christmas tree. Little red and green lights were going on and off everywhere. There were computer cabinets, consoles with lit-up video screens, and alphanumeric keyboards, and cables running all over the floor among unswept drifts of little bug-size rectangles punched out of IBM cards, and a couple of Gestetner copy machines in the corner, and towering over the scene all along the walls a number of Ampex tape reels busily twitching back and forth.

"ARPAnet," Fritz announced.

"Ah, no I'd better not, I've got to drive and stuff, maybe just give me one for later—"

"It's a network of computers, Doc, all connected together by phone lines. UCLA, Isla Vista, Stanford. Say there's a file they have up there and you don't, they'll send it right along at fifty thousand characters per second."

"Wait, ARPA, that's the same outfit has their own sign up on the freeway at the Rosecrans exit?"

"Some connection with TRW, nobody over there is too forthcoming, like Ramo isn't telling Woolridge?"

"But . . . you're saying somebody hooked up to this thing might know where Shasta is?"

"Can't know till we look. All over the country, in fact the world, there's new computers gettin plugged in every day. Right now it's still experimental, but hell, it's government money, and those fuckers don't care what they spend, and we've had some useful surprises already."

"Does it know where I can score?"

FIVE

SHASTA HAD MENTIONED A POSSIBLE LAUGHING-ACADEMY ANGLE to Mickey Wolfmann's matrimonial drama, and Doc thought it might be interesting to see how society-page superstar Mrs. Sloane Wolfmann would react when somebody brought up this topic. If Mickey was currently being held against his will in some private nuthouse, then Doc's immediate chore would be to try and find out which one. He called the number Shasta had given him, and the little woman herself picked up.

"I know it's awkward to be talking business right now, Mrs. Wolfmann, but unfortunately time is a factor here."

"This wouldn't be another creditor inquiry, would it, there've been an astonishing number already. I'm referring them to our attorney, do you have his number?" Some kind of English smoker's voice, it seemed to Doc, at the low end of the register and unspecifiably decadent.

"Actually, it's our firm who owe your husband some money. As we're talking in the mid–six figures, we felt we should bring it to your attention." He waited half a subvocalized bar of "The Great Pretender." "Mrs. Wolfmann?"

"I may have a few minutes free around noon," she said. "Whom did you say you represented?"

"Modern Institute for Cognitive Repatterning and Overhaul,"

Doc said. "MICRO for short, we're a private clinic out near Hacienda Heights, specializing in the repair of stressed personalities."

"Ordinarily I review all of Michael's larger disbursements, and I must confess, Mr.—is it Sportello?—that I am unfamiliar with any dealings he may have had with you."

Doc's nose had begun to run, a sure sign that he was onto something here. "Perhaps, given the sum in question, it might be easier after all to work through your attorney. . . ."

It took her a tenth of a second to calculate how much of a shark-bite out of the surfboard that might involve. "Not at all, Mr. Sportello. Perhaps it's only your voice . . . but you may consider me officially intrigued."

In a former en suite broom closet at the office, Doc had assembled a collection of disguises. He decided today on a double-breasted velour suit from Zeidler & Zeidler, and found a short-hair wig that almost matched the suit. He considered a glue-on mustache but figured simpler would be better—switched his sandals for standard-issue loafers and put on a tie narrower and less colorful than currently fashionable, hoping Mrs. Wolfmann would read this as pathetically unhip. Looking in the mirror, he almost recognized himself. Groovy. He considered lighting a joint but resisted the impulse.

At the print shop down the street, his friend Jake, used to rush orders, ran him off a couple-three business cards with the legend MICRO— RECONFIGURING SOUTHLAND BRAINS SINCE 1966. LARRY SPORTELLO, LICENSED ASSOCIATE, which was true enough, long as you meant a California driver's license.

On the Coast Highway about halfway to the Wolfmann residence, the Bonzo Dog Band cover of "Bang Bang" came on from KRLA in Pasadena, and Doc cranked up the Vibrasonic. As he moved up into the hills, the reception began to fade, so he drove slower, but eventually lost the signal. Before long he found himself on a sunny street somewhere in the Santa Monica Mountains, parked near a house with high stucco walls, over which flowers of some exotic creeper poured in a flame-colored cascade. Doc thought he spotted somebody looking down at him from one of the openings of a Mission-style loggia running the length of the top floor. Heat of some kind, a sniper no doubt, though federal or local, who knew?

A presentable young Chicana in jeans and an old SC sweatshirt answered the door and checked him out with dramatically made-up eyes. "She's hanging by the pool with all the police and them. Come on upstairs."

It was a reverse floor plan, with bedrooms on the entrance level and then upstairs the kitchen, maybe more than one, and various entertainment areas. The house should have been full of law enforcement. Instead the boys from Protect and Serve had set up a command post at the pool cabana, somewhere out in back. Like getting in some last-minute free catering before their federal overlords showed up. Sounds of distant splashing, rock 'n' roll radio, eating between meals. Some kidnapping.

As if auditioning for widowhood, Sloane Wolfmann strolled in from poolside wearing black spike-heeled sandals, a headband with a sheer black veil, and a black bikini of negligible size made of the same material as the veil. She wasn't exactly an English rose, maybe more like an English daffodil, very pale, blond, reedy, probably bruised easily, overdid her eye makeup like everybody else. Miniskirts were invented for young women like her.

In the time it took her to lead him through a dim sunken interior full of taupe carpeting, suede upholstery, and teak, which seemed to extend indefinitely in the direction of Pasadena, Doc learned that she had a degree from the London School of Economics, had recently begun studying tantric yoga, and had met Mickey Wolfmann originally in Las Vegas. She waved at a picture on the wall, which looked like a blowup of an eight-by-ten glossy from the lobby area of some nightclub. "Why, goodness," said Doc, "it's you, isn't it?"

Sloane made with the half-frown, half-smirk Doc had noticed among minor- and ex-showbiz people trying to be modest. "My lurid youth. I was one of those notorious Vegas showgirls, working at one of the casinos. Up onstage in those days, with the lights, the eyelashes, all the makeup, we did look fairly much alike, but Michael, something of a connoisseur in these matters as I was later to learn, said that he picked me out the minute I walked on, and after that I was really the only one he could see. Romantic isn't it, yes, certainly unexpected—next thing either of us knew, we were down at the Little Church of the West, and I had this on my finger," flashing a gigantic marquise-cut diamond up in the double digits someplace with respect to carats.

She had told the story hundreds of times, but that was all right. "Handsome stone," Doc said.

Like an actress hitting her mark, she had come to a pause beneath a looming portrait of Mickey Wolfmann, shown with a distant stare, as if scanning the L.A. Basin to its farthest horizons for buildable lots. She whirled to face Doc and smiled sociably. "Here we are, then."

Doc noticed a sort of fake chiseled stone frieze above the portrait, which read, ONCE YOU GET THAT FIRST STAKE DRIVEN, NOBODY CAN STOP YOU.—ROBERT MOSES.

"A great American, and Michael's inspiration," said Sloane. "That's always been his motto."

"I thought Dr. Van Helsing said that."

She'd found and stopped exactly inside a flattering convergence of lights that made her look like some contract star of the grand studio era, about to let loose with an emotional speech at some less expensive actor. Doc tried not to glance around too obviously to see where the light was coming from, but she noticed the flicker off his eyeballs.

"Do you like the lighting? Jimmy Wong Howe did it for us years ago."

"The D.P. on *Body and Soul* wasn't he? Not to mention *They Made Me a Criminal, Dust Be My Destiny, Saturday's Children*—"

"Those," quizzically, "are all . . . John Garfield movies."

"Well . . . yes?"

"Jimmy did film other actors."

"I'm sure he did . . . oh, and *Out of the Fog*, too, where John Garfield is this evil gangster—"

"Actually, what I find memorable about that picture is the way Jimmy lit Ida Lupino, which, now I think of it, had a lot to do with selling me on this house. Jimmy was certainly fond enough of specular highlights, all that prize-fighter sweat and chrome and jewelry and sequins and so forth . . . but his work also had such a spiritual quality—you look at Ida Lupino in her closeups—those eyes!—and instead of hard-edged lamp reflections there's this glow, this purity, almost as if it's coming from inside—. . . . Excuse me, is that what I think it is?"

"Darn! It's that Ida Lupino, every time her name comes up, so does this. Please don't take it personally."

"How curious. I can't recall ever feeling that way about John Garfield . . . but as I have a meditation appointment at one, we might find time for drinks, if we guzzle them down fast enough, and perhaps you can even tell me what you're doing here. Luz!"

The young lady who'd let him in appeared from the artfully sculpted shadows. "Señora?"

"The midday *refrescos* now, if you wouldn't mind, Luz. I do hope, Mr. Sportello, that margaritas will be satisfactory—though given your film preferences, perhaps some sort of beer and whiskey arrangement would be more appropriate?"

"Thank you, Mrs. Wolfmann, tequila's just fine—and what a welcome relief not to be offered any 'pot'! I'll never understand what these hippies see in the stuff! Do you mind if I smoke a normal cigarette, by the way?"

She nodded graciously, and Doc fished out a pack of Benson & Hedges menthol he'd remembered to bring instead of Kools, given the expected class level here and so forth, and offered her one, and they both lit up. Sounds reached them, from a pool whose dimensions he could only imagine, of policemen at play.

"I'll try to keep this brief, and you can return to your guests. Your husband was planning to endow a new wing for us, as part of our expansion program, and shortly before his puzzling disappearance he actually had tendered us a sum in advance. But somehow it just didn't seem right to keep the money while so little is known of his whereabouts. So, we'd like to refund you the sum, preferably before the end of the quarter, and if and as we all pray when Mr. Wolfmann is next heard from, why then, perhaps the process can resume."

She was squinting, however, and shaking her head a little. "I'm not sure. . . . We recently endowed another facility, in Ojai, I believe. . . . Are you somehow a subsidiary or . . ."

"Perhaps it's one of our Sister Sanatoria, there's been a program for some years. . . ."

She had stepped over to a small antique desk in the corner, bent so as to present to Doc's gaze an unquestionably alluring ass, and took some time rummaging through different pigeonholes before coming up with another publicity shot of herself. This was a photo of a ground-breaking ceremony, with Sloane sitting at the controls of a front-end loader and backhoe rig, in whose bucket could be seen one of those oversize checks that also get handed to winners of bowling tournaments. A personage in a doctor outfit was smiling and pretending to look at the amount, which ran to a lot of zeros, but he was really gazing up Sloane's skirt, which was fashionably short. She was also wearing shades, almost as if she didn't want to be recognized, and an expression conveying how much she didn't want to be there. A banner behind her carried a date and the name of the institution, though both were just out of focus enough that Doc couldn't get much more than an impression of a long, foreign-looking word. He was wondering how suspicious it would make Sloane if he asked the name, when Luz came back in with a tray holding a gigantic pitcherful of margaritas and some chilled glasses of an exotic shape whose only purpose was to make it impossible for the servants to wash them without the help of some high-ticket custom dishmop.

"Thank you, Luz. Shall I be Mother?" taking the pitcher and pouring. Doc noticed there was an extra glass on the tray, so it wasn't too much of a surprise when presently he saw reflected in the screen of a mammoth TV in the corner a large, muscular blond person coming silently down the stairs and moving toward them across the carpeting like an assassin in a kung fu movie.

Doc got up to have a look and say howdy, quickly noting that any prolonged eye contact here would mean a visit to the chiropractor for neck work, this party having three feet of altitude on him, easy.

"This is Mr. Riggs Warbling," said Sloane, "my spiritual coach." Doc didn't see them actually "exchanging glances," as Frank might put it, but if acid-tripping was good for anything, it helped tune you to different unlisted frequencies. No doubt these two had actually sat now and then on adjoining meditation mats pretending to empty their heads, just for anybody that might be nearby—Luz, the heat, himself. But Doc would bet an ounce of seedless Hawaiian and throw in a pack of Zig-Zags that Sloane and old Riggs here were also fucking regularly, and that this was the b.f. Shasta had mentioned.

Sloane poured Riggs a drink and angled the pitcher inquiringly in Doc's direction.

"Thanks, got to be back in the office. Maybe you can tell us where to send this refund, and what form you'd like it in?"

"Small bills!" boomed Riggs amiably, "with nonconsecutive serial numbers!"

"Riggs, Riggs," Sloane not as grimly as might be expected given the possibility, still open, that her husband had been kidnapped, "always making with the tasteless jokes . . . Perhaps if one of your company officers simply endorsed Michael's check back to one of his bank accounts?"

"Of course. Let us know the account number and it's as good as in the mail."

"I'll just go pop in the office for a moment, then?"

Riggs Warbling had appropriated the margarita jug, which he was taking sips from without going through the exercise of pouring anything into a glass. With no warning he blurted, "I'm into zomes."

"Beg pardon?"

"I'm a contractor, I design and build zomes? That's short for 'zonahedral domes.' Greatest advance in structure since Bucky Fuller. Here, let me show you." He had brought out from somewhere a pad of quadrille paper and begun sketching on it, using numbers, and symbols which might have been Greek, and pretty soon he was going on about "vector spaces" and "symmetry groups." Doc grew convinced of unwelcome developments inside his brain, though the diagrams were kind of hip-looking . . .

"Zomes make great meditation spaces," Riggs went on. "Do you know, some people have actually walked into zomes and not come back out the same way they went in? and sometimes not at all? Like zomes are portals to someplace else. Especially if they're located out in the desert, which is where I've been for most of last year?"

Uh, huh. "You've been working for Mickey Wolfmann?"

"At Arrepentimiento—that's a longtime dream project of his, near Las Vegas. Maybe you saw the piece on it in *Architectural Digest*?"

"Missed it." Actually, the only magazine Doc read with any regularity was *Naked Teen Nymphos,* which he subscribed to, or at least used to till he began to find the few copies that made it to his mailbox opened already and with pages stuck together. But he decided not to mention this. Sloane came sashaying back over, holding a slip of paper. "The only number I can find at the moment is for a joint account at one of Michael's S&Ls, I hope that won't present a problem for your people. Here's a blank deposit form, if that's any help."

Doc stood, and Sloane stayed where she was, which was close enough for her to be seized and violated, a thought which unavoidably crossed

Doc's mind, taking its time, in fact, and more than once looking back and winking. Who knows what lurid acts might have followed had Luz not reappeared and flashed him, unless he was hallucinating from tequila, a warning look.

"Luz, could you please see Mr. Sportello out?"

Downstairs among corridors leading off to some unknown number of bedroom suites, Doc, as if just remembering he had to piss, said, "Mind if I use a bathroom?"

"Sure, long as *you* don't steal anything."

"Oh, dear. I hope that doesn't mean any of those policemen out by the pool have been reverting to type—um, that is to say—"

She wagged a finger no, and glancing quickly around, as if the house might be bugged, crooked her arm and flexed a bicep, while rolling her eyes upstairs.

Riggs—it figured. Doc smiled and nodded and for the benefit of any audience said, "Thank you, uh . . . *muchas gracias* there, Luz, I won't be but a minute."

She slouched gracefully against a doorway and watched him, her eyes dark and busy. Doc located the door to a palatial bathroom and, guessing it was Mickey's, went in, and then on into the adjoining bedroom.

Snooping around, he came across a number of strange neckties hanging inside a walk-in closet on a rack of their own. He switched on a light and had a look. At first glance they seemed to be vintage hand-painted silk ties, each with an image of a different nude young woman on it. But these were not exactly vintage nudes. Erect clits, spread pussy lips with sort of highlights on them to suggest wetness, over-the-shoulder invitations to anal entry, each goose bump and pubic hair painstakingly set down in photographic detail. Doc became lost in art appreciation, having noticed something striking about the faces as well. They weren't just cartoon features taking on some catalog of fuck-me expressions. These seemed to be the faces, and he guessed the bodies, of specific women. Maybe some kind of a Mickey Wolfmann girlfriend inventory. Was

Shasta Fay in here, by any chance? Doc began to flip through the ties one by one, trying not to sweat on anything. He had just come across Sloane's image—inarguably Sloane and not just some blonde—lying back among tangled sheets, arms and legs open, eyelids lowered, lips shining—an almost gentlemanly angle to Mickey's character he hadn't counted on—when a hand slid around his waist from behind.

"Yaagghhh!"

"Keep looking, I'm in there someplace," Luz said.

"I'm ticklish, babe!"

"There I am. Cute, huh?" Sure enough, it was Luz in full color, on her knees, gazing upward with her teeth bared in what wasn't, it seemed to Doc, a specially inviting smile.

"My tits aren't really that big, but it's the thought that counts."

"Did you ladies all pose for these?"

"Yep, guy over in North Hollywood, does custom work."

"How about that chick what's-her-name," Doc trying to keep a tremor out of his voice. "The one that's been missing?"

"Oh, Shasta. Yeah, she's in there someplace," but as it turned out, strangely, she wasn't. Doc looked at the couple-three ties remaining, but none of them had Shasta's picture on it.

Luz was gazing over his shoulder into Mickey's bedroom. "He always used to take me in the shower to fuck," she reminisced. "I never got a chance to do anything on that groovy bed in there."

"Seems easy enough to arrange," Doc said smoothly, "maybe—" At which point, wouldn't you know, came a horrible low-fidelity screech from an intercom speaker out in the hall. "¡Luz! ¿Dónde estás, mi hijita?"

"Shit," murmured Luz.

"Another time, perhaps."

At the door Doc gave her one of the fake MICRO cards, which had his real office number on it. She slipped it in the back pocket of her jeans.

"You're not really a shrink, are you?"

"Y—maybe not. But I do have a couch?"

"*¡Psicodélico, ése!*" Flashing those famous teeth.

Doc was just getting in his car when a black-and-white came barrel-ling around the corner with all its lights going, and pulled up next to him. A window on the shotgun side came cranking down, and Bigfoot leaned out.

"Wrong part of town for scoring weed, isn't it, Sportello?"

"What—you mean my mind's been wanderin again?"

The cop driving killed the motor, and they both got out and approached Doc. Unless Bigfoot had been demoted in some strange piece of LAPD disrespect Doc knew he'd never begin to understand, this other cop could in no way have been Bigfoot's partner, though he might be a close relative—they both had the same smooth and evil look. This party now raised his eyebrows at Doc. "Mind if we have a look through that attractive purse, sir?"

"Nothing but my lunch," Doc assured him.

"Oh, we'll see you *get your lunch.*"

"Now, now, Sportello's only doing his job," Bigfoot pretended to soothe the other cop, "trying to figure out what happened to Mickey Wolfmann, just like the rest of us. Anything so far you'd like to share on that, Sportello? Who's—beg pardon, *how's*—the missus doing?"

"That's one brave little lady," Doc, nodding sincerely. He thought about getting into what Pat Dubonnet had told him about Bigfoot and Mickey being ace buddies, but there was something about the way this other cop was listening to them . . . way too attentive, maybe even, if you wanted to be paranoid about it, as if he was undercover, reporting to some other level inside the LAPD, his real job, basically, to keep an eye on Bigfoot. . . .

Too much to think about. Doc deployed his most feckless doper's grin. "There's law enforcement in there, guys, but nobody introduced me. Could even be the *federales* for all I know."

"I love it when a case goes all to hell," remarked Bigfoot with a sunny smile. "Don't you, Lester, doesn't it just remind you why we're all here?"

"Cheer up, compadre," said Lester, returning to the car, "our day will come."

Off they sped, hitting the siren just to be cute. Doc got in his car and sat staring at the Wolfmann residence.

Something had been puzzling him now for a while—namely, what, exactly, was with Bigfoot here, riding around in these black-and-whites all the time? Far as Doc knew, detectives in suits and ties rode in unmarked sedans, usually two at a time, and uniformed officers did the same. But he couldn't recall ever seeing Bigfoot out on the job with another detective—

Oh, wait a minute. Out of the permanent smog alert he liked to think of as his memory, something began to emerge—a rumor, likely by way of Pat Dubonnet, about a partner of Bigfoot's who'd been shot and killed a while back in the line of duty. And ever since then, so the story went, Bigfoot had worked alone, no replacements either asked for or assigned. If this meant Bigfoot was still in some kind of cop mourning, he and the dead guy must've been unusually close.

This bond between partners was nearly the only thing Doc had ever found to admire about the LAPD. For all the Department's long sorrowful history of corruption and abuse of power, here was at least something they had not sold but kept for themselves, forged in the dangerous life-and-death uncertainties of one working day after another—something real that had to be respected. No faking it, no question of buying it with favors, money, promotions—the entire range of capitalist inducement couldn't get you five seconds of attention to your back when it really counted, you had to go out there and earn it by putting your pitiful ass on the line, again and again. Without knowing any details of the history Bigfoot and his late partner had been through together, Doc would still bet the contents of his stash for the next year that Bigfoot if, improbably, asked to generate a list of people he loved, would have put this guy up near the top.

Meaning what, however? Was Doc about to start offering Bigfoot free advice, here? *No*nono, bad idea, Doc warned himself, bad idea, just let the man deal with his grief, or whatever it is, without your help, okay?

Sure, Doc answered himself, cool with me, man.

SIX

UNABLE TO REACH HER AT HOME, DOC FINALLY HAD TO CALL
Deputy DA Penny Kimball at her office downtown. A lunch date had
just happened to cancel, so she agreed to pencil Doc in. He showed up at
a peculiar skid-row eatery off Temple where wine abusers up from bed-
rolls in vacant lots back of what remained of the old Nickel mingled with
Superior Court judges taking recess breaks, not to mention a population of lawyers in suits, whose high-decibel jabbering rebounded off the
mirrored walls, rattling and threatening at times to knock over all the
eighty-five-cent mickeys of muscatel and tokay stacked up in pyramids
behind the steam tables.

Presently in strolled Penny, one hand loosely in a jacket pocket,
exchanging civilized remarks with any number of perfectly groomed
co-workers. She was wearing shades and one of those gray polyester business outfits with a very short skirt.

"This Wolfmann-Charlock case," is how she greeted Doc—"apparently
one of your old girlfriends is a principal?" Not that he was expecting a
friendly kiss or anything—there were colleagues watching, and he didn't
want to, what you'd call, fuck up her act. She put her attaché case on the
table and sat staring at Doc, a courtroom technique no doubt.

"I just heard that she skipped," Doc said.

"Put it another way . . . how close *were* you and Shasta Fay Hepworth?"

He'd been asking himself this for a while now but didn't know the answer. "It was all over with years ago," he said. "Months? She had other fish to fry. Did it break my heart? Sure did. If you hadn't come along, babe, who knows how bad it might've got?"

"True, you were a fucking mess. But old times aside, have you had any contact with Miss Hepworth in, say, the last week or so?"

"Well now, funny you should ask. She called me up a couple days before Mickey Wolfmann disappeared, with a story about how his wife and her boyfriend were plotting to hustle Mickey into the booby hatch and grab all his money. So I sure hope you guys, or the cops or whoever, are looking into that."

"And with your years of experience as a PI, would you call that a reliable lead?"

"I've known worse—oh, wait, I dig, you're all gonna just ignore this. Right? some hippie chick with boyfriend trouble, brains all discombobulated with dope sex rock 'n' roll—"

"Doc, I never see you this emotional."

"'Cause the lights are out, usually."

"Uh-huh, well apparently you didn't tell any of this to Lieutenant Bjornsen, when he pulled you in at the crime scene."

"I promised Shasta I'd come talk to you first, see if anybody at the DA's shop could help. Kept calling you, day and night, no reply, next thing I know Wolfmann's gone, Glen Charlock's dead."

"And Bjornsen seems to think you're as good a suspect as anyone in this."

"'Seems to—' you've been *talking*, to *Bigfoot*, about me? Wow, well never trust a flatland chick, man, prime directive of life at the beach, all we've been to each other too, hey if that's the way it must be, okay, as Roy Orbison always sez," holding out his wrists dramatically, "let's git it over with—"

"Doc. Shh. Please." She was so cute when she got embarrassed, nose-wrinkling and so forth, but it didn't last long. "Besides, maybe you *did* do it, has that crossed your mind yet? Maybe you just conveniently forgot about it, the way you do so often forget things, and this peculiar reaction of yours now is a typically twisted way of confessing the act?"

"Well, but . . . How would I forget something like that?"

"Grass and who knows what else, Doc."

"Hey, come on, I'm only a light smoker."

"Oh? How many joints a day, on average?"

"Um . . . have to look in the log. . . ."

"Listen, Bjornsen's in charge of the case, that's all, he'll be interviewing hundreds of you people—"

"Us people. Come in my fuck'n *window* again, 's basically what you're sayin."

"According to police reports, you have tended to barricade your door on previous occasions."

"You pulled my jacket and looked me up? Penny, you really *do* care!" with a glance meant to be appreciative, but which all these mirrors in here, as Doc checked out his image, were somehow presenting as just another red-eyed doper's stare.

"I'm going after a sandwich. Can I bring you something? Ham, lamb, or beef."

"Maybe just Vegetable of the Day?"

Doc watched her getting in line. What kind of DDA game was she running on him now? He wished he could believe her more, but the business was unforgiving, and life in psychedelic-sixties L.A. offered more cautionary arguments than you could wave a joint at against too much trust, and the seventies were looking no more promising.

Penny knew more about this case than she was telling Doc. He'd seen enough of that shifty way legals had of holding back information—lawyers taught it to each other, attended weekend seminars out in motels in La Puente just to work on greasiness skills—and there was no reason, sad to say, that Penny should be any exception.

She got back to the table with the Vegetable of the Day, steamed Brussels sprouts, heaped on a plate. Doc waded in.

"Yum, man! see that Tabasco a minute—hey, have you talked yet to anybody over at the coroner's? Maybe your friend Lagonda's seen Glen's autopsy?"

Penny shrugged. "Lagonda describes the matter as 'very sensitive' there. The body's already been cremated, and she won't say any more than that." She watched Doc eat for a while. "Well! And how's everything at the beach?" with a low-sincerity smile he knew enough by now to beware. "'Groovy'? 'psychedelic'? surf bunnies all as attentive as ever? Oh and how are those two stews I caught you with that time?"

"I told you, man, it was that Jacuzzi, the pumps were on too high, those bikinis just kind of mysteriously came undone, it wasn't nothin deliberate—"

As it seemed she never missed a chance to do lately, Penny was referring to Doc's off-and-on partners in mischief, the notorious stewardii Lourdes and Motella, who occupied a palatial bachelorette pad in Gordita, down on Beachfront Drive, with a sauna and a pool, and a bar in the middle of the pool, and usually an endless supply of high-quality weed, as the ladies were known to smuggle in forbidden merchandise, having by now, it was said, enormous fortunes stashed in offshore bank accounts. Yet after nightfall most any layover here, it seemed that they ended up cruising the bleak arterials of dismal L.A. backwaters, seeking out of some helpless fatality the company of low-lifes of opportunity.

"Maybe you'll be seeing them sometime soon?" Penny avoiding eye contact.

"Lourdes and Motella," he inquired as gently as he could, "they're, uh, Chicks of Interest to your shop?"

"Not so much them as some company they've been keeping lately. If in the course of bikini-related activities you should happen to hear them mention by name either or both of a pair of young gentlemen known as Cookie and Joaquin, could you try to make a note of it on something waterproof and let me know?"

"Hey, if you're thinkin of dating outside the legal profession, I can sure fix you up. If you're really desperate, there's always me."

She'd been looking at her watch. "Hectic week ahead for me, Doc, so unless any of this heats up dramatically, I hope you understand."

As romantically as he could, Doc sang her a few quiet falsetto bars of "Wouldn't It Be Nice."

She had learned the technique of pointing her face one way and her eyes another, in this case sideways at Doc, with her lids half shut, and a smile she knew would have its effect. "Walk me back to the office?"

OUTSIDE THE HALL OF JUSTICE, as if remembering something, "Do you mind if I just drop something off next door at the Federal Court-house? It won't take a minute."

They weren't two steps into the lobby before being joined, or did he mean surrounded, by a couple of feds in cheap suits who could have used a little more time in the sun.

"These are my next-door neighbors, Special Agent Flatweed, Special Agent Borderline— Doc Sportello."

"Gotta say I've always admired you guys, eight P.M. every Sunday night, wow, I never miss an episode!"

"The ladies' room is down this way, right?" said Penny. "I'll be back in a jiffy."

Doc watched her out of sight. He knew her gait when she had to piss, and this wasn't it. She wouldn't be back anytime soon. He had about a second and a half to get spiritually prepared before Agent Flatweed said, "Come on, Larry, let's find us a cup of joe." They politely but firmly steered him into an elevator, and for a minute he wondered when he'd get to smoke a joint again.

Upstairs, they waved Doc into a cubicle with framed pictures of Nixon and J. Edgar Hoover. The coffee, in sumptuous black cups with gold FBI insignia, didn't taste like it accounted for too much of their entertainment budget.

From what Doc could make out, both federals seemed newly arrived in town, maybe even straight from our nation's capital. By now he had seen a few of these back-East envoys, who landed in California expecting to have to deal with rebellious and exotic natives and either maintained a force field of contempt till the tour of duty was up, or else with blinding speed found themselves barefoot and stoned, putting their stick in their woody and following the surf off wherever it might roll. There seemed no middle range of choices. It was hard for Doc not to imagine these two as surf Nazis doomed to repeat a film loop of some violent but entertaining beach-movie wipeout.

Agent Borderline had taken out a folder and begun to look through it.

"Hey, what's 'at you got there—" Doc angling his head amiably, Ronald Reagan style, to peer at it. "A *federal file?* on me? Wow, man! The big time!" Agent Borderline closed the folder abruptly and slid it into a pile of others on a credenza, but not before Doc saw a blurred telephoto shot of himself out in a parking lot, probably Tommy's, sitting on the hood of his car holding a gigantic cheezburger and peering into it quizzically, actually *poking through* the layers of pickles, oversize tomato slices, lettuce, chili, onions, cheese, and so forth, not to mention the ground-beef part of it which was almost an afterthought—an obvious giveaway to those who knew about Krishna the fry cook's practice of including somewhere in this, for fifty cents extra, a joint wrapped in waxed paper. Actually, the tradition had begun in Compton years ago and found its way to Tommy's at least by the summer of '68, when Doc, in the famished aftermath of a demonstration against NBC's plans to cancel *Star Trek,* had joined a convoy of irate fans in pointed rubber ears and Starfleet uniforms to plunge (it seemed) down Beverly Boulevard into deep L.A., around a dogleg and on into a patch of town tucked in between the Hollywood and Harbor Freeways, which is where he first beheld, at the corner of Beverly and Coronado, the burger navel of the universe. . . .

"What's that? I was lost in thought."

"You were drooling on the desk. And you weren't supposed to see that file."

"Only wondering if you had any copies, I always like to carry some pictures around in case people want autographs?"

"These days as you may know," Agent Flatweed said, "most of the energy in this office is going into investigating Black Nationalist Hate Groups. And it's come to our attention that you had a visit yourself not long ago from a known black prison militant calling himself Tariq Khalil. We naturally became curious."

"It's the chronology, really," Agent Borderline pretended to explain. "Khalil visits your place of business, next day a known prison acquaintance of his is slain, Michael Wolfmann disappears, and you get arrested on suspicion."

"And cut loose again, don't forget that part. Have you guys talked to Bigfoot Bjornsen about this? he has the whole file on the case, way more information than I ever will, and you'd really like talking to him, he's real intelligent and shit."

"Lieutenant Bjornsen's impatience with the federal level is widely remarked on," Agent Borderline looking up from speed-reading another folder, "and his cooperation if any is likely to be limited. You on the other hand may know things he doesn't. For example, what about these two employees of Kahuna Airlines, Miss Motella Haywood and Miss Lourdes Rodriguez?"

Whom Penny had also just been asking about. What a strange and weird coincidence. "Well, what've these young ladies got to do with your Black Nationalist COINTELPRO, not I hope just 'cause they both happen to be of non-Anglo origins or nothin . . ."

"Ordinarily," said Agent Flatweed, "we're the ones who ask the questions."

"Sure thing, fellas, except aren't we're all in the same business?"

"And there's no need to be insulting."

"Why don't you just share with us what Mr. Khalil had to say the other day when he visited you," suggested Agent Borderline.

"Oh. Because he's a client, so that's privileged conversation, is why not. Sorry."

"If it has bearing on the Wolfmann case, we might have to disagree."

"Groovy, but what I can't figure is, is if your shop is really so focused on the Black Panthers and all that let's-you-and-him-fight with Ron Karenga's folks and so forth, what's with this FBI interest in Mickey Wolfmann? Somebody's been playing Monopoly with federal housing money? no, couldn't be that, 'cause this is L.A., there's no such thing here. What else, then, I wonder?"

"We can't comment," Agent Flatweed smug and, Doc hoped, lulled by his deliberately clueless cross-inquiry.

"Oh, wait, I know—after twenty-four hours it's officially a kidnap case, state lines or whatever, so you guys must be figuring it for a *Panther operation*—say they put the snatch on Mickey to make some political point, and get a shot at some nice ransom money too while they're at it."

At which the two federals, as if unable not to, had a quick nervous look at each other, suggesting they'd at least thought about this for a cover story.

"Well bummer and so forth, wish I could help, but that Khalil guy didn't even leave me a phone number, you know how irresponsible they can get." Doc stood, put out his cigarette in the rest of his FBI coffee. "Tell Penny how groovy it was of her to set up this little get-together, oh, and hey—can I be frank for a minute?"

"Of course," said Agents Flatweed and Borderline.

Snapping his fingers, Doc sang himself out the door with four bars of "Fly Me to the Moon," more or less on pitch, and added, "I know that the Director has a thing about spade penises, and I sure hope you find Mickey before any of that cell-block stuff starts happening."

"He's not cooperating," Agent Borderline muttered.

"Keep in touch, Larry," called Agent Flatweed. "Remember, as a COINTELPRO informant you could be making up to three hundred dollars a month."

"Sure. Say hi to Lew Erskine and the gang."

All the way down in the elevator, though, it was Penny that Doc was worrying about. If the best bargaining chip she had these days was to shop him to the *federales,* she had to be in some deep shit with somebody. But how deep, and who with? The only connection he saw right offhand was that both federal and county heat shared a common interest in the stewardii Lourdes and Motella, and their friends Cookie and Joaquin. Yep, he had best go look into that as soon as possible, not least because the girls were just back from Hawaii and probably had some heavy-duty dope in the house.

MEANTIME, PEOPLE WERE seeing Mickey all over the place. In the meat section at Ralph's in Culver City, shoplifting filet mignons in party-size lots. Out at Santa Anita, in earnest discussion with a person named either Shorty or Speedy. In some accounts, both. In a bar in Los Mochis, watching an old episode of *The Invaders* dubbed into Spanish, and writing urgent memos to himself. In airport VIP lounges from Heathrow to Honolulu, drinking heedless combinations of grape and grain not seen since the days of Prohibition. At antiwar rallies in the Bay Area, begging a variety of armed authorities to mow him down and end his troubles. Out at Joshua Tree, doing peyote. Ascending into the sky haloed in an all-but-unwatchable radiance toward spacecraft not of earthly origin. So forth. Doc started a file on all these reports, and hoped he wouldn't forget where he was stashing it.

Coming out of work later in the day, he happened to notice in the parking lot this tall lanky blonde plus an equally familiar *Oriental cutie.* Yes! it was those two young ladies from that Chick Planet massage parlor! "Hey! Jade! Bambi!" The girls, casting paranoid glances back over attractive bare shoulders, ran and jumped into a species of Harley Earl Impala, screeched out of the lot, and smoked away down West Imperial. Trying not to take this personally, Doc went back inside looking for Petunia, who, shaking her head reproachfully, handed him a flyer for the Chick Planet Massage Pussy Eater's Special.

"Oh. Well I can explain this—"

"Dark and lonely work," muttered Petunia, "but somebody has to do it, something like that? Oh, Doc."

On the back of the flyer, written with an applicator in hot pink toenail polish, it said, "Heard they cut you loose. Need to see you about something. I'm working weeknights at Club Asiatique in San Pedro. Love and Peace, Jade. P.S.—*Beware of the Golden Fang!!!*"

Well, actually Doc wouldn't've minded a brief word or two with that Jade, either, seeing 's how, being the last person he'd spoken with back at Chick Planet before he'd slipped, as Jim Morrison might put it, "into unconsciousness," she could have had a role in setting his unwary ass up for whoever had snatched Mickey Wolfmann and shot down Glen Charlock.

So, knowing them to be longtime Club Asiatique regulars, he headed directly for the beachfront mansion of Lourdes and Motella, who it turned out this evening were headed down to that very waterfront dive to meet their current hearthrobs, FBI Persons of Interest Cookie and Joaquin, offering Doc a chance to find out why the *federales* should be so interested, while at the same time wrecking any hopes he might've entertained for some drug-enhanced three-way among just him and the girls—now, as Fats Domino always sez, "never to be," which was how it usually worked out anyway with these two.

"Okay if I tag along?"

Motella gave him a skeptical O-O. "Those huaraches are marginal, the bell-bottoms will do, but the top needs some work. Here, have a look," leading him to a closet full of gear, from whose dimness Doc grabbed the first Hawaiian shirt he could see, parrots in psychedelic color schemes, some visible only under black light, that would have gotten them second looks even from parrot communities already noted for their extravagance of feather shades, plus hibiscus blossoms that merely snorting them would send you off onto nasal acid trips, and tubular green, phosphorescent surf. A very yellow crescent moon. Hula girls with big tits.

"You can also wear these," handing him a string of love beads from the Kahuna Airlines Duty-Free Head Shop, which opened whenever the airplane entered international airspace, "but I'll want 'em back."

"Aahhh!" Lourdes meantime in the bathroom, screaming with her nose to the mirror. "'Photo courtesy of NASA!'"

"It's this light in here," Doc hastened to point out. "You look fine, you guys, fine, really."

They did, and soon, togged out in matching dresses from the Dynasty Salon at the Hong Kong Hilton, the girls, one on each of Doc's arms, proceeded down to the alley, where, locked in a garage with a single dusty window, through the bleared old glass there glowed this dream of a supernaturally cherry vintage Auburn, maroon in color with some walnut trim, and bearing the license plate LNM WOW.

Driving down the San Diego and Harbor Freeways, the high-spirited stewardii filled Doc in on a list of Cookie and Joaquin virtues he would ordinarily have zoned out in the middle of, but since the FBI's curiosity about the boys had provoked his own, he felt obliged to listen. It was also a distraction from what seemed to Doc the unnecessarily suicidal way Lourdes was piloting the Auburn.

On the radio was a golden oldie by the Boards, in which rock critics had noticed a certain Beach Boys influence—

Thought I musta been hallu-cinating,
Waiting at the light she called to me, "Let's go!"
How am I supposed to refuse an 18-
Year-old cutie in a GTO?

We took off north, from the light at Topanga,
Tires smokin in a long hot scream,
Under the hood of my Ford Mustang, a
427 cammer runnin just like a dream—
[*Bridge*]
Grille to grille, by the time we hit
Leo Carrillo [*Horn section fill*],

And it still, wasn't over by Point Mugu—
Just a Ford Mustang and a sweet GTee-O,
In motion by the ocean,
Doin what the motorheads do.

Shoulda filled-up when I got-off, the San Diego, it's
Been pinned on empty for the last ten miles,
Next thing I know she's wavin *hasta lu-ego,* flashin
One of those big California smiles—

(Doc tried to listen to the instrumental break, and though the horn
section put some nice mariachi harmonies onto "Leo Carrillo," the tenor
player didn't seem to be Coy Harlingen, just another specialist in one- or
two-note solos.)

Bummed out on the shoulder, couldn't feel bluer,
Here comes that familiar Ram Air blast,
What's that on the front seat, right next to her,
It's a shiny red can full of hi-test gas—

So we grooved, back on down, past
Leo Carrillo [*Same horn fill*],
Grille to grille all the way down to Malibu,
Just a Ford Mustang and that sweet GTee-O,
In motion by the ocean
Doin what the motorheads do. . . .

The girls in the front seat were bouncing up and down, squealing *"¡A
toda madre!"* and "What it be, girl!" and so forth.

"Cookie and Joaquin, they are so-o-o bitchin," swooned Motella.

"¡Seguro, ése!"

"Well, actually I meant Cookie is, I can't really speak for Joaquin,
can I?"

"How's that, Motella."

"Ooh, like wondering how it must be, getting into bed with some-body, who has *another person's* name? *tattooed* on his body?"

"No problem unless all you do in bed is read," muttered Lourdes.

"Ladies, ladies!" Doc pretended to push them apart, like Moe going, "Spread out!"

Doc gathered that Cookie and Joaquin were a couple of ex-grunts newly out of Vietnam, back in the World at last though it seemed still pursuing missions of consequence, having caught wind just before they left of some demented scheme featuring connexes full of U.S. currency being transshipped, it was believed, to Hong Kong. In-country traffic in dollars ordinarily fetched many long years in the stockade, but with the money now physically in international waters, according to vari-ous bullshit artists of their acquaintance, the situation was bound to be different.

They had manifested on to Lourdes and Motella's flight to Kai Tak, heads seriously waltzed around with by Darvons, speed, PX beer, Viet-namese weed, and airport coffee, so as to be broadly incapable of the customary airplane chitchat and thus, as the ladies told it, scarcely were the seat-belt lights off than Lourdes and Joaquin, Motella and Cookie, respectively, found themselves in adjoining lavatories fucking each oth-er's brains out. The frolicking continued through the girls' layover in Hong Kong, while the containers of currency grew more and more dif-ficult to locate, not to mention believe in, though Cookie and Joaquin did try, whenever lulls in recreation allowed, to pursue an increasingly halfhearted search for them.

Club Asiatique was in San Pedro, opposite Terminal Island, with a filtered view of the Vincent Thomas Bridge. At night it seemed covered, in a way protected, by something deeper than shadow—a visual expres-sion of the convergence, from all around the Pacific Rim, of numberless needs to do business unobserved.

Glassware behind the bar, which might in some other type of saloon have been found too dazzling, here achieved the smudged cool glow of images on cheap black-and-white TV sets. Waitresses in black silk cheongsams printed with red tropical blossoms glided around on high heels, bearing tall narrow drinks decorated with real orchids and mango slices and straws of vivid aqua plastic molded to look like bamboo. Customers at tables leaned toward each other and then away, in slow rhythms, like plants underwater. House regulars drank shots of hot sake chased with iced champagne. The air was dense with smoke from opium pipes and cannabis bongs, as well as clove cigarettes, Malaysian cheroots, and correctional-system Kools, little glowing foci of awareness pulsing brighter and dimmer everywhere in the dusk. Downstairs, for those nostalgic for Macao and the joys of Felicidad Street, an exclusive fantan game went on day and night, as well as mah-jongg and dollar-a-stone Go in various alcoves behind the bead curtains.

"Now Doc my man," Motella warned as they slid into a booth upholstered with some tigerskin print in nailpolish purple and vivid rust, "remember me and Lourdes 's springin for this, so tonight it's well drinks only, none of that li'l umbrella shit." Plenty cool with Doc, considering the income-disparity situation and all.

Cookie and Joaquin showed up just as the house band was percolating into a zippy version of the Doors' "People Are Strange (When You're a Stranger)," sporting widebrim panama hats, counterfeit designer shades, and white civilian suits bought off some rack in Kaiser Estates, Kowloon, sauntering in in step, one step per beat, each waving a forefinger in the air, down into the echoless reaches of the club. "Joaquin! Cookie!" called the girls, "Oh wow! Dig it! Lookin so groovy!" And so forth. Though few men indeed can be copacetic enough with their lives that they won't go for public appreciation like this, Doc also could see Joaquin and Cookie looking at each other thinking, Shit, man, I wonder how he does it.

"May have to leave in a hurry, *mes chéries*," rumbled Cookie, burying one hand in Motella's Afro and getting into a kiss of some duration.

"Nothin personal," added Joaquin, "kind of a short-notice business trip," enveloping Lourdes in a possibly even more passionate embrace, interrupted by a well-known bass line from the band, who were hidden in a small grove of indoor palm trees.

"All right!" Motella seizing Cookie by his necktie, which had a picture of a florid Pacific lagoonscape in psychedelic colors. "Let's 'get down'!"

In two seconds Joaquin had disappeared under the table. "What's this?" Lourdes keeping her composure.

"Some psychological shit from the 'Nam," Cookie dancing away, "every time people say that, he does it."

"It's okay, folks," called Joaquin, who had spent the war trying to make some money, and wouldn't know a LZ if it ran up and started firing some rockets at his ass, "I like it down here—you don't mind, do you, *mi amor*?"

"I suppose I could think of it as being out with somebody real short?" with her arms folded and a bright smile that was maybe a little higher on one side than the other.

A small perfect Asian dewdrop in the house getup, who on closer inspection seemed to be Jade, came over to Doc. "There are a couple of gentlemen," she murmured, "real eager to see these boys, even to the point of handing out twenties right and left?"

Joaquin stuck his head out from under the tablecloth. "Where are they? We'll finger somebody else, and then we'll be twenty dollars ahead."

"Forty dollars," corrected Lourdes.

"Ordinarily a sound plan," said Motella, returning with Cookie, "except everybody here knows you two and as a matter of fact here comes the folks in question right now."

"Oh shit, it's Blondie-san," said Cookie. "He look pissed off to you? I think he's pissed off."

"Nah," said Joaquin, "he ain't pissed off, but I'm not so sure about his pardner there."

Blondie-san wore a blond toupee that wouldn't have fooled nobody's *abuelita* back in South Pas, and a black business suit of vaguely mob-connected cut. . . . Cranked up, prickly-eyed, and chain-smoking cheap Japanese cigarettes, he was accompanied by a yakuza torpedo named Iwao, the spiritual purity of whose *dan* ranking had long been compromised by a taste for unprovoked asskicking, his eyes sliding back and forth and his face wrinkling in thought as he tried to figure out who was to be his primary target here.

Doc hated to see anybody that confused. Plus which, the more deeply Cookie and Joaquin were drawn into discussion with Blondie-san, the less attention they paid to Lourdes and Motella, making the ladies that much crazier and more susceptible to those grand emotional disasters they shared such a taste for. None of which boded well.

Around then Jade happened by again. "Thought that was you," Doc said, "though we ain't exactly been wallerin in eye contact. Got your note at the office, but why'd you go runnin away like that? we could've hung out, you know, smoke some shit. . . ."

"Like there was these creeps in a Barracuda that tailgated us all the way from Hollywood? Could've been anybody and we didn't want to get you in any more trouble than you are, so we pretended we were there for the B$_{12}$ shots and I guess that made us a little speedy so when we saw you we got paranoid and split?"

"Better not be negotiating no Singapore Slings over there," Motella advised, "none of that shit."

"She's a old schoolmate, we're reminiscing about the prom, geometry class, lighten up Motella."

"What school was that, Tehachapi?"

"Oooh," went Lourdes. The girls were on edge, and strong drink was not improving their mood.

"See me outside," Jade whispered, high-heeling away.

THE NEARLY TOTAL absence of lighting in the parking lot could have been deliberate, to suggest Oriental intrigue and romance, though it also looked like a crime scene waiting on its next crime. Doc noticed a '56 Fireflite ragtop which seemed to be breathing deeply, as if it had raced all the way down here gathering pinks as it came, and was trying to think of how he could discreetly pop the hood and just have a look at the hemi beneath, when Jade showed up.

"I can't stay out here long. We're in Golden Fang territory, and a girl doesn't necessarily want to get into difficulties with those folks."

"This is the same Golden Fang you said to beware of in your note? What is it, some band?"

"You wish." She made a my-lips-are-zipped gesture.

"You're not gonna tell me, after 'beware of' and so forth?"

"No. I really only wanted to say how sorry I am. I just feel so shitty about what I did. . . ."

"Which was . . . what again?"

"I'm not a snitch!" she cried, "the cops told us they'd drop charges if we just put you at the scene, which they already knew you were so where was the harm, and I must've panicked, and really, Larry, I am, like, *so sorry?*"

"Call me Doc, it's cool, Jade, they had to cut me loose, now they just tail me everyplace, is all. Here." He found a pack of smokes, tapped it on the side of his hand, held it out, she took one, they lit up.

"That copper," she said.

"You must mean Bigfoot."

"Some warped sheet of plastic, that one."

"Did he ever come around your salon, by any chance?"

"Looked in now and then, not the way a cop would do, not like expecting freebies or whatever—if this guy was being paid off, it was more like some private deal with Mr. Wolfmann."

"And—don't take it personally, but—was it Bigfoot himself who put me on the Buenas Noches Express, or did he subcontract it?"

She shrugged. "Missed all that, Bambi and me were so freaked with that badass brigade stomping in, we didt'n stick around?"

"How about those jailhouse Nazis 't were supposed to been covering Mickey's back?"

"All over the place one minute, gone the next. Too bad. We were their damn PX there for a while, we even got to where we could tell them apart and whatever."

"They all disappeared? Was that before or after the fun started?"

"Before. Like a raid, when people know it's gonna happen? They all cleared out except for Glen, he was the only one who . . ." she paused as if trying to remember the word for it, "stayed." She dropped her cigarette on the blacktop and squashed it with the pointed toe of her shoe. "Listen—there's somebody who wants to talk to you."

"You mean I should get out of here quick."

"No, he thinks you can help each other out. He's a new face, I'm not even sure of his name, but I know he's in some trouble." She headed back inside.

Out of the onshore mists known to shroud this piece of waterfront, another figure now emerged. Doc wasn't always that easy to creep out, but still wished he hadn't waited around. He recognized this party from the Polaroid that Hope had given him. It was Coy Harlingen, newly returned from the next world, where death along with its other side effects had destroyed any fashion sense the tenor player might have had left when he OD'd, resulting in painter's overalls, a pink button-down shirt from the fifties with a narrow black knit tie, and ancient pointed cowboy boots. "Howdy, Coy."

"I would've come to your office, man, but I thought there might be unfriendly eyeballs." Doc needed an ear trumpet or something, because along with the horns and bells out in the harbor, Coy also had this tendency to fall into a nearly inaudible junkie's murmur.

"Is this safe enough for you, out here?" Doc said.

"Let's light this up and pretend we came out to smoke it."

Asian indica, heavily aromatic. Doc prepared to be knocked on his ass but instead found a perimeter of clarity not too hard to stay inside of. The glow at the end of the joint was blurred by the fog, and its color kept shifting between orange and an intense pink.

"I'm supposed to be dead," Coy said.

"There's also a rumor you're not."

"That don't come as such great news. Bein dead is part of my job image. Like what I do."

"You working for these people here at the club?"

"Don't know. Maybe. It's where I come to pick up my paycheck."

"Where are you staying?"

"House up in Topanga Canyon. A band I used to play for, the Boards. But none of them know it's me."

"How can they not know it's you?"

"Even when I was alive, they didn't know it was me. 'The sax player,' basically—the session guy. Plus over the years there's been this big turnover of personnel, like, the Boards I played with have most of them gone off by now and formed other bands. Only one or two of the old crew are left, and they're suffering, or do I mean blessed, with heavy Doper's Memory."

"Story was you came to grief behind some bad smack. You still into that?"

"No. God. No, I'm clean these days. I was in a place up near—" A long silence and a stare while Coy wondered if he'd said too much and tried to figure what else Doc might know. "Actually, I'd appreciate it if—"

"It's okay," said Doc, "I can't hear you too good, and how can I talk about what I don't hear?"

"Sure. There was somethin I wanted to see you about." Doc thought he caught a note in Coy's voice . . . not exactly accusing, but still sweeping Doc in somehow with some bigger injustice.

Doc peered at Coy's intermittently distinct face, the drops of fog condensed on his beard shining in the lights from the Club Asiatique, a million separate little halos radiating all colors of the spectrum, and understood that regardless of who in this might help whom, Coy was going to require a light touch. "Sorry, man. What can I do for you?"

"It wouldn't be nothin heavy. Just wondering if you could check in on a couple of people. Lady and a little girl. See that they're okay. That's all. And without bringing me into it."

"Where are they staying?"

"Torrance?" He handed over a scrap of paper with Hope and Amethyst's street address.

"Easy drive for me, probably won't even have to charge you for mileage."

"You don't have to go in and talk to anybody, just see if they're still livin there, what's in the driveway, who's going in or out, law enforcement in the picture, any details you find interesting."

"I'm on it."

"I can't pay you right now."

"When you can. Whenever. Unless maybe you're one of these folks who believe information is money . . . in which case, could I just ask—"

"Bearing in mind that either I don't know or it'll be my ass if I tell you, what is it, man?"

"Ever heard of the Golden Fang?"

"Sure." Was that a hesitation? How long is too long? "It's a boat."

"Off-ly in-t'resteen," Doc sang more than spoke in the way Californians do to indicate it isn't interesting at all. Since when do you beware of a boat?

"Seriously. A big schooner, I think somebody said. Brings stuff in and out of the country, but nobody wants to talk about what exactly. That blond Japanese guy tonight with the badass sidekick, who's talkin to your friends? He'd know."

"Because?"

Instead of answering, Coy nodded somberly over Doc's shoulder, across the parking lot, down the street at the main channel and the Outer Harbor beyond. Doc turned and thought he saw something white moving out there. But the fog coming in made everything deceptive. By the time he got to the street, there was nothing to see. "That was it," Coy said.

"How do you know?"

"Saw it sail in. Got here about the same time I did tonight."

"I don't know what I saw."

"Me neither. Fact, I don't even want to know."

Back inside, Doc found the light apparently shifted to more of an ultraviolet mode, because the parrots on his shirt had now begun to stir and flap, to squawk and maybe even talk, though that could also have been from smoke. Lourdes and Motella meanwhile were behaving very badly indeed, having chosen to assault a couple of local gun molls as a sort of tag team, for which waiters and waitresses, keeping semivisible, had relocated a couple of tables in order to clear a space, and customers had gathered around to give encouragement. Clothing was ripped, hairdos disarranged, skin exposed, and many holds with sexual subtexts wriggled into and out of—the usual allurements of girl wrestling. Cookie and Joaquin were still deep in conversation with Blondie-san. Iwao the torpedo was busy watching the girls. Doc edged closer into earshot.

"Just conferenced with the partners by satellite," Blondie-san was saying, "and the best offer is three per unit."

"Maybe I'll go back and reenlist," muttered Joaquin. "Make more off of the bonus than I will this."

"He's only being emotional," Cookie said. "We'll take it."

"You take it, *ése,* I ain't gonna take it."

"I need not remind you," said Blondie-san with sinister amusement, "that this is the Golden Fang."

"Best we not be messin with no Golden Fang," Cookie agreed.

"*¡Caaa-rajo!*" Joaquin in a violent double take, "what are those chicks *doín* over there?"

SEVEN

DOC CALLED SAUNCHO NEXT MORNING AND ASKED IF HE'D EVER heard of a boat called the *Golden Fang.*

Sauncho grew strangely evasive. "Before I forget—was that a diamond ring on Ginger last episode?"

"You sure you didn't, like—"

"Hey, I was on the natch, I just couldn't get a good look. And how about all those googoo eyes at the Skipper? I didn't even know they were dating."

"Must've missed that," said Doc.

"I mean I always figured she'd end up with Gilligan, somehow."

"Nah, nah—Thurston Howell III."

"Come on. He'd never divorce Lovey."

There was a pulse of embarrassed silence as both men realized that this could all be construed as code for Shasta Fay and Mickey Wolfmann and, incredibly, even Doc himself. "The reason I was asking about this boat," Doc said finally, "is, is that—"

"Okay, how about," Sauncho a little abrupt, "you know the yacht harbor in San Pedro? There's a local fish place called the Belaying Pin, meet me there for lunch. I'll tell you what I can."

From the smell that hit him when he walked in, Doc wouldn't have ranked the Belaying Pin as one of your more health-conscious seafood joints. The clientele, however, were not as easy to read. "It isn't new money exactly," Sauncho suggested, "more like new debt. Everything they own, including their sailboats, they've bought on credit cards from institutions in places like South Dakota that you send away for by filling out the back of a match cover." They threaded their way among plasticratic yachtsfolk seated at tables made from Varathaned hatch-covers to a booth by a window in back looking out on the water. "The Pin's where I like to take very special clients, and I also figured you'd want to see the view."

Doc looked out the window. "Is that what I think it is?"

Sauncho had a pair of ancient WWII field glasses on a strap around his neck. He took them off and handed them to Doc. "Meet the schooner *Golden Fang*, out of Charlotte Amalie."

"Where's that?"

"Virgin Islands."

"Bermuda Triangle?"

"Close enough."

"Sizable vessel."

Doc regarded the elegantly swept yet somehow—what would you call it, *inhuman* lines of the *Golden Fang*, everything about her gleaming a little too purposefully, more antennas and radomes than any boat could possibly use, not a flag of national origin in sight, weather decks of teak or maybe mahogany, not likely intended for relaxing out on with no fishing line or can of beer.

"She has a tendency to show up unannounced in the middle of the night," Sauncho said, "no running lights, no radio traffic." Local sophisticates, assuming her visits to be drug-related, might lurk hopefully for a day or two but would soon drift away, muttering about "intimidation." By whom was never quite made clear. The harbormaster went around in a state of nerves, as if coerced into waiving all the fees applying to transients, and every time the office radio kicked in, he was seen to jump violently.

"So who's the mob kingpin that owns this?" Doc saw no harm in asking.

"Actually, we've considered hiring you to find out."

"Me?"

"Off and on."

"Thought you guys 's all dialed in on this, Saunch."

For years Sauncho had kept a watchful eye on the yachting community of Southern California as they came and went, at first feeling the unavoidable class hatred such vessels, for all their beauty under sail, inspire in those of average income, but evolving after a while into fantasies about going in with somebody, maybe even Doc, on a boat, some little Snipe or Lido-class day-sailer at least.

As it turned out, his firm, Hardy, Gridley & Chatfield, had been keenly, almost desperately, curious about the *Golden Fang* for a while now. Her insurance history was an exercise in mystification, sending bewildered clerks and even partners clear back to nineteenth-century commentators like Thomas Arnould and Theophilus Parsons, usually screaming. Tentacles of sin and desire and that strange world-bound karma which is of the essence in maritime law crept through all areas of Pacific sailing culture, and ordinarily it would have taken no more than a fraction of the firm's weekly entertainment budget, deployed at a carefully selected handful of local marina bars, to find out anything they wanted to know from nightly chatter, yarns of Tahiti, Moorea, Bora-Bora, dropped names of rogue mates and legendary vessels, and what had happened aboard, or might have, and who still haunts the cabin spaces, and what old karma lies unavenged, waiting its moment.

"I'm Chlorinda, what'll it be," A waitress in a combination Nehru jacket and Hawaiian-print shirt, just long enough to qualify as a minidress, and with a set of vibes that didn't help sharpen anybody's appetite.

"Ordinarily I'd go for the Admiral's Luau," Sauncho more diffident than Doc expected, "but today I guess I'll just have the house anchovy loaf to start and, um, the devil-ray filet, can I get that deep-fried in beer batter?"

"Your stomach isn't it. How about you, l'il buddy?"

"Mmm!" Doc scanning the menu, "All this *good eatin'*!" while Sauncho kicked him under the table.

"If my husband dared to eat *any* of this shit, I'd throw him out on his ass and drop all his Iron Butterfly albums out the window after him."

"Trick question," Doc said hastily. "The, uh, jellyfish teriyaki croquettes I guess? and the Eel Trovatore?"

"And to drink, gentlemen. You'll want to be good and fucked up by the time *this* arrives. I'd recommend Tequila Zombies, they work pretty quick." She stalked away scowling.

Sauncho had been gazing out at the schooner. "See, the problem with this vessel is trying to find out *anything*. People back off, change the subject, even, I don't know, get creepy, head for the toilet never to reappear." Again Doc thought he saw in Sauncho's expression a strange element of desire. "Her name isn't really the *Golden Fang.*"

No, her original name was *Preserved,* after her miraculous escape in 1917 from a tremendous nitroglycerin explosion in Halifax Harbor which blew away most everything else in it, shipping and souls. *Preserved* was a Canadian fishing schooner, which later during the 1920s and '30s also picked up a reputation as a racer, competing regularly with others in her class, including, at least twice, the legendary *Bluenose*. Shortly after World War II, as fishing schooners were giving way to diesel-powered craft, she was bought by Burke Stodger, a movie star of the period who not long after got blacklisted for his politics and was forced to take his boat and split the country.

"Which is where the Bermuda Triangle comes in," recounted Sauncho. "Somewhere between San Pedro and Papeete, the ship disappears, at first everybody assumes she's been sunk by the Seventh Fleet, acting on direct orders from the U.S. government. Naturally, the Republicans in power deny all involvement, the paranoia keeps growing, till one day a couple years later, boat and owner suddenly reappear—*Preserved* in the opposite ocean, off Cuba, and Burke Stodger on the front page of weekly *Variety*, in an article reporting his return to pictures in a big-budget major-studio project called *Commie Confidential.* The schooner meantime, instantly, as if by occult forces, relocated to the other side of the planet, has been refitted stem to stern, including the removal of any traces of soul, into what you see out there. The owners are listed as a consortium in the Bahamas, and she's been renamed the *Golden Fang.* That's all we've got so far. I know why I'm so interested, but how come you are?"

"Story I heard the other night. Maybe some kind of a smuggling angle?"

"That would be one way of putting it." The ordinarily lighthearted attorney seemed a little bummed today. "Another way of putting it is, is better she should have got blown to bits in Halifax fifty years ago than be in the situation she's in now."

"Sauncho get that weird look off your face, man, you'll wreck my appetite."

"As attorney to client, this story you heard—it didn't happen to include Mickey Wolfmann?"

"Not so far, why?"

"According to scuttlebutt, shortly before his disappearance everybody's favorite developer was observed going on board the *Golden Fang.* Took a little excursion out into the ocean and back again. Like what the Skipper might call 'a three-hour tour.'"

"And wait, I'll bet he was also accompanied by his lovely companion—"

"Thought you were done with that sad bullshit, here, let me order you a boilermaker or something to go with that Zombie, you can start the whole sordid thing over again."

"Just asking. . . . So everybody got back okay, nobody pushed over the side, nothing like that?"

"Well strangely enough, my source in the federal courthouse claims he did see something go over the side. Maybe not a person, it looked to him more like weighted containers, maybe what we call lagan, which is stuff you sink deliberately so you can come back and get it later."

"They, what, put out a buoy or something to mark the spot?"

"Nowadays it's all electronic, Doc, you get your latitude and longitude fix from loran coordinates, and then when you want to zero in closer, you run a sonar scan."

"Sounds like you're plannin to go out and have a look."

"More like a civilian on a ride-along. People at the courthouse who know I'm . . ." He tried to think of the word.

"Interested."

"Putting it kindly. Long as you don't call it obsessed."

If it was a chick, maybe, Doc thought, hoping his lips weren't moving.

AS USUAL THESE DAYS, Fritz was back in the computer room, staring at data. He had that ask-me-if-I-give-a-shit look Doc had noted before in newcomers to the groovy world of addictive behavior.

"Word is that your girlfriend has split the country, sorry to be the one to hand you the news."

Doc was surprised at the intensity of the rectogenital throb that ran through him. "Where'd she go?"

"Not known. She was aboard what the federals call a vessel of interest, to them and maybe you too."

"Uh-oh." Doc looked at the printout and saw the name *Golden Fang.* "And you got this from some computer that's hooked up to your network?"

"This in particular comes from the Hoover Library at Stanford— somebody's collection of countersubversive files. Here, I printed it all down." Doc went out in the front office and drew a cup of coffee from the urn, whereupon Milton the bookkeeper, who had been acting difficult lately, got right into a hassle with Fritz about whether Doc's coffee should be charged to travel and entertainment or to company overhead.

Gladys the secretary turned up the office stereo, which happened to be playing Blue Cheer, either to drown out the argument or suggest gently that everybody pipe down. Fritz and Milton then began screaming at Gladys, who screamed back. Doc lit a joint and began to read the file, which had been put together by a private intelligence operation known as the American Security Council, working out of Chicago, according to Fritz, since around '55.

There was a brief history of the schooner *Preserved,* of keen interest to the countersubversive community for her high-seas capability. At the time of her reappearance in the Caribbean, for example, she was on some spy mission against Fidel Castro, who by that point was active up in the mountains of Cuba. Later, under the name of *Golden Fang,* she was to prove of use to anti-Communist projects in Guatemala, West Africa, Indonesia, and other places whose names were blanked out. She often took on as cargo abducted local "troublemakers," who were never seen again. The phrase "deep interrogation" kept coming up. She ran CIA heroin from the Golden Triangle. She monitored radio traffic off unfriendly coastlines and forwarded it to agencies in Washington, D.C. She brought weapons in to anti-Communist guerrillas, including those at the ill-fated Bay of Pigs. The chronology here ran all the way up to the present, including Mickey Wolfmann's unexplained day trip just before he vanished, as well as the schooner's departure last week from San Pedro with known Wolfmann companion Shasta Fay Hepworth on board.

That Mickey, known to be a generous Reagan contributor, might be active in some anti-Communist crusade came as no big surprise. But how deeply was Shasta involved? Who had arranged for her passage out of the country aboard the *Golden Fang*? Was it Mickey? was it somebody else paying her off for her services in putting the snatch on Mickey? What could she have gotten into so heavy-duty that the only way out was to help set up the man she was supposed to be in love with? Bummer, man. Bumm. Er.

Assuming she even wanted out. Maybe she really wanted to remain *in* whatever it was, and Mickey stood in the way of that, or maybe

Shasta was seeing Sloane's boyfriend Riggs on the side, and maybe Sloane found out and was trying to get revenge by setting Shasta up for Mickey's murder, or maybe Mickey was jealous of Riggs and tried to have him iced only the plan misfired and whoever had contracted to do the deed showed up and by accident killed Mickey, or maybe it was on purpose because *the so-far-unknown hitperson really wanted to run off with Sloane.* . . .

"Gahhh!"

"Good shit, ain't it," Fritz handing back a smoldering roach in a roach clip, all that was left of what they'd been smoking.

"Define 'good,'" Doc muttered. "I am, like, overthinking myself into brainfreeze, here."

Fritz chuckled at length. "Yeah, PIs should really stay away from drugs, all 'em alternate universes just make the job that much more complicated."

"But what about Sherlock Holmes, he did coke all the time, man, it helped him solve cases."

"Yeah but he . . . was not real?"

"What. Sherlock Holmes was—"

"He's a made-up character in a bunch of stories, Doc."

"Wh— Naw. No, he's real. He lives at this real address in London. Well, maybe not anymore, it was years ago, he has to be dead by now."

"Come on, let's go over to Zucky's, I don't know about you, but I've suddenly got this, what Cheech and Chong might call matzo-ball jones?"

Entering the legendary Santa Monica delicatessen, they came under the red-eyed scrutiny of a crowd of freaks of all ages who seemed to be expecting somebody else. After a while Magda showed up with the usual Zuckyburger and fries, and rolled beef on rye, and potato salad and Dr. Brown's Cel-Rays plus another bowl of pickles and sauerkraut, and looking more than ordinarily imposed upon. "Joint sure is jumpin," Doc observed.

She rolled her eyes up and down the establishment. "*Marcus Welby,*

M.D. freaks. You ever notice how the Zucky's sign shows up for half a second in the opening credits? Blink and you'll miss it, but it's more than enough for these people, who come in asking if that's, like, Dr. Steve Kiley's motorcycle parked out in front, and where's the hospital, and who also," her voice rising as she left the table, "get confused when they can't find Cheetos or Twinkies on the goldurn menu!"

"At least it ain't *Mod Squad*-ers," Doc grumbled.

"What," Fritz innocently. "My favorite show."

"Pro-cop fuckin mind control's more like it. Inform on your friends, kids, get a lollipop from the Captain."

"Listen, I came up in Temecula, which is Krazy Kat Kountry, where you always root for Ignatz and not Offisa Pupp."

They got into face-stuffing activities for a while, forgetting if they'd ordered anything else, bringing Magda back over, then forgetting what they wanted her for. "'Cause PIs are doomed, man," Doc continuing his earlier thought, "you could've seen it coming for years, in the movies, on the tube. Once there was all these great old PIs—Philip Marlowe, Sam Spade, the shamus of shamuses Johnny Staccato, always smarter and more professional than the cops, always end up solvin the crime while the cops are followin wrong leads and gettin in the way."

"Coming in at the end to put the cuffs on."

"Yeah, but nowadays it's all you see anymore is cops, the tube is saturated with fuckin cop shows, just being regular guys, only tryin to do their job, folks, no more threat to nobody's freedom than some dad in a sitcom. Right. Get the viewer population so cop-happy they're beggin to be run in. Good-bye Johnny Staccato, welcome and while you're at it please kick my door down, Steve McGarrett. Meantime out here in the real world most of us private flatfoots can't even make the rent."

"So why do you stay in the business? Why not get a houseboat up in the Sacramento Delta—smoke, drink, fish, fuck, you know, what old guys do."

"Don't forget piss and moan."

SUNRISE WAS ON the way, the bars were just closed or closing, out in front of Wavos everybody was either at the tables along the sidewalk, sleeping with their heads on Health Waffles or in bowls of vegetarian chili, or being sick in the street, causing small-motorcycle traffic to skid in the vomit and so forth. It was late winter in Gordita, though for sure not the usual weather. You heard people muttering to the effect that last summer the beach didn't have summer till August, and now there probably wouldn't be any winter till spring. Santa Anas had been blowing all the smog out of downtown L.A., funneling between the Hollywood and Puente Hills on westward through Gordita Beach and out to sea, and this had been going on for what seemed like weeks now. Offshore winds had been too strong to be doing the surf much good, but surfers found themselves getting up early anyway to watch the dawn weirdness, which seemed like a visible counterpart to the feeling in everybody's skin of desert winds and heat and relentlessness, with the exhaust from millions of motor vehicles mixing with microfine Mojave sand to refract the light toward the bloody end of the spectrum, everything dim, lurid and biblical, sailor-take-warning skies. The state liquor stamps over the tops of tequila bottles in the stores were coming unstuck, is how dry the air was. Liquor-store owners could be filling those bottles with anything anymore. Jets were taking off the wrong way from the airport, the engine sounds were not passing across the sky where they should have, so everybody's dreams got disarranged, when people could get to sleep at all. In the little apartment complexes the wind entered narrowing to whistle through the stairwells and ramps and catwalks, and the leaves of the palm trees outside rattled together with a liquid sound, so that from inside, in the darkened rooms, in louvered light, it sounded like a rainstorm, the wind raging in the concrete geometry, the palms beating together like the rush of a tropical downpour, enough to get you to open the door and look outside, and of course there'd only be the same hot cloudless depth of day, no rain in sight.

For the last few weeks now, St. Flip of Lawndale, for whom Jesus Christ was not only personal savior but surfing consultant as well, who rode an old-school redwood plank running just under ten feet with an inlaid mother-of-pearl cross on top and two plastic skegs of a violent pink color on the bottom, had been hitching rides from a friend with a little fiberglass runabout far out into the Outside, to surf what he swore was the gnarliest break in the world, with waves bigger than Waimea, bigger than Maverick's up the coast at Half Moon Bay or Todos Santos in Baja. Stewardii on transpacific flights making their final approaches to LAX reported seeing him below, surfing where no surf should've been, a figure in white baggy trunks, whiter than the prevailing light could really account for. . . . In the evenings with the sunset behind him, he would ascend again to the secular groove of honky-tonk Gordita Beach and grab a beer and silently hang out and smile at people when he had to, and wait for first light to return.

Back in his beach pad there was a velvet painting of Jesus riding goofyfoot on a rough-hewn board with outriggers, meant to suggest a crucifix, through surf seldom observed on the Sea of Galilee, though this hardly presented a challenge to Flip's faith. What was "walking on water," if it wasn't Bible talk for surfing? In Australia once, a local surfer, holding the biggest can of beer Flip had ever seen, had even sold him a fragment of the True Board.

As usual among the early customers at Wavos, there were differing opinions about what, if anything, the Saint had been surfing. Some argued for freak geography—an uncharted seamount or outer reef—others for a weird once-in-a-lifetime weather event, or maybe, like, a volcano, or a tidal wave, someplace far away out in the North Pacific, whose swells by the time they reached the Saint would have grown suitably gnarlacious.

Doc, also up early, sat drinking Wavos coffee, which was rumored to have double-cross whites ground up in it, and listening to the increasingly hectic conversation, and mostly observing the Saint, who was waiting for his morning ride out to the break. Over the years Doc had known a surfer or two who'd found and ridden other breaks located far from shore that nobody else had the equipment either under their feet or in their hearts to ride, who'd gone alone every dawn, often for years, shadows cast out over the water, to be taken, unphotographed and unrecorded, on rides of five minutes and longer through seething tunnels of solar bluegreen, the true and unendurable color of daylight. Doc had noticed that after a while these folks would no longer be quite where their friends expected to find them. Long-standing tabs at frond-roofed beer bars had to be forgiven, shoreside honeys were left to gaze mournfully at the horizons and eventually to take up with civilians from over the berm, claims adjusters, vice principals, security guards, and so forth, even though rent on the abandoned surfer pads still got paid somehow and mysterious lights kept appearing through the windows long after the honky-tonks had closed for the night, and the people who thought they'd actually seen these absent surfers later admitted they might have been hallucinating after all.

Doc had the Saint figured for one of those advanced spirits. His guess was that Flip rode the freak waves he'd found not so much out of insanity or desire for martyrdom as in a true stone indifference, the deep focus of a religious ecstatic who's been tapped by God to be wiped out in atonement for the rest of us. And that one day Flip, like the others, would be someplace else, vanished even from GNASH, the Global Network of Anecdotal Surfer Horseshit, and these same people here would be sitting in Wavos arguing about where he was.

Flip's friend with the outboard showed up after a while, and amid a clamor of anti-powerboat remarks the two split down the hill.

"Well, he's crazy," summarized Flaco the Bad.

"I think they just go out and drink beer and fall asleep and come back when it gets dark," opined Zigzag Twong, who had switched last year to a shorter board and more forgiving waves.

Ensenada Slim shook his head gravely. "There's too many stories about that break. Times it's there, times it ain't. Almost like something's down below, guarding it. The olden-day surfers called it Death's Doorsill. You don't just wipe out, it grabs you—most often from behind just as you're heading for what you think is safe water, or reading some obviously fatal shit totally the wrong way—and it pulls you down so deep you never come back up in time to take another breath, and just as you get lunched forever, so the old tales go, you hear a *cosmic insane Surfaris laugh*, echoing across the sky."

Everybody in Wavos including the Saint proceeded to cackle "Hoo-oo-oo-oo-oo-oo—Wipeout!" more or less in unison, and Zigzag and Flaco started arguing about the two different "Wipeout" singles, and which label, Dot or Decca, featured the laugh and which didn't.

Sortilège, who had been silent till now, chewing on the end of one braid and directing huge enigmatic lamps from one theoretician to another, finally piped up. "A patch of breaking surf right in the middle of what's supposed to be deep ocean? A bottom where there was no bottom before? Well really, think about it, all through history, islands in the Pacific Ocean have been rising and sinking, and what if whatever Flip saw out there is something that sank long ago and is rising now slowly to the surface again?"

"Some island?"

"Oh, an island *at least*."

By this point in California history, enough hippie metaphysics had oozed in among surfing folk that even the regulars here at Wavos, some of them, seeing where this was headed, began to shift their feet and look around for other things to do.

"Lemuria again," muttered Flaco.

"Problem with Lemuria?" inquired Sortilège sweetly.

"The Atlantis of the Pacific."

"That's the one, Flaco."

"And now you say this lost continent, is it's rising to the surface again?"

Her eyes narrowing with what, in a less composed person, could've been taken for annoyance, "Not so strange really, there's always been predictions that someday Lemuria would reemerge, and what better time than now, with Neptune moving at last out of the Scorpio death-trip, a water sign by the way, and rising into the Sagittarian light of the higher mind?"

"So shouldn't somebody be calling *National Geographic* or something?"

"*Surfer* magazine?"

"That's it, boys, I've had my barney quota for the week."

"I'll walk you," Doc said.

They moseyed south down the alleys of Gordita Beach, in the slow seep of dawn and the wintertime smell of crude oil and saltwater. After a while Doc said, "Ask you something?"

"You heard Shasta split the country, and now you need to talk to somebody."

"Readin my thoughts again, babe."

"Read mine then, you know who to see as well as I do. Vehi Fairfield is the closest thing to a real oracle we're ever gonna see in this neck of the woods."

"Maybe you're prejudiced 'cause he's your teacher. Maybe you'd like to place a small wager it's only all that acid talking."

"Throwing your money away, no wonder you can't keep your IOUs straight."

"Never had that problem when you were working at the office."

"And would I ever consider coming back, no, not without benefits including dental and chiropractic, and you know that's way beyond your budget."

"I could offer freak-out insurance maybe."

"Already have that, it's called *shikantaza,* you ought to try it."

"What I get for fallin in love outside my religion."

"Which'd be what, Colombian Orthodox?"

Her boyfriend Spike was out on the porch with a cup of coffee. "Hey, Doc. Everybody's up early today."

"She's tryin to talk me into seeing her guru."

"Don't look at me, man. You know she's always right."

For a while after he got back from Vietnam, Spike had been keenly paranoid about going anyplace he might run into hippies, believing all longhairs to be antiwar bombthrowers who could read his vibrations and tell immediately where he'd been and hate him for it, and try to work some sinister hippie mischief against him. The first time Doc met Spike, he found him a little frantically trying to assimilate into the freak culture, which sure hadn't been there when he left and had made returning to the U.S. like landing on another planet full of hostile alien life-forms. "Trippy, man! How about that Abbie Hoffman! Let's roll us a couple of numbers and hang out and listen to some Electric Prunes!"

Doc could see that Spike would be fine as soon as he calmed down. "Sortilège says you were over in Vietnam, huh?"

"Yeah, I'm one them baby killers." He had his face angled down, but he was looking Doc in the eyes.

"Tell the truth, I admire anybody's had the balls," Doc said.

"Hey, I just went in every day and worked on helicopters. Me and Charlie, no worries, we spent a lot of time in town together hanging out smoking that righteous native weed, listening to rock 'n' roll on the Armed Forces Radio. Every once in a while, they'd wave you over and go, look, you gonna sleep on the base tonight? you'd say, yeah, why? and they'd say, don't sleep on the base tonight. Saved my ass a couple times like that. Their country, they want it, fine with me. Long as I can just work on my bike without nobody hassling me."

Doc shrugged. "Seems fair. Is that yours outside, that Moto Guzzi?"

"Yeah, picked it up from some road maniac from Barstow who just rode the shit out of it, so putting it back in shape is taking up a few weekends. That and old Sortilège, they're keeping me cheerful."

"It's really nice to see you guys together."

Spike looked over at the corner of the room, thought a minute, said carefully, "We go back some, I was a year ahead of her at Mira Costa, we dated a couple times, then when I was over there we started writing, next thing anybody knew I was going, well, maybe I won't re-up after all."

"Must've been around the time I had that matrimonial in Inglewood where the b.f. tried to piss on me through a keyhole I was lookin in. Leej will never let me forget that, she was still working for me then, I remember thinking that something cool must have been happening in her life."

As time passed, Spike was able slowly to learn to relax into the social yoga positions defining life at the beach. The Moto Guzzi brought its share of admirers to hang out and smoke dope and drink beer on the cement apron in front of the garage where Spike worked on it, and he found one or two veterans back from the 'Nam who wanted more or less the same unhassled civilian afterlife he did, especially Farley Branch, who'd been in the Signal Corps and managed to boost some equipment nobody wanted, including an old Bell & Howell 16-mm movie camera from WWII, army green, spring-wound, indestructible, and only a little bigger than the roll of film it used. They would take off on their bikes from time to time looking for targets of opportunity, both discovering after a while a common interest in respect for the natural environment, having seen too much of it napalmed, polluted, defoliated till the laterite beneath was sun-baked solid and useless. Farley had already collected dozens of reels' worth of Stateside environmental abuse, especially Channel View Estates, which reminded him strangely of jungle clearings he had known. According to Spike, Farley had been out there the same day as Doc, shooting footage of the vigilante raid, and was waiting now to get it back from the lab.

Spike himself had been growing obsessed with the El Segundo oil refinery and tanks just up the coast. Even when the wind here cooperated, Gordita was still like living on a houseboat anchored in a tar pit. Everything smelled like crude. Oil spilled from tankers washed up on the beach, black, thick, gooey. Anybody who walked on the beach got it on the bottoms of their feet. There were two schools of thought—Denis, for example, liked to let it just accumulate till it was thick as huarache soles, thereby saving him the price of a pair of sandals. Others, more fastidious, incorporated regular foot-cleaning into their day, like shaving or brushing their teeth.

"Don't get me wrong," Spike said the first time Sortilège found him on the porch with a table knife, scraping off the soles of his feet. "I love it here in Gordita, mostly 'cause it's your hometown and you love it, but now and then there's just some . . . little . . . fucking detail . . ."

"They're destroying the planet," she agreed. "The good news is that like any living creature, Earth has an immune system too, and sooner or later she's going to start rejecting agents of disease like the oil industry. And hopefully before we end up like Atlantis and Lemuria."

It was the belief of her teacher Vehi Fairfield that both empires had sunk into the sea because Earth couldn't accept the levels of toxicity they'd reached.

"Vehi's okay," Spike told Doc now, "though he sure does a awful lot of acid."

"It helps him see," explained Sortilège.

Vehi wasn't just "into" LSD—acid was the medium he swam and occasionally surfed in. He got it delivered, possibly by special pipeline, from Laguna Canyon, direct from the labs of the post-Owsley psyche- delic mafia believed in those days to be operating back in there. In the course of systematic daily tripping, he had found a spirit guide named Kamukea, a Lemuro-Hawaiian demigod from the dawn of Pacific his- tory, who centuries ago had been a sacred functionary of the lost conti- nent now lying beneath the Pacific Ocean.

"And if anybody can put you in touch with Shasta Fay," Sortilège said, "it's Vehi."

"Come on, Leej, you know I had some weird history with him—"

"Well, he thinks you've been trying to avoid him, and he can't under- stood why."

"Simple. Rule number one of the Dopers' Code? Never, ever put nobody—"

"But he *told* you that was acid."

"No, he told me it was 'Burgomeister Special Edition.'"

"Well that's what that means, Special Edition, it's a phrase he uses."

"*You* know that, *he* knows that. . . ." By which point they were out on the esplanade, en route to Vehi's place.

Voluntary or whatever, the trip Vehi'd put him on with that magic beer can was one Doc kept hoping he'd forget about with time. But didn't.

It had all begun, apparently, some 3 billion years ago, on a planet in a binary star system quite a good distance from Earth. Doc's name then was something like Xqq, and because of the two suns and the way they rose and set, he worked some very complicated shifts, cleaning up after a labful of scientist-priests who invented things in a gigantic facility which had formerly been a mountain of pure osmium. One day he heard some commotion down a semiforbidden corridor and went to have a look. Ordinarily sedate and studious personnel were running around in uncontrolled glee. "We did it!" they kept screaming. One of them grabbed Doc, or actually Xqq. "Here he is! The perfect subject!" Before he knew it he was signing releases, and being costumed in what he would soon learn was a classic hippie outfit of the planet Earth, and led over to a peculiarly shimmering chamber in which a mosaic of Looney Tunes motifs was repeating obsessively away in several dimensions at once in vividly audible yet unnamable spectral frequencies. . . . The lab people were explaining to him meanwhile that they'd just invented intergalactic time travel and that he was about to be sent across the universe and maybe 3 billion years into the future. "Oh, and one other thing," just before throwing the final switch, "the universe? it's been, like, expanding? So when you get there, everything else will be the same weight, but bigger? with all the molecules further apart? except for you—you'll be the same size and density. Meaning you'll be about a foot shorter than everybody else, but much more compact. Like, solid?"

"Can I walk through walls?" Xqq wanted to know, but by then space and time as he knew it, not to mention sound, light, and brain waves, were all undergoing these unprecedented changes, and next thing he knew he was standing on the corner of Dunecrest and Gordita Beach Boulevard, and watching what seemed to be an endless procession of young women in bikinis, some of whom were smiling at him and offering thin cylindrical objects whose oxidation products were apparently meant to be inhaled. . . .

As it turned out, he was able to go through drywall construction with little discomfort, although, not having X-ray vision, he did run into some disagreeable moments with wall studs and eventually curtailed the practice. His new hyperdensity also allowed him sometimes to deflect simple weapons directed at him with hostile intent, though bullets were another story, and he also learned to avoid those when possible. Slowly the Gordita Beach of his trip merged with the everyday version, and he began to assume that things were back to normal, except for when, now and then, he'd forget and lean against a wall and suddenly find himself halfway through it and trying to apologize to somebody on the other side.

"Well," Sortilège supposed, "many of us do get uncomfortable when we discover some secret aspect to our personality. But it's not like you ended up three feet tall with the density of lead."

"Easy for you to say. Try it sometime."

They had arrived at a beach pad with salmon walls and an aqua roof, with a dwarf palm growing out of the sand in front decorated all over with empty beer cans, among which Doc couldn't help noticing a number of ex-Burgies. "Actually," Doc remembered, "I've got this coupon, buy a case, get one free, expires midnight tonight, maybe I better—"

"Hey, it's your ex–old lady, man, I'm just along for the finder's fee."

They were greeted by a person with a shaved head, wearing wire-rim sunglasses and a green and magenta kimono with some kind of bird motif on it. He was a dedicated old-school longboarder recently back from Oahu, having somehow known in advance about the epic surf that hit the north shore of that island back in December.

"Man, did you miss a big story," he greeted Doc.

"You too, man."

"I'm talkin about sets of fifty-foot waves that wouldn't quit."

"'Fifty,' huh. I'm talkin about Charlie Manson gettin popped."

They looked at each other.

"On the face of it," Vehi Fairfield said finally, "two separate worlds, each unaware of the other. But they always connect someplace."

"Manson and the Surge of '69," said Doc.

"I'd be very surprised if they weren't connected," Vehi said.

"That's because you think everything is connected," Sortilège said.

"'Think'?" He turned back to Doc, beaming. "You're here about your ex–old lady."

"What?"

"You got my message. You just don't know you did."

"Oh. Sure, Woo-Woo Telephone and Telegraph, I keep forgetting."

"Not a very spiritual person," Vehi remarked.

"His attitude needs some work," Sortilège said, "but for the level he's on, he's okay."

"Here, take some of this." Vehi held out a piece of blotter with something written on it in Chinese. Maybe Japanese.

"Oboy, now what, more through-the-wall sci-fi, right? groovy, can't wait."

"Not this," said Vehi, "this is designed expressly for you."

"Sure. Like a T-shirt." Doc popped it in his mouth. "Wait. Expressly for me, what's that mean?"

But after putting onto his stereo, at top volume, Tiny Tim singing "The Ice Caps Are Melting," from his recent album, which had been somehow fiendishly programmed to repeat indefinitely, Vehi had either left the area or become invisible.

At least it wasn't quite as cosmic as the last trip this acid enthusiast had acted as travel agent for. When it began exactly wasn't too clear, but at some point, via some simple, normal transition, Doc found himself in the vividly lit ruin of an ancient city that was, and also wasn't, everyday Greater L.A.—stretching on for miles, house after house, room after room, every room inhabited. At first he thought he recognized the people he ran into, though he couldn't always put names to them. Everybody living at the beach, for example, Doc and all his neighbors, were and were not refugees from the disaster which had submerged Lemuria thousands of years ago. Seeking areas of land they believed to be safe, they had settled on the coast of California.

Somehow unavoidably the war in Indochina figured in. The U.S., being located between the two oceans into which Atlantis and Lemuria had disappeared, was the middle term in their ancient rivalry, remaining trapped in that position up to the present day, imagining itself to be fighting in Southeast Asia out of free will but in fact repeating a karmic loop as old as the geography of those oceans, with Nixon a descendant of Atlantis just as Ho Chi Minh was of Lemuria, because for tens of thousands of years all wars in Indochina had really been proxy wars, going back, back to the previous world, before the U.S., or French Indochina, before the Catholic Church, before the Buddha, before written history, to the moment when three Lemurian holy men landed on those shores, fleeing the terrible inundation which had taken their homeland, bringing with them the stone pillar they had rescued from their temple in Lemuria and would set up as the foundation of their new life and the heart of their exile. It would become known as the sacred stone of Mu, and over the centuries to follow, as invading armies came and went, the stone would be taken away each time for safekeeping to a secret location, to be put up someplace different when the troubles were over. Ever since France began colonizing Indochina, on through the present occupation by the U.S., the sacred stone had remained invisible, withdrawn into its own space. . . .

Tiny Tim was still singing the same number. Moving through the three-dimensional city labyrinth, Doc noticed after a while that the lower levels seemed a little damp. By the time the water was ankle-deep, he began to get the idea. This entire vast structure was sinking. He went up steps to higher and higher levels, but the water level kept rising. Beginning to panic, and cursing Vehi for setting him up once again, he felt more than saw the Lemurian spirit guide Kamukea as a shadow of deep clarity. . . . We must leave now, said the voice in his mind.

They were flying together, close to the tops of the waves of the Pacific. There was dark weather at the horizon. Ahead of them a white blur began to sharpen and grow, and slowly it resolved into the sails of a topmasted schooner, running along full-spread before a fresh breeze. Doc recognized the *Golden Fang. Preserved,* Kamukea silently corrected him. This was no dream ship—every sail and piece of rigging was doing its work, and Doc could hear the snap of canvas and the creak of timbers. He angled in toward the port quarter of the schooner, and there was Shasta Fay, brought here, it seemed, under some kind of duress, out on deck, alone, gazing back at the way she'd come, the home she'd left. . . . Doc tried calling her name but of course words out here were only words.

She'll be all right, Kamukea assured him. You don't have to worry. That is another thing you must learn, for what you must learn is what I am showing you.

"I'm not sure what that means, man." Even Doc could feel now how mercilessly, despite the wind and the sails of the moment so clean and direct, this honest old fishing vessel had come to be inhabited—possessed—by an ancient and evil energy. How would Shasta be safe in that?

I have brought you this far, but now you must return through your own efforts. The Lemurian was gone, and Doc was left at his negligible altitude above the Pacific to find his way out of a vortex of corroded history, to evade somehow a future that seemed dark whichever way he turned. . . .

"It's okay, Doc." Sortilège had been calling his name now for a while. They were outside on the beach, it was nighttime, Vehi wasn't there. The ocean lay close by, dark and invisible except for luminescence where the surf broke stately as the bass line to some great uncontainable rock 'n' roll classic. From somewhere back in the alleys of Gordita Beach came gusts of dopers' merriment.

"Well—"

"Don't say it," warned Sortilège. "Don't say, 'Let me tell you about my trip.'"

"Makes no sense. Like, we were out in this—"

"I can either press your lips gently closed with my finger or—" She made a fist and positioned it near his face.

"If your guru Vehi did not just set me up . . ."

After about a minute, she said, "What?"

"Huh? What was I talkin about?"

EIGHT

THE BANK DEPOSIT FORM SLOANE WOLFMANN HAD GIVEN DOC
was from Arbolada Savings and Loan in Ojai. This, according to Aunt
Reet, was one of many S&Ls Mickey held a controlling interest in.

"And their customers, how would you describe them?"

"Mostly individual homeowners, what we in the profession refer to as
'suckers,'" replied Aunt Reet.

"And the loans—anything out of the ordinary?"

"Ranchers, local contractors, maybe some Rosicrucians and Theoso-
phists now and then—oh and of course there's Chryskylodon, who've
been doing a heap of building and landscaping and tacky but expensive
interior design lately."

As if his head was a 3-D gong just struck by a small hammer, Doc
recalled the blurry foreign word in the photo of Sloane he'd seen at her
house. "How do you spell that, and what is it?"

"Got one of their brochures someplace on this desk, down around the
Precambrian layer as I recall . . . aha! Here: 'Located in the scenic Ojai
Valley, Chryskylodon Institute, from an ancient Indian word meaning
"serenity," provides silence, harmony with the Earth, and unconditional
compassion for those emotionally at risk owing to the unprecedented
stressfulness of life in the sixties and seventies.'"

"Sure sounds like a high-rent loony bin, don't it."

"The pictures don't tell you much, everything's been shot with grease on the lens, like some girlie magazine. There's a phone number here." Doc copied it, and she added, "Call your mother, by the way."

"Oh, shit. Something happen?"

"You didn't call for a week and a half, is what happened."

"Work."

"Well, the latest is, is they think you're a dope dealer now. The impression I get, I should say."

"Right, well, seeing Gilroy's the one with the life, operations manager for whatever, grandkids and acreage and so forth, stands to reason, don't it, I should be the one with the narcs breathin down my neck."

"Preaching to the choir, Doc, I wanted out of that place before I could talk. They'd catch me pedaling a mile a minute on my li'l pink trike heading out through the beet fields, and drag me back screaming. Nothing you can tell me about the San Joaquin, kid. Then again, Elmina says she misses your voice."

"I'll call her."

"She also agrees with me you should look at that two-acre piece out in Pacoima."

"Not me, man."

"Still on the market, Doc. And like we say in the business, get a lot while you're young."

Leo Sportello and Elmina Breeze had met up in 1934 at the World's Largest Outdoor Rummy Game, held annually in Ripon. Leo, reaching for one of her discards, said something like, "Now, you're sure you don't want that," and as Elmina told it, the minute she looked up from her cards and into his eyes, she was sure as salvation about what she did want. She was still living at home then, student-teaching, and Leo had a good job at one of the wineries, known for a fortified product marketed up and down the coast as Midnight Special. Every time Leo so much as put his head in the door, Elmina's father would go into a W. C. Fields routine—"Ah? the wino's frien-n-n-d . . . ye-e-esss . . ." Leo began to make a point of bringing some over whenever he came to pick up

Elmina for a date, and before long his future father-in-law was buying the stuff by the case, using Leo's company discount. The first wine Doc ever drank was Midnight Special, part of Grandpa Breeze's concept of baby-sitting.

DOC WAS HOME watching division semifinals between the 76ers and Milwaukee, mainly for Kareem Abdul-Jabbar, whom Doc had admired since he was Lew Alcindor, when right in the middle of a fast break he became aware of a voice down in the street calling his name. For a minute he flashed that it was Aunt Reet, secretly resolved to sell his place out from under him, showing it at this inappropriate hour to some flatland couple especially selected for their pain-in-the-ass qualities. By the time he got to the window to have a look, he dug how he'd been fooled by a similarity of voices, and it was actually his mother Elmina in the street, somehow in deep discussion with Downstairs Eddie. She looked up, saw Doc, and started waving cheerfully.

"Larry! Larry!" Behind her was a double-parked 1969 Oldsmobile, and Doc could dimly make out his father Leo leaning out the window, an inexpensive cigar clamped in his teeth pulsing bright to dim and back again. Doc was now imagining himself at the rail of a long-ago ocean liner sailing out of San Pedro, ideally for Hawaii but Santa Monica would do, and he waved back. "Ma! Dad! Come on up!" He went running around opening windows and cranking up the electric fan, though the odor of marijuana smoke, having long found its way into the rug, the couch, the velvet painting, was years too late to even worry about.

"Where do I park this?" Leo hollered up.

Good question. The kindest thing anybody'd ever called the parking in Gordita Beach was nonlinear. The regulations changed unpredictably from one block, often one space, to the next, having been devised secretly by fiendish anarchists to infuriate drivers into one day forming a mob and attacking the offices of town government. "Be right down," said Doc.

"Will you look at that hair," Elmina greeted him.

"Soon as I can get to a mirror, Ma," by which time she was in his arms, not all that put out at being hugged and kissed in public by a longhaired hippie freak. "Hi, Dad." Doc slid into the front seat. "There's probably something down on Beachfront Drive, just hope we don't have to go halfway to Redondo to find it."

Meantime, Downstairs Eddie was going, "Wow, so this is your folks, far out," and so forth.

"You boys go park," said Elmina, "I'll just hang out with Larry's neighbor here."

"Door's open upstairs," Doc quickly reviewing what he knew of Eddie's rap sheet, including the hearsay, "just don't get in any kitchens with this guy, you should be all right."

"That was back in '67," Eddie protested. "All those charges got dropped."

"My," said Elmina.

Of course no more than five minutes later, having lucked into a spot just down the hill good at least till midnight, Doc and Leo returned to find Eddie and Elmina in the kitchen, and Eddie just about to open the last box of brownie mix.

"Ah-ah-ah," Doc wagging his finger.

There were beers and half a bag of Cheetos, and Surfside Slick's deli up the hill was open till midnight for whatever they'd be running out of.

Elmina wasted no time in bringing up the subject of Shasta Fay, whom she'd met once and taken to right away. "I always hoped . . . Oh, you know . . ."

"Leave the kid be," muttered Leo.

Doc was aware of Downstairs Eddie, who'd once upon a time had to listen to it all through his ceiling, throwing him a look.

"She had her career," Elmina continued. "It's hard, but sometimes you have to let a girl go where her dreams are calling her. There did use to be Hepworths over by Manteca, you know, and a couple of them moved down here during the war to work in the defense plants. She could be related."

"If I see her, I'll ask," Doc said.

There were footfalls up the back steps and Scott Oof came in by way of the kitchen. "Hi Uncle Leo, Aunt Elmina, Mom said you'd be driving down."

"We missed you at supper," Elmina said.

"Had to go see about a gig. You'll be here for a while, right?"

Leo and Elmina were staying up on Sepulveda at the Skyhook Lodge, which did a lot of airport business and was populated day and night with the insomniac, the stranded and deserted, not to mention an occasional certified zombie. "Wandering all up and down the halls," said Elmina, "men in business suits, women in evening gowns, people in their underwear or sometimes nothing at all, toddlers staggering around looking for their parents, drunks, drug addicts, police, ambulance technicians, so many room-service carts they get into traffic jams, who needs to get in the car and go anyplace, the whole city of Los Angeles is right there five minutes from the airport."

"How's the television?" Downstairs Eddie wanted to know.

"The film libraries on some of these channels," Elmina said, "I swear. There was one on last night, I couldn't sleep. After I saw it, I was afraid to sleep. Have you seen *Black Narcissus*, 1947?"

Eddie, who was enrolled in the graduate film program at SC, let out a scream of recognition. He'd been working on his doctoral dissertation, "Deadpan to Demonic—Subtextual Uses of Eyeliner in the Cinema," and had just in fact arrived at the moment in *Black Narcissus* where Kathleen Byron, as a demented nun, shows up in civilian gear, including eye makeup good for a year's worth of nightmares.

"Well, I hope you'll be including some men," Elmina said. "All those German silents, Conrad Veidt in *Caligari*, Klein-Rogge in *Metropolis*—"

"—complicated of course by the demands of orthochromatic film stock—"

Oboy. Doc went out to search through the kitchen, having dimly recalled an unopened case of beer that might be there. Soon Leo put his head in.

"I know it has to be someplace," Doc puzzled out loud.

"Maybe you can tell me if this is normal," Leo said. "We got a weird phone call at the motel last night, somebody on the other end starts screaming, at first I figure it's Chinese, I can't understand a word. Finally I can just make out, 'We know where you are. Watch your ass.' And they hang up."

Doc was having those rectal throbs. "What name are you guys checked in under?"

"Our usual one." But Leo was blushing.

"Dad, it could be important."

"Okay, but try to understand, it's this habit your mother and I have sort of fallen into, of staying at different motels up and down old 99 on weekends, under fake names? We pretend we're married to other people and having an illicit rendezvous. And I won't try to kid you, it's a lot of fun. Like those hippies say, whatever turns you on, right?"

"So the front desk doesn't really have you down as any kind of Sportello."

Leo gave him one of those hesitant smiles that fathers use to deflect the disapproval of sons. "I like to use Frank Chambers. You know, from *The Postman Always Rings Twice*? Your mother uses Cora Smith if anybody asks, but for Chrissake don't tell her I told you that."

"So it was a wrong number." Doc saw the case of beer, out in front of his face all this time. He put some cans in the freezer, hoping he'd remember he'd done this and that nothing would explode like it usually did. "Well Dad, I'm really shocked at you two." He embraced Leo and held it for almost long enough to be embarrassing.

"What's this?" Leo said. "You're laughing at us."

"No. No . . . I'm laughing 'cause I like to use that same name."

"Huh. You must get that from me."

Later, though, around three A.M., four, one of those desolate hours, Doc had forgotten his feelings of relief and only remembered how scared he'd been. Why had he automatically assumed there was something out there that could find his parents so easily and put them in danger? Mostly in these cases, the answer was, "You're being paranoid." But in the business, paranoia was a tool of the trade, it pointed you in directions you might not have seen to go. There were messages from beyond, if not madness, at least a shitload of unkind motivation. And where did that mean this Chinese voice in the middle of the night—whenever that might be at the Skyhook Lodge—was telling him to look?

NEXT MORNING, waiting for the coffee to percolate, Doc happened to glance out the window and saw Sauncho Smilax down in his classic beach-town ride, a maroon 289 Mustang with a black vinyl interior and a low, slow throb to its exhaust, trying not to block up the alley. "Saunch! come on up, have some coffee."

Sauncho took the stairs two at a time and stood panting in the doorway, holding a briefcase. "Didn't know if you were up."

"Me neither. What's happening?"

Sauncho had been out all day and night with a posse of *federales* aboard a garishly overequipped vessel belonging to the Justice Department, visiting a site previously identified as the spot where the *Golden Fang* was supposed to have left some kind of lagan. Divers went down to have a look and, as the light shifted over the ocean, presently were bringing up one connex after another full of shrink-wrapped bundles of U.S. currency, maybe the same ones Cookie and Joaquin, on behalf of Blondie-san, might still be out after. Except that upon opening the containers, imagine how surprised everybody was to find that, instead of the usual dignitaries, Washington, Lincoln, Franklin and whoever, all of these bills, no matter which denomination, seemed to have *Nixon's* face on them. For an instant a federal joint task force paused to wonder if they might not after all, the whole boatload of them, be jointly hallucinating. Nixon was staring wildly at something just out of sight past the edge of the cartouche, almost cringing out of its way, his eyes strangely unfocused, as if he had himself been abusing some novel Asian psychedelic.

According to intelligence contacts of Sauncho's, it had been common CIA practice for a while to put Nixon's face on phony North Vietnamese bills, as part of a scheme to destabilize the enemy currency by airdropping millions of these fakes during routine bombing raids over the north. But Nixonizing U.S. currency this way was not as easily explained, nor sometimes even appreciated.

"What is this? The CIA's done it again, this shit is worthless."

"You don't want it? I'll take it."

"What are you gonna do with it?"

"Spend a bundle of it before anybody begins to notice."

Some thought it was a plot by Chinese Communist pranksters to mess with the U.S. dollar. The engraving work was too exquisite not to have some Fiendish Oriental Provenance. According to others it might have been circulating as scrip for a while now throughout Southeast Asia, and even somehow be negotiable Stateside.

"And let's not forget its value on the collectors' market."

"Bit too weird for me I'm afraid."

"And dig," said Sauncho later to Doc—"the law says that before you can get your picture on U.S. currency, you have to be dead. So in any universe where this stuff is legal tender, Nixon would have to be dead, right? So what I think it is, is it's *sympathetic magic* by somebody who wants to see Nixon among the departed."

"That sure narrows it down, Saunch. Can I have some of this?"

"Hey, take whatever. Go on a shopping spree. See these shoes I've got on? Remember those white loafers that Dr. No wears in *Dr. No*, 1962? Yes dig it! same identical ones! Bought 'em on Hollywood Boulevard with one of these Nixon twenties—nobody examined it, nothing, it's amazing. Hey! my soap's almost on, do you, uh, mind?" He headed for the tube without delay.

Sauncho was a devoted viewer of the daytime drama *The Way to His Heart*. This week—as he updated Doc during lulls—Heather has just confided to Iris her suspicions about the meat loaf, including Julian's role in switching the contents of the Tabasco bottle. Iris isn't too surprised, of course, having for the duration of her own marriage to Julian taken turns in the kitchen, so that there remain between these bickering exes literally hundreds of culinary scores yet to be settled. Meanwhile, Vicki and Stephen are still discussing who still owes who five dollars from a pizza delivery weeks ago, in which the dog, Eugene, somehow figures as a key element.

Doc was in the toilet pissing during a commercial break when he heard Sauncho screaming at the television set. He got back to find his attorney just withdrawing his nose from the screen.

"Everything cool?"

"Ahh . . ." collapsing on the couch, "Charlie the fucking Tuna, man."

"What?"

"It's all supposed to be so innocent, upwardly mobile snob, designer shades, beret, so desperate to show he's got good taste, except he's also dyslexic so he gets 'good taste' mixed up with 'taste good,' but it's worse than that! Far, far worse! Charlie really has this, like, *obsessive death wish*! Yes! he, he *wants* to be caught, processed, put in a can, not just any can, you dig, it has to be StarKist! suicidal brand loyalty, man, deep parable of consumer capitalism, they won't be happy with anything less than drift-netting us all, chopping us up and stacking us on the shelves of Supermarket Amerika, and subconsciously the horrible thing is, is we *want* them to do it. . . ."

"Saunch, wow, that's . . ."

"It's been on my mind. And another thing. Why is there Chicken of the Sea, but no Tuna of the Farm?"

"Um . . ." Doc actually beginning to think about this.

"And don't forget," Sauncho went on to remind him darkly, "that Charles Manson and the Vietcong are *also* named Charlie."

When the show was over, Sauncho said, "So you, how you doing, Doc, going to be arrested again or anything?"

"With Bigfoot on my tail now, I could be calling you any minute."

"Oh. I almost forgot. The *Golden Fang*? Seems there was an ocean marine insurance policy taken out on her just before she singled up all lines, covering this one voyage only, the one your ex–old lady's supposed to be on, and the beneficiary is listed as Golden Fang Enterprises of Beverly Hills."

"If the boat sinks, they collect a lot of money?"

"Exactly."

Uh huh. What if it was a deliberate insurance hustle? Maybe Shasta could still get ashore in time, onto some island where maybe even now she'd be pulling small perfect fish out of the lagoon and cooking them with mangoes and hot peppers and shredded coconut. Maybe she was sleeping out on the beach and looking at stars nobody here under the smoglit L.A. sky even knew existed. Maybe she was learning to sail island to island on an outrigger canoe, to read the currents and the winds, and how to sense magnetic fields like a bird. Maybe the *Golden Fang* had sailed on to its fate, gathering those who hadn't found their way to shore deeper into whatever complications of evil, indifference, abuse, despair they needed to become even more themselves. Whoever they were. Maybe Shasta had escaped all that. Maybe she was safe.

THAT EVENING OVER at Penny's place, Doc fell asleep on her couch in front of the day's sports highlights, and when he woke, sometime well after dark, a face, which turned out to be Nixon's, was on the tube going, "There are always the whiners and complainers who'll say, this is fascism. Well, fellow Americans, if it's Fascism for Freedom? *I . . . can . . . dig it!*" Tumultuous applause from a huge room full of supporters, some of them holding banners with the same phrase professionally lettered on them. Doc sat up, blinking, groping around in the tubelight for his stash, finding half a joint and lighting up.

What struck him was that Nixon right now had the exact freaked-out expression on his face that he did on the fake twenty-dollar bills Doc had gotten from Sauncho. He took one out of his wallet now and consulted it, just to be sure. Yep. The two Nixons looked *just like photos* of each other!

"Let's see," Doc inhaled and considered. This same Nixonface here, live on the screen, had somehow *already* been put into circulation, months ago, on millions, maybe billions, in false currency. . . . How could this be? Unless . . . sure, time travel of course . . . some CIA engraver, in some top-security workshop far away, was busy *right now* copying this image off of his own screen and then would later somehow go slip his copy into a covert *special mailbox,* which would have to be located close to a power-company substation so they could bootleg the power they needed, raising everybody else's rates, to send information time-traveling *back into the past,* in fact there might even be *time-warp insurance* you could buy in case these messages went astray among the unknown energy surges out there in the vastness of Time. . . .

"I knew I smelled something in here. Lucky for you I don't go in to work tomorrow," Penny, squinting and barelegged in one of Doc's Pearls Before Swine T-shirts.

"This joint woke you up? Sorry, Pen, here—" offering what was by now more a friendly gesture than a real roach.

"No, all that screaming did. What are you watching, sounds like yet another Hitler documentary."

"Nixon. I think it's happening live right now, someplace in L.A."

"Could be the Century Plaza." Which was presently confirmed by the newsfolks covering the event—Nixon had indeed dropped in, as if on a whim, at the palatial Westside hotel to address a rally of GOP activists who called themselves Vigilant California. In cutaways to individuals in the audience, some seemed a little out of control, like you'd expect to find at gatherings like this, but others were less demonstrative and, to Doc at least, scarier. Strategically posted among the crowd, wearing identical suits and ties you'd have to call on the unhip side, none of them seemed to be paying much attention to Nixon himself.

"I don't think they're Secret Service," Penny sliding over next to Doc on the sofa. "Not cute enough, to begin with. More likely private sector."

"They're waiting for something—ha! look, here we go." As if linked by ESP, the robot operatives had pivoted as one and begun to converge on a member of the audience, longhaired, wild-eyed, dressed in match-ing psychedelic Nehru shirt and bell-bottoms, who was now scream-ing, "Hey, Nixon! Hey, Tricky Dick! Fuck you! And you know what, hey, fuck Spiro, too! Fuck everybody in the First Fuckin Family! Fuck the dog, hey! Anybody know the dog's name? whatever—fuck the dog, too! Fuck all of you!" And began to laugh insanely as he was seized and dragged away through the crowd, many of them glaring, snarling and foaming at the mouth in disapproval. "Better get him to a hippie drug clinic," suggested Nixon humorously.

"Giving revolutionary youth a bad name," it seemed to Doc, who was rolling another joint.

"Not to mention raising some First Amendment issues," Penny lean-ing up close to the screen. "Strange, though . . ."

"Really? Looks like typical Republicans to me."

"No, I mean—there, there's the close-up. That's no hippie, look at him. It's Chucky!"

Or to put it another way, Doc now became aware with a jolt, it was also Coy Harlingen. It took him maybe half a lungful of pot smoke to decide against sharing this with Penny. "Friend of yours," he inquired disingenuously.

"Everybody knows him—when he's not hanging out at the Hall of Justice, he's at the Glass House."

"A snitch?"

"'Informant,' please. He works mostly for the Red Squad and the P-DIDdies."

"Who?"

"Public Disorder Intelligence Division? Never heard of them, eh?"

"And . . . why's he yelling at Nixon like that again?"

"Jeez, Doc, at this rate they're going to pull your paranoia card. Even a PI can't be that naïve."

"Well, his outfit maybe is a little overcoordinated, but that don't mean there's any setup."

She sighed didactically. "But now that he's been all over the TV? he has instant and wide credibility. The police can infiltrate him into any group they want."

"You guys been watchin that *Mod Squad* again. Gives you all these *cold*-ass ideas. Hey! Did I tell you Bigfoot offered me a job the other day?"

"Astute of Bigfoot as always. He must have detected in your character some special gift for . . . betrayal?"

"Come on, Penny, she was sixteen, she was dealing, I was only trying to steer her away from a life of crime, how long are you gonna—"

"Goodness, I don't know why you always get so defensive about it, Doc. There's no reason to feel guilty. Is there?"

"Great, just what I want to do—discuss guilt with a deputy DA."

"—was identified," the TV set announced, while Penny reached to turn up the volume, "as Rick Doppel, an unemployed student dropout from UCLA."

"I don't think so," Penny muttered. "It's that Chucky."

And dang, Doc added silently, if it ain't a resurrected tenor sax player, too.

NINE

DECIDING ON A PROFESSIONAL LOOK, DOC PULLED HIS HAIR BACK
in a tight ponytail, securing it with a leather clip he only remembered
later Shasta had given him, and put a black vintage fedora on top of that,
then slung a tape machine over his shoulder. In the mirror he looked
plausible enough. He was headed up to Topanga that afternoon to visit
the Boards, pretending to be a music reporter for an underground fan
magazine called *Stone Turntable*. Denis was along posing as his photog-
rapher, wearing a T-shirt with the familiar detail from Michelangelo's
fresco *The Creation of Adam*, in which God is extending his hand to
Adam's and they're just about to touch—except in this version God is
passing a lit joint.

All the way up to Topanga, the radio cranked out a Super Surfin'
Marathon, all commercial-free—which seemed peculiar until Doc realized that nobody who would sit through this music-teacher's nightmare
of doubled-up blues lines, moronic one-chord "tunes," and desperate
vocal effects could possibly belong to any consumer demographic known
to the ad business. From this display of white-eccentric binge behavior
only once in a while, mercifully, would there be a departure—"Pipeline"
and "Surfin' Bird," by the Trashmen, and "Bamboo," by Johnny and
the Hurricanes, singles by Eddie and the Showmen, the Bel Airs, the

Hollywood Saxons, and the Olympics, souvenirs out of a childhood Doc had never much felt he wanted to escape from.

"When are they gonna play 'Tequila'?" Denis kept wondering, till just as they were pulling up the drive of the Boards' rented mansion, on it came, the Spanish modality and flamencoid roll strokes of the surfer's sworn enemy, the Lowrider. "Tequila!" screamed Denis as they slid into the last parking space.

The house had once belonged to half of a much-loved hillbilly act of the forties, and currently the Boards were renting the place from a bass player–turned–record-company executive, which trend watchers took as further evidence of the end of Hollywood, if not the world, as they had known it.

Like girls at Hawaiian airports, a couple of house groupies named Bodhi and Zinnia came forward with leis, or actually love beads, and put them around Doc's and Denis's necks, then led them off on a tour of the place, looking at which, a less tolerant person might think right away, Wow, this is what happens when people make too much money in too short a time. But Doc figured it depended on your idea of excess. Over the years business had obliged him to visit a stately L.A. home or two, and he soon noticed how little sense of what was hip the very well fixed were able to exhibit, and that, roughly proportional to wealth accumulated, the condition only grew worse. The Boards had so far managed to escape serious impairment, though Doc had his doubts about the coffee tables made from antique Hawaiian surfboards, until he saw that all you had to do was unscrew the legs to get back to a ridable plank. Thanks to ingenious porte cochere arrangements, many of the closets here were not just walk-in but drive-thru, full of costumes from past and future worlds, many obtained in Culver City at the MGM studio's historic sell-off of assets a few months back. Catered meals for twenty or thirty got trucked up here every day from Jurgensen's in Beverly Hills. There was a dope-smoking room with a huge 3-D reproduction in fiberglass of Hokusai's famous *Great Wave off Kanagawa,* arching wall to ceiling to opposite wall, creating a foam-shadowed hideaway beneath the eternally suspended monster, though now and then this would tend to freak a visitor into declining his hit whenever a joint came around, which was fine with the Boards, who were still at an arrested stage from back in their surf-punk days when every crumb of dope counted, and as greedy on the subject as ever.

Outside, on a terrace with a view across the canyon, longhaired short-skirted cuties drifted around in the sunlight tending the marijuana plants or wheeling huge trays of things to eat, drink, and smoke. Dogs came and went, some reasonably calm, others obsessive-compulsive, bringing you back the otherwise ordinary rock you had been throwing, farther and farther away each time, for the last half hour ("It's his trip, man"), and now and then one fallen afoul of that breed of human that finds amusement in feeding a dog LSD and watching what happens.

Doc was reminded for the uncountableth time that for every band like this one there were a hundred or a thousand others like his cousin's band Beer, doomed to scuffle in obscurity, energized by a faith in the imperishability of rock 'n' roll, running on dope and nerve, brother- and sisterhood, and good spirits. The Boards, though keeping their voicing—the traditional two guitars, bass and drums, plus a horn section—had changed personnel so often that only meticulous music historians had any kind of a handle on who was or had been who anymore. Which didn't matter because by now the band had evolved into pretty much a brand name, years and changes away from the tough little grommets, all related by blood or marriage, who used to stomp as a cadre barefoot into Cantor's Delicatessen on Fairfax and spend all night eating bagels, hanging out, and trying not to trigger any rock-star bodyguards into some kind of episode. When at length the once hippie-friendly eatery, growing concerned about possible lawsuits and insurance costs, started putting up signs saying Shoes Required, the Boards all went down to a tattoo parlor in Long Beach and got sandal straps tattooed on their feet and ankles, which fooled the managerial level for a while, and by then the band had moved on anyway to fancier places farther west. But there were a couple of years when you could always tell who the original members of the band were by those ink sandals.

For a week or so now, the Boards' houseguests had included Spotted Dick, a visiting British band who were getting some local airplay on those stations where the pulse was less hectic, being themselves often so laid back that people had been known to call the ambulance, mistaking the band's idea of a General Pause for some kind of collective seizure. Today they were wearing wide-wale corduroy suits in a strangely luminous brownish gold and sporting precision geometric haircuts from Cohen's Beauty and Barber Shop in East London, where Vidal Sassoon had once apprenticed and where every week the lads were piled onto a small bus, given their weekly cannabis allowance and brought out to sit in a row giggling over back issues of *Tatler* and *Queen* and getting scissor-cut asymmetric bobs. Last week in fact the lead vocalist had decided to change his name legally to Asymmetric Bob, after his bathroom mirror revealed to him, three hours into a mushroom experiment, that there were actually two distinct sides to his face, expressing two violently different personalities.

"They've got a tube in every room!" Denis reported excitedly. "A-and these zapper units you can change the channel with and not even have to leave the couch!"

Doc had a look. These control boxes, recently invented and found only in upscale homes, were large and crude, as if sharing design origins with Soviet sound equipment. Operating them required a forceful touch, and sometimes both hands, through which you could feel them buzzing, because they used high-frequency sound waves. This tended to drive most of the house dogs here crazy, except for Myrna, a wirehair who, being older and a little hard of hearing, was able to lie patiently through all sorts of programming, waiting for a dog-food commercial to come on, which because of some strange dog ESP she knew was due a minute before it actually showed up on the screen. When it was over, she would turn her head to any humans in the vicinity and nod emphatically. At first, people thought this meant she wanted dinner or at least a snack, but it seemed to be more of a social act, along the lines of, "Something, huh?"

At the moment she was lying in an unlit room of uncertain size, which smelled of potsmoke and patchouli oil, watching *Dark Shadows* along with selected Boards and Spotted Dick personnel, plus those members of the entourage who were not elsewhere in the house running their ass off indulging band whims that required deep-frying Hostess Twinkies, ironing each other's hair on the ironing board to maintain some muse image, and going through fan magazines with X-acto knives and cutting out all references to competing surf acts.

This was around the point in the Collins family saga when the story line had begun to get heavily into something called "parallel time," which was confounding the viewing audience nationwide, even those who remained with their wits about them, although many dopers found no problem at all in following it. It seemed basically to mean that the same actors were playing two different roles, but if you'd gotten absorbed enough, you tended to forget that these people were actors.

After a while the concentration level among the viewers had Doc feeling a little restless. He realized the scope of the mental damage one push on the "off" button of a TV zapper could inflict on this roomful of obsessives. Luckily he was near the door and managed to crawl out without anybody noticing. He hadn't seen Coy Harlingen around here yet, and figured this would be as good a time as any to go looking.

He began to wander the great old house. The sun went down, the groupies flocked together briefly, transitioning into nighttime mode. Denis ran around like a dog chasing pigeons in the park, snapping pictures, and girls obligingly scattered, going *eww . . . eww.* Something like a security detail appeared now and then out on the property, making perimeter checks. From an upper window came the sound of Spotted Dick's keyboard player Smedley, doing Hanon exercises on his Farfisa, a little Combo Compact model he had obtained on the advice of Rick Wright of Pink Floyd and which was never observed far from his person. He called it Fiona, and witnesses had reported him having long conversations with it. Earlier, Doc, pretending to interview him for *Stone Turntable,* asked what they talked about.

"Oh, what you'd expect. Association football, the war in Southeast Asia, where can one score, sort of thing."

"And how's, how's Fiona enjoying it here in Southern California?"

Smedley got glum. "Loves everything but the paranoia, man."

"Paranoia, really?"

His voice dropped to a whisper. "This house—" At which point a scowling young gent, maybe one of the Boards' roadies, maybe not, entered and leaned against a wall with his arms folded and just stayed there, listening. Smedley, his eyeballs oscillating wildly, fled the area.

A private eye didn't drop acid for years in this town without picking up some kind of extrasensory chops, and truth was, since crossing the doorsill of this place, Doc couldn't help noticing what you'd call an atmosphere. Instead of a ritual handshake or even a smile, everybody he got introduced to greeted him with the same formula—"Where are you at, man?" suggesting a high level of discomfort, even fear, about anybody who couldn't be dropped in a bag right away and labeled.

This seemed to be happening more and more lately, out in Greater Los Angeles, among gatherings of carefree youth and happy dopers, where Doc had begun to notice older men, there and not there, rigid, unsmiling, that he knew he'd seen before, not the faces necessarily but a defiant posture, an unwillingness to blur out, like everybody else at the psychedelic events of those days, beyond official envelopes of skin. Like the operatives who'd dragged away Coy Harlingen the other night at that rally at the Century Plaza. Doc knew these people, he'd seen enough of them in the course of business. They went out to collect cash debts, they broke rib cages, they got people fired, they kept an unforgiving eye on anything that might become a threat. If everything in this dream of prerevolution was in fact doomed to end and the faithless money-driven world to reassert its control over all the lives it felt entitled to touch, fondle, and molest, it would be agents like these, dutiful and silent, out doing the shitwork, who'd make it happen.

Was it possible, that at every gathering—concert, peace rally, love-in, be-in, and freak-in, here, up north, back East, wherever—those dark crews had been busy all along, reclaiming the music, the resistance to power, the sexual desire from epic to everyday, all they could sweep up, for the ancient forces of greed and fear?

"Gee," he said to himself out loud, "I dunno . . ."

At which point he ran into Jade just coming out of one of the bathrooms. "What, you again?"

"Drove up with Bambi—she heard that Spotted Dick were staying here, so I had to come along, try and keep her out of trouble?"

"Into these folks, is she?"

"Spotted Dick black-light posters on the walls, Spotted Dick sheets and pillowcases on the bed, Spotted Dick T-shirts, coffee cups, souvenir roach clips. And twenty-four hours a day, Spotted Dick albums on the stereo. Man. You know this English ukulele player named George Formby?"

"Sure, Herman's Hermits covered one of his."

"Well these guys have covered everything else. I mean I try to be cool with it. Spotted Dick are also known to be into some weird forms of recreation, and I think that's the main attraction for Bambi."

"Haven't seen her around tonight."

"Oh, she already split with the lead guitar, they're on the way up to Leo Carrillo looking for some cricket game."

"Night cricket?"

"Yeah, Somerset told her it was like baseball? Lights and so forth. Unless . . . oh no, do you think they were running a number on me?"

"Well if you do need a ride back, let me know. And if anybody asks, I'm a rock 'n' roll reporter, okay?"

"You? Sure, I'll tell 'em about your Pat Boone cover interview."

"Oh and hey—that guy I was talking to at the Club Asiatique the other night? You seen him around?"

"He's here someplace. Try the rehearsal rooms upstairs."

Sure enough, wandering the hallways, Doc heard the sound of a tenor sax practicing "Donna Lee." He waited for a break and put his head in the room.

"Howdy! It's me again! Remember that chore you wanted me to do?"

"Wait." Coy angled his thumb at a cluster of sound equipment over in the corner that may have had more wires than necessary running in and out of it, and he shook his head. "What was the, uh, *make and model* you looked at again?"

Doc went along. "You were asking about a older-type VW, flowers and bluebirds and hearts and shit all over it?"

"That's the one I was interested in all right. No, uhm . . ." Coy paused, improvising, "no new replacement parts, nothin like that?"

"None I could see."

"Street legal, no hassles with the registration?"

"Seemed that way."

"Well thanks for lookin into that, you know, I just . . . wondered, the way people do."

"Sure. Anytime. Any other rides you want me to check out, just let me know."

Coy was quiet for a while. Doc thought about reaching over and poking him. A look on his face so desperate, so longing, and way too nervous, as if somehow inside this house he had actually been forbidden to speak. Doc wanted to lay at least a quick *abrazo* on this guy, some reassurance, but that could be read by inquiring eyes as more emotion than anybody should invest in a used-car deal. "You have my number, right?"

"I'll be in touch." Just then a driveling of dopers burst into the room, any of whom could have been assigned to spy on Coy. Doc unfocused his eyes and allowed his face to sag into a loose grin, and next time he looked, Coy was invisible, though he might've still been in the room.

Back downstairs, a member of the company was going around jovially handing out joints. As people lit up and inhaled, he'd go, "Hey! Guess what's in this grass?"

"No idea."

"Come on, guess!"

"LSD?"

"No! it's just grass! Hahahaha!"

Approaching somebody else, "Hey! what do you think's in this dope we're smoking?"

"I don't know, uh . . . mescaline!"

"No, nothin! pure grass! Hahahaha!"

And so forth. Shredded psilocybe mushrooms? Angel dust? Speed? No, just marijuana! Hahahaha! Almost before Doc knew it, he'd gotten so stoned on the mystery weed that he flashed how it wasn't just Coy whose vital signs were debatable—somebody had definitely been out harrowing the next world for Boards personnel, because Doc knew now, beyond all doubt, that *every single one* of these Boards was a *zombie,* undead and unclean. "Dead and clean is okay?" Denis, who had materialized from someplace, wondered.

"A-and that Spotted Dick—they're zombies, too, only worse."

"Worse?"

"*English* zombies! look at them, man, American zombies are at least out front about it, tend to stagger when they try to walk anywhere, usually in third ballet position, and they go, like 'Uunnhh . . . uunnhh,' with that rising and falling tone, whereas English zombies are for the most part quite well spoken, they use long words and they glide everywhere, like, sometimes you don't even see them take steps, it's like they're on ice skates. . . ."

At which point Spotted Dick's bass player, Trevor "Shiny Mac" McNutley, with a louche smile on his face and pursuing a confused young woman, entered in exactly this way, crossing smoothly from left to right.

"You see, you see?"

"Aaahhh!" Denis running off in panic, "I'm outta here, man!"

Denis having failed to provide him much of an anchor in reality, Doc now proceeded to freak even further out. That dope with its extra ingredient which might not really have been there could also have had something to do with it—howsoever, Doc suddenly found himself fleeing through the corridors of the creepy old mansion with uncertain numbers of screaming flesh-eating creatures behind him. . . .

Down in the vast kitchen, he ran pretty much head-on into Denis again, now busy looting the fridge and cabinets and filling a Safeway bag with cookies, frozen candy bars, Cheetos, and other munchies of opportunity.

"Come on Denis, we got to split."

"Tell me about it man, I snapped a picture a couple minutes ago and they all went insane tryin to take away my camera, and now they're after me, so I figured I better grab what I can—"

"Actually, man, I think I hear them," Doc, guiding Denis by the string of love beads around his neck, dragged him out a side exit into the grounds. "Come on." They started running for where they'd parked the car.

"Jeez Doc, you said free dope, maybe some chicks, you didt'n say noth'n about no zombies, man."

"Denis," advised Doc, already out of breath, "just run." Passing a sycamore tree, he was unexpectedly descended on by somebody who'd been trying to hang on to a branch. It was Jade, in a state of panic.

"What am I, the Skipper?" Doc muttering onto his feet again, "or some shit?"

"I really need a ride out of here," Jade said, "please?"

By some piece of luck, they found Doc's car right where he'd parked it, and they piled in and went screeching out down the driveway. In the mirror Doc saw dark shapes with ghostly white incisors slithering into a 1949 Mercury woodie with a front end and split windshield that looked like the snout and pitiless eyes of a predator, which now came after them, its V-8 in a throbbing roar, gravel scattering off the driveway. At the canyon road, Doc hooked a violent left, nearly rolling them over and fishtailing once or twice before straightening out and proceeding down to Malibu on what in those days was not quite the multiple-lane suburban convenience it would later become, more you'd say of a life-threatening nightmare actually, full of blind driveways and serious hairpins, where Doc soon found himself putting to good use his refresher courses at the well-known Tex Wiener École de Pilotage, executing four-wheel drifts and more heel-and-toe double-clutching than fully foreseen by the design teams back at Chrysler Motors, while the radio played "Here Come the Hodads" by the Marketts.

Denis, despite the 3-D jolting around he was getting, sat goodnaturedly putting together a joint without hardly spilling anything, lighting and presenting it to Jade once they were all the way downhill and headed for Santa Monica.

"Nicely rolled Denis," Doc remarked when it came his way at last. "Don't know if I'd've had the presence of mind myself."

"Basically just trying to keep from freaking out?"

"Listen, Doc," Jade said, "what is with that guy from the Club Asiatique?"

"Coy Harlingen. You talk to him?"

"Yes and when they found us together, it really looked like somebody meant to do me some harm. Not like I was trying to seduce him. Normally if Bambi's around, I don't worry when they come after me like that, but she was off at that 'night cricket,' so it's a blessing you guys showed up when you did."

"Our pleasure," Denis assured her.

At some point after they were back on the Coast Highway and heading for the freeway, Doc glanced in the rearview mirror and no longer saw the headlights of the sinister woodie behind him. Like a once-troublesome pair of zits on the face of the night, they had faded away. What he couldn't also help noticing in the mirror now was that

Denis and Jade were striking up a friendship. "And what's, like, your name?" Denis was saying.

"Ashley," said Jade.

"Not Jade," Doc said.

"My working name. In the Fairfax High yearbook, I'm just one of, like, a thousand Ashleys?"

"And the Chick Planet salon . . ."

"Never considered that a career. Too fuckin wholesome. Smiling all the time, pretending it's about 'vibrations' or 'self-awareness' or anything but," sliding upward into an old-movie society-lady screech, "*hoddible fucking!*"

"Southern California," Denis chimed in. "No sympathy for weirdness, man, none of them darker type activities."

"Yeah really like where's *that* at," Jade, or Ashley, sympathized.

"And people wonder why Charlie Manson's the way he is."

"Do you eat pussy, by the way?"

They entered the transition tunnel to the eastbound Santa Monica Freeway, where the radio, which had been playing the Byrds' "Eight Miles High," lost the signal. Doc kept singing it to himself, and when they emerged and the sound came back, he was no more than half a bar off. "Denis, don't forget to leave me the camera, okay?" An eloquent silence. "Denis?"

"He's busy," Jade murmured. Remaining so all the way to the Harbor Freeway, to the Hollywood Freeway and up over the Cahuenga Pass to Jade's exit, in the course of which, in a very relaxed, occasionally drowsy voice, pausing every once in a while to send Denis down a word of encouragement, she filled Doc in on her early history of experimenting with shoplifting and grand theft auto. She had met up with Bambi in Dormitory 8000 at Sybil Brand Institute, where Bambi, observing Jade one evening furiously masturbating, offered to do her pussy for a pack of smokes. Menthol, if possible.

"Shr thing," Jade by this point was desperate enough to chirp back. Next time, lights-out arriving not a moment too soon, Bambi had brought the price down to half a pack, then, on her knees, much more thoughtful now, she found herself offering to pay Jade. "I guess," Jade said, "we could call it one token cigarette, though I'm not real comfortable even with— ohh, Bambi . . . ?" By the time they got out of Sybil Brand, they were sharing smokes out of a common stash, and what bookkeeping there was no longer included nicotine. They took a place together in North Hollywood, where they could do what they wanted all day long and all night too, which is the way things usually ran. It was possible to live cheap in those days, and it helped that the landlady had also been inside, and honored sisterly obligations that a more uptight individual might not even have recognized. Soon they had a regular dealer who made house calls, and a cat named Anaïs, and were known up and down the Tujunga Wash as a couple of righteous chicks you could trust in just about any situation. Bambi imagining that she was there to look out for her friend, Jade closer to the edge of misadventure than she knew.

Meantime, on one of these voyages of self-discovery so common at that time, in the most intensely light-bearing complexities of some now half-forgotten acid trip, Ashley/Jade saw something about herself nobody else till then had seen. Of its essence somehow, as Doc had already somehow guessed, was cunnilingus. The era, she couldn't help noticing, was conveniently providing not only eager girls but also sweetly passive long-haired boys everyplace she looked, eager to devote to her pussy the oral attention it had always deserved.

"Which reminds me, how you doing down there, Denis?"

"Huh? Oh. Well, to begin with . . ."

"Never mind. Just be advised, boys," she said, "you'll want to watch your step, 'cause what I am is, is like a small-diameter pearl of the Orient rolling around on the floor of late capitalism—lowlifes of all income levels may step on me now and then but if they do it'll be them who slip and fall and on a good day break their ass, while the ol' pearl herself just goes a-rollin on."

SPIKE'S FRIEND FARLEY had a darkroom, and when the proof sheets were ready, Doc went by to have a look. Most of the contact prints were blank frames, from Denis leaving the lens cap on, or drastically angled room fragments when he had accidentally tripped the shutter, as well as an embarrassing number of low-angle shots of microskirted groupies, and miscellaneous drug-related lapses into sleep or silliness. The only shot Coy seemed to be in was a *Last Supper*–type grouping around a long table in the kitchen, with everybody in heated discussion over a number of pizzas. Coy was saturated in a funny vibrant blur that didn't match any other part of the space, and watching the camera a little too intently, with an expression forever about to unfold into a smile.

"This one here," Doc said. "Could you make me an enlargement?"

"Sure," said Farley. "Eight-by-ten glossy okay?"

Reluctant, maybe even a little desperate, Doc figured he had to go visit Bigfoot now. On principle he tried to spend as little time around the Glass House as possible. It creeped him out, the way it just sat there looking so plastic and harmless among the old-time good intentions of all that downtown architecture, no more sinister than a chain motel by the freeway, and yet behind its neutral drapes and far away down its fluorescent corridors it was swarming with all this strange alternate cop history and cop politics—cop dynasties, cop heroes and evildoers, saintly cops and psycho cops, cops too stupid to live and cops too smart for their own good—insulated by secret loyalties and codes of silence from the world they'd all been given to control, or, as they liked to put it, protect and serve. Bigfoot's native element, the air he breathed. The big time he'd been so crazy to get away from the beach and be promoted into. At the desk in the lobby at Parker Center, owing no doubt to what he'd been smoking since he hit the freeway, Doc let loose with a long and even to him not always coherent rap about how he usually didn't spend much time hanging out with elements of the criminal-justice system? mostly getting his information from the *L.A. Times*? but how about that Leslie van Houten, huh—so cute yet so lethal, and what was the *real angle* on this Manson trial, 'cause in a strange way wasn't it something like this postseason the Lakers were having, and did he happen to catch that game with Phoenix—

The sergeant nodded. "That's 318."

Upstairs, Bigfoot, strangely jumpy today, seemed about to apologize for not having an office, even a cubicle, of his own, though in fact nobody else at Homicide had one either—everybody milled around in a single oversize room with two long tables and chain-smoked and drank coffee out of paper cups and hollered into phones and sent out for tacos and burgers and fried chicken and so forth, and half of what they threw at the wastebaskets missed, so there was an interesting texture to the floor, which Doc thought might once have included some vinyl tiling.

"Given the semi-public surroundings, I hope this will not be another of these unabridged paranoid hippie monologues I seem increasingly obliged to sit through."

Quickly as he could, Doc recapped what he knew about Coy Harlingen—the allegedly fatal OD, the mysterious addition to Hope's bank account, Coy pretending to be an agitator at the Nixon rally. He left out the part about talking to Coy in person.

"Another case of apparent resurrection," Bigfoot shrugged, "not, at first glance, a matter for Homicide."

"So . . . who around here would handle resurrections, man?"

"Bunco Squad, usually."

"Does that mean LAPD officially believes that every return from the dead is some kind of a con?"

"Not always. Could be a mistaken or false ID type of problem."

"But not—"

"You're dead, you're dead. Are we talking philosophy?"

Doc lit up a Kool, reached in his fringe bag and found Denis's photo of Coy Harlingen.

"What is this? Another rock and roll band? My kids wouldn't even have this on their wall."

"That one there is the stiff in question."

"And . . . just remind me, why do I give a shit, again?"

"He worked for the Department as a snitch, not to mention for some patriotic badasses known as Vigilant California, who might or might not have been in on the raid at Channel View Estates—you remember that place, all 'em cute li'l kids jumpin in the pools and so on?"

"All right." Bigfoot had another look at the picture. "You know what? I'll go check into this personally."

"But, Bigfoot, that isn't like you," Doc needled, "it's a cold case, where's there any glory in clearin one of them?"

"Sometimes it's about doing the right thing," replied Bigfoot, fluttering his eyelashes disingenuously.

He motioned Doc down a back corridor and into a utility room. "Just want to look in the freezer a minute." It was a corpse-size professional pathologist's model from some years back, a hand-me-down from the coroner's office, and Doc, expecting to see homicide-related body parts, was surprised instead to find several hundred frozen chocolate-covered bananas inside.

"Don't imagine for a minute I'm feeling nostalgic about the beach," Bigfoot was quick to protest. "It's an addiction, I used to deny that but my therapist says I've made amazing progress. Please, dig in, feel free. I'm told I have to share. We have this system of pneumatic message tubes here, routed all through the building, and I've been using it to send these babies everywhere it'll do some good."

"Thanks." Doc reached out a frozen banana. "Gee, Bigfoot, there certainly are a lot of these in here. Don't tell me the Department's picking up the tab."

"Actually," Bigfoot for the moment unable to look Doc in the eye, "we get them free."

"When cops say free . . . Why do I get the feeling you're about to lay some moral dilemma on me here?"

"Maybe you could give me the hippie point of view, Sportello, it's been keeping me up nights."

Bigfoot had been driving around once a week to Kozmik Banana, a frozen-banana shop near the Gordita Beach pier, creeping in by way of the alley in back. It was a classic shakedown. Kevin the owner, instead of throwing away the banana peels, was cashing in on a hippie belief of the moment by converting them to a smoking product he called Yellow Haze. Specially trained crews of speed freaks, kept out of sight nearby in a deserted resort hotel about to be demolished, worked three shifts carefully scraping off the insides of the banana peels and obtaining, after oven-drying and pulverizing it, a powdery black substance they wrapped in plastic bags to sell to the deluded and desperate. Some who smoked it reported psychedelic journeys to other places and times. Others came down with horrible nose, throat, and lung symptoms that lasted for weeks. The belief in psychedelic bananas went on, however, gleefully promoted by underground papers which ran learned articles comparing diagrams of banana molecules to those of LSD and including alleged excerpts from Indonesian professional journals about native cults of the banana and so forth, and Kevin was raking in thousands. Bigfoot saw no reason why law enforcement shouldn't be cut in for a share of the proceeds.

"What kind of extortion do you call that?" Doc wanted to know. "Ain't like it's a real drug, it doesn't get you loaded, and anyway it's legal, Bigfoot."

"Exactly my point. If it's legal, then so is taking my cut. Especially, see, if it's in the form of frozen bananas instead of money."

"But," Doc said, "no, wait—not logical, Captain . . . something I can't . . . quite . . ."

He was still trying to figure it out by the time he got back to the beach. He found Spike sitting on the alleyway steps.

"Somethin you might want to look at, Doc. Farley just got it back from the lab."

They went over to Farley's place. He had it threaded on a 16-mm projector, all set to screen.

A sunny vista in Ektachrome Commercial of half-built ranchburgers and contractor hardpan is suddenly aswarm with men in matching camo fatigues bought in lots from some local surplus store, also wearing ski masks machine-knit in reindeer and cone-bearing tree motifs. They are packing some weird and heavy shit, among which Spike points out M16s and AK-47s, both original as well as knockoffs from different lands, Heckler & Koch machine guns in both belt- and drum-fed designs, Uzis, and repeating shotguns.

The raiding party splash across the flood-control channel, secure the street bridges and footbridges, and set up a perimeter around the temporary miniplaza whose flagship tenant is Chick Planet Massage. Doc noticed his car parked out in front, but the motorcycles that were there when he arrived had vanished.

The camera tilts up and there, fleeing deeper into the tract or only riding around in circles, are Mickey's badass brigade on Harleys, Kawasaki Mach IIIs, and, as Spike points out, a Triumph Bonneville T120, with no clear idea of what their mission is anymore. It was weird to Doc watching now, weird beyond easy imagining, that somewhere inside the place, invisible, he was lying unconscious, that with an X-Ray Specs attachment of some kind he could be looking at himself inert, next door to dead, and that viewing this film of an assault that was just about to begin might qualify as what Sortilège liked to call an out-of-body experience.

Suddenly on-screen all hell broke loose. Even though there was no sound track, Doc could hear it. Sort of. The frame started bouncing around as if Farley was trying to get to cover. The old Bell & Howell he was using shot a hundred feet of film at a time, and then the reel had to be changed, so the coverage was a little jumpy. There were also three built-in turret lenses, long, normal, and wide-angle, that could be rotated as needed in front of the gate, often during the shot.

The footage, almost too clearly, showed Glen Charlock getting shot down by one of the masked gunmen. There it was, the money shot— Glen unarmed, moving in some kind of prison-yard crouch trying to look bad when all that really came through was the fear that owned him, and how much he didn't want to die. The light wasn't protecting him, not the way it will sometimes protect the actors in a movie, the way moviegoers have gotten used to. This wasn't studio light, only the indiscriminate L.A. sun, but somehow it was singling out Glen, setting him apart as the one who would not be spared. The shooter was used to handling small arms in the dutiful way of a rifle-range commando—no bravado, no shouting or abuse or firing from the crotch—he took his time, you could see him paying attention to his breath as he sighted Glen, led him, took him down with silent three-shot bursts, though several more than were needed.

"What about your lab?" Doc said, to say something. "They ever watch what they process?"

"Not too likely," Farley said, "they're used to me by now, think I'm crazy."

"Can they run off an extra print? Maybe enlarge a frame or two? I'm wonderin what's behind those masks."

"Resolution goes all to hell," Farley shrugged, "but I guess you could try."

AROUND LUNCHTIME NEXT DAY the Princess phone started jingling.

"Holy shit, *ese,* you're real."

"At least one day a week. You must've lucked out. Who is this?"

"He forgot me already. *Sinvergüenza,* as my grandma would say."

"Trick question, Luz, how you been, *mi amor?*"

"Your strange way of flirting."

"You're off today, I hope."

Close to the office, within walking distance in fact, was a small ex-neighborhood, its houses all condemned for an airport extension which may have existed only as some bureaucratic fantasy. Empty but not deserted exactly. Questionable movies were being shot inside. Drug and weapons drops were being made. Chicano bikers were having furtive noontime trysts with young Anglo executives in tax-deductible toupees that retained in their Dynel thatchwork the smell of bars downtown at lunchtime. Dopers were getting off on the airplanes a couple inches over their heads, and particularly unhappy area residents from PV to Point Dume were out scouting potential suicide sites.

Luz showed up in a red SS396 she kept saying she'd borrowed from her brother, though Doc thought he detected a boyfriend someplace in the subtext. She was wearing cutoff jeans, cowgirl boots, and a tiny T-shirt that matched the car.

They found an empty house and went inside. Luz had brought a bottle of Cuervo. There was a queen-size mattress with cigarette burns in it, a French Provincial floor-model TV with the screen all kicked in, a number of empty five-gallon joint-compound containers that people had been using for picnic furniture.

"I see in the papers that Mickey's still missing."

"Even the FBI don't come around no more, Riggs split again for the desert, and Sloane and me, we've become very close."

"How, ah, close would that be?"

"That bed downstairs Mickey would never fuck me on? That's ours now."

"Uhm . . ."

"What's this I'm lookin at here?"

"Well come on, it's a interesting thought ain't it, the two of you . . ."

"You guys and this lesbian thing . . . Why don't you just get comfortable down there—no, I meant down there—and I'll tell you all the details."

Passenger jets came thundering in every couple of minutes. The house shook. Sometimes when Luz parted her legs briefly, Doc thought he could hear landing-gear tires rolling across the roof. The louder it got, the more excited she became. "What happens if one comes in a little too low? We can be dead, right?" She grabbed two handfuls of his hair and pushed his face away from her pussy. "What's the matter, motherfucker, you can't hear me?"

Whatever he was going to say would've been drowned out in another deafening approach, and anyway what Luz wanted now was to fuck, which is what they did, and after a while they lit up a joint and she was talking about Sloane.

"These English chicks, they get to Califas they don't know how to behave. They see these people, man, all this money and real estate and none of them with any idea what to do with it. First thing anybody hears when we get across the border—*esta gente no sabe nada*. So Sloane has all this resentment. Whenever she finds out about any piece of money that's there to be grabbed, she thinks she's the one that should have it. For Riggs it's always more like, not that he should get it, but that some other asshole shouldn't."

"What the heat like to call 'theft.'"

"*They* might. Sloane likes to call it 'reallocation.'"

"So what was it, her and Riggs were skimming off Mickey, double-billing his clients, stiffing his contractors, or what?"

Luz shrugged. "Wasn't my business."

"Did they just spend their time running different hustles, or did they at least fuck once in a while?"

"Riggs said it wasn't so much that he got to fuck her as that Mickey didn't."

"Uh, huh. What'd Riggs have against her husband?"

"Nothing. They were ol' *compinches*. Riggs would have never gone near Sloane's pussy if Mickey hadt'n encouraged him."

"Mickey was gay?"

"Mickey fucked other women. He just wanted Sloane to have some fun, too. Him and Riggs worked together on different projects, Riggs stayed at the house when he was in town, couldn't keep from jerking himself off anytime Sloane was in the room, seemed like a natural choice for Mickey to fix her up with . . . along with the usual selling points, big dick, young, poor enough to keep on some kind of a leash. 'Course, Sloane wasn't too hot for the idea at first, because she hated to owe Mickey for anything."

"But . . ."

"Why are you so interested in this?"

"Carryings-on of the rich and powerful. Better than reading the *Enquirer*."

"Plus you don't get to fuck no newspaper, do you, my li'l Anglo *hijo de puta*. . . ."

"Fuckfuck," suggested Doc amiably, *"otra vez, ¿sí?"*

So he was a little late getting back to the office, and for days he would be making up explanations for all the visible hickeys and claw marks and so on. As Luz prepared to zoom away in the Super Sport, Doc said, "One thing. What do you think really happened to Mickey?"

She grew unflirtatious, almost somber. Her beauty deepening somehow. "I just hope he's alive, man. He wasn't that bad of a person."

LOOKING FORWARD TO a peaceful morning at the office, Doc had just lit up when the antique intercom started in with its guttural buzz. He moved a couple of Bakelite switches and heard somebody who might be Petunia downstairs yelling his name. This usually meant there was a visitor, most likely a chick, given the breathless interest Petunia maintained in Doc's social life. "Thanks, 'Tune—" Doc screamed back cordially, "send her right on up, and did I mention incidentally your outfit this morning is especially striking, that daffodil shade picks up the color of your eyes," knowing little if any of this would get through without heavy distortion.

On the off chance his unknown visitor might take a dim view of marijuana use, Doc ran around with a can of supermarket-brand air freshener, filling the office with a horrible thick mist of synthetic floral notes. The door opened and in stepped this, have mercy, this incredible looker, even with the reduced visibility and all. Red hair, leather jacket, tiny little skirt, cigarette stuck to a lower lip that looked more desirable the closer she got.

"Cootie food!" Doc screamed involuntarily, having been told once that this was French for "Love at first sight!"

"Remains to be seen," she said, "but what is this smell in here, it's fuckin nauseating."

He looked at the label on the aerosol can. "'Wildflower Whimsy'?"

"A gas-station toilet in Death Valley would be ashamed to smell like this. Meantime, I'm Clancy Charlock." She put her arm out full length and they shook hands.

"Glen Charlock's . . ." Doc began, about the same time she said, "sister." "Well. I'm sorry about your brother."

"Glen was a shit, and bound to have his series canceled sometime. That don't keep me from wanting to know who his killer is."

"You talk to the police?"

"More like they talked to me. Some smart-ass named Bjornsen. Can't say it was too encouraging. Would you mind not staring at my tits like that?"

"Who— Oh. Must've been trying to . . . read your T-shirt?"

"It's like a picture? of Frank Zappa?"

"So it is. . . . You say now . . . Lieutenant Bjornsen referred you to me?"

"He sounded a lot more concerned with Mickey Wolfmann's disappearance than Glen's murder, which given LAPD's priorities is no big surprise. But I guess he's a fan of yours." She had been looking around the office, and her tone was doubtful. "Excuse me, is that a half-smoked joint in your ashtray there?"

"Ah! frightfully unsociable of me, please, here's a new one, all ready to light, see?"

If he was expecting a romantic smoke sequence along the lines of

Now, Voyager (1942), this was not to be—before he could raise a sophisticated eyebrow, Clancy had seized the joint, clanked open a Zippo and fired it up, and by the time Doc got it back it was less than half its original length. "Interesting shit," she remarked when she finally got around to exhaling. Then they had a prolonged, and for Doc erectile, moment of eye contact.

Be professional, now, he advised himself. "The theory downtown is that your brother tried to prevent whoever it was from putting the snatch on Wolfmann and got shot for doing his job."

"Way too sentimental." She had slid into the green and fuchsia lunchroom booth and had her elbows on the table. "If there was a snatch in the works, Glen was more likely to be in on it. Being paid for looking bad is fine, but any real trouble and Glen's reflex was always to just split."

"Then maybe he saw something he shouldn't have."

She nodded to herself for a while. Finally, "Well . . . yep, that's how Boris has it figured, too."

"Who?"

"Another member of Mickey's muscle patrol. They've all dropped out of sight, but last night Boris called me late. We have some history. To look at him, he's nobody you'd want to get agitated, but I can tell you, right now he's scared shitless."

"What of?"

"He wouldn't say."

"Think he'd talk to me?"

"Worth a try."

"There's the phone."

"Hey, a Princess phone, man, I used to have one of these. I mean, mine was pink, but poison green is nice too. Were you planning to marry that joint or just keep hangin onto it?"

The phone had a long cord, and Clancy took it as far away from Doc as she could. Doc went in the toilet and became absorbed in something by Louis L'Amour he'd forgotten was in there, and next thing he knew, Clancy was hammering on the door. "Boris says it's got to be in person."

THAT NIGHT DOC met Clancy after she got off work tending bar in Inglewood, and they drove out to a bikers' roadhouse somewhere off the Harbor Freeway called Knucklehead Jack's. As they came in the door, the jukebox was playing the Del Shannon perennial "Runaway," which Doc took to be a hopeful sign. The low oxygen level inside was more than made up for by smoke of various national origins.

Boris Spivey had the dimensions, if possibly not the self-restraint, of an NFL lineman. The pool cue in his hand looked about the size a baton does in Zubin Mehta's. "Clancy says they popped you for Glen."

"They had to cut me loose. Wrong place at the wrong time, was all. Found unconscious at the scene, so forth. I still don't know what happened."

"Me neither, I was out in Pico Rivera, visiting my fiancée, Dawnette. You play pool? How do you feel about massé shots?"

"The usual love-hate."

"I'll break."

The pool table was host for a while to squirming ball trajectories, its playing surface repeatedly threatened by steeply driven cue angles, till Mrs. Pixley the owner finally made her way over to Doc and Boris, bearing a grim smile and a sawed-off shotgun, and a hush fell on the place.

"See that sign over the bar, fellas? You can't read it, I'll be happy to."

"Oh come on, we ain't hurtin nothin."

"I don't care, you and your li'l playmate are gonna have to leave the premises now. Ain't so much the cost of replacing the felt, I just personally fuckin hate massé shots."

Doc looked around for Clancy and saw her over in a booth, deep in conversation with two motorcyclists of a sort mothers tend not to approve of.

"She can take care of herself okay," Boris said, "she's always been into two at a time, and this looks like her lucky night. Come on, my truck's out in the lot."

His head now unavoidably teeming with lewd images, Doc followed Boris outside to a '46 Dodge Power Wagon with a mottled paint job of olive drab and primer-coat gray. They climbed in, and Boris sat checking the lot out for a while. "You think we convinced 'em back there? I figure a guy can't ever be too paranoid."

"How heavy is this, that we're talking about?" Doc lighting them a couple of Kools.

"Tell me, compadre, just between us—you ever kill anybody?"

"Self-defense, all the time. On purpose, hey, who can remember. How about yourself?"

"You packing right now?"

"Were we expecting company?"

"After a certain amount of time on the Special Needs Yard," explained Boris, "you gain the impression that there is always somebody looking to ice your ass."

Doc nodded. "Thing about these hippie getups," lifting one bell-bottom cuff to reveal a little short-barreled Model 27, "is you can almost fit a Heckler & Koch under here if you want."

"You're a dangerous hombre I can see that, too dangerous for me so I guess I better just spill the whole thing." Doc got ready to jump out and run, but Boris only continued, "Truth is, Glen got done in cold blood. He wasn't supposed to be there when they came for Mickey. The fix was in, Puck Beaverton had the duty that day, plan was to let them in the door and then disappear, but Puck got cold feet at the last minute and changed shifts with Glen, except he didn't tell Glen what was gonna happen, he just split."

"This Puck guy—you know where he went?"

"Probably Vegas. Puck thinks there's people there who'll look after him."

"Sure would've liked a word with him. Whole thing's kind of puzzling. Let's say for example that Mickey was in trouble."

"Trouble ain't the word. This was the deepest shit he could get in. All because of this idea that came to him. All the money he ever made—he was working on a way to just give it back."

Doc exhaled more than whistled through his teeth. "Can I still get my name on the list?"

"You think I'm bullshitting, that's okay, we all thought Mickey was too."

"Yeah but why would he—?"

"Don't ask me. Wouldn't be the first rich guy on a guilt trip lately. He was doing a lot of acid, some peyote, maybe it just got to a point. You must have seen that happen."

"Once or twice, but it's more like calling in sick for a couple days, breakin up with your old lady, nothing on that scale."

"What Mickey said was, 'I wish I could undo what I did, I know I can't, but I bet I can make the money start to flow a different direction.'"

"He told you that?"

"Heard him say it, him and his chick Shasta had a few of those intimate discussions, I wasn't trying to listen in or nothin, just happened to be there, price of being invisible. Shasta, she thought Mickey was crazy wanting to give all his money away. For some reason it scared her. He started in needling, like all she was worried about was losing her meal ticket. Which really *was* crazy, because she was in love with him, man. If she was scared for anybody, it was for him. I don't know if Mickey ever believed it, but every jailbird that's been in, even for a night, can tell the difference between the hustles you put on somebody you want to fuck and that other thing. That longing. All you had to do was look in her face."

They sat smoking. "Shasta and I lived together for a short while," Doc thought he should mention, "and I can't say I ever knew how she felt about me. How deep it went."

"Man," Boris glancing quickly down in the direction of Doc's ankle rig, "I hope this ain't a bummer for you to be hearin this."

"Boris, I only look like a evil motherfucker, secretly I'm as sentimental as any ex–old man. Please, forget the Smith, just tell me—who else do you think was worried about Mickey's big giveaway? Business partners? The wife?"

"Sloane? He wasn't telling her shit, 'not till it's over and done and lawyer-proof,' 's what he kept saying. Also said if she ever found out too soon, the California bar association would declare a day of thanksgiving for all the new business."

"But he'd have to bring in lawyers himself at some point, nobody just hands out millions, he would've needed some technical help."

"All's I know is, is there was suddenly a army of guys in suits around Mickey's place—only kind I can ID on sight is Mormons and FBI, if there's a difference, and I'm still not too sure what these were."

"You think they could've been some of Sloane's people? Like she found out anyway? Or began to pick up funny vibes? And how about her boyfriend, that Riggs guy?"

"Yeah, Shasta thought Sloane and him were cooking up something together. She was nervous already, but then she started to get really freaked. Mickey was renting a place for her up in Hancock Park, sometimes when I was off shift I'd drop by—nothin romantic, understand—just you could tell how much safer she felt with somebody around. Every day there was something new, cars cruising the house, phone calls that nobody on the other end would say anything, people tailing her whenever she went out in the Eldorado."

"She happen to get any license numbers?"

"Figured you'd ask." Boris took out his wallet and found a folded wheatstraw cigarette paper, and handed it to Doc. "Hope you got a way to run these without the cops knowing."

"Guy I used to work for has this computer. Why don't you want to go through the LAPD? Seems like they'd be looking to get whoever it is, too."

"What are you a doctor of, tripping? University of what planet again?"

"Almost sounds like maybe you think . . . LAPD's in on this?"

"No fuckin maybe, and Mickey was getting warned enough, too. Cop friend of his kept showing up at the house all the time."

"Let me guess—blond, Swedish, talks weird sometimes, answers to the name Bigfoot?"

"That's him. I think it was Sloane he kept coming around for, you really want to know."

"But he warned Mickey to . . . what? stay away from Chick Planet Massage? Don't trust your bodyguards?"

"Whatever—Mickey ignored all the advice, he liked it out there at Channel View, and especially that massage joint. Last place any of us expected a raid on. One minute you're gettin a nice blow job, the next it's like fuckin Vietnam, assault teams everyplace you look, scuba units climbin out of the Jacuzzi, chicks runnin around screaming. . . ."

"Wow. Almost sounds like you were there on the scene and not out in Pico Rivera."

"Okay, okay, I did drop by for a second, just to pick up some of that purple shit Dawnette likes, that you pour it in the bathtub, it makes bubbles?"

"Bubble bath."

"That's it. And just walked right in in the middle of everything, but wait, you—you said you were there, too, all that time, unconscious or whatever, so how come I didn't see you?"

"Maybe I was really out in Pico Rivera."

"Long as you weren't messin with my fiancée." They sat regarding each other quizzically.

"Dawnette," Doc said.

The characteristic long-stroke reverb of a Harley road machine approached. It was one of Clancy's dates for the evening, with Clancy riding behind him. "Everythin okay?" she called, though not exactly with keen interest.

Boris cranked down his window and leaned out. "This guy is freaking me out here, Clance, where do you find such heavy-duty hombres at?"

"Call you soon, Doc," Clancy sort of drawled.

Doc, remembering the old Roy Rogers song, came back with four bars of "Happy Trails to You" as Clancy and her new friend Aubrey thundered on out of the lot, Aubrey waving a gauntleted hand, to be followed shortly by his coadjutor Thorndyke on an Electra Glide shovelhead.

TEN

BACK AT THE BEACH, DOC COLLAPSED ON HIS COUCH AND drifted toward sleep, but scarcely had he penetrated the surface tension and sunk into REM than the phone began a god-awful clanging. Last year a crazed teenage doper of Doc's acquaintance had stolen a fire bell from his high school as part of a vandalism spree, and next morning the youth, overcome with remorse and having no idea what to do with the bell, came to Doc and offered it for sale. Downstairs Eddie, who had put in some time with the phone company and was handy with a soldering iron, had hooked the bell up to Doc's phone. It had seemed like a groovy idea at the time, but very seldom after that.

It turned out to be Jade on the other end, and she had a situation. From the background noise, it sounded like she was at a phone booth out on the street, but it didn't quite hide the anxiety in her voice. "You know FFO up on Sunset?"

"Problem is, is they also know me. What's up?"

"It's Bambi. She's been gone now two days and nights, and I'm getting worried."

"So you're up rockin and rollin on the Strip."

"Spotted Dick's playing here tonight, so if she's anywhere it'll be here."

"Okay, stick around, I'll be up soon 's I can."

East of Sepulveda the moon was out, and Doc made pretty good time. He peeled off the freeway at La Cienega, took the Stocker shortcut over to La Brea. Programming on the radio, appropriate to the hour, included one of the few known attempts at black surf music, "Soul Gidget," by Meatball Flag—

Who's that strollin down the street,
Hi-heel flip-flops on her feet,
Always got a great big smile,
Never gets popped by Juv-o-nile—
Who is it? [*Minor-seventh guitar fill*]
Soul Gidget!

Who never worries about her karma?
Who be that signifyin on your mama?
Out there lookin so bad and big,
Like Sandra Dee in some Afro wig—
Who is it?
Soul Gidget!

Surf's up, Soul Gidget's there,
Got that patchouli all in her hair,
Down in Hermosa she's runnin wild,
Back in South Central she just a child—
Uh who is it?
Soul Gidget!

So forth. Followed by a Wild Man Fischer marathon from which Doc was delivered at last by the appearance on La Brea of the lights of Pink's. He stopped in briefly for several chili dogs to go and continued on uphill, eating as he drove, found a parking space, and walked the rest of the way up to Sunset. In front of FFO was a small crowd of music lovers, handing joints back and forth, arguing with the bouncer at the door, dancing to the massively amplified bass lines coming from inside. It was the Furies, known in those days for three basses and no lead guitar, and opening tonight for Spotted Dick. Now and then during lulls, somebody was sure to go running in the door to scream, "Play 'White Rabbit'!" before being tossed back out into the street.

It wasn't long before Doc ran into Jade and the allegedly missing Bambi, lounging in front of an ice-cream store just up the street, speed-jabbering away, gesturing with gigantic cones precariously stacked with multicolored flavors of organic ice cream.

"Why, Doc!" cried Jade with a tiny warning frown, "what are you doing up here?"

"Yeah," Bambi drawled, "we had you figured for more of a Herb Alpert and the Tijuana Brass person."

Doc cupped one ear in the direction of the club. "Thought I heard somebody playing 'This Guy's in Love with You,' so I hurried over. No? What am I doing here anyway? How are you girls tonight, everything copacetic?"

"Bambi got us passes for Spotted Dick," said Jade.

"We're double-dating," Bambi said. "Time ol' Lotus Flower here got fixed up with a class act, and tonight Shiny Mac McNutley is it, baby."

A snow-white chauffeured Rolls pulled up at the curb, and a voice spoke from within. "All right girls, stay where you are."

"Oh shit," Bambi said, "it's your pimp again, Jade."

"*My* pimp, since when?"

"You didn't forget to sign that letter of intent, did you?"

"You mean all that paper in the bathroom? nah, I wiped my ass with that, it's long gone by now, why, was it important?"

"Come on you two, quit fucking around and get in the car, we got some business to discuss."

"Jason I'm not going in that car, it smells like a patchouli factory," said Bambi.

"Yeah, come on out on the sidewalk—on your feet like a man," snickered Jade.

"Guess I should be runnin along," beamed Doc.

"Stick around, Barney," said Bambi, "enjoy the show, you're in the entertainment capital of the world here."

As Jade told it later, this pimp, Jason Velveeta, probably could have used better career counseling when he was younger. Every woman he ever tried to mistreat had handed him his lunch. Some of them, usually ones not on his string, did give him money sometimes because they felt sorry for him, but it was never as much as he thought they owed him.

Reluctantly, in a cloud of patchouli, Jason stepped out onto the sidewalk. He was wearing a white suit, so white it made the Rolls look dingy.

"Need you girls inside the vehicle," he said, "now."

"Be seen riding with you? Forget it," said Jade.

"We can't afford to lose that much credibility," Bambi added.

"Ain't all you stand to lose."

"We love you, babe," said Bambi, "but you're a joke. All up and down the Strip, Hollywood Boulevard—hey, there's Jason jokes written in lipstick on toilet walls out in West fuckin *Covina,* man."

"Where? Where? I know a guy in West Covina with a bulldozer, one word from me he'll tear every one them shithouses down. Tell me the joke."

"Don't know, sweetie," Bambi pretending to snuggle close and smiling widely at the pedestrian traffic. "You know you'll only get upset."

"Ah, come on," Jason despite himself pleased by the public attention. "Jade, should we tell him?"

"Your call, Bambi."

"It says," Bambi in her most seductive voice, "'If you're paying any commission to Jason Velveeta, you can't shit here. Your asshole is in Hollywood.'"

"Bitch!" screamed Jason, by which point the girls were already running down the street, Jason in pursuit, at least for a step or two till he slipped on a scoop of Organic Rocky Road ice cream, which Jade had thoughtfully positioned on the sidewalk, and fell on his ass.

From somewhere Doc experienced a surge of sympathy. Or maybe something else. "Here, man."

"What's that?" said Jason.

"My hand."

"Man," creaking to his feet. "Do you know what it's gonna cost me to clean this suit now?"

"Bummer, really. And they both seemed like such groovy chicks, too."

"You were looking for company tonight? Believe me, we can do better for you than those two. Come on." They began to walk, and the Rolls crept along at the same pace. Jason took a withered joint from his pocket and lit up. Doc recognized the smell of inexpensive Mexican produce, and also that somebody had forgotten to remove the seeds and stems. When Jason offered him a hit, he pretended to inhale and after a while handed it back.

"Righteous weed, man."

"Yeah, just saw my dealer, he charges high but it's worth it." They walked up past the Chateau Marmont to Hollywood Boulevard, and every once in a while Jason accosted a young woman in some sub-*Playboy* idea of an alluring turnout and got insulted, screamed at, punched, run away from, and sometimes mistaken for a potential customer.

"Tough business, huh," Doc remarked.

"Ahh, lately I been thinking I should just get out of it, you know? What I really want to be is a movie agent."

"There you go. Ten percent of what some of those stars make—whoo-ee."

"Ten? That's all? You sure?" Jason took off his hat, a homburg, also dazzling white, and looked at it reproachfully. "You haven't got a Darvon on you? maybe some Bufferin? I have this headache. . . ."

"No, but here, try this." Doc lit and handed over a joint of Colombian commercial proven effective at stimulating conversation, and before

Jason knew it he was speed-rapping about Jade, on whom, if Doc was not mistaken, he had a sort of crush.

"She needs somebody watching out for her. She takes too many chances, not just this Hollywood drive-up trade. Like, these Golden Fang people, man—she's in way too deep with them."

"Yeah . . . now . . . I've heard that name someplace?"

"Indochinese heroin cartel. A vertical package. They finance it, grow it, process it, bring it in, step on it, move it, run Stateside networks of local street dealers, take a separate percentage off of each operation. Brilliant."

"That sweet young thing is dealing smack?"

"Maybe not, but she was working at a massage place that's one of the fronts they use to launder money."

If so, Doc reflected, then Mickey Wolfmann and the Golden Fang might not be all that unconnected.

Shit, man . . .

"Whatever you do," Jason was saying, maybe more to himself, "keep clear of the Fang. If they even begin to think you might get between them and their money, best you go looking for something else to do. Far away, if possible."

Doc left Jason Velveeta down on Sunset again, in front of the Sun-Fax Market, and ambled back downhill, thinking, Let's see—it's a schooner that smuggles in goods. It's a shadowy holding company. Now it's a Southeast Asian heroin cartel. Maybe Mickey's in on it. Wow, this Golden Fang, man—what they call many things to many folks . . .

Cars drove by with the windows down and you could hear tambourines inside keeping time to whatever was on the radio. Jukeboxes were playing in corner coffee shops, and acoustic guitars and harmonicas in little apartment courtyards. All over this piece of night hillside, there was music. Slowly, ahead of him someplace, Doc became aware of saxophones and a massive percussion section. Something by Antonio Carlos Jobim, which turned out to be coming from a Brazilian bar called O Cangaceiro.

Somebody was taking a tenor sax solo, and Doc, on a hunch, decided to put his head inside, where a sizable crowd were dancing, smoking, drinking, and hustling, as well as respectfully listening to the ensemble, among whom Doc, not too surprised, recognized Coy Harlingen. The change from the morose shadow he'd last seen up at Topanga was striking. Coy stood with his upper body held in an attentive arc around the instrument, sweating, loose-fingered, taken away. The tune was "Desafinado."

When the set ended, a curious sort of hippie chick approached the piano, her hair short and tightly permed, her outfit including a Little Black Dress from the 1950s and interestingly high stiletto heels. In fact, now that Doc looked closer, maybe she wasn't really a hippie chick after all. She seated herself at the keyboard the way a poker player might at a promising table, ran a couple of A-minor scales up and down, and without much more introduction than that began to sing the Rodgers & Hart lounge classic "It Never Entered My Mind." Doc was not a great admirer of torch material, had in fact been known to discreetly withdraw to the nearest toilet if he even suspected some might be on the way, but now he sat confounded and turning to Jell-O. Maybe it was this young woman's voice, her quiet confidence in the material—howsoever, by the second eight bars Doc knew there was no way not to take the lyric personally. He found shades in his pocket and put them on. After an extended piano break and a repeat of the refrain, Doc on some impulse turned, and there was Coy Harlingen at his shoulder, like a parrot in a cartoon, also wearing shades and nodding. "I can sure relate to that lyric, man. Like, you make these choices? you know for sure you're doing the right thing for everybody, then it all goes belly-up and you see it couldn't have been more wrong."

The stylish chanteuse had moved on to Dietz & Schwartz's "Alone Together," and Doc bought himself and Coy cachaça with beer chasers. "I'm not asking you to give away secrets. But I think I saw you once on the tube at a rally for Nixon?"

"And your question is, is am I really one of them screamin right-wing nutcases?"

"Somethin like that."

"I wanted to get clean, and I thought I wanted to do something for my country. Stupid as it sounds. These people were the only ones who were offering me that. It looked like an easy call. But what they really wanted was to control the membership by making us feel like we're never patriotic enough. My country right or wrong, with Vietnam goin on? that's just fuckin crazy. Suppose your mom was using smack."

"My, uh . . ."

"You wouldn't at least say somethin?"

"Wait, so the U.S. is, like, somebody's mom you're sayin . . . and she's strung out on . . . what, exactly?"

"On sending kids off to die in jungles for no reason. Something wrong and suicidal that she can't stop."

"And the Viggies wouldn't buy that."

"I never got a chance to bring it up. By then it was too late anyway. I saw what it was. I saw what I'd done."

Doc sprang for refills. They sat and listened to the rest of the-girl-who-wasn't-a-hippie-chick's set.

"Not a bad solo you took back there," Doc said.

Coy shrugged. "For a borrowed horn, I guess."

"You still stayin up at Topanga?"

"No choice."

He waited for Doc to say something, which turned out to be, "Bummer."

"Tell me. I'm lower than a groupie, fetching weed, opening beers, making sure there's only aqua jelly beans in the big punch bowl in the parlor. But there I go, complaining again."

"I do get the feeling," Doc said tentatively, "you'd rather be some-place else?"

"Back where I was would be nice," with a small break toward the end that Doc hoped was audible only to PIs who make a habit of wallowing in sentiment. The musicians were filtering back to the stand, and next thing Doc knew, Coy was deep into a complicated head arrangement of

"Samba do Avião," as if this was all he had to put between himself and the way he thought he'd fucked up his life.

Doc ended up sticking around till closing time and watched Coy getting into the sinister Mercury woodie that had chased Doc down the canyon the other night. He walked down to the Arizona Palms and had the All-Nighter Special, then sat through the dawn reading the paper and waited out the morning rush hour at a window with a downhill view into the smoglight, the traffic reduced to streams of reflective trim, twinkling ghostly along the nearer boulevards, soon vanishing into brown bright distance. It wasn't so much Coy he kept cycling back to as Hope, who believed, with no proof, that her husband hadn't died, and Amethyst, who ought to have something more than fading Polaroids to go to when she got them little-kid blues.

ELEVEN

WAITING ON DOC'S DOORSILL AT WORK WAS A POSTCARD FROM
some island he had never heard of out in the Pacific Ocean, with a lot
of vowels in its name. The cancellation was in French and initialed by a
local postmaster, along with the notation *courrier par lance-coco* which as
close as he could figure from the *Petit Larousse* must mean some kind of
catapult mail delivery involving coconut shells, maybe as a way of dealing with an unapproachable reef. The message on the card was unsigned,
but he knew it was from Shasta.

"I wish you could see these waves. It's one more of these places a voice
from somewhere else tells you you have to be. Remember that day with
the Ouija board? I miss those days and I miss you. I wish so many things
could be different. . . . Nothing was supposed to happen this way, Doc,
I'm so sorry."

Maybe she was, then again, maybe not. But what about this Ouija
board? Doc went stumbling through his city dump of a memory. Oh . . .
oh, sure, dimly . . . it had been during one of those prolonged times
of no dope, nobody had any, everybody was desperate and suffering
lapses of judgment. People were opening up cold capsules and labori-
ously sorting the thousands of tiny beads inside by color, in the belief
that each color stood for a different belladonna alkaloid, which taken in
big enough doses would get them loaded. They were snorting nutmeg,

drinking cocktails of Visine and inexpensive wine, eating packets of morning-glory seeds despite rumors that the seed companies were coating them with some chemical that would make you throw up. Anything.

One day when Doc and Shasta were over at Sortilège's house, she mentioned this Ouija board she had. Doc had a brainflash. "Hey! You think it knows where we can score?" Sortilège raised her eyebrows and shrugged, but waved a go-ahead hand at the board. The usual suspicions then arose, like how could you be sure the other person wasn't deliberately moving the planchette to make it look like some message from beyond, and so on. "Easy as pie," Sortilège said, "just do it all by yourself." Following her instructions, Doc breathed himself deeply and carefully into a receptive state, letting the tips of his fingers rest as lightly as possible on the planchette. "Now, make your request, and see what happens."

"Groovy," said Doc. "Hey—where can I find some dope, man? a-and, you know, good shit?" The planchette took off like a jackrabbit, spelling out almost faster than Shasta could copy an address down Sunset somewhat east of Vermont, and even throwing in a phone number, which Doc promptly dialed. "Howdy, dopers," cooed a female voice, "we've got whatever you need, and remember—the sooner you get over here, the more there'll be left for you."

"Yeah like who'm I talking to? Hello? Hey!" Doc looked at the receiver, puzzled. "She just hung up."

"Could've been a recording," said Sortilège. "Did you hear what she was screaming at you? 'Stay away! I am a police trap!'"

"You want to come along, keep us out of trouble?"

She looked doubtful. "I have to advise you at this point that it might not be anything. See, the problem about Ouija boards—"

But Doc and Shasta were already out the door and soon rattling up the chuckholed obstacle course known as Rosecrans Boulevard under a cloudless sky, in the sort of perfect daylight you always saw on TV cop shows, unshaded even by the eucalyptus trees that had recently all been chopped down. KHJ was playing a Tommy James & the Shondells marathon. Commercial-free in fact. What could be more auspicious?

Even before they reached the airport, something about the light had begun to go weird. The sun vanished behind clouds which grew thicker by the minute. Up in the hills among the oil pumps, the first raindrops began to fall, and by the time Doc and Shasta got to La Brea they were in the middle of a sustained cloudburst. This was way too unnatural. Ahead, someplace over Pasadena, black clouds had gathered, not just dark gray but midnight black, tar-pit black, hitherto-unreported-circle-of-Hell black. Lightning bolts had begun to descend across the L.A. Basin singly and in groups, followed by deep, apocalyptic peals of thunder. Everybody had turned their headlights on, though it was midday. Water came rushing down the hillsides of Hollywood, sweeping mud, trees, bushes, and many of the lighter types of vehicle on down into the flatlands. After hours of detouring for landslides and traffic jams and accidents, Doc and Shasta finally located the mystically revealed dope dealer's address, which turned out to be an empty lot with a gigantic excavation in it, between a laundromat and an Orange Julius–plus–car wash, all of them closed. In the thick mist and lashing rain, you couldn't even see to the other side of the hole.

"Hey. I thought there was supposed to be a lot of dope around here."

What Sortilège had tried to point out about Ouija boards, as Doc learned later back at the beach, while wringing out his socks and looking for a hair dryer, was that concentrated around us are always mischievous spirit forces, just past the threshold of human perception, occupying both worlds, and that these critters enjoy nothing better than to mess with those of us still attached to the thick and sorrowful catalogs of human desire. "Sure!" was their attitude, "you want dope? Here's your dope, you fucking idiot."

Doc and Shasta sat parked by the edge of the empty swamped rectangle and watched its edges now and then slide in, and then after a while things rotated ninety degrees, and it began to look, to Doc at least, like a doorway, a great wet temple entrance, into someplace else. The rain beat down on the car roof, lightning and thunder from time to time interrupting thoughts of the old namesake river that had once run through this town, long canalized and tapped dry, and crippled into a public and anonymous confession of the deadly sin of greed. . . . He imagined it filling again, up to its concrete rim, and then over, all the water that had not been allowed to flow here for all these years now in unrelenting return, soon beginning to occupy the arroyos and cover the flats, all the swimming pools in the backyards filling up and overflowing and flooding the lots and streets, all this karmic waterscape connecting together, as the rain went on falling and the land vanished, into a sizable inland sea that would presently become an extension of the Pacific.

It was funny that of all things to mention in the limited space of a coconut-launched postcard Shasta should have picked that day in the rain. It had stuck with Doc somehow too, even though it came at a point late in their time together, when she was already halfway out the door and Doc saw it happening but was letting it happen, and despite it there they were, presently making out frantically, like kids at the drive-in, steaming up the windows and getting the seat covers wet. Forgetting for a few minutes how it was all going to develop anyway.

Back at the beach, the rain continued, and every day up in the hills, another fragment of real estate came sliding down. Insurance salesmen had Brylcreem running down into their collars, and stewardii found it impossible even with half-gallon cans of hair spray purchased in duty-free zones far away to maintain their hairdos in anything close to a stylish flip. The termitic houses of Gordita Beach had all turned to the consistency of wet sponge, emergency plumbers reached in to squeeze the beams and joists, thinking of their own winter homes in Palm Springs. People began to go crazy even while on the natch. Some enthusiast, claiming to be George Harrison of the Beatles, tried to hijack the Goodyear Blimp, moored at its winter quarters at the intersection of the Harbor and San Diego Freeways, and make it fly him to Aspen, Colorado, in the rain.

The rain had a peculiar effect on Sortilège, who was just around then beginning to get obsessed by Lemuria and its tragic final days.

"You were there in a former life," Doc theorized.

"I dream about it, Doc. I wake up so sure sometimes. Spike feels that way, too. Maybe it's all this rain, but we're starting to have the same dreams. We can't find a way to return to Lemuria, so it's returning to us. Rising up out of the ocean—'hi Leej, hi Spike, long time ain't it. . . .'"

"It talked to you guys?"

"I don't know. It isn't just a place."

DOC TURNED OVER Shasta's postcard now and stared at the picture on the front. It was a photo taken underwater of the ruins of some ancient city—broken columns and arches and collapsed retaining walls. The water was supernaturally clear and seemed to emit a vivid blue-green light. Fish, what Doc guessed you'd call tropical, were swimming back and forth. It all seemed familiar. He looked for a photo credit, a copyright date, a place of origin. Blank. He rolled a joint and lit up and considered. This had to be a message from someplace besides a Pacific island whose name he couldn't pronounce.

He decided to go back and visit the Ouija-board address, which, being the site of a classic dope misadventure, had remained permanently entered in his memory. Denis came along for muscle.

The hole in the ground was gone, and in its place rose a strangely futuristic building. From the front it might have been taken at first for some kind of religious structure, smoothly narrow and conical, like a church spire only different. Whoever put it up must have had a pretty comfortable budget to work with, too, because the whole outside had been covered in gold leaf. Then Doc noticed how this tall pointed shape was also curved away from the street. He went down the block a little way and looked back to get a side view, and when he saw how dramatic the curve was and how sharp the point at the top, he finally tumbled.

Aha! In the old L.A. tradition of architectural whimsy, this structure was supposed to be a six-story-high *golden fang*!

"Denis, I'm gonna look around for a while, you want to wait in the car or come in and cover my back or something?"

"I was gonna go try and find a pizza," Denis said.

Doc handed him the car keys. "And . . . they did have driver ed at Leuzinger High."

"Sure."

"And you remember this is a stick, not automatic and so forth."

"I'm cool, Doc." And Denis sped off.

THE FRONT DOOR was nearly invisible, more of a big access panel that fit snugly into the curving façade. In the lobby beneath a tasteful sign in sans-serif face reading GOLDEN FANG ENTERPRISES, INC. \ CORPORATE HQ and behind a nameplate of her own that said "Xandra, hi!" sat an Asian receptionist wearing a black vinyl jumpsuit and a distant expression, who asked him in a semi-Brit accent whether he was sure he had the right place.

"This is the address they told me at the Club Asiatique in San Pedro? Just here to pick up a package for the management?"

Xandra reached for a telephone, punched a button, murmured into it, listened, gave Doc another doubtful once-over, stood, and led him across the reception area to a brushed-metallic door. It took only a step or two for him to dig that she'd logged more dojo hours in the year previous than he'd spent in front of the tube in his whole life—not the sort of young lady whose displeasure you'd go looking to provoke.

"Second office on the left. Dr. Blatnoyd will see you in a moment."

Doc found the office and looked around for something to check out his hair in but saw only a small yellow-framed feng shui mirror by the door. The face looking back did not seem to be his own. "This is not promising," he muttered. Behind a titanium desk, the window revealed a stretch of lower Sunset—taquerías, low-rent hotels, pawn shops. There were beanbag chairs and a range of magazines—*Foreign Affairs, Sinsemilla Tips, Modern Psychopath, Bulletin of the Atomic Scientists*—that gave Doc no handle on the clientele here. He started paging through *2000 Hairdos* and was just getting into "That Five-Point Scissor Cut—What Your Stylist Isn't Telling You," when Dr. Blatnoyd came in wearing a suit in a deep, nearly ultraviolet shade of velvet, with very wide jacket lapels and bell-bottom trousers and accented with a raspberry-colored bow tie and display handkerchief. He seated himself behind the desk, reached for a weighty loose-leaf manual of some kind and began consulting it, squinting over at Doc from time to time. Finally, "So . . . you have some ID, I imagine."

Doc went looking through his wallet till he found a business card from a Chinese head shop on North Spring Street he thought would do the trick.

"I can't read this, it's in some . . . Oriental . . . what is this, Chinese?"

"Well, I figured that you, *being* Chinese—"

"What? what are you talking about?"

"'The . . . the Golden Fang . . .'?"

"It's a syndicate, most of us happen to be dentists, we set it up years ago for tax purposes, all legit— Wait," peering at Doc you'd have to say diagnostically, "where'd you tell Xandra you were from again?"

"Uh . . ."

"Why, you're another one of those hippie dopefiends, aren't you. My goodness. Here for a little *perking up,* I'll bet—" In a jiffy he was out with a tall cylinder of brown glass sealed elaborately with globs of some bright red plastic—"Dig it! just in from Darmstadt, lab quality, maybe I'll even have some with you. . . ." And before Doc knew it the hectic D.D.S. had a quantity of fluffy white cocaine crystals all chopped up into snortable format and arranged in lines on a nearby copy of *Guns & Ammo.*

Doc shrugged in apology. "I try not to do dope I can't pay for, 's what it is."

"Whoo!" Dr. Blatnoyd had a soda straw and was busy snorting away. "No worries, it's on the house, as the TV antenna man always sez. . . .

Hmm, missed a little. . . ." He took it on his finger and rubbed it enthusiastically into his gums.

Doc did half a line in either nostril, just to be sociable, but somehow could not shake the impression that all was not as innocent here as it looked. He had been in a dentist's office or two, and there was a distinctive smell and a set of vibes that were as absent here as room echoes, which he'd also been wondering about. Like something else was going on—something . . . *not groovy.*

There was a quiet but no-nonsense knock at the door, and Xandra the receptionist looked in. She had unzipped the top of the jumpsuit, and Doc could now make out this exquisite pair of no-bra tits, their nipples noticeably erect.

"Oh, Doctor," she breathed, half singing it.

"Yes, Xandra," replied Dr. Blatnoyd, moist-nosed and beaming.

Xandra nodded and slid away back on out the door again, smiling over her shoulder. "And don't forget to *bring that bottle.*"

"Be right back," Blatnoyd assured Doc, speeding out after her, eyes frenziedly focused on where her ass had just been, his echoless footsteps soon vanishing into unknown regions of the Golden Fang Building.

Doc went over and had a look at the manual on the desk. Titled *Golden Fang Procedures Handbook,* it was open to a chapter titled "Interpersonal Situations." "Section Eight—Hippies. Dealing with the Hippie is generally straightforward. His childlike nature will usually respond positively to drugs, sex, and/or rock and roll, although in which order these are to be deployed must depend on conditions specific to the moment."

From the doorway came a loud, violent chirp. Doc looked up and saw a smiling young woman, blond, Californian, presentable, wearing a striped minidress of many different "psychedelic" colors and waving at him vigorously, causing enormous earrings, shaped like pagodas of some kind, to swing back and forth and actually jingle. "Here for my Smile Maintenance appointment with Dr. Rudy!"

A blast from the past. "Hey! that's 'at Japonica, ain't it. Japonica Fenway! Imagine meeting you here!"

This was not a moment he'd been either dreading or hoping for, though now and then somebody would remind him of the ancient American Indian belief that if you save somebody's life, you are responsible for them from then on, forever, and he would wonder if any of that applied to his history with Japonica. It had been his first paying gig as a licensed private eye, and pay it did, for sure. The Fenways were heavy-duty South Bay money, living on the Palos Verdes Peninsula in a gated enclave located *inside* the *already* gated high-rent community of Rolling Hills. "How am I supposed to come see you," Doc wondered when Crocker Fenway, Japonica's dad, called him at the office.

"Guess it'll have to be outside the gates and down in the flats," said Crocker, "like Lomita?"

It was a pretty open-and-shut runaway-daughter case, hardly worth daily scale, let alone the extravagant bonus Crocker insisted on paying when Doc finally brought Japonica back, one lens missing from her wire-rim shades and vomit in her hair, making the handoff in the same parking lot where he and Crocker had met originally. It wasn't clear if she'd ever clearly registered Doc then, or remembered him now.

"So! Japonica! what've you been up to?"

"Oh, escaping, mostly? There's this, like, place? that my parents keep sending me to?"

Which turned out to be Chryskylodon, the same nut plantation in Ojai that Doc remembered his Aunt Reet mentioning and which Sloane and Mickey had donated a wing to. Though Doc once may have rescued Japonica from a life of dark and unspecified hippie horror, apparently restoration to the bosom of her family had been enough to really drive her around the bend. Against the neutral surface of the wall opposite, Doc had a moment's visual of an American Indian in full Indian gear, perhaps one of those warriors who wipe out Henry Fonda's regiment in *Fort Apache* (1948), approaching with a menacing frown. "Doc responsible for crazy white chick now. What Doc planning to do about that? If anything."

"Excuse me, short man with strange hair? Are you all right?" And on she went without waiting for an answer, twinkling like a roomful of speed freaks hanging Christmas tinsel, about her different escapes. It was beginning to give Doc a headache.

Owing to Governor Reagan's shutdown of most of the state mental facilities, the private sector had been trying in its way to pick up some of the slack, soon in fact becoming a standard California child-rearing resource. The Fenways had had Japonica in and out of Chryskylodon on a sort of maintenance-contract basis, depending as always on how they themselves were feeling day to day, for both led emotional lives of unusually high density, and often incoherence. "Some days all I had to do was play the wrong kind of music, and there's my bags already packed, down in the front hall waiting for the driver."

Soon Chryskylodon had found itself attracting a type of silent benefactor—middle-aged, male, though occasionally female, more focused than usual on the young and mentally disturbed. Freaky chicks and fun-loving dopers! Why do they call it the Love Generation? Come on up to Chryskylodon for a rockin weekend and find out! Absolute discretion guaranteed! Circa 1970, "adult" was no longer quite being defined as in times previous. Among those who could afford to, a strenuous mass denial of the passage of time itself was under way. All across a city long devoted to illusory product, clairvoyant Japonica had seen them, these travelers invisible to others, poised, gazing from smogswept mesa-tops above the boulevards, acknowledging one another across miles and years, summit to summit, in the dusk, under an obscurely enforced silence. Wingfeathers trembled along their naked backs. They knew they could fly. A moment more, an eyeblink in eternity, and they would ascend. . . .

So, Dr. Rudy Blatnoyd, out on a first blind date with Japonica at the Sound Mind Café, a secluded eatery with a patio in back and a menu designed by a resident three-star organic chef, was not only enchanted, he was wondering if somebody hadn't slipped some new psychedelic into his pomegranate martini. This girl was delightful! Being a little ESP-deficient, of course Rudy failed to appreciate that behind her wide sparkling gaze Japonica was not only thinking about but at this point *actually visiting* other worlds. The Japonica sitting with the older man in the funny velour suit was actually a Cybernetic Organism, or cyborg, programmed to eat and drink, converse and socialize, while Real Japonica tended to important business elsewhere, because she was the Kozmic Traveler, deep issues Out There awaited, galaxies wheeled, empires collapsed, karma would not be denied, and Real Japonica must always be present at some exact point in five-dimensional space, or chaos would resume its dominion.

She returned to the Sound Mind to find that Cyborg Japonica had somehow malfunctioned and gone skipping into the kitchen and done something gross to the Soup of the Day, and now they would have to pour it all down the sink. Actually, it was the Soup of the Night, a sinister indigo liquid which probably didn't deserve much respect, but still, Cyborg Japonica could have showed some self-control. Naughty, impulsive Cyborg Japonica. Perhaps Real Japonica should not let her have those special high-voltage batteries she had been asking for. That would show her.

Dr. Blatnoyd, escorting her out through a roomful of disapproving faces, only grew more bedazzled. So this was a free-spirited hippie chick! He saw these girls on the streets of Hollywood, on the TV screen, but this was his first up-close encounter. No wonder Japonica's parents didn't know what to do with her—his assumption here, which he didn't examine too closely, being that he did.

"And actually, I wasn't too sure about who he was till I came in for my first Smile Evaluation. . . ." At which point in Japonica's reminiscing, in popped the lecherous toothyanker himself, zipping up his fly.

"Japonica? I thought we'd agreed never to—" Catching sight of Doc—"oh, you're still here?"

"I escaped again, Rudy," she twinkled.

Denis also now came lurching in. "Hey man, your ride's in a body shop."

"It signed itself in, Denis?"

"I sort of mashed the front end. I was looking at these chicks out on Little Santa Monica and—"

"You went to Beverly Hills for a pizza, and rear-ended somebody there."

"Needs a new . . . what do they call that, with the hoses, where the steam comes out—"

"Radiator—Denis, you said you took driver ed in high school."

"No, no, Doc, you said did they *have* Driver Ed, and I said yes 'cause they did, this dude Eddie Ochoa, that there wasn't a cop south of Salinas could get near him, and that's what everybody called him—"

"So, like, you . . . never actually . . . learned . . ."

"All that stuff they wanted you to *remember*, man?"

Xandra, visibly disheveled, now came running in after Denis, yelling, "I told you you couldn't come up here," then spotted Japonica and screeched to a halt. "Oh. Smile Maintenance Chick. How lovely," while scaling tiny glares Dr. Blatnoyd's way like the star-shaped blades in kung fu movies.

"Miss Fenway," the doctor began to explain, "may seem a little psychotic today. . . ."

"Groovy!" cried Denis.

"What?" Blatnoyd blinking.

"Being insane, man? it's groovy, where are you *at,* man?"

"Denis . . ." Doc murmured.

"It is not 'groovy' to be insane. Japonica here has been institutionalized for it."

"Yep," beamed Japonica.

"Like, in the place? Psychedelic! They put those volts in your head, man?"

"Volts 'n' volts," twinkled Japonica.

"Whoa. Bad for *la cabeza,* man."

"C'mon, Denis," said Doc, "we're gonna have to figure out how to catch a bus back to the beach."

"If you need a ride, I'm heading that way," offered Japonica.

Running a fast eyeball diagnostic, Doc could see nothing too alarming—right at the moment she was being as sane as anybody here, not too many useful remarks Doc could pass, so he settled for, "Everything cool with your brakes and lights, Japonica? license-plate lights and so forth?"

"A-OK? Just had Wolfgang in for periodic maintenance?"

"That's . . ."

"My car?" Yes, another warning buzzer, but Doc was now on to obsessing over the vast numbers of law enforcement likely to be deployed between here and the beach.

"Excuse me," wondered Xandra, who'd been staring at Denis, "is that a slice of pizza on your hat?"

"Oh wow, thanks, man, I've been lookin all over for that. . . ."

"Mind if I tag along with you people?" asked Dr. Blatnoyd. "Contingencies of the road and so forth."

Wolfgang turned out to be a ten-year-old Mercedes sedan with a roof panel passengers could slide back, allowing them, like dogs in pickups, to stick their heads out in the wind if they wanted. Doc rode shotgun, widebrim fedora down over his eyes, trying to ignore a deep foreboding. Dr. Blatnoyd climbed in the back with Denis and then spent some time trying to push a #66 market bag full of something under the front seat on Doc's side.

"Hey," exclaimed Denis, "what's in that bag you're stuffing under Doc's seat?"

"Pay no attention to that bag," advised Dr. Blatnoyd. "It will only make everybody paranoid."

Which it did, except for Japonica, who was maneuvering them smoothly up Sunset through the late rush-hour traffic.

Denis had his head out the roof. "Drive slower," he called down after a while, "I want to dig this." They were crossing Vine and about to go past Wallach's Music City, where each of a long row of audition booths inside had its own lighted window facing the street. In every window, one by one as Japonica crept by, appeared a hippie freak or small party of hippie freaks, each listening on headphones to a different rock 'n' roll album and moving around at a different rhythm. Like Denis, Doc was used to outdoor concerts where thousands of people congregated to listen to music for free, and where it all got sort of blended together into a single public self, because everybody was having the same experience. But here, each person was listening in solitude, confinement and mutual silence, and some of them later at the register would actually be spending money to hear rock 'n' roll. It seemed to Doc like some strange kind of dues or payback. More and more lately he'd been brooding about this great collective dream that everybody was being encouraged to stay tripping around in. Only now and then would you get an unplanned glimpse at the other side.

Denis waved, yelled and flashed peace signs, but nobody in any of the booths noticed. At last he slid back down into the Mercedes. "Far out. Maybe they're all stoned. Hey! That must be why they call those things *head*phones!" He put his face closer to Dr. Blatnoyd's than the dentist was really comfortable with. "Think about that, man! Like, *head*phones, right?"

Japonica was driving so skillfully that it wasn't till they were out of the white dazzle of Hollywood and across Doheny that Doc noticed (a) it was now dark and (b) the headlights weren't on.

"Ah, Japonica, like, your lights?"

She was humming to herself, a tune Doc recognized, with dawning concern, as the theme from *Dark Shadows*. After four more bars, he tried again. "Like, it would be so groovy, Japonica, really, to have some lights working is all, seeing 's how Beverly Hills cops are known to lurk uphill on these different cross streets? just waiting for minor violations, like lights, to pop folks on?"

Her humming was way too intense. Doc made the mistake of looking over, only to find her staring at him and not the road, eyes glittering ferally through a blond curtain of California-chick hair. No, this was not reassuring. Though hardly a connoisseur of the freakout, he did recognize a wraparound hallucination when he saw one and understood immediately that while she likely didn't see Doc at all, whatever she *was* seeing was indeed physically *out there,* in the gathering fog, and just about to—

"Everything all right, baby?" Rudy Blatnoyd rang in.

"Oo-*oooo*," warbled Japonica, putting some vibrato onto it and stepping on the gas, "Ooo-ooo woo-*oo*, woo-ooo . . ."

Cross traffic, neighborhood machinery such as Excaliburs and Ferraris, came blurring by at high speed, missing them by small clearances. Dr. Blatnoyd, as if wishing to start a therapeutic discussion, was glaring at Denis. "There. That's just what I've been talking about."

"You didn't say nothing about it happening while she's driving, man."

Japonica had meantime decided that she must run every red light she could find, even speeding up to catch some before they could turn green. "Um, Japonica, my dear? That was a red light?" Blatnoyd pointed out helpfully.

"Ooh, I don't *think* so!" she explained blithely. "I think that was one of Its *eyes!*"

"Oh. Well, yes," Doc soothed. "We can sure dig that, Japonica, but then again—"

"No, no, there's no 'It' watching you!" Blatnoyd now in some agitation. "Those are not 'eyes,' those are warnings to come to a full stop and wait till the light turns green, don't you remember learning that in school?"

"*That's* what those colors are for, man?" Denis said.

Suddenly, like a UFO rising over the ridgeline, the flashing lights of a police car appeared uphill and came swooping down on them, the siren screaming. "Like, shit," Denis heading for the hatch in the roof again, "I'm outta here, man," overlooking for the moment the streetscape rushing past. Feeling no sign of deceleration, Doc, trying not to think about the paper bag under the seat, kept reaching with his foot for the brake pedal, meantime trying gently to steer the car over to the shoulder. If he'd been in his own ride and by himself, he might have chosen to make a run for it, at least open a door an inch or two and get rid of the bag, but by the time he could bring himself to try even that, the Man was on top of them.

"License and registration, miss?" The cop seemed to be focused on Japonica's tits. She smiled back at him in high-intensity silence, occasionally glancing at the Smith & Wesson on his hip. His partner, a rookie even blonder than he was, came and leaned on the passenger side, content for the moment to watch Denis, who had paused in his effort to climb through the roof to gaze at the strobing array of colored lights on top of the cruiser, and now and then go, "Oh wow, man."

"Are you the Great Beast?" inquired rattling-mad Japonica in her sub-jailbait lilt.

"No no no," Blatnoyd droning desperately, "that's a policeman, Japonica, who only wants to make sure you're all right. . . ."

"Just the license and registration if you wouldn't mind," said the cop. "You know you were driving without your headlights, miss."

"But I can see in the dark," Japonica nodding emphatically, "I can see *real good*!"

"Her sister went into labor about an hour ago," Blatnoyd imagining he was charming their way out of a ticket, "and Miss Fenway promised she'd be there in time to see the baby born, so she might've been a little inattentive back there?"

"That case," said the cop, "maybe somebody else ought to be driving."

Japonica promptly jumped in the back seat with Blatnoyd, while Doc slid over behind the wheel and Denis moved up front to ride shotgun. The cops looked on beaming, like instructors at an etiquette class. "Oh and we'll need everybody's ID, too," the rookie announced.

"Sure thing," Doc bringing out his PI license. "What's it about, Officer?"

"New program," shrugged the other cop, "you know how it is, another excuse for paperwork, they're calling it Cultwatch, every gathering of three or more civilians is now defined as a potential cult." The rookie was making checkmarks on a list attached to a clipboard. "Criteria," the other cop continued, "include references to the book of Revelation, males with shoulder-length or longer hair, endangerment through automotive absentmindedness, all of which you folks have been exhibiting."

"Yeah man," Denis put in, "but we're in a Mercedes, and it's only painted one color, beige—don't we get points for that?"

Doc noticed for the first time that both cops were . . . well, not trembling, the police wouldn't tremble, but *vibrating* for sure, with the post-Mansonical nerves that currently ruled the area.

"We'll hand this all in, Mr. Sportello, it'll go in some master data bank here and in Sacramento, and unless there's wants or warrants we don't know about, you won't hear any more on this."

FOLLOWING DR. BLATNOYD'S directions, Doc turned off Sunset, braking almost immediately for a guard gate staffed by private heat of some kind. "Evening, Heinrich," boomed Rudy Blatnoyd.

"Nice to see you, Dr. B.," replied the sentry, waving him through. They went winding through Bel Air, up hillsides and canyons, arriving at a mansion with another gate, low and nearly invisible inside its landscape gardening, seeming so much constructed of night itself that at sunrise it might all disappear. Behind the gate glimmered a pale slash through the dark, which Doc finally figured out was a moat, with a drawbridge over it.

"Won't be a minute," Dr. Blatnoyd climbing out, grabbing the bag from under the front seat and getting into a cryptic discussion over the gate intercom with a voice Doc guessed to be female, before the gate opened and the drawbridge came down, rumbling and creaking. Then the night was very quiet again—not even the distant freeway traffic could be heard, or the footpads of coyotes, or the slither of snakes. . . .

"Way too quiet," said Denis, "it's freaking me out, man."

"I think we'll wait here on this side of the moat," Doc said. "Okay?" Denis rolled an enormous joint and lit up, and soon the interior of the Mercedes was full of smoke. After a while there was shrieking on the gate intercom. "Hey man," said Denis, "you don't have to yell, man."

"Dr. Blatnoyd wishes us to inform you," announced the woman at the other end, "that he will be remaining as our guest, and there is thus no further need for you to wait."

"Yeah, and you talk like a robot, man."

It took them a while to find their way back to Sunset. "I guess I'll crash with some friends in Pacific Palisades," Japonica announced.

"Mind letting us off at the Greyhound in Santa Monica? We can grab the midnight local."

"By the way, aren't you the man who found me and brought me back to my dad that time?"

"Just doing my job," Doc immediately defensive.

"Did he really want me back?"

"I've worked gigs like that a couple of times since," Doc said carefully, in case she had to drive much more tonight, "and he seemed like your standard worried parent."

"He's an asshole," Japonica assured him.

"Here, this is my office number. I don't have regular hours, so you may not always find me in."

She shrugged and managed a smile. "If it's meant to be."

THINGS WERE WEIRD for a few days with the Dart over in Beverly Hills, though Doc imagined it was having itself a nice time in the company of all those Jaguars and Porsches and so forth. When he finally went over to pick up his ride, at Resurrection of the Body, a collision emporium somewhat south of Olympic, he ran into his friend Tito Stavrou having a lively argument with Manuel the owner. Tito ran a limo service, though there was only one unit in his fleet, unfortunately not one of those limos able to Glide from the Curb, much less Insert Itself Effortlessly into Traffic—no, this one *lurched* from the curb *percussively* into traffic, being in fact garaged for at least half of any given premium period (as Tito's latest insurance carrier had just discovered, much to its own, and you can imagine how much to Tito's, dismay) or being attended to by various sand-and-fill crews around the Greater L.A. Area. One calendar year it got repainted six times. "You sure you mean limo and not *limón?*" suggested Manuel, as part of the recreational abuse he liked to lay on Tito whenever the vehicle showed up with a new set of dings. They stood out in the main shed, assembled from a Quonset hut first cut in half lengthwise and the two pieces then rearranged so that they met in a point high overhead to make a sort of churchlike vault. "It would be cheaper if you just pay me in front, small fee, anytime you want it painted, just bring it by, day or night, any color in stock includin the metallics, in and out in a couple hours."

"What worries me," said Tito, "is that 'in and out,' you know, all these high-risk elements of the auto-parts community you deal with?"

"This is Resurrection, *ése!* We're in the miracle business! If Jesus turned water into wine in front of your face? would you be goin, 'What's this I'm drinkín, I wannit Dom Pérignon,' or some shit? If I was that picky about what comes in here for a paint job? ask for what? their license and registration? Then they're *really* pissed off, they go someplace else, plus I get put on a shit list I might not want to be on?" Manuel noticed Doc for the first time. "You the Bentley?"

"The '64 Dodge Dart?"

Manuel looked back and forth between Doc and Tito for a while. "You guys know each other?"

"That would really depend," Doc was about to say, but Manuel went on. "I was gonna charge you more, but guys like Tito here, they're subsidizin guys like you." The amount on the invoice was nevertheless a

Beverly Hills type of number, and half Doc's day got blown setting up a payment schedule.

"Come on," said Tito, "I'll buy you lunch. I need your advice on something."

They went down to Pico and headed toward Rancho Park. This street was a chowhound's delight. Back when Doc was still new in town, one day around sunset—the daily event, not the boulevard—he was in Santa Monica near the western end of Pico, the light over all deep L.A. softening to purple with some darker gold to it, and from this angle and hour of the day it seemed to him he could see all the way down Pico for miles into the heart of the great Megalopolis itself, having yet to discover that if he wanted to, he could also *eat* his way down Pico night after night for a long while before repeating an ethnic category. This did not always turn out to be good news for the indecisive doper who might know he was hungry but not necessarily how to deal with it in terms of *specific food*. Many was the night Doc ran out of gas, and his munchies-afflicted companions out of patience, long before settling on where to go eat.

Today they ended up at a Greek restaurant called Teké, which according to Tito meant an old-time hashish parlor in Greek.

"I hope this won't be a problem," said Tito, "but word is around you've been working on this Mickey Wolfmann case?"

"Not how I'd put it. Nobody's paying me. Sometimes I think all it is is guilt. Wolfmann's girlfriend is my ex–old lady, she said she needed help, so I've been trying to help."

Tito, who had made a point of facing the front entrance, lowered his voice till Doc could hardly hear him. "I'm taking a chance that you ain't bent, Doc. You ain't bent, are you?"

"Not so far, but I could always use a nice envelope full of cash."

"These guys," an unhappy look crossing Tito's face, "don't hand you envelopes, it's more like, do what they want, maybe they don't fuck you up too bad."

"You're sayin this is mob-related—"

"I only wish. I mean, I know some Family badasses who scare most people, they sure scare me, but I wouldn't ever go to them with this, they'd just take a look at who it is and go, like, 'Pasadena, man.'"

"Not to mention you owe them money."

"No more, I kicked all that."

"What. No horses, no pan parlors? No Li'l T-Rex? No Salvatore 'Paper Cut' Gazzoni? No Adrian Prussia?"

"Nope, even Adrian's off my ass anymore, all paid off, the vig, everything."

"Good news 'cause sooner or later that fucker'd be reachin for his baseball bat, going to town on your head or somethin. Man gives loan-sharkin a bad name."

"They're all in my sorry past now, I been twelve-steppin it, Doc. Meetings, everythin."

"Well, Inez must be happy. How long's it been?"

"Comin up on six months next weekend. We're gonna go celebrate it in style, too, we're takin the limo to Vegas, stayin at Caesar's—"

"Excuse me, Tito, am I confusing Las Vegas with someplace *else* where all they do is fucking gamble nonstop? How do you expect to—"

"Avoid temptation? Hey that's just it, how'm I ever gonna know? Thing is to jump in, see what happens."

"Oboy. This is all cool with Inez?"

"Her idea."

Mike the owner and cook appeared with a huge plate of dolmadhes, Kalamata olives, and midget spanakopitas it looked like it would take a week to polish off. "You're sure you want to eat here," he greeted Tito.

"This is Doc, he saved my life once."

"And this is how you thank him?" Mike shaking his head in reproof. "Think long and hard, my friends," muttering back to the kitchen.

"I saved your life?"

Tito shrugged. "That time up on Mulholland."

"You saved mine, man, you're the one knew where it was," this particular "it" being a car-napped 1934 Hispano-Suiza J12 whose return Doc had been negotiating with a Lithuanian thyroid case who showed up carrying a modified AK-47 with a banana clip so oversize that he kept tripping over it, which looking back was what had saved everybody's lives, probably.

"I was doin that all for myself, man, you happened to be there when we brought it back and all that money started flyin around."

"Whatever, Doc—there's somethin now that you're the only one I can tell it to." A quick look around. "Doc, I was one of the last people to talk to Mickey Wolfmann before he dropped off the screen."

"Shit," replied Doc, encouragingly.

"And no, I haven't been near the heat with this. It would get back to these guys before I was out the door, and I'd end up a shark hors d'oeuvre."

"D and D, Tito."

"What happened, Mickey got to where he didn't always trust his drivers. They were most of 'em ex-cons, which meant they had their own IOUs to pay off that sometimes he didn't know about. So once in a while he calls me on the unlisted line, and I pick him up someplace we decide on at the last minute."

"You used that limo? Not exactly a low profile."

"Nah, we'd use Falcons or Novas, I can always score one on short notice, even a VDub if it ain't painted too funny."

"So the day Mickey disappeared . . . he called you? you took him someplace?"

"He wanted me to pick him up. He called in the middle of the night, it sounded like a pay phone, he was talking real quiet, he was scared, like somebody was after him. He gave me an address out of town, I drove up there and waited, but he never showed. After a couple hours I was getting too much attention so I split."

"Where was this?"

"Ojai, near someplace called Chryskylodon."

"I've been hearing about it," Doc said, "some nuthouse for the upper brackets. Old Indian word that means 'serenity.'"

"Ha!" Tito shook his head. "Who told you that?"

"It's in their brochure?"

"It ain't Indian, it's Greek, trust me, they talked Greek around the house all the time I was coming up."

"What's it mean in Greek?"

"Well, it's squashed together a little, but it means like a gold tooth, this one here—" He tapped at a canine.

"Oh, shit. 'Fang'? Could it be that?"

"Yeah, close enough. Gold fang."

TWELVE

DOC MADE A COUPLE OF PHONE CALLS AND TOOK THE BACK
route up by way of Burbank and Santa Paula, reaching the Ojai turnoff just before lunchtime. There were plenty of signs to point the way
to the Chryskylodon Institute. The high-rent laughing academy was
located close enough to Krotona Hill to cash in on the mystiques of
better-known spiritual facilities like the Inner School and the AMORC.
The main house, a red tile and white stucco Mission Revival mansion,
was surrounded by a hundred acres of orchards and pasture and sycamore woods. At the front gate, Doc was met by longhaired attendants in
flowing robes under which they were packing Smiths in shoulder rigs.

"Larry Sportello, I have an appointment?"

"If you wouldn't mind, brother."

"Sure, grope ahead, I ain't packing, hell I ain't even holding." The
procedure was to park in a lot by the gate and wait for an Institute shuttle
bus to run you up to the main house. The gate had a sign over it which
read STRAIGHT IS HIP.

Doc had got himself up today in an Edwardian jacket and bell-
bottoms in not quite matching and no longer fashionable shades of
brown, narrowly trimmed late-movie mustache, hair Brylcreemed into
a high pompadour with long sideburns, all meant to suggest a sleazy
and vaguely anxious go-between who couldn't himself begin to afford

the fees this place would be asking. From the looks he was getting, the put-together seemed to be working.

"We were just about to go have lunch," the associate director Dr. Threeply making with the fake-sympathetic wrinkled forehead. "Why don't you join us? Afterward we can show you around the facility."

Dr. Threeply was a shifty specimen with that quality now and then observed in aluminum-siding and screen-door salesmen of once having been through something—a marriage, a criminal proceeding—traumatic enough to have torqued him permanently out of tolerance, so that now he had to beg potential clients to ignore this unspecified character handicap.

Waiting on tables at lunch in the Administrative Lounge were inmates who seemed to be working in lieu of paying the full fee. "Thank you, Kimberly. Hands steady as a rock today, it seems."

"So happy you noticed, Dr. Threeply. More soup?"

Doc, with a forkful of some unfamiliar vegetable loaf halfway to his mouth, reflected that if these folks out here were mental cases, then what about farther back in the kitchen, well out of the public gaze? Like doing the cooking, for example?

"Try some of this chenin blanc, Mr. Sportello, right from our own vineyard." Doc had learned from his dad Leo, and later cruising supermarket shelves, that *"blanc"* meant "white," and that California whites tended to be, well, at least whiter than the queasy shade of yellow he was looking at. He squinted at the label and noticed an ingredient list several lines long, with the note, in parentheses, "Continued on back of bottle," but whenever he tried, as casually as he could, to have a look at the label on the back, he noticed he was getting these stares, and sometimes people even reached and turned the label away so he couldn't read it.

"You've . . . been here with us before?" said one of the staff shrinks. "I know I've seen your face."

"First time I've been down here, normally I never get much south of South City."

"And *ab*-normally?" Dr. Threeply chuckled.

"What?"

"I only meant that with any number of qualified facilities in the Bay Area, why bother coming all the way down here to us?" The others at the table leaned forward as if keenly interested in Doc's answer.

Time to pull out some of the stuff he'd run through with Sortilège. "I believe," said Doc earnestly, "that just as chakras can be identified on the human body, so does the body of Earth have these special places, concentrations of spiritual energy, grace if you will, and that Ojai, for the presence of Mr. J. Krishnamurti alone, certainly qualifies as one of the more blessed of planetary chakras, which regrettably cannot be said for San Francisco or its immediate vicinity."

After a small patch of silence, somebody said, "You mean . . . Walnut Creek . . . *isn't* a chakra?" which drew nodding and chuckling from colleagues.

"Some religious thing," supposed Dr. Threeply, maybe trying to restore an air of professionalism at the table, though what profession was unclear.

After lunch Doc was bustled around on a tour which included dormitories, a staff lounge with a dozen TV sets and a full-service bar, the sensory-deprivation tanks, the Olympic-size pool, and the rock-climbing wall.

"What's in here?" Doc trying to seem no more than casually curious.

"A brand-new wing for housing our Noncompliant Cases Unit," announced Dr. Threeply, "not quite operational yet, but soon to be the Institute's pride and joy. You may certainly have a look inside if you wish, though there's nothing much to see." He swung open one of the doors, and just inside the vestibule Doc caught a glimpse of the same publicity photo he'd seen at the Wolfmann home, of Sloane in a skip loader delivering an oversize check. As closely as he could, he scanned the photograph again and noticed now that none of the other faces in it seemed to be Mickey's. Mickey was nowhere in sight, but Doc was visited by the creepy feeling that somewhere close by, in some weird indeterminate space whose residents weren't sure where they were, inside or out of the frame, might indeed be some version of Mickey, not quite in the same way that the lady with the big check was a version of Sloane, but altered and—he shivered—maybe mentally or even physically compromised. Past this vestibule here, he could make out a long corridor lined with identical knobless doors receding into metallic shadow. Before the main door swung shut again, Doc just had time to notice a chunk of marble with a bronze plaque that read, MADE POSSIBLE THROUGH THE SELFLESS GENEROSITY OF A DEVOTED FRIEND OF CHRYSKYLODON.

If Sloane was endowing loony bins with Mickey's money, why not take some credit? Why be anonymous?

"Nice," said Doc.

"Come, we'll have a look outside."

As they moved out into the grounds, Doc could see, through the haze, eucalyptus trees, colonnaded walkways, neoclassic temples faced in white marble, fountains fed by hot springs. Everything looked like painted glass mattes in old Technicolor movies. Well-to-do nutcases and their attendants drifted now and then in the distance. As Aunt Reet had suggested, there was a lot of capital improvement in progress. Landscaping crews tossed through the air and neatly caught long curved stacks of clay flowerpots. Framers played hard-core acid rock 'n' roll out of truck radios and hammered along with the beat. Paving crews shoveled blacktop, and rollers rolled it smooth.

There were tennis courts and swimming pools and outdoor volleyball. The Zen Garden, according to Dr. Threeply, had been transported from Kyoto, reassembled here exactly in place, each grain of white sand, each textured rock. A ceremonial bell stood nearby, and next to it Doc noticed a strange shadowy gazebo, like a steel engraving in some old and likely forbidden book, out of which he thought he heard sounds of chanting. "Advanced therapy group," said Threeply. He led Doc to a concealed spiral stairway, and they descended into a sort of grotto, damp and dimly lit. The temperature dropped twenty degrees. From down the damp corridors, the sound of chanting got louder. Threeply led Doc into a soundproofed space behind one-way mirrors, and among underground shadows green as aquarium slime Doc immediately recognized one of a dozen kneeling figures in robes as Coy Harlingen.

Now, what the fuck?

As it turned out, this was not the only familiar face around here. Lounging by the observation window was an orderly who had apparently brought the inmates here and was waiting to take them back. He was passing the time with the age-old diversion of rolling up his necktie, holding it for a minute under his chin, and then lifting his chin and letting the tie unroll again. Hours of fun. Doc didn't notice the tie itself until he'd been watching this for a while, and then he either thought, Holy shit! or actually hollered it out loud, he wasn't sure right away which, because what this gorilla happened to be wearing was one of Mickey Wolfmann's own custom-made specials—in fact the *exact tie* Doc had failed to find in Mickey's closet, the one with Shasta hand-painted on it, in a pose submissive enough to break an ex–old man's heart, that's if he was in the mood. Doc was just able to return to the present tense in time to hear Dr. Threeply wrapping up some commentary and asking if there were any questions.

Several, in fact.

Doc wanted at least to mention to the gorilla by the window something like, "Hey, that's my ex–old lady you're fondling there," but how wise was that? The world had just been disassembled, anybody here could be working any hustle you could think of, and it was long past time to be, as Shaggy would say, like, gettin out of here, Scoob.

Loaded down with application kits and Institute literature, Doc climbed onto the shuttle back to the main gate. At the creepy gazebo stop, one passenger got on, who turned out to be Coy Harlingen in a hooded robe, making dummy-up gestures, which included, "Get off when I do."

They got off by the dodge-ball court. Some kind of Regional All-Institution Playoffs were in progress, with a lot of matching T-shirts and screaming, not all of it playoff-related, and nobody paid much attention to Coy and Doc.

"Here, put this on." One of the hooded robes people wore around here, which Doc doubted came from a religious-supply house—more like some clearance sale of no-longer-stylish beachwear. He slid into it. "Wow . . . makes a man feel like . . . Lawrence of Arabia!"

"As long as we walk slow and stoned, nobody's gonna bother us."

"Here, maybe this'll help." Producing and lighting a pinner of gold Colombian. They passed it back and forth, and after a while Coy said, "So you got to see Hope."

"For a minute. She's okay. And looks like she's been stayin clean too."

It wasn't easy to see what exactly was going on with Coy behind his shades, but his voice dropped to a whisper. "You talked to her?"

"I put my head in the front door, pretended to be one of these magazine hustlers. Caught just a glimpse of that li'l Amethyst, too, and from what I could see, they're both doing fine. And I almost sold Hope a subscription to *Psychology Today*."

"Well." Coy shaking his head slowly, as if listening to a solo. "You don't know how worried I've been." Maybe more than he meant to say. "She kicked, are you sure? Is she on a program, or how's she doing it?"

"She's back teaching, is all she said. Public health, drug awareness, something like that."

"And you're not gonna tell me where."

"Not even if I knew."

"You really think that I would ever start giving either of them shit?"

"I don't do matrimonials, man. I have a terrible history of putting in, and it's never ended well."

Coy walked along with his face in the shadow of his hood. "Don't matter, I guess."

"How's that?"

"No way I can ever go back to them."

Doc knew that tone of voice and hated it. It reminded him of too many vomit-spattered toilets, freeway overpasses, edges of cliffs in Hawaii, always pleading with men younger than himself distraught with what they were so sure was love. It was actually why he'd quit doing matrimonials. In spite of which, he now found himself prompting, "You can't go back, because if you did . . ."

Coy shook his head. "It would be my ass. Understand? My family's, too. This is like a gang. Once you're in, you're in, *por vida.*"

"Did you know that when you joined up?"

"All I knew was we couldn't do each other no good staying together. The baby was looking like shit and worse every day. We'd get fucked up and just sit there and go, 'We're draggin each other down, what're we gonna do?' and then end up doing nothing, or we'd say, 'Wait till we score again and that's out of the way, then we'll come up with something,' but that never happened either. So here came this opportunity. These people up here had money, it wasn't like it was Bible freaks wandering up and down the beach screamin at you or nothin, they really wanted to help."

It was occurring to Doc now, as he recalled what Jason Velveeta had said about vertical integration, that if the Golden Fang could get its customers strung out, why not turn around and also sell them a program to help them kick? Get them coming and going, twice as much revenue and no worries about new customers—as long as American life was something to be escaped from, the cartel could always be sure of a bottomless pool of new customers.

"They just gave me the tour here," Doc said.

"Thinkin about signin yourself in?"

"Not me. Couldn't afford it."

By now they were tuned to each other enough that Coy, if he wanted, could take this for an opening to talk about what kind of a deal he'd made. But he just paced along in silence.

"Short of actual marriage counseling," Doc said carefully, "if I did just run a fast check and happened to find some angle you maybe haven't thought of—"

"Nothing personal," was that a small tremor of anger? "but there's too much *you* haven't thought of. You want to run your check, I can't stop you, but maybe you'll wish you hadn't."

They had walked almost to the gate, and the shadows around the place were lengthening. Back at the beach, the sea breeze would be turning around about now. "I can dig you're trying to chase me off of this," Doc said, "and it's also a bad idea for me to try and phone you. But look. Whatever it is you're caught inside, I'm still out here, on the outside of it. I can move in ways you may not be able to. . . ."

"I can't come any further now," Coy said. They were in an apricot orchard near the gate. "Here, let me have the robe back."

Doc must have taken his eye off Coy for a second. Somehow in the act of shaking the robe out or folding it or something, it was taken from his grasp, flourished like a magician's cape, and when Doc looked where it had been, Coy was already gone.

Doc took 101 back and arrived at the grade up to Thousand Oaks just in time to have to brake abruptly for a paisley-painted VW bus full of giggling dopers which had materialized in front of him. The passing lane was already solid with semis trying to swerve around the VW, so there was no point trying to go there. Once Doc might have grown impatient, but with age and wisdom he had come to understand that these units never had any fucking compression to begin with, owing to engineering decisions taken long ago at Wolfsburg. He shifted down, reached for the volume knob on the radio, which was playing "Something Happened to Me Yesterday" by the Stones, and figured he'd get up the hill when he got there. Which would have been fine except that now he had time to think about Mickey's necktie and begin to wonder how the ape who was wearing it had come by it, exactly, and recall unavoidably the hand-painted image of Shasta Fay, on her back, spread and wet and, if he was not mistaken, though he'd only caught a fast glimpse, just about to come, too.

Mickey must've been wearing that particular tie when they grabbed him. Just took it out of the closet that morning at random, or maybe because of something deeper. Then when they processed him into an inmate uniform at Chryskylodon, they confiscated the tie, and that's when the ape saw it and just decided to take it. Or had Mickey exchanged it later for some mental-slam favor, a phone call, a smoke, somebody else's meds? Back in junior college, professors had pointed out to Doc the useful notion that the word is not the thing, the map is not the territory. He supposed you could extend this also to the nudie necktie is not the girl. But he wasn't rational enough right now to feel anything but ripped off, not for Mickey so much as—ancient history by now or whatever—for Shasta. Forget the fantasies her picture might've aroused in the ape—how little could she have meant to Mickey, for him to let it happen?

DOC GOT BACK to the beach just at early evening, coming up the back slope of the dunes and over, to a hazy view of bay and headlands, a pure sunset of the colors steel takes on as it heats to glowing, lights of airliners, some blinking and some steady, ascending silently from the airport in short clear curves before setting out to traverse the sky, sometimes finding brief conjunction with an early star, then moving on. . . . He decided to stop in at the office, and as he was letting himself in, the phone started ringing, quietly, as if to itself.

"Where've you been?" said Fritz.

"No place I'd recommend."

"What is it, you sound terrible."

"This thing's turnin sour, Fritz. I think I found out where they took Mickey. He might not be there any longer, or even alive, but either way he could be pretty fucked up by now."

"Better I don't know too much, but how about the po-lice, you're sure they can't help?"

Doc found a tobacco cigarette and lit up. "Never thought I'd hear that from you."

"Just slipped out."

"I wish . . ." holy shit did he feel tired, "just once I *could* trust them.

194

But it's like the force of gravity, they never pull in any but the one direction."

"Always admired your principles, Doc, specially now, 'cause I ran those plate numbers you gave me, and it turns out that some of them belong to members of the L.A. 'police reserves.' Seems a lot of those guys joined up during the Watts clambake so they could play run-nigger-run and have it all be legal. Since then they've been like a little private militia the LAPD uses whenever they don't want to look bad in the papers. You got a pencil, you can copy these down, just don't tell me what happens."

"Owe you, Fritz."

"Not at all, any excuse to feel like I'm surfin the wave of the future here, just got this new hire in, name of Sparky, has to call his mom if he's gonna be late for supper, only guess what—we're *his* trainees! he gets on this ARPAnet trip, and I swear it's like acid, a whole 'nother strange world—time, space, all that shit."

"So when they gonna make it illegal, Fritz?"

"What. Why would they do that?"

"Remember how they outlawed acid soon as they found out it was a channel to somethin they didn't want us to see? Why should information be any different?"

"I better get Sparky to hurry up, then. Today he tells me he thinks he knows a way to get into the CII computer up in Sacramento without them knowing. So pretty soon whatever the State Bureau has, we'll have, too, you can think of us as CII South."

Just then they heard the line current drop. Somebody was tapping in. "Well, he's a dang good retriever," Fritz went on unperturbed, "if it's there, ol' Sparky'll find it, he loves 'at shit."

"Remind me to pick him up some of those Liv-a-Snaps," Doc said.

Back at his place, Doc found Denis with an unlit joint hanging off his lip, sitting by the alley freaking out. "Denis?"

"Fuckin Boards, man."

"What happened?"

"They trashed my place."

Doc almost said, "How can you tell?" but saw how upset he was. "Important thing's, are *you* okay?"

"I wasn't there, but if I was, they would've trashed me too."

"The Boards—the whole band, Denis, the rhythm guitar, the bass player, they all broke in, and, and then what?"

"They were looking for those pictures I took, man, I know it. My stash was all over the floor, they cleaned out the fridge, put everything in the Ostracizer and made smoothies and didn't even leave any for anybody else."

"'Anybody else,' that's you, Denis. Why should they leave you any?"

Denis thought about this, and Doc watched him start to calm down. "Come on in the house and we'll relight that thing in your mouth there."

"Because," Denis answered Doc's question a bit later, "they are supposed to be freaks, a freak surfadelic band, that's their public image, and freaks don't rip off other freaks, and most of all if they take your food, freaks share it. Didn't you see that movie? There's this actual 'Code of the Freaks'—"

"I think," Doc said, "that was like 1932, some traveling circus story, different kind of freaks. . . ."

"Whatever—those Boards didt'n behave no better than fuckin straights do."

"You sure this was the Boards, Denis, I mean, were there any, like, witnesses?"

"Witnesses!" Denis laughed tragically. "If there were, they'd be runnin around all askin for autographs and shit."

"Look, I've got the negatives and the proof sheet, and Bigfoot's got that print with Coy in it, so whoever it was if they didn't find anything at your place, chances are they won't be back."

"All my Chinese food," Denis shaking his head. Once a month he ordered thirty meals from South Bay Cantonese out on Sepulveda and kept them in the freezer to thaw out one by one for meals over the next month.

"Why would they—"

"Even the General Tso's Broccoli left over from last night. I was *savin* that, man. . . ."

NEXT MORNING DOC threaded in to work among the usual B$_{12}$ habitués, noted an interesting bruise on Petunia's leg, and hauled on upstairs to start checking the list of cop auxiliaries he'd got from Fritz, a chore he was not looking forward to. He had run into these would-be heavies now and then, displaying an attitude typical of the overarmed, sporting paramilitary berets and camo fatigues and other Vietnam gear from surplus stores on Hawthorne Boulevard, and decorated with badges and ribbons, some even authentic though not strictly speaking earned. He could not recall one of them who'd ever looked at him kindly or even neutrally. These were neighborhood scolds licensed to carry weapons, and heaven help any male civilian with hair that ran much past Marine regulation length.

All these people had day jobs, of course. Doc called up pretending to be different kinds of salesman, or the DMV in Sacramento with a harmless question, or sometimes just an old buddy who'd drifted out of touch, and found the wives—all these guys were family men—in the mood to talk. And talk. A side effect of marriage, as Fritz had imparted to Doc when he was but newly out of the chute. "These broads are all *itchin* to talk, because nobody in their home life wants to hear anything they have to say. Sit still for two seconds and they'll be yakkin your ear off."

"They don't have sisters or other wives to talk to?" Doc wondered.

"Sure, but generally that's nothin we can use."

Doc waited till evening after everybody had had supper, settling, himself, for a quick Taco Bell burrito, a day's worth of nutrition and still a bargain at sixty-nine cents. He had on another shorthair wig, a side-parted chestnut number picked up at a sale on Hollywood Boulevard, and a thrift-store suit that looked like a Three Stooges reject. When the traffic had tapered off some, he headed down to an address in the Rossmoor-Cypress area, just over the county line.

He'd just gotten on the freeway when he heard the radio DJ saying, "Going out from Bambi, to all the Spotted Dickheads in KQAS Kick-Ass Radio Land—here's the lads with their latest single—'Long Trip Out.'"

And after a Farfisa intro from Smedley full of transatlantic Floyd Cramer licks, here came Asymmetric Bob singing,

> He's been out there sold-ierin for a
> Fascist state, so don't ex-
> Pect too much fun on the
> Very first date, he'll be
> Missin the life, he'll be
> Missin the food, he'll be
> Goin around in this pe-culi-ar mood, wond'rin
> How did he get back here in the World
> With the freaked-out hippies and the
> Dopesmokin girls, and it's a

> Long trip out, from the Ia Drang Valley,
> [*Smedley singing along in harmony,*
> *Somerset with a bottleneck guitar fill*]
> It's a sad bad ride, when you're far away
> From the good ol' boys you left behind in-country,
> Where the only thing you want is
> Just another day . . .

> Well it may sound to you like a custom exhaust,
> But that ain't what he's hearin and he's
> Flashin back, lost in the
> Middle of a night full of fire and fear, and he

Don't even know who
He's hangin with here, and that
Joint you been smokin that you thought would help
It's just makin things worse, you're even
Foolin yourself, 'cause it's a

Long trip out, from the Mekong Delta . . .
It's a last lost chance, when you need a friend,
And you're flyin on out of
Cam Ranh Bay at midnight,
And you won't know how, to
Get back home again.

Plastic trikes in the yards, people out watering the flowers and working on their cars, kids in the driveways shooting hoops, the high-frequency squeal of a TV sweep circuit through a screen door as Doc came up the path of the address he was looking for, to be followed by the more worldly sound, as he reached the front steps, of *The Bugs Bunny/Road Runner Hour*. According to Fritz, the sweep frequency was 15,750 cycles per second, and the instant Doc turned thirty, which would be any minute now, he would no longer be able to hear it. So this routine of American house approach had begun to hold for him a particular sadness.

Arthur Tweedle was a civilian machinist who worked a regular day shift at the naval weapons station. On weekends, and sometimes week-nights, too, he put on a sort of fatigue uniform from D'Jack Frost, the Manson family's favorite surplus store in Santa Monica, and went off to meetings of Vigilant California, along with his neighbor Prescott, an-other countersubversive hobbyist also on the list Fritz had run for Doc. Art wore pale horn-rims beneath a high untroubled forehead, and there was little to object to in the face he put on for company, except maybe for a slightly paralyzed look, as if it was a gear he didn't quite know how to shift out of.

Doc was posing as a rep for Hairy Rope Home Security of Tarzana, which did not, he hoped, exist. Aunt Reet had told him once long ago about the California homeowner's belief that if you run a hairy rope all around your property line, no snakes will ever cross it. "Our system works on a similar principle," Doc now explained to the Tweedles, Art and Cindi, "we set up a network of electric eyes hooked to speakers all along your property line. Anybody breaking the beam will trigger a pattern of subsonic pulses—some will produce vomiting, some diarrhea, any of it's enough to send any intruder back where he came from with a hefty dry-cleaning bill to deal with. Of course you and your family can disable the system remotely whenever you need to get on or off your property or mow the lawn or whatever."

"Sounds kind of complicated," said Art, "and besides, we've already got a system right here with a proven track record, and you're looking at him."

"But say you had to go out of town—"

"Cindi," squeezing his wife's ass as she came back in with longneck beer bottles on a tray, "is a better shot than me, and we'll be breaking the kids in on the .22s before you know it."

"Time passes by so quickly," Cindi said.

"Sounds like you're covered pretty good, but no harm I hope in dropping by like this, you're on a list of local homeowners with a history of concern for property defense . . . your service with the police reserves, for example. . . ."

"We're not technically L.A. residents, but I'm on what they call standby, car's all dialed and ready to roll, I can get anyplace they need me in under an hour," said Art.

"Every time we talk with the LAPD, there's somebody's sure to mention you guys and say how they wish there were more of you. Only so many patrol cars and men in uniform, and it's a dark ugly situation out there. They need all the help we can give them."

Which didn't turn the tap on full force right away, but little by little with the Tweedles encouraging each other, as *The Beverly Hillbillies* rolled along toward *Green Acres* and the longnecks kept arriving, Art began to bring out his collection of home defense equipment, which ran from dainty little ladies' pearl-handled .22s through .357 Magnums to Vietnam-surplus grenade launchers. "And that's just single-shot," said Art. "The full-auto inventory's back in the shop." He led Doc through the back door out into the prime-time evening and across the deep lot through sounds from neighbors through windowscreens, TVs, and after-supper clearing up and kids bickering, to an outbuilding in the shape of a midget barn holding a variety of assault rifles and light machine guns, and Art's pride and joy, the terminally illegal Gleichschaltung Model 33 Automatic Bazooka, which required a two-person team, one to aim the 75-mm launch tube itself and the other to drive the modified electric golf cart carrying the magazine, which held up to a hundred rounds.

"Won't be any darkies sneaking onto *this* watermelon patch anytime soon," declared Art.

"Quite a contraption," Doc said. "Where would a guy get hold of something like this?"

"Oh, dealers," Art demurely. "Swap meets, sensitivity-group sessions."

"How about on the job? Would the Department allow you to pack one?"

"Maybe we'll find out one day soon. Sure would've made a difference in Watts."

"Hasn't been much of *that* type of action lately. How are they keeping you fellas busy?"

"Weekend maneuvers, urban counterguerrilla training. Sometimes they'll want an individual tended to but can't commit the manpower. Not very exciting—stakeouts, maybe a rock through a window with a warning note. But it's cash on the spot, enough to keep the Pizza Man happy anyhow."

As they were leaving Art's workshop, Doc happened to spot a Nordic-themed ski mask hanging on a door hook. It looked strangely like the ones in the footage Farley Branch had taken of the assault on Chick Planet Massage.

Doc's nose started itching furiously. "Hey, I got one like that for Christmas," just dropping a random nightcrawler off the end of the pier, "well, except mine had these stuffed antlers on top, and sort of a big, red, you know, like Rudolph-type thing on the nose, battery operated, so forth . . ."

"This one here's standard issue," Art couldn't help swaggering a little, "part of the uniform, for when we're out on maneuvers."

"Was that you guys a couple weeks back, out at that wingding where Mickey Wolfmann disappeared?"

"Sure was, we ended up chasing a gang of bikers all over Channel View Estates, meanest looking bunch you ever saw, but push come to shove, no more trouble than Negroes, really."

"Yeah I keep seeing commercials for the place, with that detective fellow, what's his name . . ."

"Bjornsen—sure, old Bigfoot."

"Think I even coordinated with him once or twice, downtown, on some trespass cases."

"One of America's true badasses," said Art Tweedle.

"No kidding? Struck me as more of a college professor than a field cop."

"Exactly. That's his cover, like Clark Kent, mild mannered. But you ought to see him out on the job. Whew! Move over, Pete Malloy. Back off, Steve McGarrett."

"That dangerous, huh? Guess next time we're in touch, I'll have to watch my step."

WHICH WOULD BE almost immediately. After somehow driving under the influence back to the beach by way of surface streets, Doc went in the kitchen and was reaching for the coffee can when the phone kicked into strident alarm.

"Idiots Unlimited, First to Go, Last to Know, and how in our pathetically fucked-up way can we improve your life tonight?"

"I'm in an evil mood myself," Bigfoot informed him, "so I hope you're not expecting warmth, empathy, nothing like that?"

Clark Kent's ass. Having spent the trip home trying to stay in the correct lane and not fall asleep at the wheel, Doc hadn't got around yet to considering what, according to Art Tweedle, was now a far more sinister Bigfoot Bjornsen than he'd imagined. He also understood vaguely that right now might not be the best time to bring any of this up. Maintain, he advised himself, maintain. . . .

"Howdy, Bigfoot."

"I apologize if I've interrupted some exceptionally demanding hippie task, like trying to remember where the glue is on the Zig-Zag paper, but it seems we have yet another problem, not unconnected with this fatality of yours for introducing disaster into every life you touch, however glancingly."

"Uh-oh." Doc lit a Kool and started looking around for his stash.

"I am all too aware of the memory lapses you people must constantly struggle with, but would you happen to recall one Rudy Blatnoyd, D.D.S.?"

"One, sure—why, are there more?"

"Keen-witted as ever. Would you rather talk this over in person? We can easily dispatch a chauffeur."

"Sorry . . . you say Dr. Blatnoyd. . . ."

"Has perpetrated his last root canal, I'm afraid. We found him next to a trampoline in Bel Air scarcely an hour ago with a fatal neck injury, perhaps even suffered while bouncing in the pitch darkness on that classic resource of backyard fun, who knows? But certain details do appear inconsistent. He was wearing a suit, necktie, and loafers, seldom considered appropriate for trampoline activities. We began to entertain the possibility of foul play, though so far we have no witnesses, no motives, no suspects. Apart from you, of course."

"Not me."

"Odd, because only the other night Dr. Blatnoyd was observed riding in a vehicle full of dope-crazed hippie freaks including yourself, which got stopped by officers in Beverly Hills on suspicion of being a POFO-CAC or Potential Focus of Cult Activity."

"Okay—the owner of that car? very respectable PV family by the way? she offered me a ride? And the cops never even gave her a ticket? And Dr. Blatnoyd was her friend, not mine?"

"I don't wish to pry, Sportello, but where have you been tonight? We've been trying to call you all evening."

"I was at the movies."

"Of course you were, and where was that again?"

"Hermosa Theater."

"And the film was . . ."

"*The Good, the Bad and the Ugly*," which in fact Doc had been to see while the car was in the shop. "This chick I was with wanted to see the other half of the double feature, so we stuck around for that too, some English jailbait picture whose name I'll think of in a minute. . . ."

"Ah, *The Prime of Miss Jean Brodie*, no doubt, a splendid film for which Maggie Smith richly deserves her Oscar for Best Actress."

"She was which one again, the blonde with the big tits, right?"

"Not a fan of the British cinema, I take it."

"More of a Lee Van Cleef person, to be honest, I mean, that Clint Eastwood, he's okay, but I always end up thinking of him as Rowdy Yates—"

"Yes well there's an officer here with some evidence bags, and I'll have to get back to the really amusing part of the evening. Would you mind dropping by Parker Center tomorrow, I'd so like to chat about this fool's errand you were kind enough to send me off on, this Coy Harlingen case?"

"Yeah, by the way, some friends of Coy's came around yesterday and trashed my associate's apartment. So maybe it ain't such a cold case after all."

"There's cold and there's cold," said Bigfoot enigmatically, and hung up.

THAT NIGHT DOC dreamed he was a little kid again. He and another kid who resembles his brother Gilroy are sitting in the Arizona Palms in the middle of the afternoon with a woman who is not exactly Elmina, though she is somebody's mother. A waitress comes over with menus.

"Where's Shannon?" asks the woman who isn't exactly Elmina.

"She got murdered. I'm her replacement."

"Guess it was only a matter of time. Who did it?"

"The husband, who else?"

She brings their food in several trips, each time with some update on the slaying of her co-worker. The weapon, the suggested motives, the pretrial maneuvering. She interrupts banana-cream-pie-à-la-mode discussions with, "Known to happen, somebody kills somebody they're fucking, even in love with, shrinks and counselors and lawyers can only do so much, you go behind the boulevards and you're in the badlands again, where these people who always tell you how to behave have no jurisdiction anymore, and all the twenty-four-hour Southland belongs to the bad."

"Mom," little Larry wants to know, "when she comes back, will they let her husband out of jail?"

"When who comes back?"

"Shannon."

"Didn't you hear what the girl said? Shannon's dead."

"That's only in stories. The real Shannon will come back."

"Hell she will."

"She will, Mom."

"You really believe that stuff."

"Well what do *you* think happens to you when you die?"

"You're dead."

"You don't believe you can come back to life?"

"I don't want to talk about it."

"Well what does happen?"

"I don't want to talk about it."

Gilroy is watching them with enormous eyes and playing with his food, which annoys the Elmina woman, for whom eating is serious business. "Oh, now *you're* playing. Don't play, eat. And you," she tells Doc, "someday you're gonna have to conform."

"What do you mean?"

"Be like everybody else." Of course that's what she means. And now grown-up Doc feels his life surrounded by dead people who do and don't come back, or who never went, and meantime everybody else understands which is which, but there is something so clear and simple that Doc is failing to see, will always manage not to grasp.

He woke up into this particular season of onshore fogs and the unnatural rumbling of jets taking off and landing at LAX all night long, as if some hand at a control board had pushed the bass to an unexpected level, and he found the Indian bedspread on the couch where he crashed running red and orange dye from what could only be his tears. He walked around well into the morning with a dim paisley pattern across half his face.

THIRTEEN

TIME WAS WHEN DOC USED TO ACTUALLY WORRY ABOUT TURNING
into Bigfoot Bjornsen, ending up just one more diligent cop, going only
where the leads pointed him, opaque to the light which seemed to be finding everybody else walking around in this regional dream of enlighten-
ment, denied the wide-screen revelations Bigfoot called "hippiphanies,"
doomed instead to be accosted by freak after freak drawling, "Let me tell
you about my trip, man," never to be up early enough for what might
one day turn out to be a false dawn. Which might have accounted for
why, up till last night, he'd always been willing to cut Bigfoot a certain
amount of slack, not that he would necessarily want *that* to get around.
But now, according to Art Tweedle, there was Bigfoot's probable connection to the LAPD's private army of vigilantes, maybe even (Doc couldn't
help wondering) to the raid at Channel View Estates. By the time he got
to Parker Center, he was feeling like some allegorical statue in the park,
labeled COMMUNITY DISAPPROVAL.

"Hi, Bigfoot! been out smoking any niggers lately?" No . . . no, he
was pretty sure what he'd said out loud was, "Anything new on that Bel
Air case?"

"Don't ask. Well, actually do ask, maybe I need to vent."

The vibes around Robbery-Homicide Division this morning were
as cordial as they ever got, which was hardly at all. Maybe it was Doc,

maybe the nature of the work here, but he could have sworn that today Bigfoot's colleagues were going out of their way to avoid them both.

"Hope you don't mind if we go take a Code 7 someplace?" Bigfoot reaching under the table and dragging out a Ralph's shopping bag with what looked like several kilos of paperwork in it, getting up, and heading out the door, motioning Doc to follow. They went downstairs and out to a Japanese greasy spoon around the corner where the Swedish pancakes with lingonberries couldn't be beat, and which arrived in fact no more than a minute and a half after Bigfoot had put his head in the door.

"Ethnic as always, Bigfoot."

"I'd share these with you, but then you'd be addicted and it would be something else on my conscience." Bigfoot started in scarfing.

Those pancakes sure looked good. Maybe Doc could spoil Bigfoot's appetite or something. He found himself purring maliciously. "Aren't you ever bitter that you missed being up there on Cielo Drive? Stompin around that famous crime scene with the rest of the high-living heat, wipin out them fingerprints, leavin your own, so forth?"

Having grabbed a second fork from Doc's setup and eating now with both hands, "Minor concerns, Sportello, that's only ego and regret. Everybody's got that—well, everybody who works for a living. But do you want to know the truth?"

"Uhnnh . . . no?"

"Here it is anyway. The truth is . . . right now everybody's really, fucking, scared."

"Who—you people? All 'em burrito hounds up in Homicide? Scared of what? Charlie Manson?"

"Odd, yes, here in the capital of eternal youth, endless summer and all, that fear should be running the town again as in days of old, like the Hollywood blacklist you don't remember and the Watts rioting you do—it spreads, like blood in a swimming pool, till it occupies all the volume of the day. And then maybe some playful soul shows up with a bucketful of piranhas, dumps them in the pool, and right away they can taste the blood. They swim around looking for what's bleeding, but they don't find anything, all of them getting more and more crazy, till the craziness reaches a point. Which is when they begin to feed on each other."

Doc considered this for a bit. "What's in 'em lingonberries, Bigfoot?"

"It's like," Bigfoot had continued, "there's this evil subgod who rules over Southern California? who off and on will wake from his slumber and allow the dark forces that are always lying there just out of the sunlight to come forth?"

"Wow, and . . . and you've . . . seen him? This 'evil subgod,' maybe he . . . he talks to you?"

"Yes and he looks just like a *hippie pothead freak*! Something, huh?"

Wondering what this was about, Doc, trying to be helpful, said, "Well, what I've been noticing since Charlie Manson got popped is a lot less eye contact from the straight world. You folks all used to be like a crowd at the zoo—'Oh, look, the male one is carrying the baby and the female one is paying for the groceries,' sorta thing, but now it's like, 'Pretend they're not even there, 'cause maybe they'll mass murder our ass.'"

"It's all turned to sick fascination," opined Bigfoot, "and meantime the whole field of homicide's being stood on its ear—bye-bye Black Dahlia, rest in peace Tom Ince, yes we've seen the last of those good old-time L.A. murder mysteries I'm afraid. We've found the gateway to hell, and it's asking far too much of your L.A. civilian not to want to go crowding on through it, horny and giggling as always, looking for that latest thrill. Lots of overtime for me and the boys I guess, but it brings us all that much closer to the end of the world."

Bigfoot ran a deep scan of the place from the toilets in back out to the desert light of the street and lifted the Ralph's bag onto the table. "This Coy Harlingen matter. I didn't want to discuss it up in the office." He began to bring out ungainly wads of papers of different sizes, colors, and states of deterioration. "I pulled the tub on this expecting what we technically call zip shit. Imagine my surprise at finding how many of my colleagues, at how many far-flung outposts of law enforcement, not to mention levels of power, have had their lunchhooks all over it. Coy Harlingen not only used multiple aka's, he also had a number of offices running him, typically at the same time. Among which—I hope I don't shock or offend—have been unavoidably those elements who wouldn't mind if Coy really did end up under a granite slab with his final alias carved thereon."

"Coy's overdose, or whatever it was—there must be a lot of monthly IPRs on that by now. Any chance of having a look?"

"Except that Brother Noguchi's shop could never quite bring themselves to call it a homicide, so nobody was ever required to file any progress reports, intra-, extra-, non-, whatever. On the face of it, just one more OD, one less junkie, case cleared."

Once Doc would have said, "Well, that's that, can I go now?" But with this new fascist model Bigfoot, the one he'd recently found out maybe he couldn't trust after all, the old style of needling somehow wasn't as much fun anymore. "You mean it would be a routine case, except for all this paperwork," is what he said, carefully, "which even just eyeballing it does seem a little out of proportion. Like the one pink li'l DOA slip would've been enough."

"Ah, you noticed. It's certainly the kind of documentary attention dead folks don't see too much of. You would almost think Coy Harlingen was really alive someplace and kicking. Wouldn't you. Resurrected."

"So what have you found out?"

"Technically, Sportello, I am *not even aware this case exists*. Cool with you? Groovy? Why do you think we're down here and not upstairs?"

"Some Internal Affairs soap opera, I figure, which you're deperate to keep me away from. Now what could that be?"

"Fair enough. What I want to keep you away from is vast, Sportello, vast. On the other hand, if there is something trivial I can let you in on from time to time, why get too paranoid about it?" He rooted around in the Ralph's bag and found a long speckled box nearly full of three-by-five index cards. "Why, what have we here? Oh, but you know what these are."

"Field Interrogation Reports. Souvenirs of everybody you guys ever stopped and hassled. And this sure looks like a lot of them for one junkie saxophone player."

"Why don't you just flip through these quickly, see if there's anything that looks familiar."

"Evelyn Wood, don't fail me now." Doc began to run through the cards, trying to keep alert for one of Bigfoot's rude surprises. He had met a few close-up magicians and knew about the practice of "forcing" a card on a spectator. He saw no reason for Bigfoot to be above this kind of trickery.

And what do you know. What was this? Doc had nearly half a second to decide if the card he'd caught sight of was worth keeping from Bigfoot, and then he remembered that Bigfoot already knew which one it was. "Here," he said pointing. "I know I've seen that name someplace."

"Puck Beaverton," Bigfoot nodded, taking it out of the box. "Excellent choice. One of Mickey Wolfmann's jailbird praetorians. Let's see now." He pretended to read off the card. "Sheriff's people happen to run into him at the Venice home of the very dealer who sold Coy Harlingen the smack that killed him. Or didn't kill him, as the case may be." He pushed the FIR card across the Formica, and Doc scanned it doubtfully. "Subject, unemployed, claims to be a friend of Leonard Jermain Loosemeat, aka El Drano. 'I just came over to play a couple games of pool.' Subject seemed unusually nervous in Beaverton's company. That's it? What was Puck doing at Coy's dealer's place? Do you think."

Bigfoot shrugged. "Maybe there to buy?"

"Any record of him using?"

"Somebody'd have to look." Which must have sounded jive-ass even to Bigfoot, because he added, "Puck's file could be in storage by now, far, far away, someplace like Fontana or beyond. Unless . . ." A hustler's pause, as if a thought had just struck him.

"Let's hear it, Bigfoot."

"I seem to recall that some years ago, just before he went into Folsom, this Beaverton used to work for a loan shark downtown, named Adrian Prussia. And this dealer El Drano also happened to be one of Prussia's steady customers. Maybe Puck was there on his former employer's behalf."

Doc felt uneasy. His nose was beginning to run. "I remember Adrian Prussia from back when I had that skip-tracing job. Fuckin snake, man."

Bigfoot signaled the counterman. *"Chotto,* Kenichiro! *Dozo, motto panukeiku."*

"You got it, Lieutenant!"

"Not quite like my mother's, but still a real 'trip,'" Bigfoot confided, "though what I really go for here is the respect."

"Didn't get much of that from your mom, huh?"

Had Doc really said that or only thought it? He waited for Bigfoot to take offense, but the detective only went on, "You probably imagine I have a lot of status up in Robbery-Homicide. Who could blame you for thinking, man goes around like Prince Charles, like they're going to crown him chief any day . . . The reality, however . . ." He was shaking his head slowly, looking at Doc in this oddly beseeching way. "God help us all. Dentists on trampolines." But no, that wasn't it. Not exactly.

"Okay, Bigfoot," aware of another con job in progress, "I can tell you this—the other night, when we dropped Rudy Blatnoyd off in Bel Air, it was dark, he was giving all these directions, whole lotta turns, I don't think I could find the way back there even in daylight, or know how this connects to wherever you guys found the body, but it was about eleven P.M."—scribbling on a napkin—"and here's the address."

Bigfoot nodded. "That's just where we found the body. He was staying there as a houseguest, and this helps a little with the chronology. Thank you, Doc. Hair and drug-use issues notwithstanding, I've never thought of you as any less than professional."

"Don't get sentimental on me man, it fucks up your edge."

"I can be even more emotionally irresponsible than that," replied

Bigfoot. "Listen. There are certain polygraph keys on this case that if I told you what they were, then the only ones who'd know would be Homicide, the killer, and you."

"Good thing you're not telling me, then."

"Suppose I tell you anyway."

"Why should you?"

"Just so we know where we're 'at,' as you people say."

"You mean just so you'll have another reason to run me in. Thanks, Bigfoot. How about if I put my fingers in my ears and scream if you try to tell me?"

"You won't do that."

"Really?" Doc genuinely curious. "Why won't I?"

"Because you're one of the few hippie potheads in this town who appreciate the distinction between child*like* and child*ish*. Besides, this is right up your alley. Listen . . . we're officially calling it a fatal neck injury—don't . . . *do* that!—but more specifically, Dr. Blatnoyd had puncture wounds on his throat, consistent with bites from the canines of a midsize wild animal. That's what the coroner found. Keep it under your hat."

"Well now that's mighty weird, Bigfoot," Doc said slowly, "because Rudy Blatnoyd was one of the partners in a tax dodge that calls itself, get this, *Golden Fang* Enterprises. Huh? I don't suppose you had the SID test out those neck punctures for gold, or nothin like that?"

"I shouldn't think there'd be much trace. Gold is all but chemically inactive, as you might have learned in chemistry class if you hadn't been ditching it all the time to score dope."

"Wait, what happened to Locard's Exchange Principle, every contact leaves traces? it would sure be *ironic,* man, is all I'm saying, if it turned out Blatnoyd was bit to death by a golden fang. Or even better, like, *two* golden fangs."

"I don't . . ." Bigfoot tilting his head and hitting it like a swimmer trying to clear water from his ear, "see why . . . anything like that would be especially . . . material?"

"You mean why would the fangs have to be gold? Instead of like just some everyday werewolf fangs."

"Well . . . o . . . kay . . . ?"

"Because it's *the Golden Fang,* man."

"Yes yes the decedent's tax shelter or whatever. So what."

"No, not just a tax shelter, Bigfoot. Uh-uh. Much, much more, what you would call, vast."

"Oh. And this wouldn't," patiently enough, "just be some more of your paranoid hippie bullshit, would it, because frankly neither the Department nor, more importantly, I, have the time to waste on these pothead fantasy leads."

"Then you don't mind if I just keep lookin into it myself? I mean, there's no IA issues *here* I hope, no deliberate LAPD obstruction, nothin like that?"

"Everybody's time is precious," philosophized Bigfoot, reaching for his wallet, "in its own way."

Doc was parked down in Little Tokyo, so he walked Bigfoot to the corner of Third and San Pedro and peeled off there, flashing a peace sign. "Oh and Bigfoot."

"Uh-huh."

"Have the lab look for traces of copper."

"What?"

"Not the kind that goes stumbling all over the crime scene contaminating evidence—more like copper, the metal? See, gold teeth are never pure gold, dentists like to alloy it with copper? If you hadn't ditched forensics class to go steal hubcaps to plant on some innocent hippie, you might have known *that.*"

DOC CALLED CLANCY CHARLOCK where she tended bar, over in Inglewood. "Hi, how'd it work out with those two bikers the other night?"

"They did a lot of reds and fell asleep, thanks. Listen, have you seen

Boris Spivey lately?" There was a skip, not quite a tremor, in her voice. It could've been from smoking.

"That's just what I was gonna ask you! ESP, man!"

"Because it turns out Boris has disappeared. His place is empty, all his stuff is gone, nobody at Knucklehead Jack's has seen him."

Doc located a Kool, went to light it, then just sat staring at it instead. Could Bigfoot be right? Was Doc the kiss of death, laying bad karma on everybody he touched?

"Did you scare him or something?" Now she sounded pissed off.

"How would I do that when I can't reach higher than his knee? Maybe he owes money, maybe it's old-lady problems—do you know her, by the way? Dawnette? from Pico Rivera?"

"Actually, I tried to call her, but she seems to be missing too."

"Think they're together?"

"You have me confused with Ann Landers. What did you want with Boris?"

"The guy I'm really looking for is Puck Beaverton, and I thought Boris might've had some line on his whereabouts."

"*That* asshole."

"Almost sounds like you've . . . dated ol' Puck."

"Both him and his roommate, Einar. Don't ask me to go into details. The boys have a slightly different idea about what a three-way is. I ended up feeling, let's say, underused, and made the mistake of telling them so. Puck and Einar just murmured together for a while, and then they kicked me out. Four A.M. in West Hollywood."

"I didn't mean to—"

"Reawaken painful memories, 'course not, it's okay, just that there's bein handled and bein handled, and this wasn't even fun."

"Boris mentioned that Puck might've been headed for Vegas, and I was just trying to narrow that down a little."

"If Einar's with him, they'll be looking for girls to treat like shit, preferably ones who don't mind too much. Happy hunting."

"Maybe some tropical evening, we could play some canasta."

"Sure, bring a friend."

WAITING AT THE OFFICE when Doc got back from lunch at Wavos was a disheveled girl in a tiny skirt, whose eyes after the style of the times were hugely made up not only with mascara but also with liquid liner and shadow almost the color of the smoke from a faulty head gasket, suggesting to Doc as always a deep, unreachable innocence, all of which sent the throbbing idle of his lecherousness into overdrive.

"Trillium Fortnight," she introduced herself. "They said you could help me."

"They did, eh," suavely waving half a pack of Kools at her, which she declined. "And how many of them were there?"

"Oh, I'm sorry. Dawnette and Boris. They said—"

"Whoa." Dawnette and Boris. "How long ago was this?"

"About a week."

"You . . . wouldn't know where they are now."

She shook her head, it seemed to Doc sadly. "Nobody does."

"But you talked to them?"

"On the phone. They thought somebody was listening in, so they didn't stay on long."

"Did it sound like a local call? You know, like sometimes—"

"It sounded like they were out on the road, a pay phone on a frontage road off some interstate."

"You could hear that?"

She shrugged. "It was the way the voices combined." Doc must have been giving her a peculiar look. "Not 'voices' voices. Like parts in a musical piece?"

"Serenade for Peterbilt Rig and VW Bus," Doc guessed.

"Actually, Kenworth and Econoline van, plus a street hemi, a Harley, and some miscellaneous clunkers." This sensitivity of ear, she went on to explain, had proved useful both in her day job, teaching music theory at UCLA, and also for moonlighting as a woodwind specialist in early-music ensemble gigs. "Anything from a double-quint pommer down to a sopranino shawm, I'm your person."

Doc had a hardon, and his nose was running. That old cootie food had found him again. Trillium, on the other hand, had dropped into a peculiar silence which, if he'd been in his right mind, he would have recognized as the some-other-guy blues. He found a piece of paper from a yellow legal pad with a long shopping list of junk-food items on it in pencil, and rolled it into the typewriter, just to keep busy.

"So . . . how did Boris and Dawnette think I could help you?"

"Someone I know has disappeared, and I need . . . I'd like to find out what happened to him."

Doc typed *lucky fellow.* "We could start with name and last known address."

"His name is Puck. . . ."

"Puck." Uh, huh.

"Puck Beaverton . . . last address was in West Hollywood, but I'm not sure of the street. . . ."

Now, two or three angles were occurring to Doc at the same time, displaying themselves in a sort of hyperdimensional pattern across the piece of blank office wall he often used for these exercises. Trillium here might turn out to be some kind of hired heat herself, chasing down Puck on behalf of whoever'd made him afraid enough to split town. Of course, Puck could always be an ancient-music lover and running some kind of illicit market in hot sopranino shawms. Or, much more annoyingly, Trillium might have been deep *into some number* with Puck and unable to let it go. Doc had learned by now not to second-guess anybody's choice of romantic object, but who the hell was supposed to be looking out for this kid? How much did she know about her dream boy's job history? about Einar? Or had she actually, this smoggy-eyed innocent, found the Puck & Einar Experience trippy in a way Clancy hadn't? And was there any choice, for the moment, but to dummy up about all this? It would've almost been more comforting to think of her as a contract killer.

"Boris gave me an address in Las Vegas," Trillium said.

"You want me to what—check it out?"

"I want you to come along with me to Vegas and help me find him."

Sucker. Sap. And other old-movie terms that were sure to occur to Doc in a minute. He saw the hustle in progress but as usual was thinking with his dick. Not to mention more sentimentally. Whatever the difference was. "Sure thing," he said. "Do you happen to have a picture of this gent?"

Did she. Out of her shoulder bag, she fished one of those plastic accordion things with room for—he lost count—maybe a hundred snapshots of Puck and Trillium, walking on the beach in the sunset, dancing at different mass outdoor gatherings, playing volleyball, running in and out of the surf—it looked like a personals ad in the *L.A. Free Press*, only longer and with pictures. Doc noticed that Puck had his head shaved and tattooed with a swastika, which might help with ID'ing him, if and when. Also, in at least half the snapshots was a third presence, eyes set close together, one side of his upper lip lifted in discontent, managing usually to squeeze in between Trillium and Puck.

"And this would be . . ."

"Einar. An associate of Puck's, they met in the penitentiary."

"All right if I take a couple of these, just to show around?"

"Not at all. When can we leave?"

"Anytime. There's a shuttle flight out of West Imperial, if that's cool."

"Beyond cool," she said. "Driving freaks me out."

ACTUALLY, IT WAS FLYING that freaked Doc out, but he kept forgetting why, and didn't remember this time till the plane was touching down at McCarran. He briefly considered freaking out anyway, just to keep in practice, but then Trillium might wonder why, which could be a hassle to explain, and besides the moment had passed.

After renting a bright red '69 Camaro, they went looking for someplace to stay, preferably close to the airport, because Doc was hoping for a quick in and out, heading east on Sunset Road to Boulder Highway and cruising a neighborhood of low-end motels and locals' casinos and bars with live rock 'n' roll before settling on Ghostflower Court, a collection of bungalows dating from the fifties. They checked into a two-room unit in back with a shake roof—a little run-down maybe, but spacious and comfortable inside, with a fridge, hot plate, air-conditioning, cable TV and two king-size water beds with leopard-print sheets. "Far out," said Doc, "I wonder if these vibrate." They didn't. "Bummer."

The address Boris had given Trillium was in a neglected trapezoid of streets east of the Strip, between Sahara and Downtown. The street floor was occupied by an antiques seller who introduced himself as Delwyn Quight. "Most of it's pawnshop consignments, but have a look, half of what's here I don't even know about." He produced a Japanese stash box of black lacquer and mother-of-pearl in a crane-and-willow motif and full of prerolled joints, lit one up, and they passed it around.

"Lot of Wild West stuff here," it seemed to Doc. He remembered Bigfoot Bjornsen and his hundred pounds of barbed wire. "You got somethin I could bring a bobwire collector? Not a lot understand, maybe a small li'l piece . . ."

"Just sold off the end of my last spool, and it's all Japanese repros now anyway. But here, you might want to have a look at this—came in yesterday, direct from an archaeological dig in Tombstone."

It was an ordinary-looking coffee mug with a third of the top covered over except for a small mouth-hole, intended to keep the mustache of the drinker from getting soaked. The cup was decorated on one side with a vivid green saguaro cactus and on the other with a pair of crossed Buntline Specials above the word WYATT in that old-time wanted-poster typeface.

"Trippy," Doc said, "how much?"

"I might let it go for a thousand."

"A thousand what?"

"Please. This belonged to Marshal Earp himself."

"I was thinking more like two bucks?"

They began to discuss this and kept wandering from the subject till Doc noticed something over in the corner, how would you put it, *glowing*, sort of. "Hey, what's this?" What it was was a necktie covered with thousands, or hundreds, of magenta and green sequins in a piano-keyboard pattern and accented tastefully all around the edges with rhinestones.

"Now that," Quight said, "belonged to Liberace—during one of his shows at the Riviera, while playing Chopin's Grande Valse Brillante with one hand, Lee took this tie off with the other and flung it into the audience. Autographed on the back, see?"

Doc tried it on, looked at it in the mirror for a while and how it caught the light and so forth. Quight, still trying to sell the mustache cup, offered to throw the tie in too, and they finally settled on ten dollars for both items. "This always happens," the dealer banging his head softly but expressively against a seed-feed-and-fertilizer clerk's desk, circa 1880, "I'm smoking myself out of business."

"The other thing," Doc said, "we almost forgot is, is you have tenants upstairs, right?"

"Not at the moment, they moved out last week." He sighed. "Puck and Einar. A lot of people come and go in this neighborhood, but they were, what's the word—special."

"Did he—did they say where they were going?" Trillium's voice sliding into a darker register Doc was coming to recognize.

"Not really. No one ever does, of course."

"Anybody else been by looking for them?"

"A couple of gentlemen from the FBI, actually." Quight looked through the contents of a decorative ashtray from the Sands, said to have been thrown up into once by Joey Bishop, and located a business card, with HUGO BORDERLINE, SPECIAL AGENT printed down in the corner, and a local phone number and extension in ballpoint.

"Shit," reflected Doc. And had the Special Agent brought his running mate Flatweed along as well, a kind of government busybody twofer?

and if so, why weren't they back in L.A. setting spade revolutionaries at each other's throats? Las Vegas would seem to offer slim pickings in that direction, unless, like, the Black Nationalist story had been a front all along for something else, something aimed, let's say, at Organized Crime, which has said to own the Vegas casinos and pretty much to run the place these days. But wait—these feds had been in here inquiring after Puck, and what could Puck's connection be to any of that? Doc felt a suspicion growing, paranoid as the rapid heartbeat of a midnight awakening, that Puck's fate was included in Mickey's, and the question to be asking was what kind of business Mickey might've been doing with the Mob—or worse, with the FBI.

"During your chat—was there anything maybe you didn't share with them?"

"I did think about recommending a bar called Curly's out on Rampart, but the more they went on, the less it seemed somehow like their sort of place."

"This was, like, a Puck-and-Einar hangout?"

"Depending on the music policy week to week, that was the impression I got."

"Let me guess. Country and western."

"Broadway show tunes," Trillium said quietly.

"And how," nodded Quight.

"Puck used to do Ethel Merman," she recalled.

"They both did. They'd roll in at four A.M. singing 'There's No Business Like Show Business.' You could hear it coming from blocks away, slowly getting louder? Nobody ever complained."

Back in the car, Doc said, "Come on, I'll buy you a enchilada."

They drove toward a spectacular desert sunset and turned up South Main. El Sombrero looked to be a bit of a wait, with a line of hungry folks spilling out the door of the world-renowned taquería and well down the street, drooling on the sidewalk and so forth. Doc drove on past, and then around a couple more corners to the neon grandiosities of Tex-Mecca, unknown to guidebooks but for a network of hungry dopers and petty criminals all along the U.S.-Mexican border an object of pilgrimage.

Two steps in the door of which, who did Doc catch sight of but FBI Special Agents Borderline and Flatweed, both in the synchronized act of stuffing dimly perplexed Anglo faces with the house's celebrated Giant Burrito Special. Well, Doc supposed, the FBI did have to eat someplace. He searched his media memory for instances of Inspector Lewis Erskine ever eating anything, and came up blank. Before the brown-suited tools of justice recognized him, Doc steered Trillium quickly to a corner table out of their line of sight and hid behind a menu, resolved that not even a downer like feds in the area would get in the way of his appetite.

A waitress came over, and they ordered a lengthy combination of enchiladas, tacos, burritos, tostadas, and tamales for two called El Atómico, whose entry on the menu carried a footnote disclaiming legal responsibility.

"Do you know those men over there?" Trillium said. "They seem to know you."

Doc leaned to where he could see. The two agents, now heading out the door, kept glaring back his way.

"It's those federals that Quight was talking about."

"Is it something to do with Puck? Do you think he's in trouble with the FBI?"

"Okay, you knew he was a personal bodyguard of Mickey Wolf-mann's, right? and now Mickey is a possible kidnap. So they might have a couple of routine questions for Puck, would be all."

"He can't go back to prison, Doc. It would kill him."

She had that lovelorn look on her face. Doc had already deduced that he could be Mick Jagger, pay fees in the range of six figures per fleeting smile, even give up watching the Lakers, and nothing he did would make the least impression—for this chick it was Puck Beaverton or nobody. Not the first time Doc had run into girl-of-his-dreams unavailability. The thing right now was to be professional if not groovy and try to put her mind at rest.

"So tell me, Trillium—how did you two kids meet?"

Bless her, she thought he really wanted to know. "Well, at UCLA, as it turns out, in Pauley Pavilion."

"No kidding, hey, weren't those guys incredible last season? I'm sure gonna miss Kareem and Lucius—"

No, actually, not basketball. The L.A. Philharmonic also happened to play at Pauley Pavilion off and on, a cross-cultural music series with guest artists like Frank Zappa, and sometimes there'd be a last-minute opening for a local reedperson. One afternoon Trillium showed up at a rehearsal with an English horn and feelings of skepticism about the work in question, somebody's Symphonic Poem for Surf Band and Orchestra, featuring the Boards. Puck happened to be working security for the band. He and Trillium met back in one of the locker rooms, where people kept running in and out during breaks to light up or snort coke. She was bent over a sink, looking down into a compact mirror, felt someone close behind her, and there a little warped through a set of coke lines came looming Puck's face. He was gazing at her ass in a kind of morose fatality. Before Trillium knew what was happening she found herself in the back seat of a stolen '62 Bonneville parked in a cul-de-sac off Sunset, being seen to California Department of Corrections style. "Chicks say they don't like it this way," Puck explained later, when she had a minute to breathe, "and then before you know it they're back again, begging. With me it's just what I got used to."

"Are you apologizing?"

"I don't think so."

He was right about the begging, though. She found herself carrying rolls of coins for pay phones because she never knew at what odd moment of the day the longing would seize hold of her—between freeway exits miles away from his place in West Hollywood, in the produce section of the Safeway, during some fugue for woodwinds, all at once this humiliating heat would envelop her, and there was nothing she could think of to do but call him. He didn't always answer the phone. Once or twice she went crazy and parked outside his place, and waited, for hours, in fact overnight, till he came out, and by then, afraid of his anger, which was unpredictable both as to when and how dangerous, reluctant to face him, she followed him instead out to wherever he was working. And waited. And would fall asleep. And be awakened by the police telling her she had to move on.

"So I said, 'Puck, it's all right, I won't do anything violent, I just want to know who she is,' and Puck started to laugh and wouldn't tell me. But that was around the time I found out about Einar, and one day I was coming out of a rehearsal at the Shrine Auditorium obsessing about this particular B-flat, and there was Einar with all these Hawaiian orchids and the sweetest look on his face, and it was at least a month before he admitted he'd worked his way like a pickpocket through the crowd at a debutante ball in the Ambassador and stolen the corsages right off people's gowns. . . ."

Being the continuation of a long story Doc had forgotten, or maybe missed, the beginning of.

"I don't know why I'm telling you all this."

Doc didn't either, though he wished he had a small aggravation fee for each time somebody had spilled more than they meant to and then said they didn't know why. Sortilège, who liked finding new uses for the term "Beyond," thought this was a form of grace and that he should just accept it, because at any instant it could go away as easily as it came.

According to Trillium, Puck and Einar had met in the license-plate shop at Folsom. Sex immediately became an issue, and the boys were soon known for their ill-tempered bickering, on and on about the age-old question *¿quién es más macho?* Numberless cartons of smokes were wagered and lost all up and down the block over how long the arrangement would survive, and to everybody's surprise it outlasted both their sentences. One fine day, as the Chiffons like to put it, there they were, domiciled in West Hollywood, south of Santa Monica Boulevard, in a courtyard complex with more subtropical shrubbery than anybody could remember what half of it was, and throwing so much shade that you could lie out by the pool all day and never lose your prison pallor. . . .

"Wow Trillium, what happened to our food man, it's taking them an awful long time to bring it."

"We ate it already?"

"What. Did the check come? Who sprang for it?"

"Can't remember."

They headed out to Curly's. By the time they got there, Doc had decided he wasn't going to drive in Las Vegas any more than he had to. Everybody here drove around like a dedicated loser, expecting moment to moment to get into an accident. Doc could relate to this—it was like the beach, where you lived in a climate of unquestioning hippie belief, pretending to trust everybody while always expecting to be sold out—but he didn't have to enjoy that either, especially.

Curly's had once been a crossroads saloon, and reminded Doc of Knucklehead Jack's back in L.A., except for the slot machines in every plausible piece of floor space. The band was playing covers of old Ernest Tubb, Jim Reeves, and Webb Pierce tunes, so Doc guessed Puck and Einar might not be in tonight.

Trillium had a sort of feverish look. Doc was starting to think there was some strange vibe about her, some tattoo reading Come On In, Darlin', invisible to all but the larger, more brutal types of individual. She may've been aware of this herself, while at the same time denying it. Howsoever, over strolled this towering party in a black cowboy hat who without so much as a nod to Doc took Trillium by the hair and one bare thigh, lifted her courteously enough off the barstool and began Texas-two-stepping her away. You would've thought at least she'd scream in protest. But she only managed to whisper to Doc on the way past, "I'll see what I can find out." Doc wasn't sure but thought she was already smiling.

"You betcha," he muttered, shaking his head slowly at the longneck in front of him and wondering how John Garfield would've dealt with the situation.

"You mustn't judge Osgood too harshly," advised a voice to which Time, if it had not exactly been kind, had at least contributed some texture. "The man is a natural-born pussy hound, and there ain't a woman breathing between here and Lake Mead don't know that by now."

"Thanks, that's good to hear." Doc looked over to find an elfin geezer in a hat even bigger than Osgood's, waggling an empty beer bottle. "Sure thing." Doc went to signal the barkeep, who, blessed with extrasensory gifts, had already placed two more bottles on the bar. "All I came in for tonight," Doc pretended to sigh, "really, was to see this fella owes me some money. The ol' lady there thought I was invitin her out for a night on the town. Meantime there's the rent coming due and so forth."

"Damn," said the oldster, introducing himself as Ev, "time was a man'd sooner dry up and blow away than renege on his debts. There's a lot of deadbeats come in this place, maybe I even know the one you want."

"Somebody said he's a semiregular here. Puck Beaverton?"

A mirthless cackle which went on longer than Doc felt it should have. "Good luck with the landlord, young fella! that crazy Puck owes everybody in town and never paid a cent back that I ever heard of."

"Where's he work? Maybe I should go there and visit him."

"Puck's basically a slot hustler, him and his partner, this is the impression I get, though it ain't like we're none of us real ace buddies. The little one, Einar, has these hypersensitive hands you find in rare cases that can feel through the lever, feel the exact point where each of them reels lets go one by one, he can fine-tune the amount of spin onto each reel, get whichever symbol he wants to stop exactly at the payline. I seen him do it. Classy work."

"What about Puck?"

"Sooner or later, the house security gets on to Einar, so there's no more point him trying to collect his winnings. Puck's job is to wait nearby, playing some nickel machine, till Einar hits on his—then Einar disappears while Puck steps over and claims the jackpot."

"But then pretty soon they must get on to Puck."

"Right. Which is why they both long ago got eighty-sixed from the

Downtown and Strip casinos, so if you're lookin to find Puck, you'll want to check some local rooms, like out along Boulder Highway. The Nine of Diamonds comes to mind."

Trillium came back with a few buttons loose, an unidentified wet patch on her little skirt, and a lack of focus to her gaze. Osgood was out on the floor now with a blonde in Levi's and a cowgirl hat, and a live band was now playing "Wabash Cannonball" with psychedelic steel-guitar licks now and then. "Having a good time, Honeybunch?" Doc inquired as cheerfully as possible.

"Yes and no," in a chastened voice which despite himself he found erotic. "Buy me a beer?"

She drank in silence till Doc said, "Well! and what's 'at there Osgood got to say for himself tonight?"

"I feel kind of stupid, Doc. I should never have brought Puck's name up."

"He owes Osgood money, too, I'll bet."

"Yes, and now Osgood is all upset. He's not really as insensitive as he looks."

"He didn't happen to share any thoughts on Puck's whereabouts?"

"North Las Vegas. That's as close as he got. I don't think he knows the address, or he would have gone there by now."

"And that would have made the papers."

On the way out, they were accosted by Ev. "Leavin so early? Merle usually comes in and does a set around midnight when he's in town."

"Merle Haggard's in town?"

"No, but that's no reason to leave." Doc blinked a couple of times, bought the old-timer a Ramos gin fizz, and left anyway.

Out in the parking lot, Doc noticed a Cadillac of a certain length whose arrangement of dings seemed familiar.

"Hey Doc! I thought that was you."

"Is this another of them strange and weird coincidences, Tito, or do I have to really start getting paranoid?"

"I told you we were gonna be in Vegas. Inez is off at a show, and I'm picking up some change. You should see the way some of these guys tip, I already made more on my vacation here than a whole year back in L.A."

"And no, uh"—Doc made dice-rattling motions—"like under the spell of Vegas or nothin."

"Some spell. Look at this place. How real can any of this be? how can you take it seriously?"

"You're a fuckin gambling addict," announced an enormous voice from somewhere inside the limo, "you can't take it any other way."

"My brother-in-law Adolfo," Tito frowning. "Can't shake him. Ain't a buck comes in he don't snatch and grab it before I can."

"It's in escrow," explained Adolfo, who it turned out had been commissioned by Inez to ride along in the limo and keep Tito out of trouble.

"Lowlife Escrow Services Inc.," Tito muttered.

Trillium, appearing a litle distracted, had decided to go back to the room and get some sleep, so she took the Camaro, and Doc joined Tito and Adolfo in the limo.

"You know a place called the Nine of Diamonds, out on Boulder Highway?" Doc said.

"Sure," Tito said. "You mind if I come inside with you, just wander around a little, maybe hit the buffets, catch some of the show?"

"Sound a li'l eager there, Tito."

"Yeah, you're supposed to be kicking," Adolfo put in.

"Homeopathic doses, you guys," Tito protested.

According to Bigfoot Bjornsen, for whom this piece of western trivia had won him many a bar bet, the nine of diamonds had been the fifth card in Wild Bill Hickok's last poker hand, along with the black aces and eights. The parking lot was full of pickups with contractors' racks on them and Ford Rancheros with hay debris in the bed, ancient T-Birds and Chevy Nomads with the chrome strips long torn away, leaving only lines of rusty streaks and weld spots. The lighted marquee out front, a *Jetsons*-style polygon, mentioned an appearance tonight by a band called Carmine & the Cal-Zones.

The customers inside didn't seem to be from too far out of town, so the action was less compromised by the unthinking pursuit of "fun" as defined over on the Strip. Players here tended to play for the money, going about their business hopeful or desperate, loaded or on the natch, scientifically or gripped in superstitions so exotic they couldn't be readily explained, and somewhere out of the light the landlord, the finance company, the loan-shark community sat invisible and unspeaking, tapping feet in expensive shoes, weighing options for punishment, leniency—even, rarely, mercy.

Carmine was a longhaired lounge tenor with a Les Paul model Gibson that he may have had a few lessons on but tended to use more as a prop, often including tommy-gun gestures, while the other Cal-Zones assumed standard rock-quartet parts. A pair of cupcakes in red vinyl minidresses, black fishnet hose, and lacquered hair sang backup while doing white-chick time steps. As Doc made his way onto the casino floor, the group were performing their latest release,

JUST THE LASAGNA (semi–bossa nova)

Izzit some U, FO?
        (No, no-no!)
Maybe it's—wait, I know! it's
Just the Lasa-gna! [*Rhythm-guitar fill*]
Just the La-sa-hah-gna . . .
        (Just-the-La-sa-gna),
Out of the blue, it came,
        (Blue, it came)
Nobody knew, its name, just
"The Lasagna" . . .
Just—"The La-sagna,"
        (Just "Th' La—")
            Oh, wo, Lo-

Zon-yaaah!
Who could ever get be-
-yond ya,
Ya just sit there goin'
"Nyah, nyah!"
Whoo! Lasagna, shame
On ya! Dog-
Gone ya!

How come you're ask-in me,
                    (Ask-in me)
                         —Hey,

Ain't no big mys-tery, it's
Just th' La-sagna—
Or so they say . . . (oh,
Wo wo-oh wo)
I'm uh-under your spell, L-
A-S-A, G-N-A!

Doc spent a while chatting up change girls, bartenders, dealers and pit bosses, ladies of the evening and ladies of the later shifts, including a young woman in a wine-colored velvet minidress, who finally informed him, "Everybody knows that Puck used to work for Mickey. Nobody here's going to rat him out, especially not to a stranger, nothing personal."

A house comic, working the audience, pilot lights of malice flickering in his eyes, approached. "Evening, Zirconia, see you made bail again, who's this? Having a good time, sir? He's going, 'What planet is this? Where'd I leave the UFO?' Nah, seriously, pal, you're okay, the hair—I just adore it, it's stunning. See me in the garage later, you can buff my car. . . ."

The quipster, along with Zirconia, moved on, nearly colliding with Tito, who arrived in some agitation. "Doc! Doc! You gotta watch this guy work, he's a true genius. Come on, have a look." He led Doc in a complicated path through the casino, toward the deeper regions slotplayers avoid in the belief that machines closer to the street pay off better, till they finally rounded a corner into a remote corridor of slots and Tito said, "There."

From Tito's mental state, the least Doc had expected was an acid-trip glow surrounding the machine, but all he saw really was one more old-time unit with a faded and scuffed image from the fifties of a smiling cowgirl, presentable after the fashion of those times—oversize tits for example, plus short permed hair and bright lipstick. A long line of half-dollars went disappearing down a chute of yellowing plastic, the milling around the edges of the coins acting like gear teeth, causing each of the dozens of shining John F. Kennedy heads to rotate slowly as they jittered away down the shallow incline, to be gobbled one after another into the indifferent maw of Las Vegas. The player at the machine had his face turned away, and Doc at first noticed only the fine careful attention to how he was pulling the lever, another customer intent not so much on Fun as paying down a grocery tab somewhere in the neighborhood, until, quickly scanning the other slots nearby, Doc recognized the swastikaed head of Puck Beaverton, who was busy pretending to play a nickel machine. That would make the "genius" working the other machine Puck's running mate Einar.

No time like the present. Doc, shifting into a word-with-you-my-man mode, was just about to step forward when several kinds of hell broke loose. To a military fanfare heavy on the bass horns, plus train whistles, fire sirens, and canned athletic-stadium cheering, a quantity of JFK half-dollars began to vomit out of the machine in a huge parabolic torrent, falling onto the carpeting in a growing heap. Einar nodded and stepped away and—had Doc blinked or something?—just like that disappeared. Puck gave one last yank to the handle on his nickel machine and got up and headed over to claim the jackpot, when suddenly the laws of chance, deciding on a classic fuck-you, instructed Puck's nickel machine *also* to hit, with even more noise than the first, and there stood Puck, paralyzed between the two winning machines, and here on the run came a delegation of casino personnel to confirm and certify the two happy jackpot winners, already one short. At which point Puck, as if allergic to dilemmas, broke for the nearest exit, screaming.

With nobody else around any more plausible than Doc and Tito to step in, it took them only a tenth of a second to agree that Tito should have the jackpot from the half-dollar machine, and Doc, not being greedy, would claim what looked by now to be several cubic feet of nickels.

Adolfo took charge of Tito's, or actually Einar's, winnings, and they all drove back to Ghostflower Court, where Doc found Trillium asleep on one of the water beds. He headed for the other one and must have made it.

Next thing he knew it seemed to be early afternoon and Trillium wasn't there. He looked out the window and saw that the Camaro wasn't either. He wandered out through the desert breeze to a little store down the highway and bought smokes and several containers of coffee and some Ding Dongs for breakfast. When he got back, he flipped on the TV and watched *Monkees* reruns till the local news came on. The guest today was a visiting Marxist economist from one of the Warsaw Pact nations, who appeared to be in the middle of a nervous breakdown. "Las Vegas," he tried to explain, "it sits out here in middle of desert, produces no tangible goods, money flows in, money flows out, nothing is produced. This place should not, according to theory, even exist, let alone prosper as it does. I feel my whole life has been based on illusory premises. I have lost reality. Can you tell me, please, where is reality?" The interviewer looked uncomfortable and tried to change the subject to Elvis Presley.

As it was getting dark, Trillium finally showed up. "Please don't get angry."

"Haven't been angry since what's-his-name missed that foul shot." He searched his memory. "Name escapes me, right off hand. . . . Oh well. Where've you been?" From the look on her face and the way she'd walked in—the self-conscious gait of a punk on an exercise yard—he had an idea.

"I know I should have told you, but I wanted to see him first. I had his phone number all the time—sorry—and just kept calling and calling till finally he answered." She had showed up close to dawn at the address Puck gave her, an apartment over a garage in North Las Vegas, next to a vacant lot full of brittlebush. The boys were drinking beer and as usual discussing their machismo rankings, not to mention who'd sing melody and who harmony on "Wunderbar," from *Kiss Me, Kate.*

Trillium either grew a little dim on the details or wasn't into reminiscing, though Doc gathered that the reunion had gone on for some while, with Einar considerably stepping out at some point to make a beer run down the boulevard.

"You didn't happen to mention to Puck I'm looking for a quick word, nothin like 'at?"

"In fact, I had to go through a lengthy routine to convince him you weren't a hit man."

"We can meet wherever he feels safe."

"He suggested a casino in North Las Vegas called the Kismet Lounge. He and Einar don't like to show up till after midnight."

"You gonna be there, or . . ."

"Easier if I could take the car, actually. Run a few errands?"

Doc found a joint and lit it and called up Tito, who was just about to go to work. "You got time to run me up to North Vegas later tonight?"

"No prob-limo, as we say in the business—Inez likes to stay through the last show anyway. She can't get enough of that Jonathan Frid."

"What," Doc blinking, "Barnabas? the vampire guy on *Dark Shadows?*"

"He's got a lounge act right here on the Strip, Doc. Everybody in the business loves him—Frank, Dean, Sammy—at least one of them's in the audience every night."

"Ain't just Inez," Adolfo put in on the extension, "your kids carry lunch boxes with that guy's face on 'em, too."

"Gee, what kind of material's he sing?" Doc wondered.

"Seems partial to Dietz & Schwartz," Tito said. "His closing number is always 'Haunted Heart.'"

"He also does Elvis," added Adolfo, "singing 'Viva Las Vegas.'"

"I gave him a ride once or twice, he tips good."

Trillium sprang for dinner at one of the casino buffets over on the Strip—her idea of diplomacy, though she was clearly not in a mood to discuss anything with Doc, especially not Puck.

"You look totally gaga," he told her anyway. She smiled vaguely and gestured silently for a minute and a half with a giant shrimp as if she were conducting a chamber orchestra. Doc cupped his hand next to his ear. "Do I hear . . . wedding bells?"

"I'll be back." She slipped out of the booth and headed for the ladies' lounge, where Doc recalled there were at least as many pay phones as toilets. She was back within the hour. Doc had basically been eating. "Ever notice," she said to nobody in particular, "how there's something erotic about pay phones?"

"Why don't you drop me off at the motel, maybe I'll catch you later in North Vegas." Or maybe not.

FOURTEEN

ACCORDING TO TITO, THE KISMET, BUILT JUST AFTER WWII, had represented something of a gamble that the city of North Las Vegas was about to be the wave of the future. Instead, everything moved southward, and Las Vegas Boulevard South entered legend as the Strip, and places like the Kismet languished.

Heading up North Las Vegas Boulevard, away from the unremitting storm of light, episodes of darkness began to occur at last, like night breezes off the desert. Parked trailers and little lumberyards and air-conditioning shops went drafting by. The glow in the sky over Las Vegas withdrew, as if into a separate "page right out of history," as the Flintstones might say. Ahead presently at the roadside, much dimmer than anything to the south, a structure of lights appeared.

"Place is a dump, man." Tito wheeled into the entrance and under a weathered porte cochere. Nobody was there to notice let alone greet them, in the reduced light. Once there must have been thousands of lights, incandescent, neon and fluorescent, all over the place, but these days only a few of them were lit, because the present owners couldn't afford the electric bills anymore, several amateur gaffers, sad to say, having already been fulminated trying to bootleg power in off the municipal lines.

"We'll be back in a couple hours," Tito said. "Try not to get your ass shot at too much, okay? You bring enough to play with? Here, Adolfo, give him a black."

"That's a hundred dollars, I can't—"

"Please," Tito said. "I'll get a secondhand kick."

Adolfo handed over a chip. "It's what they tip with here," he shrugged. "We don't even know how many of these we got by now. It's fuckin crazy."

Doc got out and strolled under a Byzantine archway and into the seedy vastness of the main gaming floor, dominated by a ruinous chandelier draped above the tables and cages and pits, disintegrating, ghostly, huge, and, if it had feelings, likely resentful—its lightbulbs long burned out and unreplaced, crystal lusters falling off unexpectedly into cowboy hatbrims, people's drinks, and spinning roulette wheels, where they bounced with a hard-edged jingling through their own dramas of luck and loss. Everything in the room was lopsided one way or another. The ancient bearings on the roulette wheels made them spin erratically faster and slower. The classic three-reel slots, set long ago to payout percentages unknown south of Bonanza Road and perhaps to the world, had since each drifted in its own way, like small-town businessfolks, toward openhanded generosity or tightfisted meanness. The carpets, deep royal purple, had been retextured over the years with a million cigarette burns, each fusing the synthetic nap to a single tiny smear of plastic. The all-over effect was of wind on the surface of a lake. The level of the main floor was ten feet below that of the desert outside, providing natural insulation, so the chill in this vast indeterminate space wasn't all from air-conditioning, which had been set on low in any case to save current.

Grill cooks, tire salesmen, house framers, eye doctors, stickmen and change girls and other black-and-whites off shift from ritzier rooms where they weren't allowed to play, old horsemen fallen on faster and more crowded times, their feelings of custody now transferred to F-100s and Chevy Apaches, were ranged sparsely in the softly shadowed light, weaving in place as if trying to stay alert. Drinks here weren't free, but by way of real-life neighborhood civility they were cheap enough.

Doc had a grapefruit margarita and then, dropping into mental cruising gear, began to drift through the immense casino, scanning for Puck and Einar. At some point a presentable young lady in a paisley Qiana minidress and white plastic boots came up and introduced herself as Lark.

"And without meanin to pry or nothin, I notice you're not playing, just sort of wandering around, meanin you're either some deep guy, mysterious master of intrigue, or one more jaded sharp looking for a bargain."

"Hey, maybe I'm the Mob."

"Wrong shoes. Give me some credit, for goodness' sakes. I'd say L.A., and like every other tripper in from L.A., all you think you want to do is bet the Mickey book."

"The, uh . . . ?"

Lark explained that the Kismet offered a kind of sports book where you could bet on the news of the day, such as the recent mysterious disappearance of construction mogul Mickey Wolfmann. "Mickey enjoys some name recognition in this town, so for a limited time we've been offering even money on Dead or Alive or, as we like to call it, Pass or Don't Pass."

Doc shrugged. "Readin me like the *Herald-Examiner,* Lark. There just comes a time for the dedicated player when the NCAA don't quite do it no more."

"Come on." Motioning with her head. "I bring you back there as a guest, I get a commission."

The Kismet race and sports-book area had its own cocktail lounge, furnished in shades of purple Formica that glittered with metal-flake accents and made Doc feel right at home. They found a table and ordered frozen mai tais.

Doc knew the lilt and tessitura of most every sad song in the profession but still liked to take a glance at the sheet music. Seems Lark had grown up in La Vergne, Tennessee, outside Nashville. Besides having the same initials, La Vergne was also at the exact same latitude as

Las Vegas. "Well actually the same as Henderson, but that's where I live now anyway, me and my boyfriend. He's a professor at UNLV? And he says when Americans move any distance, they stick to lines of latitude. So it was like fate for me, I was always supposed to head due west. The second I saw Hoover Dam, I knew for the first time that I was really home."

"Ever done any pickin or singin, Lark?"

"You mean living that close to Nashville why didn't I want to go into music. You try it, darlin. Your feet'll get mighty tired waitin in *that* line." But Doc noted an evasive sparkle in her eyes.

"Not another assassination trifecta, I hope." This gent looked like a banker in an old movie, wearing a bespoke suit with one button open on each sleeve just to let you know it. Lark introduced him as Fabian Fazzo.

"Lady tells me I can bet straight up or down about whether Mickey Wolfmann is still alive."

"Yes and if your interests run to the more exotic," replied Fabian, "may I suggest an Aimee Semple McPherson–type bet, which assumes that Mickey staged his own kidnapping."

"How would a person ever prove something like that?"

Fabian shrugged. "No ransom note and he shows up alive? allegations of amnesia? Police Chief Ed Davis *doesn't* hold a press conference? If Mickey had himself snatched, even money—if he didn't, a hundred to one. More depending how many zeros in the ransom note, if and when one shows up. We can put it all in writing, with anything we forget to write down considered a push, money back and no hard feelings."

Well, said Doc to himself, well, well. The smart money—here came a brief visual of a hundred-dollar bill wearing horn-rim glasses and reading a book about statistics—for its own excellent reasons, which he would have to look into, was expecting Mickey to stage a headline-grabbing return from an exile of his own invention. For these wise folk, it was all but a sure thing. Fuck them, however. Doc found Tito's black chip in his pocket. "Here you go, Mr. Fazzo, I kind of like that long shot."

In the business Doc had learned to live with some contemptuous looks, but the one Fabian threw his way now was almost hurtful. "I'll go write this up, won't be long." Exited shaking his head.

"You must know better'n 'at," Lark fiddling with the umbrella on her drink.

"Oh, just one these naïve hippies, Lark, can't be cynical about nothin, not even the motives of a L.A. land developer. . . ."

Fabian was back shortly, with a new attitude. "You mind stepping upstairs to my office for a minute? Just one or two details."

Doc wiggled his foot discreetly. Yep the little Smith was still there in its ankle rig. "See you, Lark."

"You go careful, darlin."

Fabian Fazzo's office turned out to be as cheerful as Doc had expected it to be sinister. Framed kindergarten art on the walls, an avocado tree Fabian had planted as a pit in an institutional-size lima-bean can back in 1959 and been tending ever since, and a long photomural of Fabian flanked by the entire Rat Pack plus a number of other faces Doc could nearly recall from all-night movies on the tube. Frank Sinatra was playfully attempting to stuff a huge Cuban corona into Fabian's not-altogether-unwilling face. Sammy Davis Jr. was joking delightedly with somebody just out of the frame. Attached to the lower lip of Dean Martin, who was also brandishing a bottle of Dom Pérignon, smoldered what Doc could've sworn was a hastily rolled joint.

Fabian put Doc's hundred-dollar chip on the desk. "No offense, but you have the look of a private gumshoe, or do I mean gumsandal. As a professional courtesy, I'm offering you a chance to rethink your bet on Mickey Wolfmann, and I figured we'd have a little more privacy here, 'cause right at the moment there's FBI in the building."

"What's that to me? I'm just in town on a quick matrimonial, no interest in gambling license irregularities, improper casino ownership, none of them what Marty Robbins'd call *foul evil deeds*."

Fabian shrugged elaborately. "It's what feds do in Las Vegas I guess, this big master plan to get the casinos away from the Mob. Been going on ever since Howard Hughes bought the Desert Inn. But I'm just middle management here, nobody tells me anything."

Doc taking an educated leap, "Mickey Wolfmann—he's another big spender with a history here, isn't he? I heard someplace he met his future bride when she was working in Vegas as a showgirl?"

"Mickey dated a lot of showgirls in his day, loved the town, old Vegas dog from way back, built a house out by Red Rock. Also had this dream about putting up a whole city from scratch someday, out in the desert." Fabian took off his reading glasses and threw Doc a thoughtful squint. "Suggest anything to you?"

"Mickey's in the market for a casino too?"

"Folks in the Justice Department would love to see that happen."

"And the Kismet here's on the list?"

"You've seen this place. They're desperate for somebody non-Mob to come in and spring for the renovation. They keep bringing around their own blueprints, everything state of the art—all these old three-reel slots? forget 'em, what Uncle Sam wants is video screens, every time you play a machine, you get a little animated picture of reels spinning, something coming up on the payline. But it's all electronic, see. Plus controlled from someplace else. Old-school slot hustlers will all be shit out of luck."

"You sound a little bitter, Mr. Fazzo, if you don't mind my saying."

"I do mind, but I'm pissed off about everything these days. I try to find out what's going on, everybody clams up. You tell me. All I know is, is it was all over by '65, and it'll never be like that again. The half-dollar coin, right? 'sucker used to be ninety percent silver, in '65 they reduced that to forty percent, and now this year no more silver at all. Copper, nickel, what next, aluminum foil, see what I'm saying? *Looks* like a half-dollar, but it's really only pretending to be one. Just like those video slots. It's what they've got planned for this whole town, a big Disneyland imitation of itself. Wholesome family fun, kiddies in the casinos, Go Fish with a table limit of ten cents, Pat Boone for a headliner, nonunion actors playing funny mafiosi, driving funny old-fashioned cars, making believe rub each other out, blam, blam, ha, ha, ha. LasfuckinVegasland."

"So maybe you can appreciate the old-school appeal of a long-shot bet on Mickey."

Fabian smiled tightly and not for long. "Spend enough time here, you get these vibes. Look. What if Mickey's not as missing as we think?"

"That case I'm contributing to your renovation fund. You can name a dealer's shoe after me, put a li'l plaque down on the side."

Fabian seemed to be waiting for Doc to say something else, but finally, with a palms-up shrug he arose and escorted Doc along a corridor and around a few corners. "Right through there ought to get you where you're going." For a brief brainpulse, Doc was reminded of the acid trip he'd been put on by Vehi and Sortilège, trying to find his way through a labyrinth that was slowly sinking into the ocean. Here it was all dry desert and scuffed beaverboard, but Doc had the same sense of a rising flood, a need at all costs not to panic. He heard music someplace ahead, not the smoothly arranged sound of a showroom band, more like the ragged start-and-stop of musicians on their own time. He found what once might have been an intimate little lounge, thick with weed and tobacco smoke. There in a tiny amber spot which was sharing a few scrounged-up watts with a pedal steel while the rest of the band played acoustic, stood Lark, her bearing lively despite all the time on her feet through the shift she'd just come off of, singing a country swing number that went,

Full moon in Pisces,
Dang'rous dreams ahead,
If you're out there cruisin,
If you're home in bed,
Keep a six-pack icy,
Make sure your hat's on right,
Full moon in Pisces,
And it's a Saturday night . . .
There goes my ex–best fella,
Got on his Frankenstein shoes,

There's my girlfriend Ella,
She's got the werewolf blues,
When she hits 'em high C's,
She's gettin ready to bite,
                    (Look out!)
Full moon in Pisces,
Another Saturday night.

                    That hometown
Vampire gang's all
Flashin their fangs, it can
Do funny thangs, to your brain—and so
What if it feels,
A little head over heels,
No big deal, you're not real-
                    -ly insane—

It's just some local folks trippin,
Never lasts that long,
Good-time minutes go slippin,
Next thing you know it's dawn—
Forget the creeps and crises,
Crank up 'at neon light—
Full moon in Pisces,
Hell,
        it's Saturday night.

She couldn't see him from where she was, but Doc waved anyway,
clapped and whistled like everybody else, and then kept on with his
search for an exit through the back regions of the underlit casino. About
the time it occurred to him that Fabian Fazzo might've been trying to
steer him someplace else, he came around a corner a little too fast and
ran into big trouble in brown shoes.

242

"Oh, shit." Yes it was Special Agents Borderline and Flatweed again, along with a platoon of other suit-wearers, escorting a figure Doc recognized only too late—probably because he didn't want to believe it. And because nobody was supposed to see any of this in the first place. The blurred glimpse Doc got was of Mickey in a white suit, wearing much the same look he had in his portrait back at his house in the L.A. hills—that game try at appearing visionary—passing right to left, borne onward, stately, tranquilized, as if being ferried between worlds, or at least bound for a bulletproof car you'd never get to see in through the windows of. Hard to say if they had him in custody or if they were conducting him on what real-estate folks like to call a walk-through.

Doc had stepped back into the shadows, but not fast enough. Agent Flatweed had caught sight of him, and paused. "Little business here, you fellows go ahead, I won't be long." While the rest of the detail moved away down the corridor, the federal approached Doc.

"One, at that Mexican place over on West Bonneville, that could have been a coincidence," he observed pleasantly, pretending to count on his fingers. "All kinds of people come to Las Vegas, don't they. Two, you show up in this particular casino, and a man begins to wonder. But three, here in a part of the Kismet Lounge even most locals don't know about, well say now, that puts you somewhat out on the probability curve, and sure merits a closer look."

"How close is that, you're already upside my face here."

"I'd say you're the one who's *too close*." With his head he indicated Mickey, now almost vanished behind him. "You recognized that subject, didn't you."

"Elvis, wasn't it?"

"You're making things awkward for us, Mr. Sportello. This curiosity about the Michael Wolfmann matter. Most inappropriate."

"Mickey? no longer even a active case for me, man, fact, I never even made out a ticket on it, 'cause nobody was payin me."

"Yet you pursue him all the way to Las Vegas."

"I'm here looking into totally something else. Happened to drop by the Kismet, that's about it."

The federal gave him a long look. "Then you won't mind my sharing a thought. It's you hippies. You're making everybody crazy. We'd always assumed that Michael's conscience would never be a problem. After all his years of never appearing to have one. Suddenly he decides to *change his life* and give away millions to an assortment of degenerates—Negroes, longhairs, drifters. Do you know what he said? We have it on tape. 'I feel as if I've awakened from a dream of a crime for which I can never atone, an act I can never go back and choose not to commit. I can't believe I spent my whole life making people pay for shelter, when it ought to've been free. It's just so obvious.'"

"You memorized all that?"

"Another advantage of a marijuana-free life. You might want to try it."

"Uh . . . try what, again?"

Agent Borderline came over, an inquisitive look on his wide red face. "Ah, Sportello we meet again and a pleasure as always."

"I can see how busy you fellows are," said Doc, "so rather than keep you, I think I'll just," breaking into Casey Kasem's Saturday-morning Shaggy voice, "h'like, fuckin, *run?*" which he proceeded to do, though with no clear idea of where he was heading. What were they going to do, start shooting? yes well actually . . .

At length, nearly out of breath, he spotted a pair of toilets labeled GEORGE and GEORGETTE, and betting on FBI taboos, ducked into the ladies', where he found Lark in front of one of the mirrors, retouching her makeup.

"Damn! another one them sexually confused hippies!"

"Waitin for the feds to go mess with somebody else, darlin. Caught your number, by the way. That Dolly Parton better start gettin worried."

"Well, some of Roy Acuff's people were in last week and gave it a listen, so you keep your fingers crossed for me."

"Ordinarily I'd say let's grab us a quick beer, but—"

Federal hollering in the near distance.

She made a face. "Bad upbringin is my own theory. I'll show you the back way out, and best you avail yourself now."

Doc made his way among smells of newly sawed wood, fresh paint, and joint compound till he reached a fire door and shoved it open, whereupon a recorded voice kicked in at high volume advising him to freeze and wait for the arrival of duly authorized professionals trained to thoroughly dismantle his ass. He stepped out onto a sparsely lit loading dock of time-corroded concrete, down which he could see dark shapes already coming at him on the run.

There was the sound of an engine. Doc looked back over his shoulder, and here rounding the corner at great expenditure of tire tread came Tito's limousine, with the sunroof open and the top half of Adolfo waving some kind of submachine gun in the air. Doc's pursuers came to a halt and began to consult about this.

The limo braked next to Doc. "Hop on down!" yelled Tito. Adolfo ducked back inside long enough for Doc to step over onto the roof and slide in through it, then resumed position as Tito tached up and dropped into low, leaving a fragrant set of tracks a block long and a screech that could be heard halfway to Boulder Dam. "Where to, bro?" inquired Tito.

"You're not gonna believe who I saw," Doc said.

"Adolfo thinks he saw Dean Martin."

Adolfo slid back down inside the car. "Not exactly."

"Well . . ." Tito said, "so like . . . was it Dean Martin, or wasn't it Dean Martin?"

"See, that's just it—it was Dean Martin, and it wasn't Dean Martin."

"'And'? Don't you mean 'but'?"

Doc must have drifted away. When they let him off back at the motel, Trillium wasn't there, though her things were. He looked around for a note and couldn't find one.

He rolled a joint, lit up, and settled in in front of *All-Nite Freaky Features,* where *Godzilligan's Island,* a movie for TV in which the Japanese monster meets the sitcom castaways, was just about to begin. Over the opening credits, Godzilla, out in search of some R&R after his latest urban-demolition binge, stumbles—literally—upon the Island, causing immediate anxiety among the survivors of the *Minnow*'s historic cruise.

"We just have to stay alive," as Mary Ann explains it to Ginger, "till the Japanese Self-Defense Forces get on the case, which is usually quicker than you can say 'kamikaze.'"

"Ka-mi—" Ginger begins, but is drowned out by a skyful of jet-fighter aircraft, which begin to fire rockets at Godzilla, who as usual is no more than mildly inconvenienced. "See?" nods Mary Ann, as the laugh track also explodes in mirth. Unnoticed in the uproar, the Professor has arrived with a peculiar-looking piece of anti-Godzilla weaponry he has been working on, featuring various analog control panels, parabolic antennas, and giant helical glass coils pulsing with an unearthly purple glow, but before he can get to demonstrate it, Gilligan, mistaking the device for the Skipper, falls out of a tree on top of it, narrowly avoiding irradiation and impalement. "I just got it calibrated!" cries the Prof in dismay.

"Maybe it's still in warranty?" wonders Gilligan.

We get a crane shot from what is supposed to be Godzilla's point of view. He is looking down at the behavior on the Island, endearingly perplexed as always, scratching his head in a way meant to remind us of Stan Laurel. Fade to commercial.

At some point, Doc must have lost track of the movie, awakening next morning to Henry Kissinger on the *Today* show going, "Vell, den, ve schould chust *bombp* dem, schouldn't ve?"

The National Security Advisor was drowned out by lengthy honking from out in the lot. It was Puck and Trillium in the Camaro, which had been decorated all over with toilet paper in different fashion shades and psychedelic prints, and beer cans and a crudely lettered Just Married sign. It seemed that after a night of nonstop partying, the couple had been down to the county courthouse, obtained the license, headed straight for the Wee Kirk O' the Heather, and in short order were hitched, Einar acting as best man and deciding himself to elope with another groom-to-be who'd been waiting for a bride with what turned out to be cold feet, as, in fact, he discovered with signs of relief, were his own. For a recessional, Puck and Einar talked the electric organ player into accompanying them on a duet of the Ethel Merman favorite "You're Not Sick, You're Just in Love," from *Call Me Madam,* though there was the usual awkwardness over who would sing Ethel Merman's part.

Puck and Doc found a minute to talk. "Congratulations, man, she's a swell chick."

Marriage, even in this town, will do strange things to a man. "She can save me." Nodding wide-eyed as any bus-station runaway.

"Who's after you, Puck?"

"Nobody," his eyes almost pleading, though not with Doc necessarily.

"Salvation, see, I've got my own hangups with that, 'cause I'm feeling maybe I could have saved Mickey from what happened, whatever that was. Maybe even Glen, too?"

The swastika on Puck's head began to pulsate. "Ain't exactly been tip-toein through no tulips about that myself," he said. "Glen was a fuckup, but we were blood brothers, and that should've meant something. But if I would have stayed on that shift? it would've happened to me instead." Which wasn't saying, exactly, that he'd have sacrificed himself for Glen. He had a look in his eyes now that Doc wasn't too comfortable with. "And you, you couldn't have saved nobody."

"That much of a done deal, you think?"

"You don't want to be fuckin with this, Mr. Sportello." The swastika was throbbing furiously now. "Ain't like this is the Mob. Not even the pretend Mob you people think is the Mob."

Doc fumbled for a joint. "I'm not following."

Puck reached Doc's pack of Kools out of his shirt pocket, lit one, and kept the pack. "These Mormon fucks in the FBI. They keep preachin everything here is wops. Like end of the story, *finito,* nothin but the wops, get rid of the wops and everything's comin up roses, as Ethel always sez. Well forget that race shit, man, that's all just for cover. Howard Hughes, what's he? Aryan to the bone, right? but who's he working for? what about the *Mob behind the Mob*?"

Now, if Puck had been some average California beach-town doper, Doc might have put this down to ordinary paranoia and wished him a happy honeymoon and got back to work. But Puck still wanted to deny he knew anything about anything, and whatever that was at his back, closing in, was even too frightening for silence to do him much good either.

"Here, here's an easy one," Doc downshifted. "Did Mickey ever talk about some city he wanted to build someplace out in the desert?"

"Lately, he never did nothing but. Arrepentimiento. Spanish for 'sorry about that.' His idea was, anybody could go live there for free, didn't matter who you were, show up and if there's a unit open it's yours, overnight, forever, et cetera et cetera, and so forth as the King of Siam always sez. Here, you got a road map, I'll show you."

Trillium came over and slid her hands under one of Puck's tattooed arms, the one with the skull with the dagger in its eye socket. "We'd better be on our way, my love."

"You guys can have the car," Doc said, "which is paid up for another week, and also whatever's left on the room, consider it my wedding present. Can I have my smokes back?"

Trillium walked Doc out to where Tito was waiting with the limo. "He really is the love of my life, Doc. He needs me."

"You've got my office and home numbers, right?"

"We'll call, I promise."

"All the best, Mrs. Beaverton."

EVENING CAME, TAKING everybody by surprise. Tito drove Adolfo and Inez to the airport, and as he pulled back out onto the highway, he and Doc noticed a car just going in the airport entrance, motor-pool gray, with something unhesitant and unforgiving in its movement that told them who it was there for. Tito ascended to the freeway and headed out into the desert. "Nice town, but let's lose it."

Like spacemen in a space ship, they were pressed violently into the seat backs as Tito engaged some classified performance feature, and outside the windows city neon began to lengthen in long spectral blurs, to shift toward blue ahead while in the black distances framed by Tito's mirror each point of light grew reddish, receded, converged. Tito had Roza Eskenazi tapes playing over the car stereo. "Listen to her, I adore that chick, she was the Bessie Smith of her day, pure soul." He sang along for a few bars. *"Tiátimo meráki,* who hasn't had that, man? a need, so hopeless, so shameless, that nothing nobody can say means shit." Sounded like more addict talk to Doc, but after he got used to the scales and vocal styling he found himself thinking about Trillium, and wondering what she'd make of these *rembetissas* of Tito's and the particular kind of longing they sang about.

They drove through the night, and in the first light they got to the turnoff Puck had shown Doc on the map, and followed a state road to a county road, left the blacktop then for a ranch road of packed dirt, past battered and dangling gates and across dry washes on strumming cattle guards, past yucca and squat little cactuses, desert wildflowers at the roadside, rock outcrops in the distance, dark moving patches out in the alkaline brightness that could have been burros or coyotes or mule deer, or maybe aliens from long-ago landings, for Doc could feel evidence everywhere of ancient visitation.

They came over a ridge, and there, down a long slope into a valley whose river might've vanished centuries ago, was Mickey Wolfmann's dream, his penance for having once charged money for human shelter—Arrepentimiento. Doc and Tito lit a wake-up joint and passed it back and forth. Beyond the project stretched an expanse of desert only marginally developed, here a scatter of concrete structures, there a distant smokestack or two among the scrawls of chaparral. Later Doc and Tito wouldn't be able to agree on what they'd been looking at. There were several what Riggs Warbling had called zomes, linked by covered walkways. Not perfect hemispheres but pointed at the top. Doc counted six, Tito seven, maybe eight. The terrain between the complex and themselves was also strewn with giant almost-spherical pink rocks, though they could also have been man-made.

"Can we get down there to have a look?" Doc wondered.

"What, in this? We'd break an axle, wipe out the oil pan, some shit. You'd need a four-wheeler. Unless you think we can walk it? You got a hat?"

"I need a hat to walk?"

"Rays, man, dangerous rays." In the trunk Tito found a couple of gigantic sombreros he'd bought in Glitter Gulch for souvenirs, and he and Doc put them on and set out in the desert breeze for Arrepentimiento.

It took longer than they thought. The zomes ahead, like backdrop art in old sci-fi movies, never seemed to come any closer. It was like feeling your way through dangerous terrain at night, though Doc was conscious of the sun overhead, the star of an alien planet, smaller and more concentrated than it should have been, zapping them relentlessly with hard radiation. Lizards came out from behind the visible world and stood timeless and breathless as rock to watch Doc and Tito.

After a while it began to look more like an abandoned construction site. Scrap lumber bleaching in the sun, spools of rusted cable, lengths of plastic pipe, snarls of Romex, a wrecked air compressor. Plastic sheeting had blown away in places, revealing the skeleton underneath, struts and connectors, looking sometimes like an openwork soccer ball, sometimes patterns on a cactus, or seashells people bring back from Hawaii.

"Don't see any padlocks," said Doc.

"Don't mean we can just walk in."

Doc found a door and it opened easily, and he stepped into a soaring shadowy vault.

"All right, you can stop there."

"Uh-oh." Doc said.

"Or you can keep on coming, clear on into the next world. Ask me if I give a shit." It was Riggs Warbling with a couple weeks' start on a beard and holding a .44 Magnum, a Ruger Blackhawk, cocked and pointing at the middle of Doc's forehead, its barrel showing little if any wobble, though the same could not be said now for Doc's voice.

He took off his sombrero, respectfully. "Well, howdy, Riggs! Happened to be in the area, thought I'd take you up on that invite! Remember me? Larry Sportello? Doc? A-and this here's my friend Tito!"

"Mickey send you?"

"Um, no, as a matter of fact I've been trying to find out what happened to Mickey."

"Jesus. What *didn't* happen to him." Riggs eased the hammer back down, though he still looked plenty agitated. "Come on in."

Inside was a gigantic refrigerator full of beer and other foodstuffs, a number of slot machines, and a pool table and reclining chairs, and actually, now that Doc thought of it, more space, judging from the outside, than there could possibly be in here. Riggs saw him looking around and read his mind. "Groovy, ain't it? Kind of a switch on Bucky Fuller, basically—instead of fewer dollars per cubic foot enclosed, this is more cubic feet per dollar."

Doc's response normally would've been, "Isn't that the same thing?" But from some nuance in Riggs's behavior, perhaps the insane stare, or the tight grip he still had on his gleaming black handgun, or the inability to keep his voice from breaking into higher registers, Doc dug how dummying up might be a slightly wiser move.

Suddenly Riggs's head assumed a new angle, and he appeared to be staring through the zome wall at some point in the distant sky. After a few seconds came the sound of unmuffled jet-fighter engines, approaching from that direction. Riggs raised the muzzle of his piece a few inches and it looked for a second like he was about to start shooting. The roar overhead grew to an almost intolerable level and then faded.

"They send them over from Nellis every half hour," Riggs said. "At first I thought it was just some routine flight path, but turns out it's all deliberate, authorized buzzing. All day, all night. Someday they'll get Mickey to approve a rocket strike, and Arrepentimiento will be history— except it won't even be that, because they'll destroy all the records, too."

"Why would Mickey bomb this place? It's his dream."

"Was. You saw what it looked like out there. He's pulled the money out, stiffed all his contractors, everybody's walked but me."

"When did this happen?"

"Around the time he disappeared. Suddenly no more acid-head philanthropist. They did something to him."

"Who?"

"Whoever. And now he's back with Sloane, yes the happy couple together again, honeymoon suite at Caesar's, big heart-shaped water bed, got his hand on her ass in public all the time, like, 'This is mine folks, don't even think about it,' and Sloane going along with the whole bought-and-sold routine, not even eye contact with other men, especially not ones she's been, what's the word, seeing?"

"I thought Mickey was cool with all that," Doc almost said, but was pretty sure he didn't.

"He's a born-again family man anymore, whatever they did to his brain, they also reprogrammed his dick, and now of course she won't give me the time of day. I'm just sitting out here with a rifle across my knees, like the ghost of a crazy prospector at some old silver mine, waiting for the righteous husband to pick his moment. Dead already but don't know it. You heard he made a deal with the Justice Department."

"Some rumors, maybe?"

"Listen to what he did. Is this an example to the young, or what? Mickey buys this tiny parcel on the Strip, too small to develop even as a parking lot, but right next to a major casino, and announces plans for a 'mini-casino,' like those little convenience stores you see next to gas stations? fast in and out, one slot machine, one roulette wheel, one blackjack table. The Italian Business Men next door think of all the downscale traffic this will bring in right under the noses of their refined clientele, and they go crazy, threatening, screaming, flying their mothers in first class to stand and glare at Mickey in silent reproach. Sometimes not so silent. Finally the casino gives in, Mickey gets his asking price, some insane multiple of what he paid, which will now go to finance the renovation and expansion of the Kismet Casino and Lounge, where he's become an active partner."

"So he's another Vegas heavy now, watch yer ass Howard Hughes and so forth, well, thanks for the update, Riggs."

Another sortie of fighters came over.

When they could hear again, Tito spoke for the first time. "Can we give you a ride someplace?"

"The thing about zomes is," Riggs with a desperate grin, "is they can act as doorways to other dimensions. The F-105s, the coyotes, the scorpions and snakes, the desert heat, none of that bothers me. I can leave whenever I want." He motioned with his head. "All I have to do is step through that door over there, and I'm safe."

"Can I look?" said Doc.

"Better not. It's not for everybody, and if it's not for you, it can be dangerous."

They left him watching *Let's Make a Deal* on a little portable black-and-white TV set, whose picture each time the fighters came over got scrambled into sharp fragments it seemed would never reassemble, but in the silences between sorties they returned, as if through some form of mercy peculiar to zomes.

TITO AND DOC drove till they saw a motel with a sign reading, WEL-COME TOOBFREEX! BEST CABLE IN TOWN! and they decided to check in. Time-zone issues too complicated for either of them to understand had leveraged the amount of programming available here, network and independent, to some staggering scale, and creative-minded cable managers were not slow to exploit the strange hiccup in space-time. . . . Everybody was here to watch something. Soap enthusiasts, old-movie buffs, nostalgia lovers had driven here hundreds, even thousands, of miles to bathe in these cathode rays, as water connoisseurs in Grandmother's day had once visited certain spas. Hour after hour, they wallowed and gazed, as the sun wheeled in the hazy sky and splashing echoed off the tiles of the indoor pool and housekeeping carts went squeaking to and fro.

The remote-control units were bolted to the ends of the beds, and cycling through all the choices seemed to take longer than whatever you wanted to see was likely to stay on, but somehow about the time Doc's thumb muscles went into spasm, he happened onto a John Garfield Marathon that had been in progress for, he gathered, weeks now. And there about to begin was another John Garfield movie that James Wong Howe had also been DP on, *He Ran All the Way* (1951), not one of Doc's favorites, to tell the truth—it was John Garfield's last picture before the antisubversives finally did him in, and it had the smell of blacklist all over it—Dalton Trumbo wrote the script, but there was another name on the credits. John Garfield played a criminal on the run who picks up Shelley Winters at a public pool and proceeds to make life disagreeable for her family, obliging them at gunpoint, for example, to eat a gross-looking prop turkey ("Ya gonna eat dis toikey!"), and for his miserably misspent life he ends up, literally, dead in the gutter, though of course beautifully lit. Doc had been hoping to drift to sleep in the middle of it, but the last scene found him up and staring, sweat freezing in the air-conditioning. It was somehow like seeing John Garfield die for real, with the whole respectable middle class standing there in the street smugly watching him do it.

Tito snored away on the other bed. Out there, all around them to the last fringes of occupancy, were Toobfreex at play in the video universe, the tropic isle, the Long Branch Saloon, the Starship *Enterprise,* Hawaiian crime fantasies, cute kids in make-believe living rooms with invisible audiences to laugh at everything they did, baseball highlights, Vietnam footage, helicopter gunships and firefights, and midnight jokes, and talking celebrities, and a slave girl in a bottle, and Arnold the pig, and here was Doc, on the natch, caught in a low-level bummer he couldn't find a way out of, about how the Psychedelic Sixties, this little parenthesis of light, might close after all, and all be lost, taken back into darkness . . .

how a certain hand might reach terribly out of darkness and reclaim the time, easy as taking a joint from a doper and stubbing it out for good.

Doc didn't fall asleep till close to dawn and didn't really wake up till they were going over the Cajon Pass, and it felt like he'd just been dreaming about climbing a more-than-geographical ridgeline, up out of some worked-out and picked-over territory, and descending into new terrain along some great definitive slope it would be more trouble than he might be up to to turn and climb back over again.

FIFTEEN

AROUND NIGHTFALL TITO LET DOC OFF ON DUNECREST, AND IT was like landing on some other planet. He walked into the Pipeline to find a couple hundred people he didn't know but who were acting like longtime regulars. Worse, nobody he did know was there at all. No Ensenada Slim or Flaco the Bad, no St. Flip or Downstairs Eddie. Doc looked into Wavos and Epic Lunch, and the Screaming Ultraviolet Brain, and Man of La Muncha, where the menudo got your nose running just looking at it, and each time it was the same story. Nobody he recognized. He thought briefly about going to his apartment but started worrying that he wouldn't recognize it either or, worse, *it wouldn't know him*—wouldn't be there, key wouldn't fit or something. Then it occurred to him that maybe Tito had actually dropped him in some *other* beach town, Manhattan or Hermosa or Redondo, and that the bars, eateries, and so forth he'd been walking into were ones that happened to be *similarly located* in this other town—same view of the ocean or corner of the street, for example—so he grasped his head carefully in both hands and, mentally advising himself to *focus in* and *pay attention,* waited for the next nonthreatening pedestrian to come by.

"Excuse me, sir, I seem to be a little disoriented? could you please tell me if this is by any chance Gordita Beach?" as sanely as he could manage, and instead of running off in panic after the nearest law enforcement, this party said, "Wow, Doc, it's me, you okay? you look like you're freaking out," and after a while Doc dug how this was Denis, or somebody impersonating Denis, which, in the circumstances, he'd settle for.

"Where is everybody, man?"

"Some college break or something. A lot of junior hell-raisers in town. I'm sticking close to the tube till it's over."

Denis had some dry-ice-enhanced Mexican product, and they went down on the beach to smoke it. They watched the flashing wing lights of a single-engine plane, looking fragile and somehow already lost, taking off into the darkening glow over the water.

"How was Vegas, man?"

"Won a bucketful of nickels off a slot machine."

"Far out. Listen. Guess who's back."

The way Denis was looking at him, it couldn't be anybody else. Doc torched up a Kool but lit the wrong end and didn't notice for a while. "What's she up to?"

"Could you put that thing out, that's some evil-smelling shit."

"Or to rephrase it—who's she with?"

"Nobody, far as I know. She's staying at Flip's place over that surf shop in El Porto? The Saint split for Maui."

"How's her spirits?"

"Why ask me?"

"I mean, is she paranoid. Does the heat know she's back? Last I heard, there's all these high-priority APBs out on her, what happened to that?"

"She don't seem too worried."

"Well, that's weird." Had she made some kind of a deal too?

"We could walk up there if you want," said Denis.

For any number of reasons, Doc thought not. Denis went drifting off to watch Lawrence Welk. "What?" Doc couldn't help commenting.

"Something about Norma Zimmer," Denis called over his shoulder, "I'm still figuring out what, exactly."

The key worked, the place hadn't been robbed or rifled, the plants were still alive. Doc watered everything, put coffee on to percolate, and called Fritz.

"Your girlfriend's back," Fritz announced, and fell silent.

After a while, growing irritated, Doc said, "Yeah and her front ain't too bad either. So what?"

"According to the ARPAnet, Shasta Fay Hepworth showed up day before yesterday at LAX. Plus which, the FBI, who can somehow monitor me now when I'm jacked in, keeps coming around asking what my interest in her is. You mind telling me what the hell's going on?"

Doc recapped the trip to Vegas, or what he remembered, interrupting himself ten minutes in to point out, "Of course if they can tap your computer lines, the phone here ought to be duck soup for them."

"Oops," agreed Fritz. "But continue."

"Yeah well Mickey seems to be in one piece, the feds have got him on ice. Glen Charlock is still dead, but hey, who cares about the criminal element, right?"

He complained for a minute and a half more till Fritz said, "Well, it's your problem now. This ARPAnet trip is eating up my time, which is better spent chasing after all them hardened skips and deadbeats, so I think I'm gonna take a break. If there's anything else, maybe you better ask now, 'cause it's about to be back to the world of flesh and blood for old F.D."

"Let's see," Doc said, "there's Puck Beaverton. . . ."

"Recall doing a little business with a party of that name way back when. What about him?"

"I don't know," Doc said. "Something."

"Some weird acid vibe."

"You got it."

"Some strange inexpressible imbalance in the laws of karma."

"Knew you'd understand."

"Doc . . ."

"Don't say it. That kid Sparky still working for you?"

"Come on around, I'll introduce you. Also got some of this new shit, they call it 'Thai stick'? Kind of gummy but once you get it lit . . ."

No sooner had Doc hung up than the phone rang again, and it was Bigfoot, who started right in. "So! The elusive Miss Hepworth it seems has rejoined your little community of drug-ravaged misfits."

"Wow, no shit? News to me."

"Oh, that's right—you've been temporarily off the planet again. Phone calls, in-person visits, nothing has seemed to work. You know how anxious we get."

"Little R&R. Wish I had your work ethic."

"No you don't. Any developments on the Coy Harlingen matter?"

"Chasin down one bum lead after another, 's all."

"Any of them include young . . . what was his name again, Beaverton, I believe?"

Fuck off, Bigfoot. "Traced Puck as far as West Hollywood, but nobody's seen him since Mickey did his board fade."

"As for Dr. Blatnoyd and his unfortunate sports injury, we did mention your interesting puncture-wound theory to Dr. Noguchi's people—inquired about testing for copper-gold dental alloys and so on, and one of them smiled strangely and said, 'Mind if we call in the lab on this one?' 'Of course not,' I said. 'Wonderful. Oh, Dwayne!' and in bounded this vicious Labrador retriever with, I must say, such an unhelpful attitude that we all became rather discouraged."

"Gee and they're supposed to be such great kids' dogs—"

"We have one in this house, actually."

"Only thought it'd be a helpful tip to a fellow professional—just tryin save you some trouble down the line, 's all. . . .'"

"How's that?"

"When your own hearing comes up."

"My . . . Sportello, are you suggesting—"

Doc allowed himself one evil grin a week, and tonight was the night. "All's I'm saying is, is if it happened to Thomas Noguchi, the most brilliant medical examiner in the USA, well, who among you protect-and-servers is safe? One county supervisor with a bug up his ass is all it takes."

Total silence.

"Bigfoot?"

"I had been enjoying a quiet family evening with Mrs. Bjornsen and the children, and the dog, watching Lawrence Welk, and now see what you've done."

Doc heard an extension being picked up. A woman's voice with a steep front edge to it and very short decay time said, "Is everything all right, Kitkat?"

"What's this," Doc said.

"*This* is Mrs. Chastity Bjornsen, and if *that* is one more sociopathic 'special employee' of my husband, I'll thank you to stop harassing him on his day off, as he has quite enough to do all week trying to keep dopers and lowlifes like yourself off the streets."

"There there, my lit-tle boysenberry. Sportello's only been indulging in his idea of humor."

"*Doc* Sportello? *The* Doc Sportello? So! at last! Mr. Moral Turpitude himself! Have you any idea of the therapist bills around here for which you are directly responsible?"

"Now, Snookums, the Department picks up most of that—"

"After a deductible that would choke a horse, and meanwhile, Christian, I quite fail to understand *your* spineless response to this wretched hippie freak with his unending provocations—"

Doc discovered he was out of cigarettes. He put the receiver on the kitchen table and went looking for his carton of Kools, which after a lengthy search turned up in the icebox, next to the remains of a pizza he'd forgotten about, not all of whose ingredients, though colorful, he could identify any longer. Feeling despite this a little hungry, he decided to make a peanut butter and mayonnaise sandwich, located a cold can of Burgie, and started into the other room to flip on the television when he noticed strange noises coming from the phone, whose receiver, actually, seemed to be off the hook. . . .

"Oh." He went to put the instrument to his ear, though the Bjornsens, now in full screaming confrontation, had actually been audible across the kitchen, reviewing some recent personal history, with footnotes, unfamiliar to Doc but still embarrassing, and after a minute or two of calculating how likely were his chances of getting in even another word, he replaced the receiver in its cradle as gently as if he were about to sing it a lullaby and went in to watch the last couple minutes of *Adam-12*.

The Saturday horror movie tonight was Val Lewton's *I Walked with a Zombie* (1943), hosted by subcultural superstar Larry Vincent, aka "Seymour," who liked to address his population of faithful viewers as "fringees" and also hosted the annual Halloween show at the Wiltern Theatre, which Doc tried never to miss. He had seen this zombie picture a couple of hundred times and still got confused by the ending, so he spent the news hour rolling joints to help him through, especially with the calypso singing, but somehow despite his best efforts fell asleep in the middle, as so often before.

NEXT MORNING—OCEAN SMELL, fresh coffee, a cool edge—Doc was in Wavos, going through the Sunday *Times* to see if there was anything new about the Wolfmann case, which there wasn't—though of course with twenty or thirty different sections you never knew what might be hiding among the real-estate ads—and was about to dig in to a specialty of the house known as Shoot the Pier, basically avocados, sprouts, jalapeños, pickled artichoke hearts, Monterey jack cheese, and Green Goddess dressing on a sourdough loaf that had first been sliced lengthwise, spread with garlic butter, and toasted, seventy-nine cents and a bargain at half the price, when who should stroll in, who else, but Shasta Fay. She was wearing, near as Doc could tell, unless she owned a drawerful of them now, the same old Country Joe & the Fish T-shirt as in the olden days, same sandals and bikini bottom. Strangely, his appetite did not produce a hall pass and ask to be excused, but on the other hand, what was this? was he having an acid flashback, was he about to run into James "Moondoggie" Darren in *The Time Tunnel* or something? Last Doc knew, his ex–old lady here had been at least a person of interest to countless levels of law enforcement, yet here she was now, same getup, same carefree attitude, as if she still hadn't even met Mickey Wolfmann, as if some stereo needle had been lifted and set back down on some other sentimental oldie on the compilation LP of history.

"Hi, Doc."

Which of course was all it ever took, and sure enough, would you look at this. Suavely positioning the Book Review over his lap, he grinned as sincerely as possible. "Heard you were back. Got your postcard, thanks."

One of those little puzzled frowns she may have perfected around kindergarten. "Postcard?"

Well, that's probably significant too, he thought, and I better write it down or I'll forget. Ouija-board pranksters at work again, no doubt.

"Thought it was your handwriting, must have been somebody else's . . . so! where've you been?"

"Had to go up north? Family stuff?" Shrug. "Anything been happening down here?"

Bring up Mickey? Don't bring up Mickey? "Your . . . friend in the construction business . . ."

"Oh, that's all over." She didn't look specially sad about it. Or happy either.

"Maybe I missed something on the news—he isn't . . . back, by any chance?"

She smiled and shook her head. "I've been away." Around her neck on a piece of thong, she was wearing a seashell, maybe even brought back from a distant Pacific island, whose shape and markings reminded Doc of one of the zomes in Mickey's now-abandoned project in the desert.

Ensenada Slim came in. "Howdy, Shasta. Hey Doc, Bigfoot's been looking for you."

"Oboy. How long ago?"

"Just saw him over to the Brain. Seemed pretty intense about something."

"Either of you like to finish this?" Doc crept out the back way, only to find Bigfoot lounging in the alley with a peculiar smile.

"Don't look so nervous. I'm not planning to inflict bodily harm, much as I'd like to. Part of this godforsaken hippie era and its erosion of masculine values I expect. Wyatt Earp would have been using your head for sledgehammer practice by now."

"Hey, that reminds me—my bag, just going to reach in my bag here, okay? two fingers? slowly?" Doc brought out the antique coffee cup he'd found in Vegas.

"Though one grows hardened in police work," said Bigfoot, "occasionally one's sensibilities are profoundly challenged. What is . . . this . . . supposed to be?"

"It's Wyatt Earp's personal mustache cup, man. See, it's got his name on it and everything?"

"May I, without wishing to cause offense, inquire as to the provenance of this . . ." He paused as if groping for the right term.

"Antique dealer in Vegas named Delwyn Quight. Seemed respectable enough."

Bigfoot nodded bitterly and for some time. "You obviously don't subscribe to *Tombstone Memorabilia Collectors' Alert*. Brother Quight poses for its centerfold at least every other month. The man is a byword of fraudulent Earpiana."

"Wow." And worse, what if that also meant the *Liberace necktie* was a fake, too?

"It's the thought, isn't it," said Bigfoot. "Listen," and exactly in cadence with Doc saying the same thing, "I'm sorry about last night." They paused for exactly the same number of pulses, and again in unison said, "You? Why should you be sorry?" This could have gone on all day, but then Doc said, "Weird," and Bigfoot said, "Extraordinary," and the spell was broken. They went ambling down the alley in silence till Bigfoot said, "I'm not sure how to tell you this."

"Oh, shit. Who is it this time?"

"Leonard Jermaine Loosemeat, whom you might recall as a minor-league heroin dealer in Venice. Floater. Found him in one of those canals."

"El Drano. Coy Harlingen's dealer."

"Yes."

"Funny coincidence."

"Define 'funny.'" Doc heard something in his voice and looked over, and thought for a second that Bigfoot had finally arrived at his own long-overdue cop-related nervous breakdown. His lip was trembling, his eyes moist. He caught and held Doc's gaze. Finally, "You don't want to be fucking with this, Doc."

Puck Beaverton had issued the same free advice.

WHICH DIDN'T KEEP Doc from driving up to Venice that evening to see what he could see. Leonard had been living in a bungalow beside a canal with a rowboat tied up at a little pier in the backyard. Periodically a dredge came through, and all the dopers who'd hidden their stashes in the canal could be observed the night before running around frantically trying to remember who'd put what where exactly. Doc happened to arrive in the middle of one of these exercises. In the soft and bath-warm night, half a dozen stereos were going at once out the open windows and sliding glass doors. Low-voltage garden lights glowed through the night foliage, up and down driveways and in the yards. Neighborhood people wandered around with beer bottles or joints in their hands or lounged on the little bridges watching the fuss.

"What? You forgot to put it in something waterproof again?"

"Ups."

Doc had El Drano's address from Bigfoot's field interrogation card. Almost before he had time to knock, the door was opened by a fat guy with thick eyeglasses and a little tiny mustache, holding and chalking a pool cue handsomely inlaid with mother-of-pearl.

"What, no camera crew?"

"Actually, I'm here representing HULK, that's Heroin Users

Liberation Kollective? we work out of Sacramento, and we're basically a lobby in the state assembly for junkie civil rights? May I offer our condolences for your loss."

"Hi, I'm Pepe, and junkies, in fact dopers in general, are diseased human trash who wouldn't know what to do with civil rights if it walked up and bit them on the ass, not that civil rights actually does that, understand, oh come on in, by the way, do you happen to play eight ball?"

The walls inside were fiberboard and painted Prison Pink, a shade at that time believed to produce calm among the institutionalized. Every room had a pool table in it, including little bar-size units for the bathrooms and kitchen. There were nearly as many TV sets. Pepe, who appeared to've had nobody to talk to, or at, since El Drano's passing, kept up a monologue into which Doc now and then tried to slip a question.

". . . not that I begrudged him the money he borrowed or even owed me because I was always the consistently better one in terms of pool playing, but what really annoyed me was the loan sharks, and the thugs they used to send around, if money at high interest was the whole story, well that would have its own integrity I suppose, but they also deal in pain and forgiveness—their forgiveness!—and they traffic with agencies of command and control, who will sooner or later betray all agreements they make because among the invisible powers there is no trust and no respect."

He had paused briefly in front of one of the TV sets to flip through the channels. Doc took the occasion to ask, "Do you think it could have been one of those loan sharks who killed Leonard?"

"Except that all that was over. For the first time since I knew him, Lenny was free of debt. My impression is that up at some level somebody had decided to forgive everything he owed. But then, in addition, every month a check also started coming for him in the mail. Once or twice I would sneak a look at the amount. Serious money, my friend—what was your name again?"

"Larry. Hi. This money—you think it was from a client?"

"I asked, naturally, and sometimes he'd say operating expenses, and sometimes he called it a retainer fee, but one night—he shouldn't have been using, but it was the Christmas holidays—he was in this mood, being nice to everybody, putting a little extra weight in the bags— around three in the morning he started freaking out, and that's when he mentioned 'blood money,' and I asked about that later and he pretended he didn't remember, but I knew his face by then, every pore, and he remembered, all right. Something was corroding him from inside. You'd never know to look at him, but he had a conscience. One of those checks showed up last week and normally Lenny would've been out to the bank first thing to deposit it, but this one he just let sit, he was very upset about something . . . here, look, this is it, no use to me, not like I ever had any power of attorney."

The check was drawn on the Arbolada Savings and Loan in Ojai— one of Mickey Wolfmann's, Doc recalled, also used by the Chryskylodon Institute—and signed by a financial officer whose name neither of them could read.

"Worse than a forged prescription," Pepe said.

"A nice piece of change here, Pepe. There has to be some way you can cash this."

"Maybe I should just donate it to your organization, in Leonard's name, of course."

"I'm not going to pressure you one way or the other, though it might help with our new Save a Rock 'n' Roller program. You know how many musicians have been overdosing in recent years, it's an epidemic. I've noticed it especially in my own area, surf music. I happen to be a huge fan of the Boards—fact it's how I got personally involved in overdose prevention, ever since one of their sax players passed away. . . . Remember Coy Harlingen?"

It could've been some unexpected side effect from all the dope he'd been smoking, but Doc now felt an ice-cold electric shock blasting through the room—Pepe went rigid, his face, even with all the pink reflection in here, drained suddenly to an alarming white, and Doc saw the pain he must have been in all this time, how much Leonard must have meant to him, how he must have thought all the desperate talking would get him through this . . . but here was something he'd been forbidden to talk about, maybe even suspicions of his own that he could not allow himself to go into, with Coy Harlingen clearly at the heart of it. Pepe's silence went on, the multiple voices of the TV sets in all the rooms combined in jagged disharmony, till far too late he finally said, "No, that name doesn't register. But I understand. Too many needless losses. Your people are in a position to do something wonderful, I'm sure."

If El Drano, on somebody's orders, had switched the 3-percent shit he'd been selling Coy for something that was sure to kill him, then it seemed clear that nobody had bothered to tell him later about it being a scam, and that Coy was still alive. All this time they'd let him think he was a murderer. Was it finally too much for this conscience Pepe said he had? Was he about to go confess to somebody? Who wouldn't have wanted him to do that?

On one of the pool tables lay an impossible arrangement of balls ready for some superhero of the sport to address. "One of Lenny's safety shots," Pepe said. "It's been there ever since he stepped out and never came back. I keep meaning to finish the game, I know I could run the table, but somehow . . ."

Doc walked back to his car through a slightly more calmed neighborhood, the dopers were all back indoors heading for the bedding, the uproar had died down, the moon was out, what had been found again was found, what was lost was gone for good except for what some lucky dredgefolks tomorrow would happen across. Lost, and not lost, and what Sauncho called lagan, deliberately lost and found again . . . and there was something now scratching like a rogue chicken at the fringes of the unkempt barnyard that was Doc's brain, but he couldn't quite locate it, let alone account for the critter when evening rolled around.

HE THOUGHT HE'D better go discuss Adrian Prussia with Fritz, who'd had more of a history with the loan shark than Doc did. Sparky, who worked the vampire shift, hadn't come in yet.

"I wouldn't go near Adrian," Fritz advised. "He's no longer the wholesome Chamber of Commerce bigshot we used to know in the olden days, Doc, he's bad shit anymore."

"How can he be worse than he was? He's the reason I quit being a pacifist and started packing."

"Something happened to him, he made a deal with somebody bigger than him, bigger than anything he was into up till then."

"I heard something about him along the same lines out in Venice tonight. 'Agencies of command and control,' is how it went. Seemed strange at the time. Who've you been talking to?"

"State attorney general's office, they've been after him for years. But nobody can touch him, partly because of this interesting portfolio of IOUs he's holding. The amounts themselves aren't all that huge, but taken one at a time, it's always enough to guarantee obedience."

"Obedience to . . ."

"Commanders. Controllers. Prussia gets the money, plus the vig, and the others get what they want done done."

"But there's loan sharks everywhere. Are they all in on this, too?"

"Maybe not. Prussia's allergic to competition. Anybody started threatening his share, they'd be apt to suddenly wind up in distress."

"Dead?"

"If you want to put it that way."

"But the more of that he does—"

"The better his chances of being popped, yeah you'd think. But not if he's running the ones most apt to do the popping."

"LAPD?"

"Oh, heaven forfend."

"And Prussia's immunity from them would also extend to the people he sends around to collect?"

"How it usually works."

"Then something here is ungroovy." Doc ran down Puck Beaverton's history briefly. "The last time he got popped? I looked it up. One seed they found in his vacuum-cleaner bag, my little nephew who's five could've got him off. But nobody fixed it, he still got arrested and with his record he could've been in for a zip six at least."

"Maybe some cop he offended?"

"Not likely any of the cops who borrowed from Prussia—that was all easy terms and friendly relations. But, just about the only one of Prussia's people that ever got run in was Puck."

"So it was really personal."

"Bummer. Means I have to talk to Bigfoot again."

"You should know how to do that by now."

"No, I mean human to human."

"Jesus. Don't tell me how *that* comes out."

DOC FIGURED HE'D be likely to run into Bigfoot out at the Waste-a-Perp Target Range down off South La Brea. For some reason Bigfoot liked to use civilian ranges. Had the LAPD 86'd him from cop facilities? Were there too many colleagues looking to shoot him down and pretend it was an accident? Doc wasn't about to ask why.

He went out to the range after suppertime, as soon as it got dark. He knew that Bigfoot preferred the Urban, Gang-related and Hippie (UGH) section, where full-length plastic images of black, Chicano, and longhaired menaces to society came lurching at you on a 3-D shooting-gallery-type arrangement while you blew the 'suckers to shreds. Doc himself liked to spend most of his time on the low-light part of the range. Lately he'd come to regard these visits as not so much about exercising night vision as John Garfield dead in the gutter, and dead from real-world Hollywood betrayal and persecution, and the controlling order under which outcomes like this were unavoidable, because they ran off of cold will and muzzle velocity and rounds discharged in the dark.

Sure enough, there was Bigfoot at the cash register, just settling up.

"Need to talk," Doc said.

"I was headed for the Raincheck Room."

This esteemed West Hollywood saloon was known in those days for a thrifty approach to light bills. Doc and Bigfoot found a booth in back.

"Mrs. Bjornsen sends her regards, by the way."

"What're you talking about, she hates me."

"No actually you quite intrigue her now. If I weren't so confident in my marriage, I'd almost be jealous."

Doc tried to remove all sympathy from his face while thinking, ah you poor Swedish Fish, and I hope you're keeping that service .38 out of everybody's reach. Far as Doc could see, the woman was dangerously unbalanced, and he estimated a week and a half before apocalypse descended upon the Bjornsens. "Well sure, tell her howdy."

"Anything else I can do for you this evening?"

"Correct me if I'm mistaken here, Bigfoot, but it's been clear to me for some time that you're desperate to have a word with Puck Beaverton but can't let on, because otherwise you're in deep shit with powers unnamed, so instead you keep putting me out there on point for all 'em AKs in the jungle to open up on—have I got that more or less right so far?"

"We're in sensitive territory here, Sportello."

"Yes, I know all that man, but somebody's gonna have to be less sensitive for a minute and just wipe off their chin and stand up and *deal* with it, 'cause I'm tired of this bein jacked around all the time, if there's something you need just come on out and say it, how hard can that be?"

With Doc this passed for an outburst, and Bigfoot gazed back in what, with him, passed for astonishment. He nodded at Doc's shirt-pocket. "Mind if I have one of those?"

"You don't want to start smoking, Bigfoot, smokin's bad for your ass."

"Yes well I wasn't planning to smoke it in my ass, was I?"

"How I'm spoze to know that?"

Bigfoot lit up, puffed without inhaling in a way Doc found annoying, and said, "Among certain of my colleagues, Puck Beaverton—for a felony offender with conspicuous impulse-control issues and a swastika

on his head—was always considered rather a charming fellow, really."
He took half a beat. "For any number of reasons."

"And now I'm supposed to say—"

"Throwing you a cue. I'm sorry. It's a habit."

"Like smoking."

"All right." Bigfoot squashed out the cigarette irritably and glared at
Doc, who by reflex was already looking covetously at the lengthy butt.
"Puck's former employer, AP Finance, did regular business with many
officers in the Department, all of it friendly and as far as I know above-
board. Perhaps with one unhappy exception."

A name which must not be spoken aloud. Doc shrugged. "Part of
that IA hangup you keep mentioning." Breezily enough, he hoped.

"Please understand, without a preeminent need to know . . ."

"Groovy with me, Bigfoot. And this unnamable cop—how did Puck
happen to feel about him?"

"Hated him, and the hatred was mutual. For—" Dropping then into
second thoughts.

"For good reason. But you have an Eleventh Commandment about
criticizing a fellow flatfoot, I can dig that." Doc then had a thought. "Is
it okay to ask if this party is still on the job?"

"He's—" The silence was as clear as the word withheld. "His status is
Inactive."

"File's unavailable too, I bet."

"The IA's locked it all down till the year 2000."

"Don't sound like it was natural causes somehow. Uh who do you
thank, as Elvis always sez, when you have such luck?"

"Aside from the obvious, you mean."

"Puck, sure, it could've been him. But tell me now, this cop—what
do we call him?—Officer X?"

"Detective."

"Okay, let's say this mystery cop was actually the one who arrested
Puck on that chickenshit dope-seed charge, hoping with his record he'd
be put back in Folsom for a while. If it wasn't Puck who did him, then

let's see, who else . . . oh! how about Adrian Prussia, who can't afford to look bad in front of the community, if even one of his former people gets arrested, maybe convicted. That's a shot somebody's taking not just at Puck but at him. Almost as bad as some deadbeat refusing to pay back a loan. What happens in those cases again. I forget."

"You begin to see?" Bigfoot glumly nodding. "You think it's all one big monolithic funfest at the LAPD, don't you, nothing to do all day but figure out new ways to persecute you hippie scum. Instead it might as well be the yard at San Quentin. Gangs, addicts, butches and bitches and snitches, and everybody's packing."

"Can I say something out loud? Is anybody listening?"

"Everybody. Nobody. Does it matter?"

"Say Adrian Prussia iced this Detective X, or had it done. And what happens? nothing. Maybe everybody in LAPD knows he did the deed, but there's no back-channel outcries in the paper, no vigilante revenge by horrified fellow officers. . . . No, instead IA locks it all up tight for the next thirty years, everybody pretending it's another cop hero fallen in the line of duty. Forget about decency, or respecting the memories of all the real dead-cop heroes—how can you people be that fuckin unprofessional?"

"It gets even worse," Bigfoot said in a slowly stifled way, as if trying in vain to call to Doc out of years of history forbidden to civilians. "Prussia has been prime suspect in . . . let's say a number of homicides—and each time, upon intervention from the highest levels, he's walked."

"And you're saying what? 'Ain't it awful'?"

"I'm saying there's a reason for everything, Doc, and before you get too indignant you might want to look at why Internal Affairs should even be duked into this in the first place, let alone be the office that's sitting on the story."

"I give up. Why?"

"Figure it out. Use what's left of your brain. The trouble with you people is you never know when somebody's doing you a favor. You think whatever it is, you're entitled because you're cute or something." He got up, dropped a handful of shrapnel on the table, tossed a disgruntled salute to the barkeep, and prepared to step out into the street. "Go look in a mirror sometime. 'Dig' yourself, 'man,' till you understand that nobody owes you anything. Then get back to me." Doc had seen Bigfoot out of sorts now and then, but this was getting downright emotional.

They stood on the corner of Santa Monica and Sweetzer. "Where were you parked?" said Bigfoot.

"Off of Fairfax."

"My direction as well. Walk with me, Sportello, I'll show you something." They begin to stroll along Santa Monica. Hippies were thumbing rides up and down the street. Rock 'n' roll was blasting from car radios. Musicians who'd just come awake were drifting out of the Tropicana looking for evening breakfast. Reefer smoke hung in pockets up and down the street, waiting to ambush the unwary pedestrian. Men were murmuring to each other in doorways. After a few blocks, Bigfoot turned right and ambled down toward Melrose. "This looking familiar yet?"

Doc had an intuition. "It's Puck's old neighborhood." He started looking for the overgrown courtyard complex Trillium had told him about. His nose began to run and his clavicles to shiver, and he wondered if somehow one or all of the happy threesome were about to appear, to what Sortilège liked to call manifest, and from the corner of his eye he noticed Bigfoot watching him closely. Yes and who says there can't be time travel, or that places with real-world addresses can't be haunted, not only by the dead but by the living as well? It helps to smoke a lot of weed and to do acid off and on, but sometimes even a literal-minded natchmeister like Bigfoot could manage it.

They approached a courtyard apartment building nearly dissolved in the evening. "Go have a look around, Sportello. Sit out by that pool there under the New Zealand tree ferns. Experience the night." He made a show of looking at his watch. "Regretfully, I have to be moving along. The missus will be expecting me."

"One special lady for sure. Pass on my regards."

No lights, either incandescent or cathode-ray, showed in any of the apartment windows. The whole place might have been deserted. The traffic on Santa Monica was scarcely audible. The moon rose. Small critters went running around in the undergrowth. What came creeping out of the shrubbery after a while actually were not ghosts but logical conclusions.

If Internal Affairs was hushing up the murder of an LAPD detective, then somebody in the Department must have wanted him dead. If they were unwilling to do it themselves, then they were hiring contract specialists, and the list plausibly could've included Adrian Prussia. It would be interesting to look into the other murder raps Bigfoot claimed that Prussia had beaten. But even on the remote chance Bigfoot had access to it, there might be no direct way for him to get the information to Doc. Which might explain why it looked so much like he'd been hustling Doc, from the jump, into discovering some other way into the loan shark's history.

Doc wondered what way that might be. Fritz's ARPAnet would be too much of a crap shoot—according to Fritz, you never knew from one day to the next what you'd find on it, or wouldn't find. Which left Penny. Who had already shopped him to *los federales* and might have little if any problem reshopping him to the LAPD. Penny who might not even want to see him anymore. That Penny.

SIXTEEN

DOC HAD NEVER KEPT COUNT, BUT HE'D PROBABLY SPENT WAY more time in the Hall of Justice on the upper floors, in the men's lockup, than downstairs on the other side of the law. The elevators were run by a squad of uniformed women commanded and terrified by a large, jail-matronly lady with an Afro who stood in the lobby with a pair of castanets dispatching the individual cars with different signals. *Tkk-trrrrrkk-tk-tk* might mean, for example, "Elevator Two's up next, that's forty-five seconds in and out, let's be movin it," and so forth. She gave Doc a serious once-over before letting him aboard.

Penny shared her cubicle with another deputy DA named Rhus Frothingham. When Doc put his head in the door, Penny did not exactly gasp but did start hiccupping uncontrollably. "Are you all right?" said Rhus.

Between hiccups Penny explained, though all Doc could make out was ". . . the one I was telling you about . . ."

"Should I call Security?"

Penny threw Doc an inquiring look, like, so, should she? It might as well be stewardii out at the beach around here. Rhus sat rigidly at her desk, pretending to read through a file. Penny excused herself and headed for the ladies' lounge, leaving Doc immersed in Rhus's glare like an old car radiator in an acid bath. After a while he got up and ankled his way down the corridor and met Penny coming out of the toilet. "Only wondering when you'd be free for dinner. Didn't mean to freak you out. I'll even spring for it."

That sideways look. "Thought you'd never want to speak to me again."

"The FBI has actually been fantastically stimulating company, so I figure at least I owe you some ribs or somethin."

What it turned out to be was a recently opened gourmet health-food joint off Melrose called The Price of Wisdom, which Doc had heard about from Denis, who'd given it a rave. It was upstairs from a dilapidated bar where Doc remembered hanging out during one of his seedier phases, he forgot which. Penny looked up at the flickering red neon sign and frowned. "Ruby's Lounge, uh-huh, I remember it well, it used to be good for at least one felony arrest per week."

"Groovy cheeseburgers as I recall."

"Voted unanimously by local food critics the Southland's Most Toxic."

"Sure, but it kept down the health-code violations, all those mice and roaches every morning with their li'l feet in the air, stone dead next to the burgers that done the deed?"

"Getting hungrier by the minute." Directed by a hand-lettered sign reading, THE PRICE OF WISDOM IS ABOVE RUBY'S, JOB 28:18, Doc and Penny ascended into a room full of ferns, exposed bricks, stained glass, tablecloths on the tables and Vivaldi on the sound system, none of these for Doc too promising. Waiting for a table, he eyeballed the clientele, many of whom seemed to have fitness issues, gazing at each other over and around salads detailed as the miniature mountains in Zen gardens, trying to identify various soybean-derived objects with the aid of pocket flashlights or magnifying lenses, sitting with knife and fork gripped in either fist regarding platters of Eggplant Wellington or rhomboids of vivid green kale loaf on plates too big for them by an order of magnitude.

Doc began to wonder, too late, just how stoned Denis had been when he came in here. It didn't get any more encouraging when the menus finally arrived. "Can you read any of this?" Doc said after a while. "I can't read this, is it me, or some foreign language thing?"

She gave him a smile he had learned not to trust too heavily. "Yes, so clear something up for me, Doc, because taking me out to a place like this could be construed as a hostile act—are you pissed off at me? Not pissed off?"

"That's the choice? Well, give me a minute. . . ."

"Those federal guys helped me out with something once. This seemed like an easy way to return the favor."

"That's me," said Doc. "Always easy."

"You *are* pissed off."

"I'm over it. But you didn't ask me beforehand."

"You would've said no. You people all hate the FBI."

"What are you talking about, us people? I was a Dick Tracy Junior G-Man, sent away for this kit? Learned how to snoop on all the neighbors, fingerprinted everybody in first grade, got the ink all over everything, they sent me to the principal's office—'But I'm a Junior G-Man! They know about me in Washington, D.C.!' I had to stay after school for a month, but it was Mrs. Keeley and I got to look up her dress now and then, so that was cool."

"What a horrible little boy."

"See, it was way before they invented miniskirts—"

"Listen, Doc, the feds really want to know what you were doing in Vegas."

"Hanging with Frank and the gang, playing a little baccarat, more important, what were your two cheap-suit idiot friends doing there getting in my face?"

"Please. They can subpoena you. They have permanent grand juries that have been known to indict a bean burrito. They can put you in a world of heartache."

"Just to find out why I went to Vegas? That sounds really cost-effective."

"Or you can tell me, and I'll tell them."

"As one Junior G-Person to another, Penny, what are you getting out of this?"

She grew solemn. "Maybe you don't want to know."

"Let me guess. It isn't something nice they'll do *for* you, it's something shitty they won't do *to* you."

She touched his hand, as if she did it so seldom she wasn't sure of how. "If I could believe for one second . . ."

"That I could protect you."

"At this point even a practical idea would help."

Midnight, pitch dark, can't remember whether they drained the pool or not, hey, what the fuck's it matter? He bounced once, twice, then off the end of the board and down in a blind cannonball. "You probably know your pals have Mickey Wolfmann."

"The FBI." There might've been a question mark on the end, but Doc didn't hear it. Her eyes narrowed, and he noticed enough of a pulse in her temple to make one of her drop earrings begin to flash like a warning light. "We've suspected, but can't prove anything. Can you?"

"I saw him in their custody."

"You saw him." She thought for a few seconds, tapping a high-school marching-band beat on the tablecloth. "Would you be willing to depone for me?"

"Sure babe, you bet! . . . Uh wait a minute, what does that mean?"

"You, me, a tape machine, maybe another DDA to witness it?"

"Wow, I'll even throw in a few bars of 'That's Amore.' Only thing is . . ."

"All right, what is it *you* want."

"I need to look at somebody's jacket. Ancient history, but it's still under seal. Like till 2000?"

"That's it? No big thing, we do that all the time."

"What, break into officially sealed records? And here I had such faith in the system."

"At this rate you'll be ready for your bar exam any day now. Listen, would you mind if we just went back to my place?" and immediately

Doc—though he would have wagered against it—got a hardon. As if she'd noticed it, she added, "And we can pick up a pizza on the way."

There was a time, back in his period of impulse-control deficit, when Doc's reply would've had to be, "Marry me." What he said now was, "Your hair's different."

"Somebody talked me into seeing this hotshot on Rodeo Drive. He puts in these streaks, see?"

"Groovy. Looks like you've been living at the beach for a while."

"They were promoting a Surfer Chick Special."

"Just for me, huh?"

"Who else, Doc."

Back at Penny's place it took maybe a minute and a half to deal with the pizza. Both of them reached at the same time for the last slice. "I believe this is mine," said Doc.

Penny let go of the pizza and slid her hand down, took hold of his penis, and gave it a squeeze. "And this, I believe . . ." She reached over a stash box with some Asian buds in it he'd been smelling since he came in the room. "Roll us one while I go find an appropriate outfit." He was just twisting the ends of the joint when she came back wearing nothing at all.

"There you go."

"Now, you're sure you're not pissed off."

"Me? pissed off, what's that?"

"You know, if somebody I cared about, even in a casual-sex sort of way, had shopped *me* to the FBI? I'd certainly think twice. . . ." Doc lit up and passed her the joint. "I mean," she added thoughtfully when next she exhaled, "if it was *my* dick? and some self-satisfied lady prosecutor thought she was getting away with something?"

"Oh," said Doc. "Well, you've got a point. . . . Here, let me. . . ."

"Just try it," she cried, "you drug-crazed hippie freak, get your hand out of there, who said you could do that, let go of my, what do you think you're—" By which time they were fucking, you could say, energetically. It was quick, not too quick, it was mean and nasty enough, it was great stoned fun, and in fact for an untimably short moment Doc believed it was somehow never going to be over, though he managed not to get panicked about that.

Normally Penny would've jumped right up again and gotten reimmersed in some straight-world activity, and Doc would have found his way to the TV set on some chance the playoffs, even though it was Eastern Division tonight, might still be on. But instead, as if both appreciated the importance of silence and embrace, they just lay there and lit up again and took time to finish the joint, which owing to its high resin content had considerably gone out the instant it hit the ashtray. Too soon, however, like Reality marching into the room, flipping on the lights, taking a gander, and going "Hrrumph!" it was time for the eleven-o'clock news, taken up, as always and for Penny more and more annoyingly, by developments in the Manson case, about to go to trial.

"Give it a rest, Bugliosi," she snarled at the screen while the lead prosecutor was having his nightly couple of minutes with the cameras.

"Would've thought all this pretrial stuff'd be right up your alley," Doc said.

"It was, for a while. They let me get in on a couple of depositions, but it's too much like boys up in a tree house. The only part I enjoy anymore is hearing how all these hippie chicks did everything Manson told them to do. That master-slave thing, you know, it's kind of cute?"

"Oh yeah? you never told me you were into that, Penny, you mean all this time we could've been—"

"With you? forget it, Doc."

"What."

"Well . . ." Was that what they call a *mischievous gleam* in her eye? "You're almost short enough. I guess. But, see, it isn't only the hypnotic stare, Charlie's big appeal is that he's down there eyeball to eyeball with the ladies he's ordering around. It might be about fucking Daddy, but the really perverse thrill is that Daddy's only five foot two."

"Wow man, well . . . I could work on that?"

"Keep me up to date, anyway."

A promo came on for the late movie, which tonight happened to be *Ghidrah, the Three-Headed Monster* (1964).

"Hey Penny, were you going in tomorrow?"

"Maybe around midday. Unless you have a better idea, I'm just going to go crash, I think."

"No wait a minute, here's something you might really like." He tried to explain that this Japanese monster movie was actually a remake of the classic chick flick *Roman Holiday* (1953), both movies featuring a stylish princess visiting another country who meets a working-class protag who becomes sweet on her, although, despite having some adventures together, the two at the end must part, but somewhere in the middle of this review, Penny having slid gracefully to her knees and begun sucking his cock, next thing either of them knew, there they were fucking again. Afterward, as they were sitting on the couch, the movie came on. Doc must have drifted away somewhere in the middle, but toward the end he woke up to find Penny sniffling into a Kleenex, transfixed by the human or romantic part of the plotline after all.

NEXT DAY WAS as they say another day, and by the time Doc found himself in the Hall of Justice again sitting on a chair from some long-ago yard sale in front of a tape recorder mike back in a neglected cubicle among brooms, mops, cleaning supplies, and an antique floor-waxing machine which may have been assembled from WWII tank parts, he'd begun to wonder if the affectionate Penny of last night hadn't just been another wishful hallucination. She kept calling him Larry, for one thing, and avoiding eye contact. The witness she brought along naturally turned out to be her cubicle-mate Rhus, whose glare had intensified overnight from suspicion to loathing.

Doc ran through for them what he'd seen in Vegas, having stopped by his office earlier to pick up a logbook, a sign not so much of professionalism as of Doper's Memory. There was uncommon interest in Mickey's white suit, for some reason. Lapel-notch location and so forth.

Ready-made or bespoke. And how was his attitude? they wanted to know. Who was present besides the FBI? Who appeared to be in charge?

"No way to tell. There was casino security, and all kinds of civilians in suits moving around, but in terms of Mob folks, if that's what you're getting at, were they wearing black fedoras, making with Eddie Robinson remarks? no, not that I know of?"

This county-DA exercise really looked to Doc like pissants versus elephants. You could catch the FBI in the act of sodomizing the president in the Lincoln Memorial at high noon and local law enforcement would still just have to stand around and watch, getting more or less nauseated depending which president.

On the other hand, nobody asked about Puck Beaverton, and Doc didn't volunteer anything. Now and then he caught the two deputy DAs giving each other significant looks. What about, he had no idea. Finally the tape ran out and Penny said, "I think we're done here. On behalf of the DA's office, Mr. Sportello, thank you so much for your cooperation."

"And thank you, Miss Kimball, for not thanking me while the tape was on. And Miss Frothingham, may I add, that skirt length on you today is especially attractive."

Rhus screamed and picking up a galvanized trash can prepared to throw it at Doc's head, but Penny intervened and coaxed her out the door. Just before she disappeared herself, she looked back at Doc and pointed at the phone, making phone-call gestures. Who was supposed to call whom was less clear.

The clock up on the wall, which reminded Doc of elementary school back in the San Joaquin, read some hour that it could not possibly be. Doc waited for the hands to move, but they didn't, from which he deduced that the clock was broken and maybe had been for years. Which was groovy however because long ago Sortilège had taught him the esoteric skill of telling time from a broken clock. The first thing you had to do was light a joint, which in the Hall of Justice might seem odd, but surely not way back here—who knew, maybe even outside the jurisdiction of local drug enforcement—though just to be on the safe side he also lit a De Nobili cigar and filled the room with a precautionary cloud of smoke from the classic Mafia favorite. After inhaling potsmoke for a while, he glanced up at the clock, and sure enough, it showed a different time now, though this could also be from Doc having forgotten where the hands were to begin with.

The phone rang, he picked up and heard Penny say, "Come down to my cubicle, there'll be a package waiting for you." No hello or nothing.

"Will you be there?"

"No."

"How about what's-her-name?"

"Nobody'll be there but you. Take all the time you need."

"Thanks babe, oh hey and by the way I was wondering, if I could find you a Manson-chick type wig to wear? would it be, like, a problem"— the change in sound ambience as she hung up echoed for a while—"I was thinking in terms of Lynette 'Squeaky' Fromme, you know, sort of long and curled at the same time, and—Oh. Uhm . . . Penny?"

DOWNSTAIRS IN PENNY'S cubicle, waiting for Doc on a beat-up old wood table and decorated with all kinds of top-secret stickers, sat the record of Adrian Prussia's strange history with the California Public Code, including his numerous escapes from punishment for murder one. Doc lit a Kool, opened the folder, and started reading, and it was clear right away why the Department didn't want any of this known. His first thought was how much danger Penny might've put herself in the way of for unsealing this—maybe not even aware of how much. For her it was just more ancient history.

Detective X's name turned out to be Vincent Indelicato. Adrian's law-yers had argued justifiable homicide. Their client Mr. Prussia, a widely respected businessman, believing someone was breaking in to his beach apartment on Gummo Marx Way, had mistaken the decedent for the irate husband of a female acquaintance and, swearing further that he'd seen a gun, thereupon fired his own. No one was more upset than Mr. Prussia to find he'd plugged an LAPD detective, one he had even in fact met occasionally in the course of his normal day's business.

The body was identified by the arresting officer, Detective Indelicato's partner of many years, Lieutenant Christian F. Bjornsen.

"What," Doc wondered aloud, "the fuck, is going on here?"

Bigfoot's partner. The one he didn't ride with these days, or talk about, or even mention by name. Bigfoot's air of possessed melancholy now began to make sense. This was mourning all right, and it was deep.

And where else could the events have taken place but Gummo Marx Way—GMW, as it was known locally, the hard-luck boulevard everybody living along Doc's piece of shoreline sooner or later ended up on, though nobody Doc knew had ever lived there, or knew anybody else who did. Yet somehow there it always lay, between the populations of the South Bay beach towns and other places they thought at some point in their lives they needed to be. The home of a girlfriend whose psychopathic parents wanted her back before curfew. A dealer shifty as a rat up a palm tree, whose less-wary clients found themselves putting oregano and Bisquick to uses they were never meant for. A pay phone in a bar that a friend of a friend, in peril and without resources, had called you from, the hope in his voice already fading, too late at night.

"Okay, wait a minute," Doc muttered, maybe out loud, "is what this is now, is . . ." Bigfoot's partner is murdered by Adrian Prussia, with the apparent collaboration of elements in the department. How does Bigfoot react? Does he check out an appropriate-size cannon and some extra clips and go looking for Adrian? Does he plant a bomb in the loan shark's car? Does he keep it all inside the LAPD and embark on a nonviolent and lonely crusade for justice? No, none of the above, instead what Bigfoot does is, is he finds some dumb-ass sucker of a civilian PI who'll keep nosing on into the case, maybe even clumsily enough to call some attention.

And then what? What did Bigfoot expect to happen? Somebody

would decide to come after Doc? Groovy. And where'd be the nameless, unspoken-of partner to watch Doc's back for him?

As if looking for something he knew he didn't want to find, Doc leafed quickly through the other arrests in the folder. It became clear as vodka you keep in the icebox that whatever the connection was between the LAPD and Adrian Prussia, he might as well have been working for them as a contract killer. Time after time he was pulled in, questioned, arraigned, indicted, no matter—somehow the cases never quite got to trial, each being bargained down in the interests of justice, not to mention of Adrian, who invariably walked. The thought did flit on fragile mothlike wings in and out of Doc's consciousness that the DA's office had to be aware of all this, if not outright complicit. Sometimes there wouldn't be enough evidence for a case, or what there was would be inadmissible, or too circumstantial, or the body couldn't be found, or sometimes a third party would come forward and plead to some make-believe offense like voluntary manslaughter. One of these thoughtful patsies in particular caught Doc's attention, turning out to be who but his old parking-lot Q&A buddy Boris Spivey, currently on the run out in the U.S. someplace with his fiancée Dawnette. From Pico Rivera. Curiously, after pulling reduced time on the Semi-Honor Block at San Quentin, Boris had then been cut loose to go directly to work for Mickey Wolfmann. Making him, along with Puck, the second AP Finance alumnus Doc knew of who'd hired on with Mickey. Was Adrian Prussia also running a talent agency?

Doc was about to shut the folder and go looking for a cigarette machine when something more recent caught his eye. It was a brightly lit photograph which didn't look attached to anything else, as if it had been tossed in in some miscellaneous way. It showed a group of men standing on a pier next to an open box about the size of a coffin, full of U.S. currency. Among them was Adrian Prussia in some idea of a yachting costume, holding up one of the bills and making with the shit-eating grin which had endeared him to so many. The bill was a twenty and looked strangely familiar. Doc rooted around in his fringe bag till he found a Coddington lens and squinted through it at the picture. "Aha!" Just as he thought. It was that CIA Nixonhead funnymoney again, like the bills Sauncho and his pals had fished out of the drink. And in the background, riding calmly at anchor in some nameless harbor, slightly out of focus as if through the veils of the next world, the schooner *Golden Fang*. There was a date on the back of the photo. Less than a year ago.

ON THE WAY back to the beach, Doc looked in at the offices of Hardy, Gridley & Chatfield. Sauncho was there, but mentally for the moment not available, having the other night happened to watch *The Wizard of Oz* (1939) for the first time on a color TV set.

"Did you know it starts off in black and white," he informed Doc with some anxiety, "but it changes to color! Do you realize what that means?"

"Saunch . . ."

No use. "—the world we see Dorothy living in at the beginning of the picture is black, actually brown, and white, only *she thinks* she's seeing it all in color—the same normal everyday color we see our lives in. Then the cyclone picks her up, dumps her in Munchkin Land, and she walks out the door, and suddenly *we* see the brown and white shift into Technicolor. But if that's what *we* see, what's happening with Dorothy? What's her 'normal' Kansas color changing into? Huh? What very weird *hyper*color? as far beyond our everyday color as Technicolor is beyond black and white—" and so on.

"I know I should . . . be worried about this, Saunch, but . . ."

"The network ought to've at least run a disclaimer," Sauncho by now quite indignant. "Munchkin Land is strange enough, isn't it, without adding to the viewer's mental confusion, and in fact I think there's a pretty good class-action suit here against MGM itself, so I'm gonna bring it up at the firm's next weekly get-together."

"Well, can I ask you something that's sort of related?"

"You mean about Dorothy and the—"

"Y—sort of. You recall that stash of Nixon bills you guys hauled out of the drink. I just ran across a photo of a loan shark named Adrian Prussia posed next to a box full of the stuff. Maybe from the same batch you found, maybe not. Did anybody keep a record of what happened to it after you hauled it in?"

"I'd certainly like to think most of it's safe and sound in a federal evidence room someplace."

"You'd like to, but . . ."

"Well, for a while out on deck there, it all got into a happy-go-lucky type atmosphere. . . . Federals are like everybody else, you can't expect them to live on their salaries."

"Thing about this picture is, is they all look like they just got off, or were maybe about to get on, the *Golden Fang*."

"Swell. So how does this relate again to Dorothy Gale and her color-vision situation?"

"What?"

"You said this photo you saw was 'sort of' related."

"Oh. Oh, well it was in this, this strange color process? Yeah. Colors looked like they do on acid?"

"Nice try, Doc."

FIGURING TO CHECK in at his office, Doc left the Marina by way of Lincoln Boulevard, slid across the creek and down Culver to Vista del Mar. Even in the parking lot, he felt something was strange, not only in the afternoon hush of the building but also in Petunia's demeanor. "Oh Doc, do you really have to go upstairs right away? It's been ages since we had one of our interesting chats." She was perched attractively on a sort of high barstool next to her check-in station, and Doc couldn't help noticing that her lilac turnout today didn't seem to include matching, or in fact any, underwear. Good thing he was wearing shades, which allowed him to gaze for longer than usual. "Um, Petunia, are you trying to tell me I have visitors waiting?"

She lowered her gaze and voice. "Not exactly."

"Not exactly visitors?"

"Not exactly waiting?"

The door upstairs was unlocked and slightly ajar. Doc stooped and reached the little snub-nose Magnum out of his ankle rig, though it did not take a sharp ear to identify what was going on inside. He eased through the door, and the first thing he saw was Clancy Charlock and Tariq Khalil down on his office floor, fucking.

After a while Tariq looked up. "Hey. Doctor Sportello, my man. This is all right, isn't it?"

Doc raised his sunglasses and pretended to scrutinize the scene. "Looks all right to me, but you'd know better'n I would. . . ."

"What he means is," Clancy, from somewhere underneath, clarified, "is it all right that we're using your office." Seems while Doc was in Vegas, they had showed up here separately one day looking for him, and Petunia decided they were a cute couple, so she gave them a spare key. Doc excused himself and headed back downstairs to have a word with Petunia, the particular word on his mind being "cute."

"I know you have the soul of a matchmaker, Petunia, and normally I'm groovy with intimacy of all kinds, but not between elements in a case I'm workin on. Too much information I end up never seeing. . . ."

And so on. Fat lot of good this did against the perhaps-insane sparkle in her eyes. "But it's too late, can't you see? they're in love! I'm just the karmic facilitator, I really have the gift for knowing who's supposed to be together and who's not, and I'm never wrong. I've even been staying up late night after night, studying for my degree in Relationship Counseling so I can make some contribution no matter how tiny to the total amount of love in the world."

"The total what?"

"Oh, Doc. Love is the only thing that will ever save us."

"Who?"

"Everybody."

"Petun-*ya?*" screamed Dr. Tubeside from some back region of the suite. "Well, maybe not him."

"I think I'm gonna go back upstairs now and see if they're really there. . . ."

After a couple of careful taps on his office door, Doc put his head gingerly around the edge of it and this time observed Tariq and Clancy with their clothes back on, playing a quiet game of gin rummy and listening to a Bonzo Dog Band album which to his knowledge Doc didn't own. Obviously hallucination wasn't out of the question here, but then again if it really was happening, all the average pothead had to do was look at them to see that their common element, Glen Charlock, had been gathering presence and energy, like a ghost slowly becoming visible.

Clancy noticed Doc and whispered something to Tariq. They put down their cards and Tariq said, "Figured on you showin up sometime, man."

Doc headed for the electric coffeepot and started in making coffee. "I had to go to Las Vegas," he said. "I thought I was looking for Puck Beaverton."

"Clancy mentioned something. Any luck?"

"Nothin but," Doc shrugged. "It was Vegas."

"He's pissed off," Clancy said.

"Am not."

"I wanted to talk to you about Glen," Tariq said.

"So did I," added Clancy.

Doc nodded, looked in his shirt for a cigarette, came up empty-fingered.

"Here," said Clancy.

"Virginia Slims? what is this?" But Clancy was holding out her lighter like the Statue of Liberty or something. "All right," Doc said, "it's menthol at least."

"I should've told you the whole thing," Tariq said. "Too late now, but I still could've trusted you more."

"Some white detective you never met before, and you didn't trust me? Wow, now I *am* pissed off."

"You need to tell him," Clancy pointed out to Tariq.

"But—" Doc went to supervise the coffeemaker. "Wait a minute man, didn't you say you had to take some oath of silence about that?"

"That don't count," Tariq said. "I thought it did once, but Puck and them other Nazis took a oath too, to watch each other's back no matter what, and look how much good it did Glen. Am I uh spoze to respect *that* shit? I'm off the hook now. They don't like it, they can see how far they get with it."

"Okay. So what was it Glen owed you, exactly?"

"First you got to take a oath."

"What? You just said that was bullshit."

"Yeah, but you a honky. You got to sign off in blood, Blood, that you won't ever tell *nobody*."

"Blood?"

"Clancy did."

"I'm in the middle of my period, darlin," she pointed out.

"So . . . could I borrow some of yours?" Doc wondered.

"Hey, fuck this," Tariq heading for the door.

"Emotional, ain't he?" Doc going over to the file cabinet and retrieving his emergency stash. Like, if this wasn't an emergency . . .

Around the second or possibly third joint, everybody began to relax. Tariq got into the business he and Glen had done together while inside.

It was complicated. The original beef was between two Chicano factions, Nuestra Familia, who were based out of Northern California, and the Sureños, who were from down south here. At that moment among the prison population, there had been active a snitch known as El Huevoncito, who had brought grief to many inmates, black and white as well as Chicano. Everybody hated this little rat, everybody knew he'd have to be dealt with, but for reasons of gang history, which grew very tangled especially when you were smoking weed, none of the Chicano population north or south could conveniently do the deed, so they finally subbed it out to the Aryan Brothers, who just then also happened to have an opening for a new member and were trying to recruit Glen Charlock for the slot. Part of the initiation being that you had to kill somebody. Sometimes giving them a cut on the face was enough, but then that meant they'd eventually have to come after you looking for payback, so it was better, Tariq explained, to just kill they ass and get it over with.

Glen wanted to be in the Brotherhood but didn't want to kill anybody. He knew he would fuck up somehow and get caught, because somehow he always did, and if he wasn't killed on the spot by associates of El Huevoncito, he'd either get a trip upstate to the San Quentin Green Room or be kept in the joint forever, when all he really wanted, sometimes desperately, was to be outside. On the other hand, the Brothers were being really pains in the ass about it. So Glen went looking for a way to sub-subcontract the hit, take credit for it among the Brothers, but escape retaliation from anybody else.

Tariq enjoyed a reputation as a shank artist who never got caught, but approaching him took almost more caution than Glen knew how to use. Black and white did not routinely mix, nor were they encouraged to. "Sounds like fun," Tariq admitted, "but it'll cost a lot. 'Less I'm mistaken, more than you got or be likely to have."

True as far as it went, except that Glen had some unusual connections on the outside, though he'd been careful not to share this information unless he had to. Now it looked like he had to.

"How would you be wanting payment? in cash? Dope? Pussy?" Tariq just stared back. "Help me out. Watermelons?"

Tariq thought about taking offense, shrugged, and made a minimal gesture with his trigger finger, to indicate firearms.

"What do you know. My friends just happen to specialize in that area. What kind of weight we be talking about?"

"Oh, enough for somewhere between a platoon of niggers and a company."

Glen looked around for eavesdroppers. "You don't mean for in *here*, man?"

"Shit no, I'm bad, not stupid. But we all got friends outside, and mine, that's what they could use right now."

"How soon?"

"How soon you want them 'woods suckin all on you dick in gratitude?"

A blur, a shadow, passed, and neither Tariq nor Glen was sure what they saw, but they knew who it was. "Some rat runnin for his hole," Glen said.

"Means we been walkin and talkin too long. Better from here on we keep it short."

By and by, El Huevoncito, rest his soul, was found mysteriously deceased after an early-morning shake-and-bake on Tariq's block, which gave Tariq a perfect alibi and never got traced to him. Glen, with his time also accounted for, was likewise in the clear, though he made a point of asking for brotherly assistance in disposing of a mess-hall shank he'd first put some of his own blood on. He was accepted into the Aryan Brotherhood and shortly after Tariq's release found himself also on the outside, with a job offer from Mickey Wolfmann.

As it turned out, because of the logistics, Tariq's people, Warriors Against the Man Black Armed Militia (WAMBAM) had had to wait awhile for Glen to set up the small-arms part of the deal and by now were growing fretful.

"Which is about the time I come to see you," Tariq said.

"I can dig why you didn't want to get too specific," Doc said. "Maybe I should've took that oath."

"I understand you been gettin some shit from the local FBI, Brother Karenga's bed buddies."

"Yeah but I couldn't tell them much 'cause I didn't know all this. Now I guess I'll have to start worryin about the Red Squad and the P-DIDdies, too."

"How's that?"

"See technically, it's black armed rebellion, ain't it, gets us into heavy Charles Manson fantasy material, and there's idiots enough in the

LAPD who take ol' Charlie seriously when he starts in screamin about all that."

"Yeah over at the WAMBAM office too, I been seein these T-shirts and shit? Like Manson's mug shots with Afros airbrushed onto them, that's real popular."

"How about Lynette 'Squeaky' Fromme?"

"Yeah, ain't *she* some righteous-ass bitch."

"No I meant, like Squeaky T-shirts, where she has a Afro?"

"Oh . . . not that I know of. You want me look around for one?"

"Actually maybe Leslie van Houten, too, what do you think?"

"Fellas," muttered Clancy.

"Right," Doc said, "then . . . I guess what I really need to know from you is who these 'friends' of Glen's were, that were arranging this arms deal."

"Some bunch of honky dentists out on lower Sunset. Worked out of some weird-ass building look like a big tooth?"

"Uh-huh," Doc trying not to betray the hollowness of soul that hit him now. "Well. Maybe I can think of one or two places to look."

Questions arose. Like, what in the fuck was going on here, basically. If Glen all along had had "friends" in the Golden Fang, what was he even doing in the pen? Was he taking the fall for somebody else, some higher-level figure in the Fang organization? Had they put him in there as a deliberate plant, the Fang's man on the inside, as if they had a master scheme to station their agents in all areas of public life? And how deeply implicated did that make the Fang in Glen's murder? Was Glen another Rudy Blatnoyd, had he touched some acupressure point forever uncharted on the mysterious body of the Golden Fang so uncomfortably he had to be dealt with?

And would this be multiple choice?

By now it was dark and they were all hungry, and somehow they ended up at the Plastic Nickel on Sepulveda. Inside, the walls were decorated with silvery plastic reproductions of the heads side of a U.S. five-cent coin, each about the size of a giant pizza. An artificial hedge about two feet high, very green and also of plastic, separated the rows of booths. Crews of unknown hedge-assembly specialists had carefully fitted together thousands of small modular leafy twig imitations plug-and jackwise in nearly infinite complexity to produce this strangely entertaining shrubbery. Over time all manner of small articles got lost down inside of it, including roach clips and roaches and hash pipes, loose change, car keys, earrings, contact lenses, tiny glassine packets of coke and heroin and so forth. Life below, say, one gram. Customers had been known to spend hours while their coffee got cold, carefully going through the hedge inch by inch, especially when on speed. Now and then, late at night, they would be interrupted by one of the plastic images up on the wall, as Thomas Jefferson turned from left profile to full face, unfastened the ribbon that held his hair back, shook everything out into a full-color redheaded freak halo, and spoke to selected dopers, usually quoting from the Declaration of Independence or the Bill of Rights, which had actually been of great help with many legal defenses focusing on search-and-seizure issues in particular. Tonight he waited till Clancy and Tariq had both headed back to the toilets, turned quickly to Doc, and said, "So! the Golden Fang not only traffick in Enslavement, they peddle the implements of Liberation as well."

"Hey . . . but as a founding father, don't you get freaked out a little with this black apocalypse talk?"

"The tree of Liberty must be refreshed from time to time with the blood of patriots and tyrants," replied Jefferson. "It is its natural Manure."

"Yeah, and what about when the patriots and tyrants turn out to be the same people?" said Doc, "like, we've got this president now . . ."

"As long as they bleed," explained Jefferson, "is the thing. Meantime, what are you going to do with the information you've just acquired from Mr. Khalil?"

"Let's see, what are the choices? Go to the FBI and rat out Tariq and WAMBAM. Sic the feds onto the Golden Fang, after giving Tariq enough warning to keep his own ass clear. Tell Bigfoot Bjornsen everything and let him present it to the PDID or whoever, and let them deal with it. What am I leaving out?"

"Do you begin to detect a common thread here, Lawrence?"

"I can't trust any of those people?"

"Remember too that Glen's weapons deal never went through. So you don't really have to *tell* anybody anything. What you *do* have to do, however, is—" He fell abruptly silent and turned back into his ponytailed profile.

"Talking to yourself again," said Clancy. "You need to find true love, Doc."

Actually, he thought, I'll settle for finding my way through this. His fingers, with a mind of their own, began to creep toward the plastic hedge. Maybe if he searched through it long enough, late enough into the night, he'd find something that might help—some tiny forgotten scrap of his life he didn't even know was missing, something that would make all the difference now. He said, "I'm happy for you, Clancy, but what happened to that two at a time?"

She gestured with her head back at Tariq, on his way to rejoin them. "Doc, this guy is at *least* two at a time."

SEVENTEEN

BACK AT HIS PLACE, DOC FOUND SCOTT AND DENIS IN THE
kitchen investigating the icebox, having just climbed in the alley window after Denis, a bit earlier, down at his own place, had fallen asleep
as he often did with a lit joint in his mouth, only this time the joint,
instead of dropping onto his chest and burning him and waking him up
at least partway, had rolled someplace else among the bedsheets, where
soon it began to smolder. After a while Denis woke, got up, and wandered into the bathroom, thought he would take a shower, sort of got
into doing that. At some point the bed burst into flame, burning eventually up through the ceiling, directly above which was his neighbor Chico's water bed, luckily for Chico without him on it, which being plastic
melted from the heat, releasing nearly a ton of water through the hole
that had by now burned in the ceiling, putting out the fire in Denis's
bedroom while turning the floor into a sort of wading pool. Denis came
drifting back from the bathroom, and not able right away to account for
what he found, plus getting the fire department, who had now arrived,
confused with the police, went running down the alley to Scott Oof's
beach place, where he tried to describe what he thought had happened,
basically deliberate sabotage by the Boards, who had never stopped plotting against him.

Doc found a White Owl cigar most of whose contents he had tweezed out and replaced with Humboldt sinsemilla, lit up, inhaled, and started passing it around.

"I don't see how it could be the Boards, man, really," exhaled Scott.

"Hey, I saw them," Denis insisted, "just the other day, lurking in the alley."

"That was only the bass player and drummer," Scott said, "we were hanging out. There's going to be a free concert at Will Rogers Park, they're calling it a Surfadelic Freak-In? and the Boards want Beer to open for them?"

"Groovy," said Doc, "congratulations."

"Yeah," added Denis, "except they're totally evil, of course."

"Well, maybe the label they're signed with," Scott admitted, "but . . ."

"Even Doc thinks they're zombies."

"That's probably true," Doc said, "but you can't always blame zombies for their condition, ain't like there's guidance counselors going around, 'Hey, kid, you ever consider career opportunities with the undead—'"

"Mine told me I should go into real estate," said Scott, "like my mom."

"Your mom's not a zombie," Denis pointed out.

"Yeah, but you should see some of her co-brokers. . . ."

"Just so's you examine her regularly for bites," Doc advised, "which is how it gets transmitted."

"Anybody understand why they call it 'real' estate?" wondered Denis, who was now rolling a joint.

"Hey Doc," Scott remembered, "I saw that Coy again, that used to play with the Boards, who was supposed to be dead only later he wasn't?"

Doc was just barely not too loaded to ask, "Where?"

"In Hermosa, standing in line outside the Lighthouse?"

Sending Doc off down the Toilet of Memory to when he and Shasta were first dating, evenings hanging out in front of the Lighthouse Café, neither of them able to afford the prices, listening to the jazz from inside and eating hot dogs from the renowned Juicy James stand around the corner, whose sign featured a giant hot dog with a face, arms and legs, cowboy hat and getup, firing a pair of six-guns and to all appearances enjoying itself. On Sundays there was always a jam session. Studio musicians showed up in rides they had bought with their first big paychecks, to be redeemed in years to follow from impound lots, winched out of mudslides, preserved from the depredations of divorce lawyers, all replacement parts kept authentic for resales that would never happen, fantasies of the eras when the longings began, Morgans from the showroom up in Westwood with hoods held down by leather straps, Cobra 289s and '62 Bonnevilles and that supernatural DeSoto in which James Stewart, gone round the bend of love, tails Kim Novak in *Vertigo* (1958).

Up at Ojai, Doc and Coy had parted under strange circumstances, with Coy doing an abrupt fade into the evening, half angry, half desperate, after Doc's sort of half promise that he'd look for some way for Coy to cut loose of the countersubversives who were running him. Except for the quick once-over Bigfoot let him have at Coy's LAPD file, Doc hadn't made much progress with this, and he may have been feeling guilty, because technically he was supposed to be working for Hope, too.

So he thought he'd take a stroll down to Pier Avenue. The palm trees along the Strand cast shadows through the fog with its usual chemical smell, the Juicy James sign glowed cheerfully smudged at some uncertain distance, and there in front of the Lighthouse, sure enough, was Coy, among a ragged line of hipsters nodding to the music, Bud Shank today and some rhythm section.

Doc waited for a break between sets and said howdy, expecting another Invisible Man number, but right now Coy had the look of a sailor on liberty, willing to live inside the moment till he had to be back in some condition of servitude.

"I got to take the day off." He checked the light over the ocean. "But it looks like maybe I'm about to be AWOL."

"You need a ride back up to Topanga? Long as I don't have to come in with you, that is."

"Oh, that all got fixed. Now everything's cool."

"'Drac's a part of the band'?"

"Seriously. It was the chicks. None of them could handle it anymore, so they all got together and kicked in and hired an exorcist. Some Buddhist priest from the Temple downtown. He came up one day and did his thing, and now the Boards and the house are all officially dezombified. They gave him a maintenance contract to run regular psychic perimeter checks."

"Did any of the band, like, suddenly recognize you?"

He shrugged. "Maybe. It don't matter as much as it used to."

The fog had thickened by the time they reached the car. Doc and Coy got in, and Doc put the wipers on for a couple of cycles, and they headed up Pier Avenue.

"Chisel one of your smokes?" Coy said. Doc reached him the pack off the dashboard and pushed in the lighter and took a left on Pacific Coast Highway. "Hey, what's this button here?"

"Uh, maybe not, that's the—" They were submerged in the bone-shaking reverberations of Pink Floyd's "Interstellar Overdrive." Doc found the volume knob. "—the Vibrasonic. Takes up half the trunk, but it's there when you need it."

Going under the runway at the airport, they lost the music for a minute and Doc said, "So the Boards really aren't so evil anymore?"

"Maybe confused now and then. You know a band that isn't?"

"You back playin with them now?"

"Workin on it." Doc knew there was more coming. "See, I always needed to think somebody gave a shit. When the call came from Vigilant California, it was like, somebody's been watching all the time, somebody who wants me, sees something in me I never guessed was there. . . ."

"A gift," they told him, "for projecting alternate personalities, infiltrating, remembering, reporting back."

"A spy," Coy translated. "A snitch, a weasel."

"A very well-paid actor," they replied, "and without groupies or paparazzi or know-nothing audiences to worry about."

It would mean kicking heroin, or at least the kind of habit he had then. They told him stories about junkies who had gained control of their addictions. It was called "the Higher Discipline," more demanding than religious or athletic or military discipline because of the abyss you had to dare successfully every moment of every day. They took Coy to meet some of these transcended junkies, and he was amazed at their energy, their color, the bounce in their stride, the improvisational quickness of mind. If Coy performed up to spec or beyond, there would also be the bonus incentive of a once-a-year fix of Percodan, then regarded as the Rolls-Royce of opiates.

Of course, it would mean leaving Hope and Amethyst for good. But nobody at home, he kept reminding himself, had been happy for a real long time, and the Viggies promised to send Hope an anonymous one-time payment, suggesting strongly that it was from Coy. It would have to look like something he'd left them in a will, however, because in order to carry out this particular job he must assume one or more new identities, and the old identity of Coy Harlingen must cease to be.

"Fake my death? Oh, I don't know, man, I mean, that's really bad karma. Don't know if I want to what Little Anthony & the Imperials call 'tempt the hand of fate,' you know?"

"Why think of this as death? why not reincarnation instead? Everybody wishes they had a different life. Here's your opportunity. Plus you get to have fun, to take chances with your ass unparalleled even in the world of heroin abuse, and the pay is far, far better than scale, assuming you ever worked for scale."

"Can I get some new choppers?"

"False teeth? That could be arranged."

The fix was also in, they assured him, with Coy's dealer, El Drano, to provide some especially lethal unstepped-on China White to be found at the scene of the overdose. Coy was advised to use only enough to be plausible in the emergency room but not enough to kill him.

"Not my favorite part of the caper," Coy confessed to Doc. "It was like, I better not fuck up this time, I better have my wits about me, and of course I didn't. As it was, I nearly ate the Big Wiener anyway."

"Where'd your dealer get this heroin from?" Doc asked as pretty much a formality.

"Some bunch of heavies who bring it in direct—not the connection El Drano usually dealt with. Whoever they were, they had him scared shitless, even though he was just the cutout guy, in there to keep it from being traced back to this other source. But they kept telling him, 'Never say a word.' Silence, that was their big thing. So when he showed up floating in the canal the other day, you know, naturally I couldn't help but wonder?"

"Could've been anything, though," Doc said, "he had a long history."

"Maybe."

Eventually, like other turned souls before him, Coy put in some discomfort time at the Chryskylodon program kicking heroin, from which visits to the Smile Maintenance Workshop of Rudy Blatnoyd, D.D.S., seemed almost like vacations. The new teeth meant a new embouchure, and that also took some adjusting, but finally, one night there he was in a toilet stall at LAX, passing compromising notes on toilet paper under the partition to a state legislator with hidden sexual longings whom the Viggies wished to have, as they put it, "on the team." After this—he guessed—audition, the assignments gradually got more demanding—preparation sometimes included reading Herbert Marcuse and Chairman Mao and the comprehension issues that came along with that, plus daily workouts at a dojo in Whittier, dialect coaching in outer Hollywood, evasive driving lessons out in Chatsworth.

It didn't take long for Coy to become aware that the patriots who were running him were being run themselves by another level of power altogether, which seemed to feel entitled to fuck with the lives of all who weren't as good or bright as they were, which meant everybody. Coy learned they'd labeled him an "addictive personality," betting that once committed to snitching for his country, he would find the life as hard to kick as heroin, if not harder. Pretty soon they had him hanging around campuses—university, community college, and high school—and slowly learning to infiltrate antiwar, antidraft, anticapitalist groups of all kinds. For the first months, he was so busy he didn't have time to think about what he'd actually done, or if there was any future in it. One night he was in Westwood shadowing elements of a group at UCLA called the Bong Users' Revolutionary Brigades (BURBs), when he noticed a little girl who would have been about Amethyst's age, breathless with excitement in front of a lighted bookstore window, calling to her mother to come and look. "Books, Mama! Books!" Coy stood nailed in his tracks, while his quarry went on with their evening. It was the first time since signing on with the Viggies that he'd given any thought to the family he had abandoned for something he must have believed was more important.

In that moment everything was clear—the karmic error of faking his own death, the chances that people he was helping to set up were looking at deep possibilities including real death, and clearest of all how much he missed Hope and Amethyst—more, desperately more, than he'd ever thought he would. With no resources, sympathy or support, Coy all of a sudden, too late, wanted his old life back.

"And that's around the time you asked me to look in on them?"

"Yep, that's how desperate I was."

"This is it here, right?"

Doc pulled over on the shoulder near the apron of the Boards' driveway. "One thing."

"Uh-oh."

"The original job offer from Vigilant California—who was it that called you?"

Coy looked Doc over, as if for the first time. "When I started spying, I used to wonder why people ask the questions they do. Then I began to notice how often they already know the answer but just want to hear it from another voice, like outside their own head?"

"All right," Doc said.

"Better go talk to Shasta Fay, I think."

DRIVING BACK DOWN to the coast road, Doc managed to put himself on a full-scale paranoid trip about Shasta, and how she must have been using, all the time she and Doc were together, maybe since before they'd met, a devoted junkie taking every chance she could to slip out into the fine breezy nights and go someplace they'd've been looking after her outfit for her so she wouldn't have to hide it at home from Doc . . . just to be back for a while among the junkie fellowship, to have a break from this hopeless stooge of the creditor class she was already planning to split on and so forth. It took him nearly all the way to Gordita to remember that once again he was being an asshole. By the time he got back to his place and reconfigured his hair into something halfway groovy, and set off up the esplanade to El Porto, with night fallen and the surf invisible, he was back to his old wised-up self, short on optimism, ready to be played for a patsy again. Normal.

The surf shop downstairs had closed early, but there were lights up in the Saint's windows, and Doc didn't have to knock but two or three times before Shasta opened the door and even smiled at him before saying hi, c'mon in. She was barelegged in some kind of Mexican shirt, pale purple with some orange embroidery on it, and had her hair wrapped in a towel, smelling like she did just out of the shower. He knew there was a reason he'd fallen in love with her back then, he kept forgetting it, but now that he half-remembered, he had to grab himself mentally by the head and execute a quick brainshake before he could trust himself to say anything.

Shasta introduced him to her dog Mildred and took some time rattling around in the kitchen. Flip had covered most of one living-room wall with an enlarged photo of a gigantic monster wave at Makaha last winter, with a tiny but instantly recognizable Greg Noll cradled in it like a faithful worshipper in the fist of God.

Shasta came in with a six-pack of Coors from the fridge. "You know Mickey's back," she said.

"Some rumor, yeah."

"Oh, he's back home all right, yep, back home with Sloane and the kids, and so what? *C'est la vie.*"

"Que sera sera."

"You got it."

"Have you seen him?"

"How likely is that? These days I'm only an embarrassment."

"Sure, but maybe if you did something about your hair . . ."

"Fucker." She reached, undid the towel and threw it at him, shook her hair out—he didn't want to say violently, exactly, but there was a look in her eye he remembered, or thought he did. "How's this?"

He angled his head as if she'd asked a serious question. "Darker than it was."

"Back to my old dirty-blond ways. Mickey liked it almost platinum, used to spring for this colorist down on Rodeo Drive?" and Doc knew beyond all doubt that she and Penny had met at that same hair salon, where at least one topic of discussion had been him, and sure enough, "Word's around that you have this thing about Manson chicks?"

"Y—well, 'thing,' guess it depends what you— Are you sure you want to be doing that?"

She had unbuttoned her shirt and now, looking him in the eye, began unhurriedly to stroke her nipples. Mildred glanced up in momentary interest, then, shaking her head slowly side to side, got off the couch and left the room. "Submissive, brainwashed, horny little teeners," Shasta continued, "who do exactly what you want before you even know what that is. You don't even have to say a word out loud, they get it all by ESP. Your kind of chick, Doc, that's the lowdown on you."

"Hey. You the one's been stealin my magazines?"

She slid out of the shirt and down on her knees, and crawled slowly over to where Doc was sitting with an untouched can of beer and a hardon, and, kneeling, she carefully took off his huaraches and gave each bare foot a soft kiss. "Now," she whispered, "what would Charlie do?"

Probably not what Doc would do, which was find half a joint in his shirt pocket and light it up. Which he did. "You want some of this?" She raised her face, and he held the joint to her lips while she inhaled. They smoked in silence till Doc had to put what was left in a little alligator clip he carried with him. "Look, I'm sorry about Mickey, but—"

"Mickey." She gave Doc a good long look. "Mickey could have taught all you swingin beach bums a thing or two. He was just so powerful. Sometimes he could almost make you feel invisible. Fast, brutal, not what you'd call a considerate lover, an animal, actually, but Sloane adored that about him, and Luz—you could tell, we all did. It's so nice to be made to feel invisible that way sometimes . . ."

"Yeah, and guys love to hear shit like this."

". . . he'd bring me to lunch in Beverly Hills, one big hand all the way around my bare arm, steering me blind down out of those bright streets into some space where it was dark and cool and you couldn't smell any food, only alcohol—they'd all be drinking, tables full of them in a room that could've been any size, and they all knew Mickey there, they wanted, some of them, to be Mickey. . . . He might as well have been bringing me in on a leash. He kept me in these little microminidresses, never allowed me to wear anything underneath, just offering me to who-ever wanted to stare. Or grab. Or sometimes he'd fix me up with his friends. And I'd have to do whatever they wanted. . . ."

"Why are you telling me this?"

"Oh I'm so sorry, Doc, are you getting upset, do you want me to stop?" By now she was draped across his lap, her hands beneath her playing with her pussy, her ass irresistibly presented, her intentions, even to Doc, clear enough. "If my girlfriend had run away to be the bought-and-sold whore of some scumbag developer? I'd just be so angry I don't know what I'd do. Well, no, I'm even lying about that, I know what I'd do. If I had the faithless little bitch over my lap like this—" Which was about as far as she got. Doc managed to get in no more than a half dozen sincere smacks before her busy hands had them both coming all over the place. "You fucker!" she cried—not, Doc guessed, at him—"you bastard . . ."

He only remembered later to look for telltale zombie symptoms, in case wherever she'd been they'd processed her somehow, the way they'd done to Mickey, but it seemed like the same old Shasta. Of course, she still could have made a deal to escape Mickey's fate, in which case who was it with, and what was the payback? Before he could ask about any of that, she was talking, quietly, and he knew he'd better listen.

"I said I was up north with family stuff, but what really happened was, was a couple of apes found me and took me to San Pedro and put me on this boat? and I never knew what their real plans for me were, because when we got to Maui, I hustled my way off."

"Some first mate who digs beautiful asses no doubt."

"Chief cook, actually. Then at Pukalani I ran into Flip hitchhiking, and he handed me the keys to this place and asked me to house-sit. Why are you looking so weird all of a sudden?"

"Around the same time that was happening, Vehi Fairfield gave me some acid and while I was tripping I saw you, on that same boat, the *Golden Fang*. I was out in the wind someplace, I don't know, kept tryin to get on board, kept close as long as I could . . . now it's you that's lookin weird."

"I knew it! I felt something then, and all I could think of was that somehow it might be you. It was so creepy."

"Must've been me, then."

"No, I mean it felt like . . . being haunted? It's why the first island we got to, I sent you that card."

"Vehi's spirit guide said you weren't on the ship by choice, but that you'd be okay."

"I wonder if he knew that everybody on board was packing. Officers, crew, passengers."

She didn't exactly ask about it, but Porfirio, the chief cook, had been happy to explain. "Pirates."

"Excuse me?" she said.

"The cargoes we carry, señorita, are highly desirable, particularly in the Third World."

"Think I could borrow something from the ship's armory to carry with me, just in case?"

"You are a passenger. We will protect you."

"You're sure that's what I am, and not just more desirable cargo."

"But this is flirting, yes?"

"Yeah, yeah?" Doc said after a while. "So you said . . ."

"I said, 'Ooh, Porfirio, I hope they're not planning to sell me to some horrible Chinese Communist gang of perverts who'll do all kinds of horrible Chinese stuff to me. . . .'"

Doc found some of Fritz's Thai weed and lit up. "Yeah," after offering her a hit, "and Porfirio said?"

"'Allow me do it all to you first, señorita, with your permission of course, so that you will at least know what to expect.'"

"Uh huh?"

"Well, you know these sailing ships, all the ropes and chains and pulleys and hooks and things. . . .'"

"Okay, that does it—let's see that cute red ass there."

"But . . . Doc . . . what did I say?" She knelt on the couch, put her face down on a pillow, and presented herself.

"You need a tattoo right here. How about 'Bad, Bad Girl'?"

She looked back, her eyes slitted and pink. "Figured you'd go more for a marijuana leaf. . . ."

"Hmm. Maybe I better—"

"No . . ."

"What kind of a ChiCom sex slave are you anyhow? You want to just . . . arch your back—yeah, beautiful, like that. . . ."

They started fucking, and it didn't take very long this time either. A little later she said, "This doesn't mean we're back together."

"No. No, course not. Can I tell you something anyway?"

"Sure."

"I wasn't really pissed off at you, you know, ever, Shasta, not about us, I never felt like I was any kind of a injured party or nothing. Fact, for a while, when Mickey really looked like another one of these straight-to-freak converts, I was even willing to cut him some slack for that. I trusted you on how sincere he was."

"Trouble is," a little sadly, "so did I."

"And if anybody should be revenging themself on anybody's ass around here . . ."

"Oh," said Shasta. "Oh. Well. Let me give *that* some thought."

She went in the kitchen and found a box of Froot Loops, and they put on the TV and sat companionably eating dry cereal and watching the Knicks and the Lakers, Doc would have said just like in the old days, except this was now and he'd come to know a lot less than he thought he did then.

"Don't you need the sound on?"

"Nah, it's all those sneakers, when they squeak like that?"

At halftime she looked over and said, "Something's on your mind."

"Coy Harlingen. I ran into him down in Hermosa."

"So he really didn't OD like everybody said."

"Even better'n that, he's clean now."

"Glad to hear it. Long may he wave."

"But he's caught in something he doesn't want to be in. He's been working as a snitch for the LAPD, and I also saw him on the tube at some Fascism for Freedom rally, pretending to scream at Nixon, working undercover for this outfit called Vigilant California?"

"Then," Shasta murmured, "I guess that one's on my ticket, 'cause it was me who put Coy in touch with Burke Stodger, and it was Burke who set him up with the Viggies." No excuse, she went on, it was during that very freaky time for everybody up in Hollywood right after Sharon Tate. It had occurred to very few in the hopeful-starlet community that regular features and low body weight might not after all be counted on to buy you a thing that mattered. The shock of the Cielo Drive murders was bad enough out in civilian life, but the impact on Shasta and her friends was paralyzing. You could be the sweetest girl in the business, smart with your money, careful about dope, aware of how far to trust people in this town, which was not at all, you could be nice

to everybody—focus pullers, grips, even writers, people you didn't even
have to say hello to—and still be horribly murdered for your trouble.
Once-overs you'd found ways to ignore now had you looking for the
particular highlight off some creep's eyes that would send you behind
double and triple locks to a room lit only by the TV screen, and whatever
was in the fridge to last you till you felt together enough to step outside
again.

"Which is about when I met Burke Stodger. We were neighbors and
used to walk our dogs at around the same time every morning, and I
sort of knew who he was but hadn't seen any of his pictures till one night
I couldn't sleep, went switching around the channels and came across
.45-Caliber Kissoff. Normally I don't watch that type of movie, but something about this one . . ."

"I can relate!" cried Doc. "That picture made me who I am today.
That PI that Burke Stodger played, man, I always wanted to be him."

"I thought you wanted to be John Garfield."

"Well, and that all came true, but guess what, John Garfield also happens to show up uncredited in that same movie—remember there's a
funeral scene, where Burke is sort of discreetly fondling the widow at
graveside, usin a umbrella for cover, well if you look closely, just past her
left tit, that's screen left, a little out of focus, next to a tree, there's John
Garfield in a pinstriped mobster suit and a homburg hat. He was pretty
much blacklisted by that point and must have figured a gig's a gig."

"Burke ran into that same problem but said he found another
solution."

"One that didn't get him hassled into a fatal heart attack. . . . Ups,
but there I go, being bitter again."

To the dismay of many in the business, Burke had let himself be gathered into the embrace of the same Red-hunting zealots who'd once forced
him to split the country. He testified before subcommittees, and donated
his boat to the countersubversive cause, and was soon working again in
modestly budgeted FBI dramas like *I Was a Red Dope Fiend* and *Squeal,
Pinko, Squeal!* a run of luck which lasted as long as anti-Communist

themes kept putting asses in seats. By the time Shasta met Burke, he was pretty much semiretired, content to go eighteen low-stakes holes at the Wilshire Country Club (even nine, if he could find a member who was half Jewish), or hang out at Musso & Frank's spinning showbiz yarns with other old-timers, at least the percentage in the industry who didn't cross the street and sometimes the freeway with a nauseous look on their face to avoid him.

Burke knew a back way onto the golf course, and he and Shasta had fallen into the habit of making it part of their morning stroll. For Shasta this was often the best part of the day, busy with early deliveries, yard and pool work, hosed pavement—still, cool, smelling like the desert after rain, garden exotics, shadows everywhere to shelter in for a bit before the day's empty sky asserted itself.

"I saw you on that *Brady Bunch* episode," she said one morning.

"I just read for another one, waiting now to hear, something about Jan gets a wig." Burke found an almost-unplayed ball in the grass, retrieved it, and slipped it in his pocket.

"What kind of a wig?"

"Brunette, I think. She gets tired of being a blonde?"

"Tell me about *that*. Still not the same as changing your politics, I guess."

She was afraid she'd been too blunt, but he scratched his head elaborately and pretended to think. "Well sure, I have second thoughts, third and fourth, up in the middle of the night, all that old-guy stuff. But they've treated me well. I still get out on the boat, sometimes there's even work." Despite the ease and promise of the morning, the jaunty straw hat, pastel-striped shirt, and pale linen shorts, some sorrowful veteran-actor note had crept into his voice. "Thanks for not bringing up Vietnam, by the way. We get started on that, you really might begin to think less of me."

"Right now that's all, like, kind of remote?"

"No boyfriends out in the street screaming 'Death to the pig,' rolling bombs, whatever it is they do?"

She shook her head, smiling. "Forget about political guys, in this business how many datable guys do I ever run into?"

"Catch as catch can, and ever thus, kid. Only big difference I see today is the drugs. Pretty much everyplace I look, so many of these wonderful, promising young folks either ending up in stir or else dead."

By then of course she was thinking about Coy. He was not, could never be, the love of her life, but she had enough of an ear for music to respect what he did for a living, if you could call it a living. He was a good friend, free so far of assholery, and even strung out most of the time on smack had never looked at her in that creepy Mansonoid way. He sure needed a break in his life.

"There is this sax player I've been sort of worried about?" Going on to tell Burke more than she meant to about Coy's history with heroin. "He can't afford to be on a program, but that's what he needs. It's the only thing that'll save him."

Burke walked quietly awhile in the sun. The dogs came over, and Burke's dog Addison looked up at him and raised one eyebrow. "See that? too much sitting in front of the TV, watching George Sanders movies. No, no—'You're too short for that gesture.' . . . But now I think of it, there is a recovery program, one they tell me really works. Of course I have no idea if it's anywhere up your friend's street."

Next time she talked to Coy, she passed along Burke's phone number. "And then Coy just disappeared. Nothing unusual, he was always disappearing, one minute he's there, maybe even in the middle of a solo, next minute, like, whoa, where'd he go? But this time the silence was like something you could almost hear?"

"That must've been the first time he went inside that joint up at Ojai," Doc said.

"The first? How many times has he been in?"

"Don't know, but I got the feeling he's a regular up there."

"So maybe he's still using." With an unhappy look on her face.

"Maybe not, Shasta. Maybe something else."

"What else could it be?"

"Whatever those people are really into, it ain't helping junkies back on the straight and narrow."

"I should be saying, 'Well, Coy's a grown person, able to take care of himself. . . .' Only, Doc, he really can't, and that's why I'm worried. Not just for him but for his wife and baby, too."

The first time she saw Coy, he was out hitchhiking on Sunset with Hope and Amethyst. Shasta was driving the Eldorado, couldn't recall how many times up and down this street she could have used a ride herself, so she gave them a lift. They had some car trouble, Coy said, and were looking for a garage. Hope and Amethyst got in the front, and Coy sat in back. The baby, poor little thing, was so flushed and listless. Shasta recognized the soiled hand of smack. It occurred to her that the baby's parents might only be in Hollywood to score, but she held off from lecturing. Even by then she had learned enough being Mickey Wolfmann's g.f. to know she didn't qualify for any grand-lady parts—it was luck, dumb luck, that had put them each where they were, and the best way to pay for any luck, however temporary, was just to be helpful when you could.

"And you and Mickey were already, like, into it by then?" Doc couldn't help asking.

"Nosy fuck, ain't you?"

"Put it another way—how'd you and Coy's wife get along?"

"That was the only time I ever saw her. They were staying down in Torrance someplace, Coy was hardly ever home. Did I give him my phone number, no, couple days later I was on La Brea, Coy was in the line at Pink's, saw the Eldorado, came running into traffic, the rest is history. Were we an item? Was I running around on Mickey? What a thing to ask."

"When did I—"

"Listen, in case you haven't figured it out, I was *never* the sweetest girl in the business, there was no reason for me to waste half a minute on a sick junkie like Coy, who was clearly headed for a bad end. He was not my charity project, and we didn't shoot up together, and anyway, if you stop to think about some of the chicks *you've* hung out with—"

"Okay. Whatever you meant to do, you ended up saving his life. And then he went on to be a snitch for the LAPD and a undercover agent for the Viggies and maybe the Golden Fang—the outfit, not the boat—and there's three stiffs so far that may or may not be on his karmic ticket."

"Wait. You think Coy—" She got up on an elbow and peered at him red-eyed. "You think *I'm* in on this, Doc?"

Doc stroked his chin and gazed off into space for a while. "You know how some people say they have a 'gut feeling'? Well, Shasta Fay, what I have is *dick feelings,* and my dick feeling sez—"

"So glad I asked. I'm making coffee, you want some?"

"You bet . . . but now, I *was* sort of wondering . . ."

"Uh-oh."

"When I said I saw Coy in Hermosa? You didn't seem too surprised."

There was a long silence from the kitchen, except for coffeemaking sounds. She came back in and paused in the doorway, one hip out, one knee bent, beautiful naked Shasta. "I saw him once in Laurel Canyon, and he made me swear never to mention it to anybody. He said it would be his ass if anybody found out. But he didn't get into details."

"Sounds like even then somebody was desperate to keep that cover story from falling apart. Which it did anyway, right from the first time Coy ever tried to use it. What the hell did he think was going to happen?"

"I don't know. What did you think, back when you got into your PI trip?"

"Different situation."

"Oh? far as I can see, you and Coy, you're peas in a pod."

"Thanks. How's that."

"Both of you, cops who never wanted to be cops. Rather be surfing or smoking or fucking or anything but what you're doing. You guys must've

thought you'd be chasing criminals, and instead here you're both working for them."

"Ouch, man." Could that be true? All this time Doc assumed he'd
been out busting his balls for folks who if they paid him anything it'd
be half a lid or a small favor down the line or maybe only just a quick
smile, long as it was real. He began to run through the cash customers he
could remember, starting with Crocker Fenway and going on through
studio executives, stock-market heroes of the go-go years, remittance
men from far away who needed new pussy or dope connections, rich old
guys with cute young wives and vice versa. . . . It sure was a piss-poor
record, not too different after all, he guessed, from the interests Coy had
been working for.

"Bummer!" Could Shasta be right? Doc must have looked depressed
enough. Shasta came over and put her arms around him. "Sorry, being
actressy. Love those zingers, can't resist 'em."

"You think this is why I'm going crazy trying to figure a way to help
Coy cut loose of these people? even if I can't do it for myself? *Because* I
can't—"

"*Courage*, Camille—you're still a long way from LAPD material."
Nice try. But now it had him wondering.

Later they went outside, where a light rain was blowing in, mixed
with salt spray feathering off the surf. Shasta wandered slowly down to
the beach and through the wet sand, her nape in a curve she had learned,
from times when back-turning came into it, the charm of. Doc followed
the prints of her bare feet already collapsing into rain and shadow, as if
in a fool's attempt to find his way back into a past that despite them both
had gone on into the future it did. The surf, only now and then visible,
was hammering at his spirit, knocking things loose, some to fall into the
dark and be lost forever, some to edge into the fitful light of his attention whether he wanted to see them or not. Shasta had nailed it. Forget
who—*what* was he working for anymore?

EIGHTEEN

AS DOC APPROACHED DOWNTOWN L.A., THE SMOG GREW THICKER till he couldn't see to the end of the block. Everybody had their headlights on, and he recalled that somewhere behind him, back at the beach, it was still another classic day of California sunshine. Being on the way to visit Adrian Prussia, he'd decided not to smoke much, so he was at a loss to account for the sudden appearance, rising ahead, of a dark metallic gray promontory about the size of the Rock of Gibraltar. Traffic crept along, nobody else seemed to see it. He thought about Sortilège's sunken continent, returning, surfacing this way in the lost heart of L.A., and wondered who'd notice it if it did. People in this town saw only what they'd all agreed to see, they believed what was on the tube or in the morning papers half of them read while they were driving to work on the freeway, and it was all their dream about being wised up, about the truth setting them free. What good would Lemuria do them? Especially when it turned out to be a place they'd been exiled from too long ago to remember.

AP Finance was tucked somewhere between South Central and the vestigial river, hometown of Indians and bindlestiffs and miscellaneous drinkers of Midnight Special, up a wasted set of what looked like empty streets, among pieces of old railroad track brickwalled from view, curving away through the weeds. Out in front and across the street, Doc noted half a dozen or so young men, not loitering or doing substances but poised and tonic, as if waiting for some standing order to take effect. As if there was this one thing they were there to do, one specialized act, and nothing else mattered, because the rest would be taken care of by God, fate, karma, others.

Inside, the woman at the front counter gave Doc the impression of having been badly treated in some divorce settlement. Too much makeup, hair styled by somebody who was trying to give up smoking, a minidress she had no more idea of how to carry than a starlet did a Victorian gown. He wanted to say, "Are you okay?" but asked to see Adrian instead.

On Adrian's office wall was a framed picture of a bride and groom, taken long ago somewhere in Europe. On top of the desk was a half-eaten glazed doughnut and a paper container of coffee, and behind it was Adrian, silent and staring. Heated downtown smoglight filtered in from the window behind him, light that could not have sprung from any steady or pure scheme of daybreak, more appropriate to ends or conditions settled for, too often after only token negotiation. It would be hard to read anybody, let alone Adrian Prussia, in light like this. Doc tried to anyway.

Adrian had short white hair parted at the side to reveal a streak of pink scalp. Ignoring the hair and focusing on his face, Doc saw that it was really more of a young man's face, not too distant from the amusements of youth, not yet, perhaps not ever, fated to grow into the austere competence the hair seemed to be advertising. He wore a sky blue suit of some knit synthetic with a slovenly drape to it and a Rolex Cellini which didn't seem to be working, though that didn't keep him from consulting it now and then to let visitors know how much of his time they were wasting.

"So you're here about Puck? Wait a minute, this is bullshit—I remember you, the kid from Fritz's shop out in Santa Monica, right? I lent you my special edition Carl Yastrzemski bat once, to collect from that child-support deadbeat you chased down the Greyhound and pulled him off of, and then you wouldn't use it."

"I tried to explain at the time, it had to do with how much I've always admired Yaz?"

"No place for that shit in this business. So what you up to these days, still skip tracing or 'd you go into the priesthood?"

"PI," Doc saw no point in denying.

"They gave *you* a license?" Doc nodded, Adrian laughed. "So who sent you here? Who you working for today?"

"All on spec," Doc said. "All on my own time."

"Wrong answer. How much of your own time you think you got left, kid?" He checked the dead wristwatch again.

"I was just about to ask."

"Let me buzz my associate in here a minute." In through the door in a way that suggested indifference about whether it was open, closed, or locked, came Puck Beaverton.

This was not going to end well. "Howdy, Puck."

"I know you? I don't think I do."

"You look like somebody I ran across once. My mistake."

"Your mistake," said Puck. To Adrian Prussia, "What do I do with . . . uh," angling his head at Doc.

"Busy day ahead," said Adrian, going out the door, "I know nothing about any of this."

"Alone at last," Doc said.

"Helps to have a bad memory sometimes," Puck advised, sitting in Adrian's executive chair and producing a joint a bit longer than the usual, to Doc's eye likely rolled with an E-Z Wider paper. Puck lit up, had a long hit, and handed it over to Doc, who unthinkingly took it and inhaled. Little knowing till too late that Puck after years of faithful attendance at a ninja school in Boyle Heights had become a master in the technique known as False Inhaling, which allowed him to seem to be smoking the same joint as his intended victim, thus lulling Doc into thinking this number was okay when in fact it was full of enough PCP to knock over an elephant, which had no doubt been Parke-Davis's original idea when inventing it.

"Acid invites you through the door," as Denis liked to say—"PCP opens the door, shoves you through, slams it behind you, and locks it."

After a while Doc finds himself walking along beside himself in the street, or maybe a long corridor. "Hi!" sez Doc.

"Wow," Doc replies, "you look just like you do in th' mirror!"

"Groovy, because you don't *look like anything,* man in fact you're *invisible!*" so commencing a classic and, except for the Doper's Memory factor, memorable bummer. It seemed there were these two Docs, Visible Doc, which was approximately his body, and Invisible Doc, which was his mind, and from what he could make out, the two were in some kind of ill-tempered struggle which had been going on for a while. To make matters worse, this was all being accompanied somehow by Mike Curb's score from *The Big Bounce* (1969), arguably the worst music track ever inflicted on a movie. Fortunately for both Docs, over the years they had been sent out on enough of these unsought journeys to have picked up a useful kit of paranoid skills. Even these days, though occasionally surprised by some prankster with a straight-looking nose inhaler full of amyl nitrate or a rosy-cheeked subadolescent offering a bite of a peyote-bud ice cream cone, Doc knew he could count on the humiliation if nothing else to pilot him, and his adversary Doc, safely through any trip, however disagreeable.

At least till now. But here, out of, well, not exactly nowhere, but some badlands at least that unmerciful, came this presence, tall and cloaked, with oversize and wickedly pointed gold canines, and luminous eyes scanning Doc in a repellently familiar way. "As you may have already gathered," it whispered, "I am the Golden Fang."

"You mean like J. Edgar Hoover 'is' the FBI?"

"Not exactly . . . they have named themselves after their worst fear. I am the unthinkable vengeance they turn to when one of them has grown insupportably troublesome, when all other sanctions have failed."

"Okay if I ask you something?"

"About Dr. Blatnoyd. Dr. Blatnoyd had a fatality for rogue profit-sharing activities, of which his coadjutors have taken an understandably dim view."

"And you actually . . . what's the word . . ."

"Bit. Sank these," smiling horribly, "into his neck. Yes."

"Huh. Well. Thanks for clearing that one up, Mr. Fang."

"Oh, call me 'The Golden.'"

"He's freaking out," somebody said.

"Am not," protested Doc.

"Here, this ought to calm him down," and next thing he knew, a needle was going into his arm, and he had time to begin the reasonable inquiry, "What the—" but not to complete it until he woke up, mercifully not too many hours later, in a room, handcuffed to an institutional iron bed.

"—fuck? Or, to put it another way, what was in that joint?"

"Feeling better?" There was Puck, leering at him in a particularly evil way. "No idea you were only a weekend warrior, could've gone cheap and just used beer."

Doc found this hard to follow, but gathered that Puck had deliberately put him on a bad trip, giving somebody a pretext to sedate him and bring him here. Which was where? He thought he heard surf nearby . . . maybe was feeling it through beams and joists.

"That you again, Puck? how's the missus?"

"Who told you about that?"

"Uh-oh. What happened?"

"The paramedics gave her a good chance, better than you got right at the moment."

"What'd you do to her, Puck?"

"Nothin she didn't want. What fuckin business is it of yours?"

"How quickly they forget. I'm the one that got you two lovebirds together."

"Don't worry about her. I know what to do about her. I even know what to do about you. But there's still something I think you should know. About Glen."

"Glen."

"Listen, Sportello, I really did warn him just before they nailed him."

"Before they what?"

"Glen was the target all along, smart-ass. That outfit he was runnin guns for didn't trust him any more than the Brothers who shitlisted him for being a traitor to his race."

"And you're telling me this because . . ."

"You're the only one I know who ever gave a shit about Glen. Him and me, we were road dogs once, I took shank cuts for him, he did times in the hole for me, then I turned around and helped set him up anyway. Shitty of me ain't it. But I owed him the phone call at least, didn't I?"

"You warned him? Why didn't he split, then?"

"First straight job he ever had, 'It's my duty to protect Mickey.' The dumb fuck. Fact, you and Glen are basically the same kind of dumb fuck."

"Don't mean to interrupt, but where are we again? and when I can split this place?"

"When you've been neutralized as a threat."

Doc briefly took in the situation. He was handcuffed, and somebody had taken away his Smith. "I'm not sure, but I'd say zero threat potential?"

"Adrian had some business in town, but he'll be along soon, and then we can get on with our own business. Like a cigarette?" He waited for Doc to nod yes. "Too bad—I quit smokin, and so should you, asshole."

Puck brought over a folding chair and straddled it backwards. "Let me tell you something about Adrian. Up on first degree murder more times than anybody can remember, gone free every time. Loan sharking's really only his day job. After the shutters go down, the last numbers get posted, the sweatshop people and the bums off the nickel go where they're goin and the street is empty and quiet again—that's when Adrian gets to work."

"He's a hit man."

"Always was. He just didn't know it till a couple years ago."

Adrian understood from the jump, Puck explained, that what people were buying, when they paid interest, was time. So anybody that failed to come up with the vigorish, the only fair way to deal with that was to take their own personal time away from them again, a currency much more precious, up to and including the time they had left to live. Severe injury was more than just pain, it was taking away their time. Time they thought they had all to themselves would have to be spent now on stays in hospitals, visits to doctors, physical therapy, everything taking longer because they couldn't move around so good. So it wasn't as if Adrian hadn't been working up to homicide for hire all his career.

One day out on his rounds, Adrian dropped in on a client from the LAPD Vice Squad who, just bullshitting, happened to mention a certain pornographer and pimp at the fringes of the movie business, with interests in nudie bars, modeling agencies, and "specialty publishing," whom the Department seemed uncommonly eager to be done with. As it turned out, he had also kept lengthy and detailed files on a sex ring based in Sacramento, and was threatening now to blow the whistle unless he got paid a sum he was too small-time to understand was out of the question, though even the minor allegations in his story, proven or not, would be enough to bring down the administration of Governor Reagan.

"The Governor has some great momentum right now, the future of America belongs to him, somebody can be doing American history a big favor here, Adrian."

Though there were by now any number of souls already on Adrian's ticket, many Louisville Slugger–related, in fact, something in him did a silent and fateful double take. It may have helped that he had always voted Republican.

"Well, simply as a good American," said Adrian, "I'd like to volunteer my services, and my only condition is that I shouldn't do any jail time."

"How would you feel about being charged but then going free on a plea bargain before it got to trial?"

"Great, but why even bring me into it, why not just leave it an unsolved crime?"

"Federal money. The amount we get depends on our yearly clearance rate. There's a formula. The more cases we clear, the better we make out." Adrian must have looked uncomfortable, because the cop added, "We can guarantee—zero consequences for you, legal or otherwise."

Though he didn't care much for the arrest and arraignment process, and especially not the legal fees, Adrian supposed that was the price he had to pay for the cold keen-edged thrill that overtook him the closer it got to the actual moment. There was something sexy about it. Like, a seduction.

He arranged for his target to be kidnapped and brought to a vacant warehouse in the City of Commerce and hired a couple of professionals who specialized in gay S&M. "Nothing too heavy," Adrian said, "just work him into a mood. Then you fellas can split."

They looked at Adrian, then at the client, then at each other, shrugged, and on the principle of No Telling What People Will Go For, set to work. When they had been paid off and gone, Adrian had his turn.

"You corrupt the innocent," he addressed his victim, who by now, covered with bruises and welts, had grown unappeasably erect, "plus you keep millions of freaks and losers addicted to their stupid-ass appetites for bleach-blond pussy and oversize cock, you ruin their family life, you get 'em to piss so much of their money away they end up coming to me—me, for shit's sake—just to cover the rent. And then you have the fuckin nerve to go after a man like Ronald Reagan? To even put yourself in the same league as him? Big mistake, pal. Fact, there ain't enough left of your life to make a bigger one. So start praying, asshole, for truly I say unto you, your hour is at hand."

Adrian had spent the previous weekend out visiting different suburban shopping plazas, going in home-improvement stores and assembling the kit of tools he now set to work with. The victim's penis, needless to say, came in for extra attention.

When the job was over, Adrian took the mutilated corpse and drove it to a freeway under construction miles away and dropped it inside the forms for a concrete support column about to be poured. A liberally compensated cement-mixer operator known to friends of Adrian's then helped encase the remains in what would become a vertical tomb, an invisible statue of someone the authorities wished not to commemorate but to wipe from the Earth. Even today, Adrian could still not drive the freeway system without wondering how many of the columns he saw might have stiffs inside them. "Brings new meaning," he remarked jovially, "to the expression 'pillar of the community.'"

Besides making sure he was seen with the victim at a West Hollywood bar earlier in the evening, Adrian had set himself up with a shitload of circumstantial evidence. His two assistants from the warehouse were encouraged to come forward as witnesses, and Adrian left blood and fingerprints around the warehouse for the cops to find and, being who they were, to contaminate as much of it as they could. Though the cement-mixer operator had unaccountably disappeared, a number of hardware clerks were able to identify Adrian as having purchased items later found at the warehouse, with blood on them assumed to be the victim's. However, no body meant no case. Adrian signed a statement acceptable to the federal nickel-and-dimers, and walked.

Simple as that. It felt like his life had turned a corner. As he was about to discover, there seemed no end to the list of wrongdoers the Department would happily see out of the way, and secret Rolodexes filled with the names of private contractors eager for the business, for whom the price, given federal policies of bountiful aid to local law enforcement, was, more often than not, right.

In the months and eventually years that followed, Adrian found himself specializing in politicals—black and Chicano activists, antiwar protesters, campus bombers, and assorted other pinko fucks, it was eventually all the same to Adrian. The weapon of choice was usually from his collection of baseball bats, though he could now and then be persuaded to use a firearm which had mysteriously vanished from some other crime scene remote in time and space. He became a regular around Parker Center, where they didn't always know his name but never questioned his presence. It was like finding a life in the military. After years of blind alleys and false starts, Adrian had discovered his calling and reclaimed his identity.

Imagine his surprise, however, when one day his silent benefactors the LAPD came to him with a request to hit one of their own. What was going on? They knew he was the political guy.

"Doing a cop, I don't know. Doesn't have quite that, what do you call it, magic. Unless there's something I'm missing. . . ."

"On the job," his contact explained, "there's a code. There has to be trust. Everything depends on it, it's nonnegotiable."

"And this detective . . ."

"Let's say he's in violation."

"A federal snitch, something like that?"

"Better we don't get into details."

As a matter of fact, Adrian recognized the name of this detective, Vincent Indelicato, who had borrowed from APF now and then—not a problem client, always came up with payments plus the vig on time. Adrian also happened to know that Puck Beaverton hated Indelicato from way back and was in fact currently out on bail pending sentence for some penny-ante infraction that Indelicato had just busted him on. Something about a pot seed.

Adrian had tried to work himself up into the same lethal indignation he'd felt toward pinkos and pornographers, but somehow his heart just wasn't in it. Finally he summoned Puck.

"Look, I've been trying to fix this chickenshit arrest for you, Puck, but they're just being so hard-ass about it."

"Don't worry, Mr. P.," replied Puck. "One of those cases of wrong cop at the wrong time. Vincent Indelicato is the one member of the Department that I flat-out fuckin hate, and he feels the same about me, so he ain't about to let nothing go."

"This have anything to do with Einar?"

"This fuckin cop, every chance he gets . . . pullin him over, bringin him in for nothing . . . Pure hatred of homos. And Einar, like he's so innocent, man, he's like a little kid, he can't see how evil it is, how systematic. Son of a bitch Indelicato really needs to be lined up and shot.

Too bad I couldn't've got popped for . . . I don't know, something real? maybe that would get me some respect inside?"

"Now that you mention it . . ." Adrian explained about his history as a contract employee, his get-out-of-jail-free card, "And what I don't have this time is any true desire. I mean, this Indelicato, he's a customer, he's a shit, but he's nothin to me. I could do him, but so what? Where's the passion, see what I'm saying? Whereas somebody who really truly hates his ass—"

"So you mean . . . I'd get to do it—"

"But they arrest me. And if you do go in on this other little two-bit charge, word gets around on the jailhouse grapevine it was really you that iced the same copper who put you in there, and your yard credibility gets a big speed injection."

So it came about—Adrian solicited the act, Puck performed it, in a perfect justice system both would have gone down for murder one, but there is no overestimating the lengths to which a force with such deep insecurities as the LAPD will go to act them out. "To top it off," Puck concluded, "that fuckin seed thing got dealt before it ever came to trial, so I never even had to go inside. Somethin, huh?"

"Leaving a question open," Doc said. "Since we're only chatting here and all. Who was it that hired Adrian?"

"Who gives a shit? Cop on cop, just a waste of time to ask."

"No, no, it's fascinating as Mr. Spock would say, tell me more."

But they'd both heard the sound of a car pulling in to the garage, and doors slamming. Soon Adrian, muffled but recognizable, was calling, "Puckie . . . I'm home. . . ."

Puck was on his feet, and Doc saw from the look on his face, too late as usual, how totally, dangerously insane Sunshine Boy here had always been. "Special treat for you today, Doc, we just got in a shipment of pure number four, not a white guy's finger laid on it between the Golden Triangle and your own throbbin vein, and there's worse ways to be removed forever from a major-pain-in-the-ass list. Just let me step out here and get you some."

He noticed Doc's glance down toward his ankle and the empty holster rig and smirked, and Doc thought he saw the swastika on Puck's head twinkling too. "Yep, got it right here," patting his inside jacket pocket. "You'll have it back soon, though I can't say you'll be in much condition to use it. Don't go away now." The door closed behind him, and a dead bolt slammed into place.

There is a fairly straightforward way to get out of handcuffs, which Doc had learned as soon as he began having regular run-ins with the LAPD. A metal clip snapped off a ballpoint pen would have worked, but they'd taken his pen away when they took the Smith. Doc always made a point, however, of carrying in different pants pockets, loose and he hoped unnoticeable, two or three plastic shims he'd cut long ago from an expired Bullocks charge card that Shasta had left behind. The idea was to slide the plastic strip into one cuff to disengage the locking pawl and also cover the ratchet teeth so the pawl couldn't reengage.

It took a lot of squirming and muscle strain and semi-headstands to get even one of the shims to fall out of his pocket, but finally Doc worked himself out of the cuffs, creaked up off the bed, and had a look around. There wasn't much to see. The door was designed not to open from the inside, and there was nothing to force it with. He pulled the folding chair under the overhead light fixture, stood on it, and unscrewed the bulb. Everything went very dark. By the time he managed to get back down off the chair, he was in the middle of some kind of flashback, possibly from that elephant dope they'd given him. He saw old familiar images, like spirit guides sent to help him out, Dagwood and Mr. Dithers, Bugs and Yosemite Sam, Popeye and Bluto, rotating violently inside intensely saturated green and magenta clouds of dust, and he understood for a second and a half that he belonged to a single and ancient martial tradition in which resisting authority, subduing hired guns, defending your old lady's honor all amounted to the same thing.

He heard movement outside the door, but no conversation. An even chance that Puck was alone. Doc held one of the cuffs and let the other swing free and waited. By the time Puck got the door open far enough to register the darkness inside, before he could say "Uh-oh," Doc was on his ass, slamming him in the head back and forth with the loose handcuff, smashing his foot into Puck's knee to bring him down, and then going down after him, giving in to a fury Doc understood would provide the balance he needed to coast through this, grabbing Puck's head and continuing to beat it almost silently against the marble doorsill till everything was too slippery with blood.

Puck had dropped a tray with a spoon, needle, and syringe on it, but nothing had broken. "Good. Here you go, then." He went through Puck's pockets and recovered his own handgun, a ring of keys, and a pack of smokes and a lighter—the mean-ass shit had even been lying about that—and, keeping an ear out for Adrian, carefully cooked up the heroin, drew some into the syringe, and without bothering to clear the air from the spike drove it into Puck's neck about where he thought a jugular might be, pushed the plunger the rest of the way down, handcuffed Puck in case he came to, grabbed his huaraches, and slid out into the corridor. It looked empty. He lit up one of Puck's prison menthols, cautiously inhaled in case there was some more PCP in the story, and using the sound of the surf as a guide moved away from it toward what he hoped would be the street.

"Puck?" It was Adrian down at the end of the hallway, holding a pistol, and Doc dove out of the way just as he raised and fired it. The round bounced off a gigantic Vietnamese nipple gong hanging nearby. A note, pure and bell-like, filled the house. Doc found himself in a large indoor patio leading into a room with a conversation pit and a picture window with drapes over it. Some late light off the ocean came through crevices in the drapes. He could see, but only just. He slid into the room and rolled behind a couch, took off one huarache and threw it back in Adrian's direction. This drew a shot from the patio. The muzzle flash filled the room. The gong was still ringing. Doc felt more than heard Adrian creeping toward him. He waited till he saw a dense patch of moving shadow, sighted it in, and fired, rolling away immediately, and the figure dropped like an acid tab into the mouth of Time. Then there was no more shooting. Doc waited five minutes, or maybe ten, until he heard crying somewhere in the long invisible room.

"That you, Adrian?"

"I'm fuckin lunch meat," sobbed Adrian. "Oh, shit . . ."

"Did I get you?" said Doc.

"You got me."

"Fatal, I hope?"

"Feels like it."

"How can I know for sure?"

"Maybe it'll be on the news at eleven, asshole."

"Stay there, try not to croak, I'll call this in."

He went looking for a phone. Nobody seemed to be shooting at him. He was calling the ambulance when he heard sounds of activity from directly beneath the floor, in what he guessed to be the garage. He found some stairs and cautiously crept down them to have a look.

Busy offloading a twenty-kilo parcel from the trunk of a Lincoln Continental was Bigfoot Bjornsen, who regarded him without surprise. "Did you take care of them okay? Anything I can—"

"You fuckin set me up, Bigfoot, what's the matter, you don't have the balls to do this yourself?"

"Sorry about that. I'm in enough shit personally with the captain, and I've seen you on the range."

"And that there, is that what I think it is?"

A brief beat, as if a congested mass of snow high on a mountainside were waiting permission to avalanche. Bigfoot shrugged. "Well . . . it's only one. There's more. Enough left for evidence."

"Uh-huh, and the one you're taking here has a street value higher than you think only cops know how to count. Bigfoot, Bigfoot, I saw the movie, man, and as I recall, that character comes to a bad end."

"I have obligations."

The garage door was open. Bigfoot brought the package over to a '65 Impala parked on the apron, popped the trunk, and put it in.

"This is the Golden Fang you're about to rip off here, man. The fully fuckin weird outfit, if you recall, that iced one of their own board members up in Bel Air the other night?"

"That's according to your own delusional system, of course. Our current thinking in the Division is focused more on an Irate Husbands list of, admittedly, considerable length. Can I offer you a lift?"

"Naah, you know what, fuck this . . . in fact, fuck you, I'm gonna walk." He turned and started off.

"Ooh," went Bigfoot. "Sensitive."

Doc kept going. The sun was just down, a sinister glow fading out above the edge of the world. As he walked, he began to notice something increasingly familiar about this stretch of stucco bungalows and beach shacks, and after a while remembered that it was Gummo Marx Way, where according to the files Penny had let him see, Adrian had a house, and Bigfoot's partner had been shot down. Major arterial to the impulsive and already forsaken, and uphill, no matter what anybody's geometry teacher had told them, in both directions. Who knew how many times Bigfoot had been out here since the death of his partner? In how helpless a state of passion?

Doc resisted the impulse to look back. Let Bigfoot go about his business. It couldn't be more than a couple of miles to a bus stop, and Doc needed the exercise. He could hear wind up in the palm trees and the regular beat of the surf. Now and then a car came zooming by on yet another thankless chore, sometimes with the radio on, sometimes honking at Doc for being a pedestrian. Pretty soon he spotted a dolled-up surfer's cabana across the street with a '59 Cadillac hearse parked in front with its windows blacked out and its chrome, from what Doc could see, rigorously authenticated, and a couple of longboards where the stiffs used to ride. He went over to have a look.

All at once something flickered at the edge of his vision, like the things you see in houses that are supposed to be deserted. He ducked down behind the hearse, reaching for his Smith, just as Adrian Prussia emerged from a cone of streetlight ahead.

What?

Either Doc had hallucinated killing Adrian, which was always possible, or only wounded him, and Adrian had managed to go out the back and down to the beach, and make his way as far as the next path up through the ice plant to the street again.

"Fucking hippies, you're so easy to fool." Adrian actually didn't sound that good, but Doc at the moment couldn't afford much wishful thinking.

"Go on ahead Adrian, you can still get away, go in peace man, don't let me keep you or nothin."

"Not after what you did to Puck. I'm coming over there, asshole." Doc crouched beneath the last of the skyglow, considering possibilities like rolling under the hearse and trying to shoot Adrian in the foot. "Maybe you'll have time for one shot. But you're going to have to stand up in the open to take it, and it'll have to be perfect. Meantime I'm gonna blow your head off the minute I see it."

From back down Gummo Marx Way, Doc heard sirens now. Seemed like more than one, and getting louder. "See? I called you an ambulance and everything."

"Thanks," said Adrian, "mighty thoughtful of you," and fell on his face in the street, and when Doc finally edged out to have a look, appeared not to be moving. Dead enough.

Doc looked back and saw flashing lights in front of Adrian's house— an ambulance and two or three black-and-whites. Having a word with Bigfoot, no doubt. Better just keep on with this evening stroll here, up Gummo Marx Way. Wasn't like he was running away from the scene of a crime or nothing, was it. They'd see Adrian's body, they'd either come after Doc or they wouldn't, pop him now, pop him later, what'd it matter. In theory he knew he'd just killed two people, and that months, maybe years, of hassle awaited him, but then again, it wasn't him back there in the street.

He was trying to remember the lyrics to "The Bright Elusive Butterfly of Love" when behind him he heard a roar nearly as melodious, which he recognized as a V-8 exhaust by way of a Cherry Bomb Glasspack. It was

Bigfoot, who slowed, paused next to Doc, and rolled his window down. "You coming?"

You bet. Doc got in. "Where's the El Camino?"

"In the shop, needs rings. This is Chastity's."

"And . . . we're just gonna split now."

"Quit worrying, Sportello, it's all taken care of."

"¿*Palabra?*"

Bigfoot put three fingers up like the Boy Scout Oath, except they were sort of, well, bent. "Semi *palabra.*"

BIGFOOT DIDN'T SPEAK again till they were on the San Diego Freeway, headed north. "You're right. I know I should have done it myself."

"That's between you and whoever, man. Your partner's ghost, maybe."

Bigfoot turned on the car radio, which was tuned—probably welded—to an easy-listening station. Some sort of Glen Campbell medley was in progress. Bigfoot in his mind remained back on GMW. "Vinnie was out here from New York, you know, it took me a week before I could understand anything he was saying, not so much the accent as the tempo. Then I was starting to talk like that too, and nobody could understand *me.* I still keep asking myself now if I couldn't've bought him some time that day, but as usual he was too fast. We came down to GMW on a tip he said he had, and before I even stopped the unit he was already out the door and into the house. I knew what was going to happen. I was calling in for backup when I heard the shots. For a while I just kept stupidly yelling, Vinnie, you in there? And he was, and he wasn't. Poor fucker. Doomed to a bad end sooner or later. Crazy as they make them, but my back never felt so safe before or since. Hard to explain to a civilian, but I really . . . I owed him so much."

Bigfoot drove for a while. Doc said, "You know what? Total honesty? I thought it was you."

"Thought what was me? That I was the one who did Vinnie? my own partner? Jesus, Sportello. Don't you ever stop with this paranoid pothead routine?"

"Call it what you want, Bigfoot, it's a normal reaction ain't it? How do I ever know what goes on with any of you people, all creepin around behind your blue steel curtain there playing your fucked-up power games?"

Bigfoot didn't answer but there were times Doc could hear his silences, and this one was saying Too Much You Can't Know About So Fuck Off.

Might as well keep pushing it. "Like maybe the Department had you both on the same shit list, I mean bein his partner and all, cashin him in'd be a good way to get your own cred back wouldn't it?"

"You don't know what you're talking about. Thanks so much for your concern, but I've got it covered, okay? I'm a Renaissance cop, remember, I get to be all things to all interested parties here."

"No, Bigfoot . . . no, you know what I think you really are? Is you're the LAPD's own Charlie Manson. You're the screamin evil nutcase right at the heart of that li'l cop kingdom, that nothin and nobody can reach, and God help 'em if you wake up someday in a mood to bring it all down, 'cause then it'll be run copper run, and when the gunsmoke clears, there'll be songbirds building their nests in all the empty corners of the Glass House. Plus broken glass and shit."

Looking pleased with this character update, Bigfoot accelerated to eighty-five or ninety miles per hour and went gleefully, one might almost say suicidally, weaving in and out of traffic in traditional freeway style. Onto Chastity Bjornsen's car radio came the drawling irreverent brass and subhip syncopation of a Herb Alpert arrangement, which Doc realized with growing horror was a cover of Ohio Express's "Yummy Yummy Yummy." He reached for the volume knob but Bigfoot was ahead of him.

"If you're interested," Doc said, "Puck told me it was him that fired the actual shots. Adrian got paid for doing it, and took the rap, and then they cut him loose. The usual. But maybe you knew all that. Maybe you also know who inside the LAPD was paying Adrian to do it."

Bigfoot looked over at Doc and then back at the freeway. "Either I do know, which means I won't tell you, or I don't know, in which case you'll never find out on your own."

"Right, forgot. I'm just the stupid-ass civilian out there drawin unfriendly fire."

"My job offer is still on the table. Join up, maybe you'll learn a thing or two. You might even be Academy material." They were nearing the Canoga Park exit and Bigfoot put on his signal.

"Don't tell me," Doc said.

"Yes we had to impound your short once again, it was parked illegally down there in Adrian's neighborhood."

"Wait. You're letting me drive away, you're not taking me in or booking me or nothin? How are we supposed to square this?"

"Square what?"

"All that—you know," angling his head back in the direction of Gummo Marx Way and making vague blam-blam gestures with thumb and index finger.

"No idea what you're trying to say, Sportello, something you've been hallucinating no doubt."

"I don't get it. Adrian must've been one of the Department's key assets. How are they just gonna shine it on that he's been eliminated?"

"All I can safely tell you is that Adrian was getting cute. Way too cute, but don't press me for details, just rest assured the boys are only too happy to be rid of him. And Puck too, because now they can say Vinnie's murderer's been ID'd at last, met a violent end but justice was served, the clearance rate jumps another notch and we pick up x million more from the feds. Everybody downtown's what you would call groovy with that."

"Maybe I should take a small commission."

"But that would put you on the payroll, wouldn't it."

"Right . . . then maybe you could just toss me a small tip instead? It's these cases I'm working on? Puck was kind enough to mention that all that commotion at Chick Planet Massage that day was really to cover a hit on Glen Charlock. Said it never was about Mickey. Did you know any of that? 'Course you did. Why didn't you tell me?"

Bigfoot smiled. "Did that slip my mind? Jeepers, I'm getting worse than a doper. Yes, well Mickey just stumbled into something he shouldn't have seen, and the boys in the John Wayne outfits panicked and hustled him away for a while. Then the feds found out—here's an acidhead billionaire about to give all his money away, and of course they had their own ideas on how to spend it. Being tight with this Golden Fang of yours by way of scag-related activities in the Far East, they got Mickey programmed into Ojai for a little brain work."

"Looks like they got what they wanted, too. My bad luck and lousy timing. Man sees the light, tries to change his life, my one big chance to rescue somebody like that from the clutches of the System, and I'm too late. And now Mickey's back to them old greedy-ass ways."

"Well, maybe not, Sportello. What goes around may come around, but it never ends up exactly the same place, you ever notice? Like a record on a turntable, all it takes is one groove's difference and the universe can be on into a whole 'nother song."

"Been doing a little acid, there, Bigfoot?"

"Not unless you mean the stomach variety."

At the lot, Bigfoot paused in front of the office, went in and came back out with a release form. "You can start this, I'm just going to go check something out, I'll be right back to sign off on everything." With the Glasspack pulsating like the bass line of an up-tempo blues, he rolled away into glaring mercury-vapor light saturating a lot full of outward and visible civic annoyance. He wasn't gone that long, but Doc began to feel nervous anyway. Doper's ESP again no doubt, which only got more intense when he saw his car in some totally unreal gesture of civility being brought right up to the office doorsill. "What's this?" said Doc.

"Drive safely," advised Bigfoot, touching an invisible hatbrim. He got back in the Impala, revved the engine throbbingly a number of times, and prepared to depart. "Oh, I nearly forgot."

"Yeah Bigfoot."

"Chastity and I had an appraiser over last weekend to look at some pieces. And that Wyatt Earp mustache cup? Turns out it's real. Yeah. You could've kept that 'sucker and turned it for *big bucks*." Cackling sadistically, he roared away.

Pulling out of the lot, Doc happened to take a sharper left than he meant to over a piece of curb onto the street and heard an ominous thump from the trunk. His first thought was that something on the Vibrasonic had come loose. He pulled over and got out to look.

"Ahhh! Bigfoot, you motherfucker." How could he have expected the ol' mad dog to be satisfied with only Adrian and Puck? They'd all been tools in somebody else's crib, including Doc. Now he had twenty kilos of No. 4 China White bouncing around in his trunk, Bigfoot no doubt at this very moment was putting word out to that effect, and once again Doc was bait, with only the keen brainpower of the LAPD between him and incorporation into some freeway overpass. He had to ditch this Asian shit someplace secure, and fairly quick.

Keeping to surface streets, Doc headed east, pulled in briefly at a shopping mall, went around back by the dumpsters and found two card-board cartons about the same size, put Bigfoot's dope in one and filled the other with garbage sacks and renovation debris, and then proceeded to Burbank Airport, parked near a phone booth and used up most of a roll of quarters trying to get patched through a mobile operator to the two-way radio in Tito's limo, on the off chance Tito was working late.

"Inez how many times I got to swear to you, it ain't the name of a horse, it ain't a bookie's phone number, it's only this cocktail waitress—"

"No, no, Tito, it's me!" Doc hollering on account of the connection.

"Inez? You sound funny."

"It's Doc! and I need a untraceable ride!"

"Oh, it's you, Doc!"

"I know it's short notice, but if you could find me some kind of Falcon—"

"Hey, I don't do no pimpin, man?"

This went on for a while, jet takeoffs and landings kept interrupting, reception faded in and out. Doc was obliged to dig up more quarters and soon found himself screaming through his teeth like Kirk Douglas in *Champion* (1949). But they finally worked it out that Adolfo would be there within the half hour with another ride, and Doc was ready for phase two of his plan, which required rapidly smoking some Hawaiian weed rolled into a joint of a certain diameter and bringing the box full of dumpster trash to the counter of Kahuna Airlines, where he bought a ticket for Honolulu on a dubious credit card he'd taken once in lieu of a fee, checked the dummy carton in as baggage, and watched it roll away into what stewardii of his acquaintance had described as a bureaucratic nightmare, hoping it would take the Fang some time to sort out.

"You're sure it'll be safe, now."

"You've asked that several times, sir."

"Call me Larry . . . is it's only that you guys have the worst reputation in the industry for losing shit, so I'm a little anxious is all."

"Sir, we can assure you—"

"Oh forget that. What I really need to know about *now* is the Land of the Pygmies."

"Excuse me?"

"You have a flight atlas handy? Look it up, 'Pygmies, Land of the.'"

This being a California airline, with standing instructions to be as accommodating as possible, somebody in a uniform and short haircut soon appeared with a flight atlas and stood leafing through it, growing perplexed and apologetic. "Whichever of these it is, sir, it has no landing facilities."

"But I, wanna go, to the Land, of the *Pygmies*!" Doc kept sort of whining.

"But, sir, the Land of the, the Pygmies seems to have no, um, runways?"

"Well then, they'll just have to *build* one, won't they—gimme that—" He seized the PA microphone from behind the desk, as if it were on some shortwave frequency being attentively monitored by Pygmies waiting for a message just like this. "All right, now listen up!" He began barking orders to an imaginary Pygmy construction crew. "Is it a what? of course it's a Boeing, shorty—got a problem with that?"

Security people began to drift into Doc's visual perimeter. Supervisorial personnel were hovering in a sort of sick fascination. Customers queued behind Doc found reasons to step out of line and wander away. He unplugged the microphone, set his hat at a jaunty Sinatroid angle, and in a not-totally-embarrassing lounge voice began to work the crowd, singing,

> There's a skyful of hearts,
> Broken in two,
> Some flyin full fare,
> some non-revenue,
> All us bit actors
> Me him and you,
> Playin our parts,
> In a skyful of hearts . . .

> Up there in first class,
> Ten-dollar wine,
> Playing canasta,
> Doin so fine,
> Suddenly, uh-oh,
> Here's 'at No Smokin sign
> That's how it starts,
> In a skyful of hearts . . .

> [*Bridge*]
> To the roar of the fanjet . . .
> You went on your way . . .
> I'll sure miss you, and yet . . .
> There ain't much to say . . .

> Now I'm flyin alone
> In economy class,
> Drinkin the cheap stuff,

Till I'm flat on my ass,
Watchin my torch song
Fall off the charts,
But that's how it goes
In a skyful of hearts . . .

This tune had in fact been on the radio briefly a couple weeks back, so by the last eight bars there were actually people singing along, some lead, some backup, and stepping in rhythm. Enough witnesses to keep the Fang busy for a while. Doc meanwhile had slowly been making his way toward the exit and now, tossing the mike to the nearest customer, slid away out the door and ran back to find Adolfo behind the wheel of a 442 Olds with the motor idling in the space next to his own car, and on the radio Rocío Dúrcal with her heart about to break.

Doc got in his car, and they pulled out of the lot, drove till they found a reasonably dark street in North Hollywood, and quickly shifted the twenty-kilo inconvenience from Doc's trunk to the Olds. Doc handed his own keys to Adolfo. "They'll have this plate number and the car description, all I need's like an hour or two, try to keep 'em busy as long as you can—"

"I was going to switch after a while with my cousin Antonio 'Bugs' Ruiz, who the word '*peligro*' is not in his phrase book, plus he don't give a shit," replied Adolfo.

"More than I can repay, *vato*."

"Tito thinks it's him that owes you. You guys work it out, don't bring me in."

This Oldsmobile didn't have power steering, and well before he reached the San Diego Freeway, Doc felt like he was back in PE class doing push-ups for Mr. Schiffer. On the bright side, nobody seemed to be following him. Yet. He still had to work out the interesting question, how does one keep twenty kilos of heroin hidden and safe for a short period of time, when vast resources are being mobilized to discover it, repossess it, and exact retribution for ripping it off?

Back in Gordita, looking for someplace to park, he happened to pass Denis's place, which was still decorated with heaps of soggy plaster and splintered laths and wiring and plastic pipes, like somebody had spilled a giant bowl of fucked-up novelty cereal. And with Denis, Doc knew, living somehow down in the middle of it, bootlegging the power he needed for the fridge and TV and the lava lamp off of the neighbors next door. Until the landlord, who in any case was vacationing down in Baja, could figure out how to collect enough insurance to pay for repairs, nothing was likely to change here. "Psychedelic!" exclaimed Doc. A perfect stash site. It was about this point that he noticed he was wearing only one huarache anymore.

The bars hadn't closed yet, and Denis didn't seem to be home. Keeping an ear out for funseekers in the vicinity, Doc brought the carton with the heroin inside it down into the remains of Denis's living room and hid it behind a section of collapsed ceiling, draping the giant plastic rag of what had been Chico's water bed over it. Only then did he happen to notice that the carton he'd pulled out of that dumpster in the dark had once held a twenty-five-inch color TV set, a detail he had no cause to think about till next day when he dropped in on Denis about lunchtime and found him sitting, to all appearances serious and attentive, in front of the professionally packaged heroin, now out of its box, and staring at it, as it turned out he'd been doing for some time.

"It said on the box it was a television set," Denis explained.

"And you couldn't resist. Didn't you check first to see if there was something you could plug in?"

"Well I couldn't find any power cord, man, but I figured it *could be* some new type of set you didn't need one?"

"Uh huh and what . . ." why was he pursuing this? "were you watching, when I came in?"

"See, my theory is, is it's like one of these educational channels? A little slow maybe, but no worse than high school . . ."

"Yes Denis thanks, I will just have a hit off of that if you don't mind. . . ."

"And dig it, Doc, if you watch long enough . . . see how it begins to sort of . . . change?"

Alarmingly, Doc after a minute or two did find minute modulations of color and light intensity beginning to appear among the tightly taped layers of plastic. He sat down next to Denis, and they passed the roach back and forth, eyes glued to the package. Jade/Ashley showed up with a giant Thermos full of Orange Julius and paper cups and a bag of Cheetos.

"Lunch," she greeted them, "and color-coordinated, too, and— Whoa, what the fuck is that, it looks like smack."

"Nah," said Denis, "I think it's like a . . . documentary?"

They all sat there in a row, sipping, crunching, and gazing. Finally Doc tore himself away. "I hate to be the bad guy, but I've got to do a repo on this?"

"Just till this part's over?"

"Till we see what happens," added Jade.

DOC HAD BEEN on the phone with Crocker Fenway, Japonica's dad, who had called around noon, interrupting a dream Doc was having about the schooner *Golden Fang*, which had reassumed its old working identity, as well as its real name, *Preserved*. Somehow the Zen exorcist Coy had told Doc about, the one who'd dezombified the Boards' mansion up in Topanga, had also been at work on the schooner, clearing away the dark residues of blood and betrayal . . . conducting the unquiet spirits of those who'd been tortured and assassinated aboard her safely to rest. Whatever evil had possessed her was now gone for good.

It was toward sunset, after some rain, the dark lid of clouds rolled back a few fingers' widths from the horizon, revealing a strip so clear and luminous that even homebound traffic out on the freeway was slowing down for it. Sauncho and Doc were out on the beach. Last apricot light flooded landward and brought their shadows uphill, past the lifeguard towers, into terraces of bougainvillea, rhododendrons, and ice plant.

Sauncho was giving a kind of courtroom summary, as if he'd just been handling a case. ". . . yet there is no avoiding time, the sea of time, the sea of memory and forgetfulness, the years of promise, gone and unrecoverable, of the land almost allowed to claim its better destiny, only to have the claim jumped by evildoers known all too well, and taken instead and held hostage to the future we must live in now forever. May we trust that this blessed ship is bound for some better shore, some undrowned Lemuria, risen and redeemed, where the American fate, mercifully, failed to transpire . . ."

From the beach Doc and Sauncho saw her, or thought they saw her, heading out to sea, all sails glowing and spread. Doc wanted to believe that Coy, Hope, and Amethyst were somehow on board, bound for safety. At the rail, waving. He almost saw them. Sauncho was not so sure. They began to bicker about it.

At which point Crocker had fire-gonged Doc back into another petroleum-scented day at the beach. "Not me," Doc croaked into the receiver.

"Sure been a long time!" the Prince of Palos Verdes way, way too chirpy for this time of the morning.

"Just a second while I see about a pulse here," Doc rolling off the couch and staggering into the kitchen. He wandered in small loops, trying to remember what he was supposed to be doing, somehow got water on to boil and instant coffee in a cup, and after a while also remembered that the phone was off the hook. "Howdy. And your name was . . ."

Crocker reintroduced himself. "Some people I know have lost something, and there's a theory developing that you might know where it is."

Doc drank half a cup of coffee, scalded his mouth, and finally said, "You wouldn't also happen to be one of the principals in this, man."

"Not that it's any of your business, Mr. Sportello, but over the years I've become known in this town as something of a fixer. My problem today is that you may be holding in gratuitous bailment an item whose owners wish to reclaim possession, and if this can be arranged quickly enough, there will be no penalties attached."

"Like, I won't get wasted or nothing."

"Luckily for you, that's a sanction they prefer to exercise only against their own. Given the sorts of business they engage in, without absolute trust in one's associates all may too swiftly revert to anarchy. Outsiders like yourself tend to get the benefit of the doubt, and you in turn may trust their word without any hesitation."

"Groovy. Want to meet at the same old place?"

"A parking lot in Lomita? Think not. Too much like your turf. It's probably been replaced with something else by now anyway. Why don't we meet this evening at my club, the Portola." He gave an address near Elysian Park.

"I bet there's a dress code," Doc said.

"Jacket and tie if possible."

NINETEEN

ON THE WAY OVER, DOC KEPT AN EYE ON THE REARVIEW MIRROR
for inquisitive El Caminos or Impalas. One of many basic things he had
failed to learn about Bigfoot was what kind of motor pool he had access
to. About the time he reached the Alvarado exit, it occurred to him to
start worrying about helicopters, too.

Crocker Fenway's club was housed in a Moorish Revival mansion dating from the Doheny-McAdoo era. In a room off the lobby where they
sent Doc to cool his heels was a mural depicting the arrival of the Portolá
expedition in 1769 at a bend of the river near what became downtown
L.A. Pretty close to here, in fact. The pictorial style reminded Doc of
labels on fruit and vegetable crates when he was a kid. Lots of color,
atmosphere, attention to detail. The view was northward, toward the
mountains, which nowadays people at the beach managed to see only
once or twice a year from the freeway when the smog blew away, but
which here, through the air of those early days, were still intensely visible, snow-topped and crystal-edged. A long string of pack mules wound
into the green distance along the banks of the river, which was shaded
by cottonwoods, willows, and alders. Everybody in the scene looked
like a movie star. Some were on horseback, packing muskets and lances
and wearing leather armor. On the face of one of them—maybe Portolá himself? there was an expression of wonder, like, What's this, what

unsuspected paradise? Did God with his finger trace out and bless this perfect little valley, intending it only for us? Doc must have got lost then for a while in the panorama, because he was startled by a voice behind him.

"An art lover."

He blinked a couple-three times, turned and saw it was Crocker, looking what they call tanned and fit, and as if somebody had just run a floor buffer all over his face.

"It's sure some picture," Doc nodded.

"Never noticed it really. Why don't we go up to the visitors' bar. Nice suit, by the way."

Nicer than Crocker knew. Doc had found it at the big MGM sell-off not long ago, having headed for it unerringly among the thousands of racks of more humdrum movie outfits that filled one of the soundstages. It was calling to him. A note pinned to it said that John Garfield had worn it in *The Postman Always Rings Twice* (1946), and it turned out to fit Doc perfectly, but not wishing to compromise what mojo might still be active among its threads, Doc saw no point in telling Crocker any of this. He'd worn the Liberace necktie as well, which Crocker kept looking at but seemed unable to comment on.

Not Doc's kind of bar, really. Full of fake-Mission furniture and so much somber wood you couldn't see what you were sitting on or drinking off of. Some jungle-print upholstery, not to mention more colored lights, would have livened things up.

"Here's to peaceful resolution," Crocker raising a squat glassful of a West Highland malt made exclusively for the Portola and angling it toward Doc's rum and coke.

A subtle reference, no doubt, to recent events out on Gummo Marx Way. Doc beamed insincerely. "So . . . how's the family?"

"If you mean Mrs. Fenway, I remain as devoted to her as I was the day she came down the aisle at St. John's Episcopal Church looking like the Gross National Product. If you mean my lovely daughter Japonica, on whom I hope you are not idiot enough ever to have considered laying so much as a finger, why, she's fine. Fine. In fact, it's only because of her, and our own small transaction a few years ago, that I am even cutting you as much slack as I am now."

"Ever so grateful, sir." He waited till Crocker was about to swallow some Scotch and said, "By the way—did you ever run into a dentist named Rudy Blatnoyd?"

With as little choking and sputtering as possible, Crocker replied, "The son of a bitch who until recently was corrupting my daughter, yes I do seem to recall the name, perished in a trampoline accident or something, didn't he?"

"The LAPD's not so sure it was an accident."

"And you're wondering if I did it. What possible motive would I have? Just because the man preyed on an emotionally vulnerable child, tore her from the embrace of a loving family, forced her to engage in sexual practices that might appall even a sophisticate like yourself—does that mean I'd have any reason to see his miserable pedophile career come to an end? What a vindictive person you must imagine me."

"You know . . . I did suspect he was fucking his receptionist," Doc in his most innocent voice, "but I mean, what dentist doesn't, it's some oath they all have to take in dentist school, and anyhow that's a long way from strange and weird sex. Isn't it?"

"How about when he forced my little girl to listen to *original cast albums* of Broadway musicals while he had his way with her? The tastelessly decorated resort hotel rooms he took her to during endodontist conventions? the wallpaper! the lamps! And I won't even get into his secret collection of vintage snoods—"

"Yeah but . . . Japonica's legal age now, isn't she?"

"In a father's eyes, they're always too young." Doc took a quick glance at Crocker's eyes but didn't see much fatherly emotion. What he did see made him thankful he'd decided not to smoke too much on the way over.

"To the matter at hand—those I represent are prepared to offer you a generous compensation package for the safe return of their property."

"Groovy. Suppose it didn't even have to be in the form of, like, money?"

Crocker for the first time appeared to be taken aback. "Well . . . money would be a lot easier."

"I've been more concerned about the safety of some people."

"Oh . . . people . . . Well, that would depend, I suppose, on how much of a threat they represent to my principals."

"I'm thinking about those who are close to me in my life, but there's also this saxophone player named Coy Harlingen, who's been working undercover for different antisubversive outfits, including the LAPD? He's come to feel lately that he made the wrong career choice. It lost him his family and his freedom. Like you, he has an only daughter—"

"Please . . ."

"Okay, well anyway now he wants out. I think I can square it with the heat, but there's this other bunch called Vigilant California. And whoever's running them, of course."

"Oh, the Viggies, yes a fairly contemptible lot, useful in the street but no political sense beyond simple hooliganism. My guess is that they'd prefer he didn't disclose any confidential information."

"Last thing he'd ever do."

"Your personal guarantee."

"He tries anything, I'll go after him myself."

"Barring surprises, then, I don't see why some amicable separation shouldn't be arranged for him. That's all you wanted? No money, now, you're sure?"

"How much money would I have to take from you so I don't lose your respect?"

Crocker Fenway chuckled without mirth. "A bit late for that, Mr. Sportello. People like you lose all claim to respect the first time they pay anybody rent."

"And when the first landlord decided to stiff the first renter for his security deposit, your whole fucking class lost everybody's respect."

"Ah. So you're looking for what, a refund? Plus how many years' interest? That'd be a bookkeeping issue, of course, but I expect we could come up with that."

"'Course. Nothin to you, couple hundred bucks, just something to roll up and snort coke through. But see, every time one of you gets greedy like that, the bad-karma level gets jacked up one more little two-hundred-dollar notch. After a while that starts to add up. For years now under everybody's nose there's been all this class hatred, slowly building. Where do you think that's headed?"

"Sounds like you've been talking to His Holiness Mickey Wolfmann. You've been out to have a look at Channel View Estates? Some of us moved heaven and earth, mostly earth, to keep that promise of urban blight from happening—one more episode in a struggle that's been going on for years now—residential owners like me against developers like Brother Wolfmann. People with a decent respect for preserving the environment against high-density tenement scum without the first idea of how to clean up after themselves."

"Bullshit, Crocker, it's about your property values."

"It's about *being in place*. We—" gesturing around the Visitors' Bar and its withdrawal into seemingly unbounded shadow, "we're in place. We've been in place forever. Look around. Real estate, water rights, oil, cheap labor—all of that's ours, it's always been ours. And you, at the end of the day what are you? one more unit in this swarm of transients who come and go without pause here in the sunny Southland, eager to be bought off with a car of a certain make, model, and year, a blonde in a bikini, thirty seconds on some excuse for a wave—a chili dog, for Christ's sake." He shrugged. "We will never run out of you people. The supply is inexhaustible."

"And you don't ever worry," Doc grinned back cordially, "that someday they'll all turn into a savage mob screamin around outside the gates of PV, maybe even looking to get in?"

Shrug. "Then we do what has to be done to keep them out. We've been laid siege to by far worse, and we're still here. Aren't we."

"And thank heaven for that, sir."

"Oh. You people do irony, I wasn't aware."

"More like practicality. If you and your friends and lunch companions don't all remain 'in place,' how will average PIs like me ever make a living? We can't get by on matrimonials and car theft, we need those high-level felony activities you folks are so gifted at."

"Yes. Well." Crocker flicked a glance at his Patek Philippe moonphase. "Actually . . ."

"Sure. Don't want to hang you up. Where and when do we do the handoff this time?"

Easy enough. Parking lot at the May Company shopping mall out at Hawthorne and Artesia, tomorrow evening. Transfer of goods to be made only after verification that certain individuals have been allowed to go their ways unmolested. Future guarantees of personal safety not to be unreasonably withheld.

"Your reputation as a fixer's on the line here, Crocker. I may not be as well connected, and for sure not as much into revenge as you folks are, but if you been jivin with me here my good man, I say unto you, best watch your ass."

"Revenge," protested the sensitive tycoon, "me?"

DOC BROUGHT DENIS along for, well maybe not muscle, but something like that, some kind of protection he hadn't realized till lately he needed, a boost for his immunity against the shopping plazas of Southern California, for a desire not to desire, at least not what you found in shopping malls.

"Huh?" said Denis while they were waiting for the drop and handing a joint back and forth and Doc was trying to explain this. "So why are you giving back that TV set?"

Doc looked closely at Denis. "It— Denis, it's not a . . ."

Denis started giggling. "It's okay, Doc, I knew it was smack. I know you're not dealing smack and probably not making any money out of this trip tonight either. But you should be getting something for your trouble."

"I'm getting their word they won't hurt anybody. My friends, my family—me, you, a couple others."

"You believe that? Comin from whoever it is handles this kind of weight? Their word?"

"What, I should only trust good people? man, good people get bought and sold every day. Might as well trust somebody evil once in a while, it makes no more or less sense. I mean I wouldn't give odds either way."

"Wow, Doc. That's heavy." Denis sat there pigging on the joint as usual. "What does that mean?" he said after a while.

"There they are."

The Golden Fang operatives were cleverly disguised tonight as a wholesome blond California family in a '53 Buick Estate Wagon, the last woodie that ever rolled out of Detroit, a nostalgic advertisement for the sort of suburban consensus that Crocker and his associates prayed for day and night to settle over the Southland, with all non-homeowning infidels sent off to some crowded exile far away, where they could be safely forgotten. The boy was six and already looked like a Marine. His sister, a couple years older, had a possible future in drug abuse but wasn't saying much, content to sit staring at Doc while focused inside on thoughts of her own he was just as happy not to know about. Mom and Dad were all business.

Doc got out and opened the trunk. "Need a hand with this?"

"I'm good." The dad had on a short-sleeved shirt which revealed, maybe by design, a complete absence of tracks. The mom was a sleek-enough California blonde in a species of tennis dress, smoking some white-chick filter cigarette. The smoke kept getting into one of her eyes, but she didn't bother to take the cigarette out of her mouth. When hubby had the dope stashed securely in back, she squinted Doc half a smile and held out a flat rectangle of plastic.

"What's this?"

"A credit card," the daughter piped up from the back seat. "Don't hippies have them?"

"I must have meant, why's your mom handing me this?"

"It isn't for you," said the mom.

Doc took the object doubtfully. It seemed normal, though issued by a bank he didn't recognize right away. Then he saw Coy Harlingen's name on it. The husband watching him out of narrowed eyes. "You're supposed to tell him, 'Well done, welcome back to the main herd, safe journeys.' That's 'journeys,' plural."

"Guess I can remember that." He noticed that Denis was writing it down anyway.

A minute or two after the Buick drove away toward Hawthorne Boulevard, Doc saw a beat-up El Camino which could only be Bigfoot's creeping along after them. It sounded different. Bigfoot must've put new headers in or something.

But where was this tail he was on going to take Bigfoot finally? How far in this weird twisted cop karma would he have to follow the twenty kilos before it led him to what he thought he needed to know? Which would be what again, exactly? Who hired Adrian to kill his partner? What Adrian's connection might be to Crocker Fenway's principals? Whether the Golden Fang, which Bigfoot didn't believe in to begin with, even existed? How smart was any of it, right now for example, without backup, and how safe was Bigfoot likely to be, and for how long?

"Here," Denis said after a while, passing a smoldering joint.

"Bigfoot's not my brother," Doc considered when he exhaled, "but he sure needs a keeper."

"It ain't you, Doc."

"I know. Too bad, in a way."

TWENTY

WEDGED UNDER THE KITCHEN DOOR WHEN HE GOT BACK WAS
an envelope Farley had left, with some enlargements of the film from
the shindig at Channel View Estates. There were close-ups of the gun-
man who'd nailed Glen, but none were readable. It could have been Art
Tweedle under the Christmas-card ski mask, it could've been anybody.
Doc got out his lens and gazed into each image till one by one they began
to float apart into little blobs of color. It was as if whatever had happened
had reached some kind of limit. It was like finding the gateway to the past
unguarded, unforbidden because it didn't have to be. Built into the act of
return finally was this glittering mosaic of doubt. Something like what
Sauncho's colleagues in marine insurance liked to call inherent vice.

"Is that like original sin?" Doc wondered.

"It's what you can't avoid," Sauncho said, "stuff marine policies don't
like to cover. Usually applies to cargo—like eggs break—but sometimes
it's also the vessel carrying it. Like why bilges have to be pumped out?"

"Like the San Andreas Fault," it occurred to Doc. "Rats living up in
the palm trees."

"Well," Sauncho blinked, "maybe if you wrote a marine policy on
L.A., considering it, for some closely defined reason, to be a boat . . ."

"Hey, how about a ark? That's a boat, right?"

"Ark insurance?"

"That big disaster Sortilège is always talking about, way back when Lemuria sank into the Pacific. Some of the people who escaped then are spoze to've fled here for safety. Which would make California like, a ark."

"Oh, nice refuge. Nice, stable, reliable piece of real estate."

Doc made coffee and punched on the tube. *Hawaii Five-0* was still on. He waited through the end credits, with the footage of the giant canoe, which he knew Leo liked to watch, and then rang up his parents in the San Joaquin.

Elmina filled him in on the latest news. "Gilroy got promoted again. He's regional manager now, they're sending him to Boise."

"They're all gonna pack up and move to Boise?"

"No, she'll be staying here with the kids. And the house."

"Uh, huh," Doc said.

"Gil sure picked a lulu, that one. Can't stay away from the bowling alley, out dancing with Mexicans and some of them you can't tell what they are to all hours and of course we're always happy to sit our grand-babies but they need their mama, too, don't you think?"

"They're lucky to have you guys, Ma."

"I just hope when you get married, you'll be thinking a little more clearly than Gil was."

"I don't know, I always tended to cut Vernix some slack 'cause of that first husband and all."

"Oh, the jailbird. He was just her type. How she ever kept out of Tehachapi herself, I'm sure I don't know."

"Funny, you always sounded like her biggest fan."

"Do you see much of that pretty Shasta Fay Hepworth?"

"Once or twice." And no harm in adding, "She's living back at the beach now."

"Maybe it's fate, Larry."

"Maybe she needs a break from the picture business, Ma."

"Well, you could do worse." Doc could always tell when his mother was taking a beat on purpose. "And I hope you've been *staying out of trouble.*"

Leo had been on the extension for a while. "Here we go."

"I only meant—"

"She thinks you're dealing grass, and she wants to score some, but she's too embarrassed to ask."

"Leo, now, I swear—" Scuffling and thumping sounds could be heard.

"Should I be callin the riot squad in?"

"He's never going to drop this," Elmina said. "You remember our friend Oriole, who teaches junior high. She confiscated some pot the other day, and we decided we'd try a little."

"How'd that go?"

"Well, there's this soap that we watch, *Another World*? but somehow we couldn't recognize any of the characters, even though we've been following them every day, I mean it was still Alice and Rachel and that Ada whom I have never trusted since *A Summer Place* [1959] and everybody, their faces were the same, but the things they were talking about all meant something different somehow, and meantime I was also having some trouble with the color on the set, and then Oriole brought in chocolate chip cookies and we started eating and couldn't stop with those, and next thing we knew, *Another World* had changed into a game show, and then your father came in."

"I was hoping there'd be some reefer left, but those two had smoked it all up."

"Bummer," said Doc sympathetically. "It sounds like you're the one who wants to score, Dad."

"Actually," Leo said, "we were both sort of wondering . . ."

"Your cousin Scott is coming up next weekend," Elmina said. "If you could find some, he says he'll be happy to bring it."

"Sure. Just do me a favor, you guys?"

Elmina reached down the miles of phone line to take his cheek in a pinch and wobble it back and forth once or twice. "Best of the bunch! Anything, Larry."

"Not when you're baby-sitting, okay?"

"'Course not," growled Leo. "Ain't like that we're dope fiends."

NEXT MORNING THE fire bell went off, and it was Sauncho. "Thought you might want to be in on this. Had a tip the *Golden Fang* put in last night at San Pedro, and there's been activity all night long, and this time it looks like a quick turnaround. *Los federales* are making shadow-and-intercept noises. The firm's runabout is down at the Marina and if you drive fast, you can make it here in time."

"In time to stop you from something crazy, you mean?"

"Oh and you might want to wear some Sperry Topsiders instead of that one huarache?"

Traffic cooperated, and Doc found Sauncho at Linus's Tavern drinking a Tequila Zombie, but he didn't even have time to get one himself before the phone behind the bar rang. "For you, honey," Mercy the bartender passing the phone to Sauncho, who nodded once, then twice, then, moving faster than Doc had ever seen him, threw a twenty on the bar and ran out the door.

By the time Doc caught up with him, Sauncho was down on the pier casting off lines from a little fiberglass inboard-outboard belonging to Hardy, Gridley & Chatfield. Sauncho had the motor going and had begun easing away from the berth in a haze of blue exhaust when Doc just managed to stagger aboard.

"What am I doing on this Clorox bottle again?"

"You get to be the mate."

"Like Gilligan? That makes you . . . wait a minute . . . the Skipper?"

They steered south. Gordita Beach emerged from the haze, gently flaking away in the salt breezes, the ramshackle town in a spill of weather-beaten colors, like paint chips at some out-of-the-way hardware store, and the hillside up to Dunecrest, which Doc had always thought of, especially after nights of excess, as steep, a grade everybody sooner or later wiped their clutch trying to get up and out of town on, looking from out here strangely flat, hardly there at all.

The waves were pretty good today for this stretch of the coast.

Offshore winds had slackened enough to bring some surfers out, and they waited in a line, bobbing up and down, like Easter Island in reverse, it had always seemed to Doc.

Through Sauncho's old binoculars he observed a CHP motorcycle cop chasing a longhaired kid along the beach, in and out of folks trying to catch some midday rays. The cop was in full motorcycle gear—boots, helmet, uniform—and carrying assorted weaponry, and the kid was barefoot and lightly dressed, and in his element. He fled like a gazelle, while the cop lumbered behind, struggling through the sand.

Doc flashed how this was the time machine and he was seeing Bigfoot Bjornsen at the outset of his career as a young cop in Gordita. Bigfoot had always hated it here and couldn't wait to get away. "This place has been cursed from the jump," he told anybody who'd listen. "Indians lived here long ago, they had a drug cult, smoked *toloache* which is jimsonweed, gave themselves hallucinations, deluded themselves they were visiting other realities—why, come to think of it, not unlike the hippie freaks of our present day. Their graveyards were sacred portals of access to the spirit world, not to be misused. And Gordita Beach is built right on top of one."

From watching Saturday-night horror movies, Doc understood that building on top of an Indian graveyard was the worst kind of bad karma, though developers, being of evil character, didn't care where they built as long as the lots were level and easy to get to. It wouldn't have surprised Doc at all to learn that Mickey Wolfmann had committed this desecration himself more than once, calling down curse after curse on his already miserable soul.

They were hard to see and hard to catch hold of, these Indian spirits. You plodded along in pursuit, maybe only wanting to apologize, and they flew like the wind, and waited their moment. . . .

"What're you looking at?" Sauncho said.

"Where I live."

They rounded Palos Verdes Point, and there in the distance, out from San Pedro with all her staysails and jibs set, blooming like a cubist rose, came the schooner. The look on Sauncho's face was of pure unrequited love.

Doc had seen *Preserved* under full sail only once before, during the acid trip that Vehi and Sortilège had put him on. Now, more or less on the natch, he noticed an interesting resemblance to the schooner in *The Sea Wolf* (1941), aboard which John Garfield is assaulted and in fact decked by Edward G. Robinson going, "Yeah! yeah I'm the Sea Wolf, see? I'm the boss on this ship, and what I say goes, yeah . . . 'cause nobody messes with the Sea Wolf, see—"

"Everything all right, Doc?"

"Oh. Was . . . I doing that out loud?"

They fell in astern and followed. Soon a pair of greenish blobs appeared on the radar, moving closer with each sweep, and Sauncho got on the radio. Some of the transmissions sounded like a Gordita Beach bar any night of the week.

"Your buddies from the Justice Department," Doc guessed.

"Plus the Coast Guard." Sauncho looked at the schooner for a while through the binoculars. "She's seen us now. Pretty soon . . . yup. Some smoke. She's switching over to diesel power. Well, that lets us out."

Soon they were looking at the ass end or, as Sauncho liked to call it, fantail, of a Coast Guard cutter pursuing the *Golden Fang* at flank speed, and before long the DOJ vessel also had caught up with Sauncho and Doc. Young attorneys in amusing hats waved cans of beer and hollered remarks. Doc saw at least half a dozen cuties in bikinis scampering forward and aft. KHJ was on at top volume, playing Thunderclap Newman's rousing revolutionary anthem "Something in the Air," to which a number of DOJ passengers and guests were actually singing along, with every appearance of sincerity—though Doc wondered how many would have recognized revolution if it had come up and said howdy.

"Mind if I just kick back here?" Doc said. "Don't suppose your law firm happens to keep any fishing gear aboard."

"Actually, if you go look in that locker . . . They even sprang for a fathometer so they could track schools of fish." Sauncho lit off the instrument and began to gaze at its display. After a while he began muttering and reaching for charts. "Something funny here, Doc. . . . According to this, look—there isn't much out here in the way of a bottom, it's all like hundreds of meters deep. But this fathometer—unless the electronics are fucked up—"

"Saunch, do you hear something?"

From ahead of them somewhere now came a rhythmic murmur which, if they were on land, could easily be taken for surf. But this far out at sea couldn't possibly be.

"Something," Sauncho said.

"Good."

The sound grew louder, and Doc started to time the interval in his head. Unless he was nervous and counting too fast, it seemed to be around thirty seconds, which normally—which this wasn't—suggested waves up to about that many feet high. By now the little craft was beginning to pitch around in the swell, which had become, you'd say, pronounced. Something was also happening to the light, as if the air ahead of them were thickening with unknown weather. Even with binoculars it was hard to keep the schooner in view.

"Your dreamboat there trying to lead us into something?" Doc hollered, not quite in panic.

The surf—if that's what it was—had grown to a day-splitting roar. Caustic salt spray lashed at them, driving into their eyes. Sauncho throttled back the engine, screaming, "What the fuck?"

Doc had been on his way aft to vomit but decided to wait. Sauncho was pointing off the port bow in some agitation. There were no rocks visible, no shoreline, open ocean all around, but what they now beheld made the north shore of Oahu at its most majestic look like Santa Monica in August. Doc put the sets rolling in at them from the northwest at thirty and maybe even thirty-five feet from crest to trough—curling massively, flaring in the sun, breaking in repeated explosion.

"Can't be Cortes Bank," Sauncho squinting at his charts, "we haven't come that far. But there's nothing else around here, so what the hell is it?"

They both knew. It was St. Flip of Lawndale's mythical break, also known to old-timers as Death's Doorsill. And the schooner was headed straight into it.

Sauncho had been tracking her course with a yellow grease pencil on the radar screen. "They're committing either suicide or barratry here, hard to say which—why don't they turn?"

"Where's the feds now?"

"Justice Department look like they're hove to, but the Coast Guard is still trying to intercept."

"That takes some balls."

"It's what they tell you when you join up—you have to go out, but you don't have to come back."

They were close enough now to see two, make it three, dark narrow shapes detach from the schooner, seem to hover a moment above the surface, then go roostertailing away, their engines for a short while louder even than the crashing surf. "Cigarette boats," hollered Sauncho. "Five hundred HP, maybe a thousand, don't matter, nobody's about to engage in hot pursuit here."

Doc watched the schooner through the smeared oceanlight. She kept fading in and out of the spray. It may have been the visibility, but she looked all at once older, more sea-beaten, more like the ship in his dream the other morning. The dream of Coy's escape with his family to safety. *Preserved.*

"They've abandoned her," Sauncho cried into the dimness and roar.

"Shit, man, I'm really sorry."

"Don't be. At least they stopped the engines. We've just got to pray she doesn't strand on whatever that is down there." In the lulls between wavecrashes, he explained that if she could be brought back in, into some kind of safe receivership, and the owners didn't come and claim her within a year and a day, then she was officially abandoned, and who the ownership would pass to then became a matter of all kinds of marine law Doc had trouble following.

Meantime the Coast Guard were putting a boarding party on the schooner, shortening sail, getting out trip lines and storm anchors to keep her head to the wind, rigging range and towing lights. According to radio traffic, an oceangoing tug was on the way.

"Good thing we came out," Sauncho said.

"We didn't do much."

"Yeah, but suppose we hadn't come out. There'd be only the government story then, and that old boat could kiss her transom good-bye."

AT THE TERMINAL Island Coast Guard base, Sauncho had to go in the office and do some paperwork, and arrange for overnight moorage for the inboard-outboard, then he and Doc grabbed a lift with a carload of sailors heading up to Hollywood on liberty, who let them off at the Marina. At Linus's Tavern they found Mercy just going off shift. "Never got to finish that Zombie," Sauncho realized.

"You're probably in a mood to celebrate," Doc said, "but I should look in at the office, it's been a while."

"I know—I have to calm down, we shouldn't jinx this, a lot can happen in a year and a day. Everybody starts coming out of the woodwork, multiple insurers, particular average claims, ex–old ladies, who knows what-all. But say there was a legal marine policy in force, allowing ownership to go back to the underwriter. . . ."

Hell, call it Doper's Intuition. "You didn't happen to take out a policy yourself, Saunch."

Was it the light in here? Did somebody have to go run and call up the Pope to report a miraculous case of some lawyer actually blushing? "If there's litigation, I'll be in on it," Sauncho admitted. "Although it's more likely one of your lowlife millionaire friends will end up stealing her at auction."

On some sentimental impulse, Doc went to hug him, and as usual

Sauncho flinched. "Sorry. Hope it works out, man. That boat and you really do belong together."

"Yep, like Shirley Temple and George Murphy." Before anybody could stop him, Sauncho began singing "We Should Be Together," from *Little Miss Broadway* (1938), actually doing a fair vocal impression of the curly-headed moppet. He got to his feet, as if about to tap-dance, but by now Doc was pulling nervously at his sleeve.

"I think that's your boss over there?"

It was indeed the intimidating C. C. Chatfield, in propria persona. Moreover, he was aiming meaningful looks Sauncho's way. Sauncho stopped singing and waved.

"Didn't know you were a Shirley Temple fan too, Smilax," boomed C.C. across what, helpfully, wasn't yet a quitting-time crowd. "When you're done with your client there, come on over. I need a word with you about that MGM idea."

"You didn't," said Doc.

"It was a class-action suit waiting to happen," Sauncho protested. "If it isn't us, it'll be somebody else. And think of the potential. Every studio in town's vulnerable. Warners! What if you could find enough pissed-off viewers who *don't* want Laszlo and Ilsa to get on the airplane together? Or what if they want Mildred to strangle Veda at the end, like she does in the book? A-and—"

"I'll call you soon," Doc as carefully as possible patting Sauncho on the shoulder and making his way out of Linus's.

THINGS WERE WINDING down for the day at Dr. Tubeside's energy shop. Petunia, mighty fetching today in pale fuchsia, was murmuring intimately with a longhaired older gent in very dark wraparound shades. "Oh, Doc, I don't think you've ever met my husband? This is Dizzy. Honey, this is Doc, that I've told you about?"

"My brother," Dizzy slowly advancing a hand with bass-player cal-luses on the fingers, and the next thing Doc knew, they were deep in a complex handshake, including elements from Vietnam, a number of state prisons, and fraternal organizations that post their weekly meeting times at the city limits.

Dr. Tubeside joined them from the back office and handed Petunia a large prescription bottle. "If you're *really* going *ahead* with this *vegetarian-diet* thing," punctuating this by rattling the pills in the bottle, "you'll *need* a *supp*lement, Pe*tun*-ya."

"We have news, Doc," said Petunia. "Pregno," said Dizzy.

Doc did a quick radiance check on her and felt a stupid smile taking over his face. "Well what do you know. I thought that glow in the room was just some flashback I was havin. Congratulations, you guys, that's wonderful."

"Except for this nutcase here," said Petunia, "who thinks now he has to drive me to and from work. Just what I need, a freaked-out chauffeur. Take your shades off, darling, let everybody see them pretty eyeballs pinwheelin around."

Doc headed upstairs. "Put the lights out and lock up!" hollered Dr. Tubeside.

"I never forget," replied Doc. An old routine.

There was a pile of mail fanned out on the other side of the doorsill, most of it pizza-delivery menus, but one sumptuous envelope, embossed in gold, caught Doc's eye. He recognized the fake-Arabic typeface of the Kismet Lounge and Casino, North Las Vegas.

The first thing he saw inside the envelope was a check for ten thousand dollars. It looked real enough. "After exhaustive review," said the cover letter, "in which the best—and incidentally the most expensive—legal, psychological, and religious experts have been consulted, it has been determined that Michael Zachary Wolfmann was in fact abducted against his will, and, like the space aliens of nearby Area 51, his abductors remain inaccessible to ordinary legal remedy. The amount enclosed reflects our quoted odds of 100 to 1, though the betting lines at certain other casinos to the south of here would have provided a vastly more lucrative payoff. 'Tough luck, high roller!'

"Look for further mailings, including your exclusive invitation to the Grand Opening of the new and totally reconceptualized Kismet Lounge and Casino, sometime in the spring of 1972. We look forward to seeing you again. Thank you for your continued interest in the Kismet.

"Cordially, Fabian P. Fazzo, Chief Operating Officer, Kiscorp."

The Princess phone rang, and it was Hope Harlingen. "God bless you, Doc."

"I sneeze or something?"

"Seriously."

"Really. Like sometimes I forget if I did or not? and then I have to ask. It's embarrassing."

There was a short silence. "Rewinding," she said. "Was that you who slid those passes under my patio door?"

"No. What passes?"

Seems somebody had given her and Amethyst backstage passes to the massive Surfadelic Freak-In up at Will Rogers Park last night.

"Oh wow, did I miss that? My cousin's band, Beer? was supposed to open for the Boards."

"Beer? Really? Doc, they were so far out? like they're the next Boards."

"Scott will be happy to hear that. I don't know if I am. Did Coy play?"

"He's back, Doc, he's really alive and back and I've been tripping for twenty-four hours now, and I don't know what to believe."

"How's old what's-her-name doin?"

"She's still asleep. I'd say she's been a little spaced. I don't think she's really made any connections about Coy yet. But the one thing at the concert she keeps going back to is when Coy picked up a baritone sax, took the mike off the mike stand, and put it down in the bell of the sax and started just blasting. She loved that. He scored all kinds of points with that."

"So . . . you guys are . . ."

"Oh, we'll see."

"Groovy."

"We're also going to Hawaii next weekend."

Doc remembered his dream. "You takin a boat?"

"Flying over on Kahuna Airlines. Coy got tickets someplace."

"Try not to check too many bags."

"He just came in. Here, talk to him. We love you."

There were sounds, annoying after a while, of prolonged kissing, and Coy finally said, "I'm officially off of everybody's payroll, man. Burke Stodger called in person to tell me. Did you get to the concert last night?"

"No, and my cousin Scott's gonna be so pissed off. I just forgot. Heard you really kicked ass."

"I got some long solos on 'Steamer Lane' and 'Hair Ball' and the Dick Dale salute."

"And I guess your daughter had fun."

"Man, she's . . ." And he just went silent. Doc listened to him breathing for a while. "You know what the Indians say. You saved my life, now you've got to—"

"Yeah, yeah, some hippie made that up." These people, man. Don't know nothin. "You saved your life, Coy. Now you get to live it." He hung up.

TWENTY-ONE

WHEN IT BECAME TRAGICALLY OBVIOUS TOO LATE IN THE FOURTH quarter that the Lakers would lose Game 7 of the finals to the Knicks, Doc began thinking about who he'd bet on it with, and how much, and then the ten thousand dollars, and then everybody else he owed money to, which he now remembered included Fritz, so he popped off the tube and, deciding to take his disappointment out on the road, got in the Dart and headed up to Santa Monica. By the time he arrived at Gotcha!, there were still one or two lights on inside. He went around the back and tapped at the door. After a while it opened an inch, and a kid with very short hair peered out. Had to be Sparky.

Which it was. "Fritz said you'd be by sometime. Come on in."

The computer room was hopping. All the tape reels were spinning back and forth, and there were now twice as many computer screens as Doc remembered, all lit up, plus at least a dozen TV sets on, each tuned to a different channel. A sound system that must have been looted from a movie theater was playing "Help Me, Rhonda," and the beat-up old percolator in the corner had been replaced with some gigantic Italian coffee machine covered with pipes and valve handles and gauges and enough chrome that you could drive it slowly along any boulevard in East L.A. and fit right in. Sparky went to a keyboard and typed in some series of commands in a peculiar code Doc tried to read but couldn't, and the coffee machine started to—well not breathe, exactly, but begin to route steam and hot water around in a purposeful way.

"Where's Fritz got to?"

"Down in the desert someplace, chasing deadbeats. As usual."

Doc took a joint out of his shirt pocket. "Mind if I, uh . . ."

"Sure," just this side of sociable.

"You don't smoke?"

Sparky shrugged. "It's harder for me to work. Or maybe I'm just one of those people shouldn't be goin in for drugs."

"Fritz said after he'd been on the network for a while it felt like doing psychedelics."

"He also thinks the ARPAnet has taken his soul."

Doc thought about this. "Has it?"

Sparky frowned off into the distance. "The system has no use for souls. Not how it works at all. Even this thing about going into other people's lives? it isn't like some Eastern trip of absorbing into a collective consciousness. It's only finding stuff out that somebody else didn't think you were going to. And it's moving so fast, like the more we know, the more we know, you can almost see it change one day to the next. Why I try to work late. Not so much of a shock next morning."

"Wow. Guess I better learn something about this or I'll be obsolete."

"It's all pretty clunky," waving around the room. "Down here in real life, compared to what you see in spy movies and TV, we're still nowhere near that speed or capacity, even the infrared and night vision they're using in Vietnam is still a long way from X-Ray Specs, but it all moves exponentially, and someday everybody's gonna wake up to find they're under surveillance they can't escape. Skips won't be able to skip no more, maybe by then there'll be no place to skip to."

The coffee machine burst into a loud synthesized vocal of "Volare."

"Fritz programmed that in. I might have gone more for 'Java Jive.'"

"Little before your time."

"It's all data. Ones and zeros. All recoverable. Eternally present."

"Groovy."

The coffee wasn't bad considering its robotic origins. Sparky tried to show Doc a little code. "Oh hey," Doc remembered then, "this network of yours, does it include hospitals? Like if somebody went in an emergency room, could you find out their status?"

"Depends where."

"Vegas?"

"Maybe something by way of the University of Utah, let me look." There was a flurry of plastic percussion and green space-alien glyphs on the screen, and after a while Sparky said, "Got Sunrise here, and Desert Springs."

"She'd either be under Beaverton or Fortnight. Pretty recent, I think."

Sparky typed some more and nodded. "Okay, Sunrise Hospital shows a Trillium Fortnight, home address in L.A., admitted with a concussion, cuts, and bruises. . . . In for observation and treatment two . . . three nights, released in the custody of her parents . . . looks like last Tuesday."

"That's her." He looked over Sparky's shoulder at the screen. "What do you know, that is her. Well. Thanks, man."

"You all right?" Seeming impatient now to be back to work.

"Why shouldn't I be?"

"I don't know. You look a little weird, and most people your age call me 'kid.'"

"I'm headin over to Zucky's, can I bring you somethin back?"

"Don't really get hungry till after midnight, then I usually just call up Pizza Man."

"Okay. Tell Fritz I owe him money. And would you mind if I look in here once in a while if I try not to be too much of a pain in the ass?"

"Sure. Help you set up your own system if you want. It's the wave of the future, ain't it."

"Tubular, dude."

At Zucky's, Doc sat at the counter and ordered coffee and a full-size chocolate cream pie, and for a while went through the exercise of actually cutting forty-five-degree slices and putting them on a plate and eating them one by one with a fork, but finally he just picked up what was left with his hands and went ahead and finished it that way.

Magda came over to have a look. "Like some pie with that?"

"You're workin nights now," Doc observed.

"Always been more of a night person. Where's that Fritz, I haven't seen him for a while."

"Out in the desert someplace, is what I heard."

"Looks like you've been copping some rays yourself."

"I know this guy has a boat, we went out on it the other day?"

"Catch anything?"

"Drank beer mostly."

"Sounds like my husband. They figured one time they'd go to Tahiti, ended up at Terminal Island."

Doc lit an after-dinner cigarette. "Long as they all got back safe."

"Can't remember. You have some whipped cream on your ear there."

DOC GOT ON the Santa Monica Freeway, and about the time he was making the transition to the San Diego southbound, the fog began its nightly roll inland. He pushed his hair off of his face, turned up the radio volume, lit a Kool, sank back in a cruising slouch, and watched everything slowly disappear, the trees and shrubbery along the median, the yellow school-bus pool at Palms, the lights in the hills, the signs above the freeway that told you where you were, the planes descending to the airport. The third dimension grew less and less reliable—a row of four taillights ahead could either belong to two separate cars in adjoining lanes a safe distance away, or be a pair of double lights on the same vehicle, right up your nose, no way to tell. At first the fog blew in in separate sheets, but soon everything grew thick and uniform till all Doc could see were his headlight beams, like eyestalks of an extraterrestrial, aimed into the hushed whiteness ahead, and the lights on his dashboard, where the speedometer was the only way to tell how fast he was going.

He crept along till he finally found another car to settle in behind. After a while in his rearview mirror he saw somebody else fall in behind him. He was in a convoy of unknown size, each car keeping the one ahead in taillight range, like a caravan in a desert of perception, gathered awhile for safety in getting across a patch of blindness. It was one of the few things he'd ever seen anybody in this town, except hippies, do for free.

Doc wondered how many people he knew had been caught out tonight in this fog, and how many were indoors fogbound in front of the tube or in bed just falling asleep. Someday—he figured Sparky would confirm it—there'd be phones as standard equipment in every car, maybe even dashboard computers. People could exchange names and addresses and life stories and form alumni associations to gather once a year at some bar off a different freeway exit each time, to remember the night they set up a temporary commune to help each other home through the fog.

He cut in the Vibrasonic. KQAS was playing Fapardokly's triple-tongue highway classic "Super Market," ordinarily ideal for driving through L.A.—though with traffic conditions tonight Doc might have to settle for every other beat—and then there were some Elephant's Memory bootleg tapes, and the Spaniels' cover of "Stranger in Love," and "God Only Knows" by the Beach Boys, which Doc realized after a while he'd been singing along with. He looked at the gas gauge and saw there was still better than half a tank, plus fumes. He had a container of coffee from Zucky's and almost a full pack of smokes.

Now and then somebody signaled a right turn and cautiously left the line to feel their way toward an exit ramp. The bigger exit signs overhead were completely invisible, but sometimes it was possible to see one of the smaller ones down at road level, right where the exit lane began to peel away. So it always had to be one of those last-possible-minute decisions.

Doc figured if he missed the Gordita Beach exit he'd take the first one whose sign he could read and work his way back on surface streets. He knew that at Rosecrans the freeway began to dogleg east, and at some point, Hawthorne Boulevard or Artesia, he'd lose the fog, unless it was spreading tonight, and settled in regionwide. Maybe then it would stay this way for days, maybe he'd have to just keep driving, down past Long Beach, down through Orange County, and San Diego, and across a border where nobody could tell anymore in the fog who was Mexican, who was Anglo, who was anybody. Then again, he might run out of gas before that happened, and have to leave the caravan, and pull over on the shoulder, and wait. For whatever would happen. For a forgotten joint to materialize in his pocket. For the CHP to come by and choose not to hassle him. For a restless blonde in a Stingray to stop and offer him a ride. For the fog to burn away, and for something else this time, somehow, to be there instead.